PRAISE FOR RUTH GLICK, WRITING AS REBECCA YORK

"Rebecca York's writing is fast-paced, suspenseful, and loaded with tension." —Jayne Ann Krentz

"Glick's prose is smooth, literate and fast-moving; her love scenes are tender yet erotic; and there's always a happy ending." —*The Washington Post Book World*

"A true master of intrigue." —*Rave Reviews*

"No one sends more chills down your spine than the very creative and imaginative Ms. York!" —*Romantic Times*

"She writes a fast-paced, satisfying thriller." —UPI

EDGE OF THE
MOON

REBECCA YORK

BERKLEY SENSATION, NEW YORK

THE BERKLEY PUBLISHING GROUP
Published by the Penguin Group
Penguin Group (USA) Inc.
375 Hudson Street, New York, New York 10014, USA
Penguin Group (Canada), 90 Eglinton Avenue East, Suite 700, Toronto, Ontario M4P 2Y3, Canada
(a division of Pearson Penguin Canada Inc.)
Penguin Books Ltd., 80 Strand, London WC2R 0RL, England
Penguin Group Ireland, 25 St. Stephen's Green, Dublin 2, Ireland (a division of Penguin Books Ltd.)
Penguin Group (Australia), 250 Camberwell Road, Camberwell, Victoria 3124, Australia
(a division of Pearson Australia Group Pty. Ltd.)
Penguin Books India Pvt. Ltd., 11 Community Centre, Panchsheel Park, New Delhi—110 017, India
Penguin Group (NZ), 67 Apollo Drive, Rosedale, North Shore 0632, New Zealand
(a division of Pearson New Zealand Ltd.)
Penguin Books (South Africa) (Pty.) Ltd., 24 Sturdee Avenue, Rosebank, Johannesburg 2196,
South Africa

Penguin Books Ltd., Registered Offices: 80 Strand, London WC2R 0RL, England

This is a work of fiction. Names, characters, places, and incidents either are the product of the author's imagination or are used fictitiously, and any resemblance to actual persons, living or dead, business establishments, events, or locales is entirely coincidental. The publisher does not have any control over and does not assume any responsibility for author or third-party websites or their content.

EDGE OF THE MOON

A Berkley Sensation Book / published by arrangement with the author

PRINTING HISTORY
Berkley Sensation mass-market edition / August 2003

Copyright © 2003 by Ruth Glick.
Excerpt from *Witching Moon* copyright © 2003 by Ruth Glick.
Cover design by Brad Springer.

ISBN: 978-0-425-19125-5

BERKLEY® SENSATION
Berkley Sensation Books are published by The Berkley Publishing Group,
a division of Penguin Group (USA) Inc.,
375 Hudson Street, New York, New York 10014.
BERKLEY SENSATION and the "B" design are trademarks belonging to Penguin Group (USA) Inc.

PRINTED IN THE UNITED STATES OF AMERICA

15   14   13   12   11   10   9   8   7

EDGE OF THE
MOON

PROLOGUE

HIS NAME WAS Ayindral, and he lived somewhere between the realm of earth and ageless emptiness. In a plane of existence not of this universe.

Some might have called him a demon, a chimera, an imp, a spirit, or a jinni. Others might see him as a dark god and prostrate themselves before him.

But he was none of those. He was a being of energy. Of light and shadow. Of mental power. A being that humankind would never understand, even in a nightmare.

He had lived since before the planet Earth formed from cosmic dust. He would live on into eternity—if left to himself.

But there were channels of power between his world and the world of humankind, channels that could spell his destruction.

Like a rift in the fabric of time, one of those passageways had begun to open. In his incorporeal fashion, he raised his head and sniffed the air—catching the scent of danger the way an animal of the forest might sense the presence of a hunter.

There was no choice. He must act to save himself. And quickly, before it was too late. Delicately, desperately he cast his mind outward, searching for human beings he could bend to his will—use as his defensive shield.

CHAPTER
ONE

KATHRYN REYNOLDS SWEPT a lock of fiery red hair away from her forehead and rocked back in her chair.

Rolling the tension out of her shoulders, she stared critically at the computer screen. Two days ago she'd been happy with the brochure she was designing for Sunrise Realty.

Now . . .

Now she had the nagging feeling there was something wrong. Was the text readable enough against the background of rising suns? Should she use a bolder font?

She had just clicked on the color chart when she heard footsteps on the front porch of the white Victorian she'd inherited from Grandma O'Shea.

Heather! Thank God. She hadn't realized until that moment how worried she was. But her sigh of relief evaporated with the sound of the doorbell. Heather wouldn't ring the bell. Unless she'd lost her key—and forgotten about the one she'd hidden under a rock in the bushes. Which, actually, she wouldn't put past her friend and downstairs tenant. Heather had a lot of excellent qualities, but she was also a bit of a flake.

Speaking of which—

The bell sounded a second time, and a male voice called out, "Anybody home?" Kathryn looked down at the long, bare legs protruding from beneath her Redskins tee shirt. Damn! She'd done it again—gotten up and started working, then lost track of the time.

Now it was afternoon, and she wasn't exactly dressed for company. Sprinting into the bedroom, she grabbed the pair of knit shorts she'd left on the chair, pulling them on as she crossed the worn Oriental rug.

After unlocking the door to her apartment, she hurried barefoot down the stairs to the sound of pounding on the front door, then looked through the beveled glass window.

A dark-haired man in a blue uniform stood on the porch, and her mouth went dry.

It was him!

No. She canceled the spurt of panic. It wasn't him. He was too young. Too heavy. It wasn't the guy with the white van she'd seen off and on around the neighborhood for the past week—acting busy. He'd given her a creepy feeling, and she'd asked a couple of neighbors if they knew what he was doing. Nobody had been sure. She hadn't seen him for a few days; and, for a moment, she'd thought . . . But it wasn't him.

Slipping the door on the chain, she opened it and asked, "Can I help you?"

"Heather DeYoung?"

"She's not home right now."

The man looked annoyed. "She's supposed to be here between three and six."

"I'm sorry. Can I help you?" she asked again.

"Mr. Fisher asked me to bring over these carpet samples she wanted to see."

Heather had complained about the carpet in the bedroom, and Kathryn had said she'd go in with her on replacing it. But obviously she couldn't make the selection by herself.

"I'm sorry, you'll have to come back when she gets home."

He jutted out his jaw. "And when will that be?"

"I don't know."

"Yeah, well, I'm late for an installation job because of her, so tell her to get back to Mr. Fisher."

"I'll give her the message."

He picked up a vinyl case he'd set down and stamped back across the porch, leaving Kathryn standing in the vestibule that led to both apartments. Turning to her right, she stared at her friend's door.

When had she last seen Heather? Saturday night? She wasn't sure, because she'd been working on a couple of jobs, and she hadn't been paying attention. It wasn't unusual for Heather to take off for the weekend. And it wasn't even unusual for her to extend a minivacation into the next week—since she worked as a substitute teacher and could turn down assignments if she wanted. But usually she was back by Monday afternoon. Now it was Tuesday. And she still wasn't home.

Kathryn pressed her hand against the wall, running her fingers over the raised strips in the wallpaper, staring at Heather's door. She owned the apartment. She could go in if she wanted and look around, but her own sense of privacy was very strong. So she wasn't going to invade Heather's space just because she was feeling jumpy.

And what would she be looking for if she did go inside? A body? Signs of a struggle?

She grimaced, knowing she was letting her imagination run away with her now.

Slowly she climbed back up the stairs, stepped into her apartment, and locked the door—looking around at the cozy space where her graphic design business shared her living quarters. After Gran had died, she could have moved down to the first floor. But she liked being up here, liked the extra light and the view of the garden—and not having anyone walking around above her. She loved the high ceilings and the old wooden floors and the carefully crafted woodwork that made her home so different from the tract housing developers were slapping up these days. More than that, she was comfortable here. Maybe too comfortable. Sometimes she knew she had a tendency to close herself off like a hermit crab ducking into its shell.

Which was why her friendship with Heather De-Young, who rented the apartment downstairs, had been so good for her.

The woman could be maddening. Exasperating. A total flake. And at the same time a really good friend. In the year and a half that Heather had lived downstairs, they'd gotten into the habit of hanging out together—taking power walks in the afternoons, going on shopping expeditions. Talked long into the evening about movies and books and the guys in their lives. Shared their problems.

So did her friend have a problem now? Something she hadn't felt comfortable bringing up? Like that little episode last year?

She crossed to the window, ducked under The Spider Plant That Took over the World, and stared down at the bright pink and red azaleas in full bloom, then flicked her gaze back to the empty space in the driveway where her tenant's burgundy Honda was usually parked.

"Dammit, Heather," she muttered. "Where are you? Atlantic City, cleaning up at the slot machines? Why don't you take a minute to give me a call and let me know you're okay?"

Like magic, the phone rang, and she blinked—then sprinted back to the desk and snatched up the receiver.

"Hello?"

There was no answer.

"Hello?"

The silence stretched, and she carefully replaced the receiver in the cradle as she looked at the caller I.D.

It said "Unavailable." So it was probably just one of those automated telemarketing calls. Not Heather trying to check in. Or calling to say her car had broken down because she'd forgotten to change the oil.

Like she'd forgotten to charge the battery on her cell phone. Which was probably why there was no answer when Kathryn had called that number.

She grimaced. Maybe it was time to check in with Heather's boyfriend, Gary Swinton. He was a strange guy. Secretive. Always acting superior, like he knew something Kathryn didn't. Privately she called him The Swine, and she'd told Heather she could do better; but Gary was still in and out of her bed on a semiregular basis.

After looking up his number in her Rolodex and dialing, she counted five rings before an answering machine picked up.

"Hey, this is Gary. I really want to talk to you. So leave a message."

Yeah, sure, she thought. Probably she was the last person he wanted to talk to, because she'd made her feelings about him pretty clear.

She almost hung up. Then she took a breath and said in an upbeat voice, "Hi. This is Kathryn Reynolds. I'm trying to reach Heather. She needs to set up an appointment to look at the bedroom carpet samples. If she's with you, could you ask her to give me a call?" She finished by leaving her number, all the time picturing Gary sitting by the machine, listening to her talk.

She considered driving down to his place. But he lived in D.C., in Adams Morgan—not a neighborhood she liked to walk through alone at night. And it would be dark by the time she got there.

With a sigh, she picked up the magic wand sitting on the desk. Too bad she couldn't wave it, say "abracadabra," and command her tenant to appear. Unfortunately, the wand was just a hollow plastic tube about a foot long, one of the toys she liked to play with while she was thinking. It was filled with shiny stars and moons floating in a viscous blue liquid. Turning it on end, she watched the heavenly bodies shoot upward in a swirl of blue, but they didn't give her any insights into Heather's whereabouts.

Her hand tightened on the plastic as she seesawed the cylinder back and forth, watching the moving shapes, trying to banish the feeling of uneasiness that had been hanging over her since she'd opened her eyes that morning. Well, longer than that—if she were honest.

With a small *thunk*, she set down the wand.

What was wrong with her? She was usually rock steady. In charge of her life. She'd been on her own since Gran died five years ago. She'd paid for her own college education with work-study and student loans. After apprenticing for a couple years at one of the big ad agencies downtown, she'd gone out on her own. Her graphic design business was doing really well, and her client list was growing as satisfied customers recommended her to their friends. She'd worked hard to get where she was. And she was proud of her achievements.

But for the past few days, a kind of free-floating anxiety had been hanging over her. Not just because of Heather. It was something else—something she couldn't identify. Like a storm gathering, its low, dark clouds hanging directly over her.

"Really, that's a pretty over-the-top image," she muttered. With a quick shake of her head, she crossed to the window, staring down again at the empty space in the driveway. Heather would be home tomorrow morning, she told herself firmly. But if she wasn't, it was time to get in touch with the Montgomery County Police.

JACK Thornton pulled his unmarked into the driveway of his gray colonial, cut the engine, and sat with his hands wrapped around the wheel for several moments.

All day he'd felt something hovering over him, something that grated on his nerves. And now that he was home, he felt as though he'd made a miraculous escape.

From what?

He didn't know. But he did know he'd had a hell of a day. He'd walked into the middle of a domestic case. The kind that made him wonder if he was a police detective or a mental health worker.

It started out when he'd been driving down Democracy Boulevard and seen a woman dressed in a nightgown and robe, sobbing and running in and out of the traffic. No one else was on the scene, so he'd called in a report, then stopped and identified himself.

By the time a couple of uniformed officers had arrived, Mrs. Westborn had apparently bonded with him.

But seeing the uniforms got her sobbing again, begging him to stay with her, and he'd ended up taking her to Montgomery County Hospital, where he'd interviewed her in an emergency room cubicle.

He'd sensed from the first that she was holding back information—which was one of the reasons he'd stuck with her.

With a good deal of patience and reassurance, he'd finally gotten Mrs. Westborn to admit that her husband was at home—dead. He'd slit his own throat, and the wife had freaked out.

Slit his throat! That had riveted Jack's attention. Slitting a throat wasn't so easy to do, despite its popularity with producers of slasher movies. It took a bit of effort to cut through tough muscles, cords, and rubbery tendons, unless you had a rather large and exceptionally sharp surgical scalpel. Besides, throat-cutting was a kind of slow and painful death, one that normally didn't appeal to suicidal folks.

Jack had sent a couple of uniforms to check out the story while he'd waited with the woman until psychiatric services arrived.

Then he'd gone over to the house to investigate the scene—and found the guy was dressed in a woman's lacy gown and robe.

So much for domestic tranquillity in Montgomery County, Maryland, one of the richest counties in the nation. But he'd learned that more money sometimes meant more problems. Like the bored teenager who had hacked up his friend a few years ago, or the group of boys who'd raped a mentally retarded girl in the woods.

Now he was thinking that murder was as likely as suicide in the Westborn case. Tomorrow he'd start questioning the neighbors, to find out how the couple had been getting along. But he wasn't going to dismiss the possibility of suicide out of hand. Suppose, for example, that Westborn was in serious financial trouble, and he'd seen only one way out?

Six months ago, Jack might have started checking up on Westborn from his home computer. But he'd been smart enough to recognize the signs of burnout. He'd pulled back, vowed to leave the job at the office.

As he stepped inside the door, he was enveloped by the smell of baking chocolate chip cookies. For a heart-stopping moment, he thought that Laura was in the kitchen with the kids. Then reality came slamming back. Almost three years ago, a drunk driver on I-270 had crossed the median and crashed into his wife's car with enough force to ram the engine block into the front seat.

He closed his eyes, banishing the terrible image. He didn't need it. Not now.

He took several measured steps down the hall, focusing on the conversation coming from the kitchen. Craig was talking to their housekeeper, Emily Anderson, and he remembered that seven-year-old Lily was at a friend's for dinner. Emily was going to pick her up later.

Nine-year-old Craig was enthusiastically helping with the cookies.

"You promised I could lick the bowl. If you keep on scraping like that, there won't be anything left," Craig complained.

"I think you like cookie dough better than cookies."

"Yeah. And you got those eggs that come in a carton so I could eat the dough."

"Mm-hmm." The housekeeper chuckled. "I suppose

I liked the dough better, too, when I was your age," she admitted.

"Not you, Mrs. A."

"Oh, yes."

Jack set down his briefcase and leaned his shoulder against the wall, enjoying the domestic eavesdropping. His children had gone through a pretty rough patch, and it was gratifying to hear Craig having a normal good time, thanks to Mrs. Anderson. A plumber's widow, she was the perfect grandmother substitute for two kids who needed as much stability in their lives as they could get. And she ran the house with quiet, unobtrusive efficiency.

The timer rang. From the hallway, Jack watched the housekeeper bend to open the oven and take out a cookie sheet. Deftly she used a metal spatula to transfer the cookies to wire racks.

"When can I have one?" Craig asked.

"Well, we both know it's supposed to be dinner first and then dessert."

"Aw . . ."

Emily lowered her voice to a conspiratorial whisper. "You can have a cookie first, if you have it with a glass of milk. Just be sure to eat your dinner—so your dad won't think I'm a bad influence."

"You're a good influence! I've heard him say that."

She made a *tsk*ing sound as she set the boy up at the table with his before-dinner treat, then popped the last sheet of cookies into the oven.

Jack was about to join them when Craig stopped him in his tracks with a question. "Does a girl have to be married to have a baby?"

He saw Mrs. Anderson set down her pot holder and turn slowly, saw his son watching her intently.

"Uh, why do you want to know?" she asked.

Craig scuffed his foot against the chrome leg of his chair. "Dad tries to be real cool, but he'd probably get uptight if I asked him."

"What made you think of the question?" the house-keeper asked carefully.

"On the playground today, this kid, Billy Patterson, was talking about his sister. He says she's going to have a baby and that her and her boyfriend are probably going to get married."

"She and her boyfriend," Mrs. Anderson corrected. "Craig, this is the kind of thing you *should* talk to your dad about."

"Oh, he got me and Lily this book that explains all about . . . you know . . . about how the mom and dad . . . you know. But I can't imagine anyone doing something that yucky unless they were married and . . . you know . . . had to have a baby."

"Well, some people . . . uh . . . try it out before they get married."

Jack felt a stab of guilt, because he was glad Emily was handling this for him. One of the things he dreaded about single fatherhood was coping with the sensitive stuff.

"Oh." Craig thought about that. "Do you think my mom and dad did it before they got married?"

"I don't know."

"But they did it after. Twice."

Jack took a step back, his stomach knotting. God, what he wouldn't give to do it with Laura again!

Closing his eyes, he took a quick emotional inventory. His wife's loss was no longer a raw wound. Maybe he was even ready to think about a relationship with another woman—although he hadn't met anyone that interested him.

With an inaudible sigh, he returned to the front door, opening it silently, then closing it loudly to announce his arrival before striding down the hall.

Both occupants of the kitchen looked toward the door, embarrassment painted across their faces. Mrs. Anderson bent and checked the oven again. Craig took a gulp of milk.

"What a great surprise. Cookies," Jack said, grabbing one and taking a bite.

HE was slender and of medium height, with pale gray eyes that darkened when he was excited or when he wore his special contact lenses. His hair was fine and blond as corn silk. When he combed it carefully, the medallion-sized bald spot on his crown was invisible.

He called himself many names. Simon Gwynn was his alias today, although that wasn't his real name, of course. He was careful to keep his real identity hidden, because to have possession of a name was to have power over that thing or person.

No one had questioned the legitimacy of Simon Gwynn or any of his other names. They gave him protection—from the police, from those few men who still knew and practiced the ancient magic arts. And from other more powerful forces.

But names weren't his only safeguard. He had many homes, so that he could switch his residence if need be. And there were many disguises that he put on when he ventured forth into the world of ordinary men and women. Not just the clothing—the whole persona, he thought with a self-satisfied laugh. He could look and sound like an old man in a dirty button-down shirt, baggy pants, and a white Albert Einstein wig. He could play a plumber in a visor cap and blue coveralls with the name Jerry embroidered on the breast pocket. A fast-talking salesman in a crisp blue suit, horn-rimmed glasses, and a mustache. He had a wardrobe that filled an enormous closet. And the theater courses he'd taken had taught him the art of makeup. Once or twice, he'd even passed as a woman, although that certainly wasn't his preferred mode of disguise.

Alone at home, he dressed quite simply and all in black. This afternoon he was clad only in loose-fitting silk trousers that slid sensuously against the skin of his legs as he climbed the stairs from the basement.

He'd been down there to check on the prisoner in the soundproof cell behind the locked door in the laundry room. She had been spaced out when he'd scooped her up. Spaced out and all too trusting. Stupid, actually. Too caught up in a relationship to pay attention to little warning signs. But most people were like that. You simply had to understand how to manipulate them. How to assert your will over theirs.

She was still sleeping from the drugs he'd put in her food. If she figured out what he'd done, she wouldn't eat the next time he fed her. But that was okay. If she didn't eat, she'd get weak. And that would only make it easier to handle her when he brought her into the black chamber and used her in the most important ceremony of his career.

As he ascended the stairs, he stroked his fingers gently over the skin of his narrow chest. It was pale, except where it was crisscrossed with a network of fine, raised red lines. He stroked those faint lines, loving the way they felt under his sensitive fingertips. The scars were the product of the lash he'd taken to his own flesh. The lash that was part of the discipline of his studies.

The lines that remained were symbols of his acquisition of knowledge, and he was justifiably proud of them.

When he reached the second floor, he walked with measured paces to the library. The walls were lined with volumes, old and new. *The Golden Dawn* as revealed by Israel Regardie; *The Black Arts*, the brilliant biography of Aleister Crowley; *The Great Beast*, Hopper's *Mediaeval Number Symbols; The Kabbalah*, Butler's *Ritual Magic*. Most of the standard works in his field. He was still looking for *Portal to Another World* on the off chance that it still existed somewhere. But he didn't need it; he'd learned enough on his own from the books he had hunted down in private libraries and dusty shops. Along with the ancient texts and the histories of magic rituals were the other branches of knowledge he had explored. Psychology, pharmacology, economics, social history, anthropology, physics.

He had studied long and hard, delved into mysteries that few understood. He had practiced the rituals he needed, memorized the words of power. And soon he would be ready to put all his hard work to the test.

A tingle of excitement rippled over his skin, and he struggled to regain his composure. There was no room in his life for euphoria. Not yet. Not until he had achieved his goal.

CHAPTER
TWO

IN HIS DREAMLESS realm, Ayindral felt a ripple in the current of time, a moment in which he could catch the leading edge of the wave and change the course of events.

The woman was the key. The woman who had captured the magician's interest.

But he needed to be sure of the man as well. Delicately his mind probed the world of humans. Sight and sound were alien to Ayindral. Yet he could simulate the tools that humans used.

Through the shrouded fog of his own universe, he opened a window into the world of men. It was only a narrow slit in the time–space continuum, and yet there was an immediate rush of mental energy from one state to another, like a rush of wind, a pulling sensation that turned the core of his being cold.

A soundless scream rose within him. Soundless because he had no mouth, no vocal cords. He was a being of pure energy, and pain was alien to him. Yet he felt it.

Ruthlessly, he ignored the frightening sensation. The

danger would come, yet the time of greatest risk had not arrived.

Now he entered the mind of Police Captain James Granger and sent the man a new idea—reinforcing it with a clenching cramp in the gut.

JACK looked up to see Captain Granger standing beside the blotter. "What are you working on?" his supervisor asked.

Jack gestured toward the papers spread across his desk. "I'm doing a background check on Harold Westborn, the guy whose wife says he slit his throat."

"Yeah. I think we can turn that one over to the medical examiner."

Jack blinked. "We're not going to investigate it as a possible murder?"

"Let's see what the M.E. says. If he confirms suicide, then we can cross it off our caseload."

"Okay." That wasn't the way Granger usually worked. Usually he assumed a suspicious death was murder, until the facts showed otherwise. But he figured the captain must have his reasons this time.

Granger's next words confirmed the speculation. "I've got something more important for you. Come into my office."

Jack pushed back his chair, then followed his supervisor to the private enclosure in the corner of the squad room.

When they were both seated, Granger said, "I'd like you to interview a woman named Kathryn Reynolds." He consulted a file on his desk. "She turned in a missing person report two days ago on her tenant, Heather DeYoung. One of the uniforms at the Rockville station, Chris Kendall, took the initial report."

"Uh-huh."

"We have several other missing person reports in the county. Another woman named Brenda Quinlin. A young man named Stewart Talber. And an eight-year-old boy, Kip Bradley."

Jack felt his chest tighten. A kid. About the age of his own children. He remembered reading about it. There was some evidence that the boy had been abducted by his noncustodial father, but neither the man nor the boy had turned up in a month of beating the bushes for them. Jack was still hoping it was the father, because the alternative hit too close to home.

"The missing guy is a mentally-ill man," Granger was saying. "On the surface these incidents don't seem related to each other—or to Heather DeYoung. But you're good at digging information out of witnesses and making correlations. DeYoung was just reported missing. I want your impressions, and then I want you to see if you can find any patterns."

Basically, there was nothing strange about Granger's request. Jack knew he was good at connecting the dots on crimes that might not seem related. Still, Granger's manner put him on the alert. There was something else in play here. Had a bigwig with an interest in one of the cases leaned on the captain?

Jack knew he might never find out. So he simply said, "Okay," took the offered case files, and went back to his own desk to study them.

AN hour later, he pulled up in front of Kathryn Reynolds's nicely preserved Victorian on Davenport Street. Out of habit, his appraising eye took in details. It was early in the season, but the flower beds were dressed with a fresh layer of mulch. Pink and red azaleas and a variety of daffodils were in bloom, along with white dogwoods.

The plantings were mature, like the house. They might say nothing about Reynolds's tastes. On the other hand, she hadn't ripped out the bushes and paved the yard with antique brick, the way he'd seen with homeowners who didn't want to be bothered with the great outdoors.

His gaze flicked back to the structure. The white siding looked like it had been painted recently. And the paving in the driveway was fresh, which suggested that the owner was doing well financially. The house and garden definitely looked better than some of the other properties in this older Rockville neighborhood of mature trees and wide lawns.

Rockville had once been a sleepy rural community about forty minutes north of D.C. Years ago, its chief claim to fame was that F. Scott Fitzgerald was buried on the outskirts of town. Now the country church and its graveyard were surrounded by a tangle of highways—a symbol that suburban sprawl had moved out to envelop the area. But there were still neighborhoods, like this one, that looked pretty much the way they had seventy-five years ago.

He sat for several more minutes, still grappling with the odd, disquieting feeling that had settled over him in Granger's office. He might have ignored it, but long ago he'd learned to trust his spider senses.

He'd worked with Chris Kendall, the officer who had taken Reynolds's report, back when they were both at the Bethesda station, and he would have liked to talk to him before coming out here. But the patrolman had left the building for a doctor's appointment before Jack had gotten the assignment. Too bad, because the initial police contact was a good source of additional information. The uniforms put down what was required in writing. But there was usually a whole lot they didn't get onto paper. Jack liked to do a little probing into their casual observations, stuff they didn't think was important enough to go in the report, or stuff they didn't even know they'd noticed, until he asked about it. He also paid attention to their opinions, which gave them a chance to express "gut feelings" that were often useful later.

Of course, Jack suspected Granger was probably

planning to do the same thing with him. More than
once, the captain had sent him out on an interview that
hardly seemed top priority, then quizzed him on his
impressions.

After climbing out of the unmarked and locking the
door, he glanced toward the second floor of the house
and caught a flash of red. Red hair, he realized—as fiery
as flames flickering behind the windowpanes.

Was that Reynolds? Or someone else? Whoever it
was had pulled back the moment he'd looked up. So
she was nervous about getting caught peering out or
curious about who had pulled up in front of her house?

He hadn't called ahead. She'd said she worked at
home, so he'd taken a chance on catching her in—
catching her off-balance if there was something going
on that she hadn't shared with Officer Kendall.

He tucked the folder unobtrusively under one arm
and started toward the front door. According to the initial report, Ms. Reynolds owned the house and lived
on the upper story. The missing woman had an apartment on the ground floor.

Jack rang the bell and listened to footsteps coming
down an inner stairway. He prepared to confirm the
name of the female who opened the door; but the moment the door opened, the breath froze in his lungs so
that it was impossible to speak.

He was caught and held by a pair of emerald green
eyes, a sweep of wild red hair, and skin like rich dairy
cream.

His muscles went rigid. His arm clamped on the
folder tucked against his body.

Time seemed to stop, like a scene from a videotape
frozen on a TV screen. Unable to move forward or back
away, he stared into her eyes, seeing her pupils dilate
and then contract.

Everything around him was out of focus, with the
exception of the slender young woman standing in the
doorway. She remained sharp and clear. Details came
to him: the way her breasts filled out the front of her

wildflower-printed tee shirt. The smell of strawberries wafting toward him. The startled look in those green eyes.

Along with the physical awareness came a jolt of pure sexual energy, like nothing he had ever experienced in his life. Lust at first sight. It was almost palpable—arching between them like electricity between two contact points. Dangerous and at the same time so compelling that he would have leaped through a wall of fire to reach this woman if she had been on the other side.

The whole out-of-kilter experience lasted only seconds. Then the world as he knew it clicked back into real time. The moment had passed so quickly that it was easy to tell himself that it had all been in his imagination.

He clung to that theory, because if it wasn't imagination, he was hardly equipped to deal with what had happened.

The woman in the doorway took a quick step back, as if trying to escape from the same emotions bolting through him.

For several heartbeats, neither of them spoke.

Finally, Jack dragged air into his lungs and let it out before asking, "Kathryn Reynolds?" He was surprised that his voice sounded normal.

"Yes. And you are?"

"Detective Jack Thornton, Montgomery County P.D."

Reynolds's hands clenched in front of her. "The police? Have you come to tell me something about Heather? Is it bad news?"

"Are you expecting bad news?" he asked, slipping back into his professional mode, carefully watching her reaction.

"No . . . I mean, I don't know. I hope not. I don't know what to expect."

"Can I come in? Then you can tell me what brought you to the station house."

"Can I see some identification?" she countered, as if she'd just realized she should have asked.

"Of course." While he pulled out his I.D. and shield, he was still mentally shaking his head at his out-of-character reaction in those first few seconds after she'd opened the door.

She studied his I.D, then said, "I already filed a report with Officer . . ." She stopped and fumbled for the name. "Officer Kendall."

"Yes." Jack put away his credentials, then pulled the folder from under his arm, opened it, and showed her the forms. "I have the report right here. So can we talk?"

This time she nodded and stepped back to let him into a vestibule. He followed her through a second doorway, then up a flight of steps, watching the unconscious sway of her hips in faded jeans.

He was accustomed to making assumptions about people based on their personal spaces. Seconds after stepping into her apartment, he was thinking that Kathryn Reynolds was a study in contradictions.

In one corner of the room was an antique desk with a computer under a set of mahogany wall shelves. Catty-corner to the desk area were more shelves piled with neatly labeled folders and plastic boxes. The office atmosphere was broken by all manner of whimsical objects that adorned the work area. He saw ceramic cats, a papier-mâché rooster, at least ten fancy glass paperweights, a white unicorn. On her computer screen was an underwater scene with swimming fish and coral. When the computer made a belching, bubbling noise like a toilet flushing, she crossed the room and cranked the sound down.

He turned to hide his grin and saw that the opposite side of the room showed even more of her personality.

Intrigued, he walked closer. She had a flowered humpback sofa, several overstuffed chairs, and a coffee table that looked like it might have started life as a packing case. A ceramic pitcher of dried flowers shared the marble top of a low chest with several Mexican carved and painted animals. A Victorian whatnot held paperback books and antique toys. The pictures on the walls reflected the same eclectic mix.

Looking from the decor to her tense face, he strove to put her at ease. Or perhaps he just wanted her to know he wasn't a total ignoramus when it came to culture.

"You're a fan of Sir Lawrence Alma-Tadema?" he asked, peering at a picture of some very handsome young men and women dressed in classical Greek outfits relaxing around a circular marble structure.

"You like his work?"

He laughed. "Actually, yes. I once caught a burglary case where a whole bunch of his prints were stolen. I started off rolling my eyes at his stuff, but he grows on you."

"Yes. He was out of style for years. But I always did like his combination of realism and romanticism."

He nodded, not sure exactly what she meant, and thinking it was time to get back to business.

He cleared his throat. "So when did you first notice that Heather DeYoung was missing?"

She walked toward one of the easy chairs, picked up a paisley pillow, and clutched it to her middle as she sat down. "It kind of crept up on me. Two days ago I realized she hadn't come home since Sunday night."

"She was missing for five days before you reported it?"

Her fingers clamped on the pillow. "You're making it sound like an accusation."

"I didn't mean to. I'm just trying to get the full picture," he said, still watching her reactions, thinking that facts were never the whole story.

"Sometimes she stays away for several days. It suddenly dawned on me that I hadn't seen her in a while."

"Okay," he answered, noting her discomfort. He still didn't know if it was because of her friend or because of him.

For a split second he thought about what had happened when she'd opened the door. Should he say something to clear the air? Or to find out if she'd experienced the same thing that he had?

The latter would be his primary motive, he silently admitted. A very unprofessional motive.

Usually he had an excellent sense of what questions to ask a witness or a suspect. Today he fumbled for the right approach.

"Let's see. Ms. DeYoung works for the Montgomery County school system as a substitute teacher. That pays enough to support her?"

"She says it does."

"But she could have some other source of income?"

"I don't know."

He set finances aside for the moment. He had other ways of poking into the woman's fiscal solvency. Instead, he quickly switched topics. "So Ms. DeYoung is unreliable?"

She tipped her head to one side. "Where did you get that impression?"

"It isn't unusual for her to take off for several days—on a whim?" He waited for her to answer the question.

"Yes, but she pays her rent on time. She doesn't give me any problems."

"What kind of problems are you referring to?"

"She doesn't play loud music. She doesn't have wild parties. She doesn't wake me up at two in the morning if the toilet's stopped up. She gets out a plunger."

He nodded, thinking about what she was saying and what she was leaving out. "Does she have any bad habits? Drugs, alcohol? Something that could get her into trouble."

"No," she said, but could have sounded more sure.

"But?"

Reynolds swallowed. "I don't like to make judgments. And I don't like to talk about people."

"I understand. But if it will help us find Heather, I'd appreciate your insights."

She hesitated, then answered. "Okay, I don't like her boyfriend."

"Because?"

"He takes advantage. She loves him, but he doesn't love her."

"How do you mean, 'takes advantage'?"

"He's borrowed money from her." She stopped, played with the fringe of the pillow. "I wouldn't tell you this if it weren't important. He told her he'd stop dating her if she didn't have an abortion last year, but she was the one who had to pay for it."

The guy sounded like a real winner, but Jack still didn't know whether or not Reynolds was exaggerating her assessment. "She discussed all that with you?"

"Yes. We've gotten to be good friends."

"What's his name?"

"Gary Swinton."

"Could she be at his house?"

"His apartment," she corrected. "I thought of that. I called and left a couple of messages on his answering machine."

"Do you have a phone number for him, an address?"

"In my Rolodex." She stood, set the pillow down on the chair, and crossed to the desk, where she flipped through cards, then gave him the requested information.

"What about a work address?"

She thought about that. "I know he works at Circuit City. The one in Bethesda. I think he's in small electronics—because he got a good deal for her on a floor model tabletop stereo. But I don't have the address."

"I know where it is. Can you give me a description? Some way I'll recognize him?"

Her hand skimmed across the desk, settled over a footlong clear plastic rod with colored liquid and shiny stars and moons inside. When she tipped it on end, the liquid and the glitter began to flow up and down the tube.

She stared at the bobbing glitter, her brow wrinkling. "He's about thirty years old. Blond hair. Light eyes.

They're set close together. His hair is usually just one beat too long—maybe to hide his bald spot. He's average height. Not too heavy. He's got a small scar on the left side of his chin. I guess that would be the most identifying mark."

"Okay. That's great," he said, writing it down. "You're good at detail."

"My art background."

"Yeah."

She was still playing with the plastic tube. He watched the swirl of colors. "What's that?"

She gave a small, embarrassed laugh. "A magic wand."

"Where did you get it?"

"Don't tell me you need one."

"Sometimes I'd like to have one. But I was thinking my daughter would like it."

"Oh, you're married."

"I was. . . ." He let the sentence trail off. Probably she thought he was divorced, and he didn't want her thinking that he couldn't make a marriage work. Then he reminded himself that it didn't matter what she thought about him. He was interviewing her about a missing person—that was all.

"Oh," she said again, twirling the plastic rod in her hand.

His eyes were drawn to the bits of glitter and the swirling blue liquid. For a moment they both watched the shifting motion inside the beveled plastic.

"What would you do with a magic wand if you had one?" she asked.

"Solve Stone Who Done Its."

"What's a Stone Who Done It?"

"A case where there are no solid suspects and no leads."

"Um."

He watched her lips form the syllable, then roused himself from his study of her—a very unprofessional study. "Would it be possible for me to see Ms. De-Young's apartment?"

She hesitated. "I'd feel like you were invading her privacy."

"Maybe I'd see something that would give me a clue."

"I went down there before I filed the missing person report. I didn't see anything."

"You're not a trained police detective."

She thought that over, then gave a small nod. After putting down the wand, she opened a desk drawer and extracted a key with a pink ribbon threaded through the key chain hole.

She went back down the stairs to the vestibule.

"Did you have the house converted into a duplex?" he asked, already knowing the answer, since he could tell that the work was more than twenty years old.

"No. Grandma O'Shea did it after my grandfather died. She didn't need such a big place, and she needed the income."

"So how did you end up with the property?"

"My parents got divorced. Dad took off for parts unknown. Mom and I moved into the downstairs apartment. I was just starting college when she got a pulmonary embolism. She died."

"I'm sorry."

"It could have been worse. Grandma O'Shea and I were always close, and I moved in with her."

"She died, too?"

"In her sleep. Five years ago. A heart attack. She was ninety-two and able to take care of herself until the end. I guess that's the way to live—and the way to go."

"Yes," he answered, wondering what his own chances were of dying in bed.

They were still standing in the hallway. "I took the upstairs flat and rented out this one," she said, unlocking the door. She stepped into an apartment that was similar to her own in layout. But the similarity ended there.

Her abode had been quirky but orderly. DeYoung

was—to put it politely—a slob. There were stacks of mail, newspapers, and other paper on every flat surface, including the floor. When he walked farther into the room and looked toward the kitchen, he saw dirty dishes in the sink and on the counter.

"You say she didn't give you any trouble. It looks like you're going to have to blast this place out when she moves."

"Okay, she's not so neat. But she's a good person. She likes children and animals."

"Mm hmm," he said, thinking it was probably lucky she didn't have custody of either.

He scanned the apartment. To his practiced eye, the owner had stepped out and intended to come back.

He started with the answering machine, pressed the rewind button and listened to the messages. There were several—two from Ms. Reynolds, both asking De-Young to call.

And a message from the boyfriend, Swinton, two days ago. Which proved nothing. If he'd done something to her, he might have left the message to establish his innocence.

The rest of the messages were at least four days old. One was apparently from the office that handled substitute teachers, asking if she was available to take a biology class at Wootton High School on Monday. Another was from her mother with some chatty news about various friends and relatives.

"Did she go to work on Monday?" Jack asked.

"I don't know."

He nodded, then strode down the hall to the bedroom and opened the closet. The hanging rack was full of blouses and jackets, packed so tightly together that they had to come out wrinkled.

"I'd ask if you thought anything was missing, but I imagine it's hard to tell," he said over his shoulder.

"I looked in her storage closet. Her suitcases are there."

"Did you check her dresser drawers?"

She swiped back a lock of fiery hair. "I opened some, yes. But I felt like a sneak, so I gave it up."

He opened a drawer and found sweaters in a messy pile. Reaching underneath, he discovered nothing hidden. The next drawer held panty hose and nothing else. The third was a mass of women's underpants and bras. This time, when he slid his hand underneath, he felt several magazines and a book. When he pulled them out, he saw that they were pornography—S and M oriented. One magazine cover showed an almost naked woman chained to a crossbar. A man was standing over her with a whip. The other magazines were similar. And the book looked like a dominance and submission how-to manual. He made a snorting sound. It seemed that a routine case had just gotten more interesting.

Before he lost the chance to catch Reynolds's unvarnished reaction, he glanced up. She was standing stock-still, staring at the literature as if he'd pulled a box of rattlesnakes out of the drawer.

CHAPTER
THREE

KATHRYN MANAGED TO draw in a breath.

She felt Detective Thornton's gaze on her.

"You said you and Ms. DeYoung are friends. Did you know she was interested in . . . unusual . . . sexual practices?" he asked.

"No!"

He continued to stare at her like he didn't believe her, like he thought maybe she and Heather were into some kind of dirty little games together. She shifted her weight from one foot to the other, resisting the impulse to flee the room. "Honestly, I wouldn't have thought . . ." Her voice trailed off.

"Do you mind if I take this stuff?" he asked, waggling the book and magazines in his hand. "And a piece of her clothing."

"Do what you want!" Turning, she fled the room, fled from the apartment and up the stairs. It was several moments before she realized that Detective Thornton had followed her. He'd put the magazines into a paper grocery bag, which he must have found in Heather's kitchen. She assumed there was also a piece of Heather's clothing in there.

His eyes stayed fixed on her, and she made an effort to calm down, although her pulse was pounding.

"Why are you so upset?" he asked.

"I'm not."

He continued to stare at her, letting that obvious lie hang in the air between them.

She sighed. It was none of his business, yet she felt compelled to say, "Apparently my . . . my father was interested in that kind of stuff. That's why my mom divorced him."

It was his turn to say "Oh."

She focused on the fish swimming across her computer monitor, thinking that her parents' screwed-up relationship was none of this man's business. Mom was dead. Her father was, too, for all she knew. What had happened between him and Mom was a long time ago, so long ago that Kathryn had locked the knowledge in some deep, hidden corner of her mind. Maybe she'd actually forgotten about it.

Then the door to the memories had blasted open—when she'd seen the "literature" from the bottom of Heather's underwear drawer. She remembered her mother standing in the bedroom, holding a magazine that looked remarkably similar to the one Thornton had found. She remembered the mixture of anger and sadness on her mother's face.

A few months later, Mom had moved them out of the house and into Grandma's. And she and Mom had never talked about why they'd cleared out. It had stayed buried—a family secret that had finally sunk into the swamp of bad memories.

Until a few minutes ago when Thornton had pulled those magazines from the drawer.

Lord, did other families have similar stuff they didn't talk about? Probably, she told herself. Maybe even Jack Thornton. His marriage had ended. There must have been reasons.

Well, that was none of *her* business, she thought as she watched a sea horse bob up and disappear again, aware that Thornton was watching her, hoping that she'd divulge something he could sink his teeth into. But there wasn't anything—at least with regard to Heather. And she wasn't going to share more about her background than she'd already blurted out.

"Do you have any additional questions for me?" she asked, hearing the hard edge in her voice. She wanted Jack Thornton out of her apartment.

He cleared his throat. "Do you have a picture of Ms. DeYoung? And could you give me the phone number of her next of kin?"

Next of kin. In case Heather was dead. "Her mother is Margaret DeYoung. She lives in Philadelphia." Once again she opened her Rolodex and found the number.

"Are they on good terms?"

"She doesn't see her often. But I think they get along."

"Would she go there if she were in trouble?"

"Maybe."

"Okay. Thanks. If you can just give me a picture, I'll get out of your hair."

In fact, she was easily able to accommodate the detective. A couple of weeks ago, she and Heather had been out in the yard enjoying the azaleas, and they'd decided that the bright masses of flowers would make a nice backdrop for some pictures. She'd gone back inside for her camera, then ordered double prints when she had the roll processed. Shuffling through the shots, she handed one to Thornton.

"Thanks. I appreciate it," he said, slipping it into the folder with the missing person report.

Now that he was leaving, she was able to raise her eyes to his and asked the question that had been gathering in her mind. "Do you think you're going to find her? I mean—find her alive."

"I hope so."

"But you're not counting on it."

"We've barely gotten into the investigation. I should ask, is there anyone besides the boyfriend that you think might want to do her harm?"

"I didn't exactly put it that way!"

"Noted." He stared at her, making it impossible for her not to speak.

She took a calming breath before answering. "Okay, there is one other thing I should tell you. Some things have happened around here. Vandalism, I guess you'd call it."

"Such as what?"

"Little things. Trash from my trash cans spread around the driveway. Some black spray paint on the white lattice at the bottom of the porch. Stuff like that."

"Did you report it to the police?"

"It didn't seem worth it."

"So—are you having a fight with any of the neighbors?"

"Not that I know of. I don't know if it has to do with me—or Heather."

"Thanks for telling me," he said, but she had the feeling he was reproaching her for holding back until the last minute. She swallowed. "Okay, there's one more thing—since you're asking. There was a workman in a white van hanging around the neighborhood last week. I never found out what he was doing. But he gave me a . . . creepy feeling."

"Did you get his license number?"

"It was smeared with dirt," she said, suddenly feeling as if she should have tried harder.

He wrote that down, then said, "I may get back to you with more questions. Here's my card, in case you think of anything."

She accepted the small white rectangle, flexing it in her hand as he walked toward the door.

He hesitated for a moment, as though he wanted to say something more, and she felt her nerves jangle as she waited to find out what he was thinking. Was he going to mention that first charged moment when they'd faced each other at the door?

To her relief, he remained silent, then left.

She closed and locked the door behind him, then moved to the window, standing back where she thought he couldn't see her, since he'd already caught her watching him when he arrived. But he didn't look back as he climbed into his car and drove away. When the vehicle was out of sight, she let out the breath she hadn't known she was holding. She'd wanted him to leave, but now that he was gone, she felt strangely let down. Backing away from that part, she went over the rest of the encounter. After those first few moments, she'd kept herself together while he was here, until she'd seen that magazine he'd pulled from Heather's drawer.

Before that, she hadn't known that Heather had any interest in sadomasochism. If she'd had a clue, she would have told her to run—not walk—away from that sick bastard Gary as fast as she could.

Unfortunately, Heather hadn't said anything. Or asked for help. And now Kathryn was left with a clenched feeling in her gut. And the sneaking suspicion that she didn't know Heather DeYoung as well as she'd thought. Or Gary Swinton. She'd had bad feelings about the guy. What else was he hiding?

Stiff-legged, she crossed to the kitchen and filled the kettle at the sink. While she waited for the water to boil, her mind flashed back to Detective Thornton.

Something had happened when she'd first opened the door to him and they'd stood facing each other across four feet of charged space, something she couldn't explain—a sudden awareness of the man that had taken her breath away.

So many impressions had assaulted her at once—with no time to sort them out. Now she took a mental step back and tried to analyze why the encounter had been so arresting.

He'd been wearing a tweed sports jacket over a light

blue shirt and dark slacks. She wasn't the kind of woman who went around mentally undressing men. But she sensed that there were taut muscles under the conventional outfit.

She stopped thinking about his body and called up his head and face. His hair was dark and thick and probably a little too long for a police detective. His eyes were dark, too. Dark hazel, almost black. And she'd have to describe his features as chiseled.

With her art training, she was interested in faces, in what they told about people. She'd guess he was in his early thirties. Yet there were lines fanning out at the corners of his eyes. Laugh lines, although she had the feeling he didn't laugh often. Along with the deep creases carved between his nose and mouth—they told her he'd done some hard living.

Everything about him—small and large details—had riveted her attention in the few seconds he'd stood there in the doorway. Not just visual impressions. She'd caught the scent of his body, too, a mixture of soap and man and subtle aftershave. She'd heard his indrawn breath. And for a moment out of time, she'd thought she sensed the beating of his heart.

She shook her head. Now *that* was going a little far.

Yet she'd felt a connection that went far beyond a conventional first meeting. An emotional connection. A sexual connection. Oh, yes, sexual. That had been a strong component.

She could remember no other incident like that in her life. It was like being caught in a sudden cyclone, wind whirling around them, cutting them off from everything but the taut, sharp awareness of each other.

And it wasn't just her. Detective Thornton had stared at her as if she were the focus of every need he'd ever felt—every longing that had ever made his chest clench.

He wasn't married. He'd told her that while they were talking about the magic wand. She knew his marital status shouldn't matter. But it did. More than she wanted to admit.

She sighed, picked up the mug of tea, and cupped her hands around the smooth porcelain, feeling the warmth seep into her bones. Then she lifted the mug to her lips, taking small sips, focusing on the soothing flavor of the tea.

As she started back toward her desk, the Alma-Tadema painting caught her attention. She knew the title. It was called *Under the Roof of Blue Ionian Weather*. She also knew it had been called one of the artist's finest paintings of sunny indolence.

The description made her grin. She'd always liked the picture. Now she focused on details that she'd simply skimmed over in the past. Taking up most of the picture was a circular, tiered white marble structure called a lounge. Sir Lawrence had so meticulously rendered the marble that she could imagine running her fingers over the smooth surface. The sea was in the background. And, as in many of the artist's works, a flowering bush softened the hard lines of the marble. In this case, she saw it was a pink oleander, rising from behind a low marble wall. Six handsome young men and women lounged in various comfortable poses. Some wore flower garlands in their hair. All were dressed in flowing classical raiment.

Her eye went to the two women at the center of the painting. One was dark. The other had curly red hair and creamy skin—similar to Kathryn's own. Nobody in ancient Greece would have had that coloring. But Alma-Tadema had been famous for mixing women from his own Victorian England with darker Mediterranean types.

It had been a long time since she'd studied a painting with such attention to detail. She leaned forward, admiring the exacting depiction of the scene. It was so very real that she suddenly had the odd feeling that she could step right into the sunny afternoon scene and mingle with the men and women there.

What an idea!

And all because Thornton had drawn her attention to

the picture that she'd walked past dozens of times every day.

She made a small sound. Determined to get her mind off Thornton, reminding herself that she didn't particularly like the man—even if she wanted to make wild, primitive love with him.

PERHAPS money couldn't buy happiness, but it could buy all the creature comforts of the twenty-first century, Simon thought as he climbed the wide stairs to the second floor of his primary residence, running his hand along the smooth wooden banister.

He loved the polished wood. Loved everything about his house. It was full of little details that made life here so fulfilling.

The place was a mansion, really. The most opulent of his houses and apartments. He used the others at his convenience, but this was his real home—on five prime acres in eastern Montgomery County, in a development where every edifice was custom built. There was a wide green lawn in front and natural woods in back, and the house was set in the center of the property. Far enough from his neighbors for the privacy he needed, the mansion had been built for a guy who was flush with success in the dot-com boom of the late nineties. He'd sold drugstore products online. But he'd had to give big discounts and free shipping to get sales. When his financial structure collapsed, he sold off his estate to pay his debts.

Mr. Dot-Com's financial crisis had been Simon's windfall. He'd scooped up the house for a fraction of its value.

The exterior was classic redbrick Georgian, with graceful white Ionic columns supporting a triangular portico.

Entering the library, he stood for a moment, breathing in the scent of old books—a mixture of leather, paper, and mold. A pleasing combination to his senses.

After absorbing the atmosphere of the room, he crossed to the sculpted leather chair where he liked to read and practice the rituals he used in his ceremonies. Propping his feet on the footstool, he leaned back and closed his eyes, chanting the words of power that he had memorized, making sure he had the difficult syllables and the intonation right.

"SOTOU AR ATHOREBALO MRIODOM ARO-GOGORUABRAO AEOOU OOO PHOTETH MA GAIA."

His voice was sonorous, the words beating and swelling and reverberating in the room as he gave them a life of their own. He knew how to perform an effective ritual. The words themselves must have importance—they must flow like an epic poem from the mouth of the master magician. They must roll from his lips like water coursing down a mountain channel.

He knew the meaning of each word, knew their derivation from his study of the ancient texts. SOTOU. Thou, the Savior! From the Greek *soter*. ATHORE-BALO. Thou Goddess of Beauty and Love, whom Satan beholding, desireth!

The ritual was called *Liber Samekh*. He was only practicing now, only making preparations for the real event. Yet he felt his own excitement. Reaching down to the soft silk of his pants, he stroked his fingers along the hard shaft of his cock. Only a light, teasing stroke. Because he was a man of discipline. Because this was only foreplay. Only a rehearsal for the real thing—the ritual in the basement ceremonial chamber that would end with a blood sacrifice and his own shattering sexual climax—releasing the energy that would bring him unimagined power. Power kings and dictators had only dreamed of. Because he would command the obedience of a demon. The creature would be forced to steal for him. Spy for him. Terrorize his enemies. Kill them if he asked. Do *anything* if he wished it.

From Ayindral. He had spoken the other words of

power in a strong, clear voice. But he only whispered the demon's name.

As always, when he uttered the syllables, he felt the hairs on the back of his neck stir. The reaction sent a surge of anger coursing through him. Anger at himself, because he was never less than honest—on his own terms.

A tiny kernel of fear still lodged within the strong fortress he had built around his negative emotions. Fear he should have conquered long ago, through the hard work and discipline that had been the focus of his life for the past ten years.

He had studied long hours to divine the demon's name. He knew that the name was the key to enslaving the supernatural being—to harnessing his incredible power. Yet each time he thought about the capturing ceremony, a small prickle of doubt scratched at his will.

His hands balled into fists at his sides, and he willed himself to be calm. Willed himself to that place where he knew that victory would be his—very soon.

Despite his efforts at self-control, the unsettled feeling hung over him like a cloud of poison gas.

He knew how to make it go away. Rising from the chair, he crossed the room and switched on the monitor that gave him a view of the basement cell.

The woman was huddled on the narrow bunk, dressed in the white cotton gown he'd left in the cell for her. While she'd been asleep from the drug in her food, he'd taken away all her clothing and her jewelry, stripping the rings from her fingers and removing her ankle bracelet. When she'd awakened, she'd had a choice. She could stay down there naked and exposed. Or she could put on the gown he'd left for her. She'd chosen the latter. It wasn't a sexually provocative garment. It was like a gown a child might wear for a baptism. Modest, long, embroidered with lace. It would be her shroud.

Watching her lying on her side with her head bent and her arms clasped around her knees soothed him. She was helpless. She was his to use as he desired.

And he would—when he was ready.

Of course, she hadn't been the one he'd really wanted, not in the beginning. The object of his desire had been her good friend. The redhead. The moment he'd seen her, she'd reminded him of the girl in school he'd . . . liked.

"Patience Hampton." He whispered her name aloud.

He'd never forgotten her. Never. They'd both been lonely, and they'd studied together in the school library, where they'd shared some of their secrets. He'd thought she liked him, but then an older guy had showed an interest in her, and she'd shut her friend Simon off. Well, not Simon. That wasn't his name back then. He'd been . . .

He clenched his teeth and bit off the memory. He wasn't that pitiful boy.

Today he was Simon Gwynn, self-made man.

But no matter how far he'd come, he'd never forgotten Patience Hampton. His first victim had looked a lot like Patience. Red hair. Creamy skin. Green eyes. Every time he saw a woman who reminded him of her, he felt that tug in his chest, that tug to use her in a ceremony. But it was too dangerous to repeat a pattern. He never repeated himself.

So he'd done the next best thing—switched his focus to the redhead's friend. Because he knew it would hurt her. Disturb her. Frighten her.

JACK figured there were probably two hundred Starbucks in the Washington, D.C., area, all with the same moss green and beige interior appointments and the map and compass stuff printed on the rounded platform where you picked up your order.

How many of them were there around the world? Five thousand? There must be a whole factory set up in Mexico or some other cheap labor country where they produced Starbucks furniture twenty-four, seven.

On the way back to police headquarters, he stopped

at one of the coffee shops and indulged in the blend of the day—laced with a good shot of half-and-half. A little rich for his blood—but he figured he could use it this morning instead of the crankcase sludge in the squad room.

He took the steaming paper cup out to the unmarked and sat with his eyes unfocused, still trying to understand what had happened between himself and Kathryn Reynolds. Something weird. Something he might have explained away as a delusion sixteen months ago.

Back then, he'd been the kind of guy who didn't believe in anything beyond his own experience in the rock-solid natural world. Then he'd started investigating a private detective named Ross Marshall, who often brought him information on hard-to-solve cases. Missing person cases and murders, usually.

Jack took a small sip of the hot coffee, thinking back to the events of the spring evening that had changed his perceptions of the universe.

When Dr. Megan Sheridan, the woman Ross loved, had been kidnapped by a serial killer, he and Jack had sped to her rescue. And he'd discovered a startling fact about his friend. Ross Marshall was a werewolf.

If he hadn't seen the wolf in action, he wouldn't have believed it possible. That night, he'd become a believer. The knowledge might have sent him running as fast as he could in the other direction. But he'd known that Ross was governed by his humanity, not his werewolf heritage. They were still good friends and still working together, the two of them solving cases where the enhanced faculties of a wolf made the difference between success and failure.

In fact, the shirt he'd taken from DeYoung's closet was for Ross, who used his wolf sense of smell to track people who seemed to have disappeared off the face of the earth.

Now his knowledge of Ross Marshall's double life made it possible for him to wonder if there was something extraordinary about Kathryn Reynolds.

Like—was she a witch? Did she have some sort of supernatural powers, different from those of Ross Marshall but no less potent?

Was there a quirk in her genetic makeup that set her apart from other human beings? Something besides that wild red hair that his fingers itched to stroke? Simply standing in front of her, meeting her for the first time, he'd wanted her with a strength that rocked him to the core.

Had she snared him in a net? Was she a temptress making the first move on another victim? He snorted and almost spilled the coffee. Carefully he set the cup down on the console as he thought back over that astonishing first encounter.

Maybe her feelings hadn't exactly matched his. But she'd looked startled and confused, as if she'd been caught up in an encounter completely beyond her previous experience. Something strange. Like an obscuring cloud of smoke from a peyote fire that had enveloped the two of them—then just as quickly blown away.

So where did that leave him with Kathryn Reynolds? He didn't know. Part of him wanted to run as fast as he could in the other direction. And part of him wanted to explore what had happened between them in those strange, out of reality moments—and go beyond them, to something more substantial.

His face contorted. Whatever personal connection the two of them had felt was hardly the point of their meeting. She'd called the police because her tenant, Heather DeYoung, was missing.

His mind jumped to the cache of porn in DeYoung's drawer. Reynolds had reacted strongly. She'd given him a plausible reason for her response. She'd seemed surprised. And he was a pretty good judge of people's reactions. But she still might have known about DeYoung's interest in S and M. And been shocked that the woman was keeping such literature in a dresser drawer.

He'd like to find out what Reynolds really knew. Was

she telling him the truth—or was she an accomplished liar?

He was still mulling that over when his cell phone beeped. He saw from the number that it was Granger calling.

"Where are you? I want to know what you've dug up on that suicide," the captain said as soon as Jack identified himself.

"The suicide. Isn't the coroner's office handling that?"

There was a small pause on the other end of the line. "Yeah, that's right. You were interviewing that woman who reported her tenant missing."

"I'll start doing a background check as soon as I get to my desk."

"Right. And you're going to look for a connection to those other cases."

"Yeah."

The captain clicked off, and Jack lowered the phone, staring at the speaker, his brow wrinkled. It sounded like Granger had had some kind of memory lapse. Was the guy just working too hard, or was he due for some medical leave?

AFTER Starbucks, the coffee in the squad room tasted as bad as he'd expected. Still, Jack was used to having the stuff available on his desk. So he poured himself a mug and got down to work, putting in requests for information on Heather DeYoung.

He might have done some more poking around DeYoung's apartment, but he'd had the feeling that finding any coherent records would take hours.

And then there had been Kathryn. She'd watched him as though he were committing burglary, not conducting an official police investigation.

Kathryn. He brought himself up short. A half-hour ago she'd been Reynolds. And she'd better stay Reynolds.

His mouth set in a firm line, he got to work. First he made requests to utility companies, phone companies, credit card companies.

Next he pulled up DeYoung's motor vehicle records. She seemed to get pulled over for a moving violation at regular intervals—just far enough apart to keep from getting enough points to suspend her license.

There was also a notation that she'd received a second request to bring her car in for an emissions test. But he already knew she wasn't the most responsible person in the world.

While he was checking DeYoung's background, his mind kept straying back to Kathryn Reynolds.

He'd be justified in investigating her, too, he told himself. In some cases, the individual who reported a person missing was the person responsible for that disappearance. He didn't want that to be true of Kathryn, but he couldn't dismiss it out of hand.

The phone on his desk rang, and he picked up the receiver.

"Thornton."

"Jack, I'm sorry to bother you."

It was Emily Anderson, his housekeeper, who made a point of not interrupting him at work, except in an emergency.

Instantly on the alert, he asked, "What's wrong?"

"Jack, it might not be anything."

"Tell me why you called."

"Lily's missing."

CHAPTER
FOUR

IT WAS HARD to speak when his heart had leaped into his throat, blocking his windpipe. But Jack managed to croak out a request for more information.

"You know she was supposed to go to a friend's after school. Jessica Barrett."

He didn't remember, but he managed a small affirmative sound.

Emily rushed on. "She was supposed to call me when she got there. Sometimes she forgets, so I finally called the Barrett house. Mrs. Barrett said that she thought the girls had changed their minds and come here."

Jack cursed under his breath, thinking that the woman's irresponsibility was beyond comprehension. He'd naturally assumed she was picking the girls up from school.

"So Lily and her friend still aren't at the Barretts'. And they're not at our house, either?"

"Yes."

"And when should they have gotten home?"

"School was out at three. They should have been there by a quarter after three."

"Okay. I'm going to look for them. What's the address?"

Emily gave him the street and number, which he wrote on a sheet of notepaper and shoved in his pocket.

"Call me on my cell phone if they show up," he said. "And I'll keep in touch with you, too."

He saved his work, turned off his computer, and made a rapid escape from the building, glad he had a job where he could come and go without having to sign in and out.

As he climbed into the unmarked, he was thinking how much things had changed in a few hours. He'd gone to interview Kathryn because her tenant was missing. Heather DeYoung had been purely a professional concern. Now his daughter was missing, and his pulse was pounding so loudly in his ears that that was all he could hear.

WELL, she hadn't been missing for days. Only a little over an hour. Not long in the grand scheme of things. But he was a cop, and he knew what could happen to a child in a very short time. A mom could turn her head away for a few seconds, and some bastard could scoop up her kid at the mall.

He tried not to think about all the terrible possibilities. But he couldn't stop his mind from flashing back over old cases. Cases that made his stomach tie itself in knots when he thought about them in terms of Lily.

He forced himself not to drive more than ten miles above the speed limit. The elementary schools were out. And the middle schools would be dismissed soon—which meant lots of kids on the streets, kids who weren't so careful about watching where they were going.

As he headed toward his neighborhood, he phoned Emily again.

"Have you heard from her?"

"No, Jack, I'm sorry."

"Not your fault," he answered, then focused on getting more information. "Jessica Barrett—what kind of kid is she? Has Lily gotten into trouble with her before?"

"She's a nice child. I wouldn't have let Lily go there after school if I was worried about her."

"Right. I wasn't questioning your judgment."

"Jack, I know you're worried. We both are."

"Yeah. Don't let me take it out on you," he answered, thinking that if he stayed on the line much longer, that was exactly what would happen.

At the school, he made himself take several deep breaths before jogging around the redbrick, one-story structure.

On the playground at the back and side of the building, he scanned the blacktop, the climbing equipment, the soccer field. His heart stopped when he thought he caught a glimpse of Lily's light brown hair. But when he sprinted closer, it turned out to be another girl.

"Shit!" The reflexive expletive drew stares from the children and a mother who happened to be on the scene. He flushed as she pulled out a cell phone. Probably the cops were about to get a call about a suspicious guy hanging out around the school.

Hurrying back to the unmarked, he climbed inside and pressed his palms against his eyes, picturing the likely route that Lily and Jessica would have taken.

By the time he reached the Barretts' place, frustration and fear bubbled inside him. Jumping out of the unmarked, he strode to the door and banged on it loudly.

After half a minute, a scrawny teenage boy with shaggy hair and a torn Grateful Dead tee shirt came to the door. Jack sniffed, pretty sure he detected the aura of pot clinging to the kid's clothing.

"Where's your mother?" he demanded, looking into the boy's muddy brown eyes. When the kid shrugged, Jack pulled open the screen door, resisting the urge to grab the boy by the shoulders and shake him till his eyeballs fell out of his head.

He settled for taking one menacing step forward. "Listen, son, your sister is missing. Along with my daughter. Why aren't you out looking for them?"

The kid blinked, taking a good look at Jack for the first time. "Sally was supposed to walk them home. But she didn't. M . . . Mom told me to stay here, in case they showed up. I'm supposed to phone her if I see them."

"Yeah. If they *do* show up, call me first." He pulled out one of his cards, wrote the cell phone number on the back, and tossed the card into the hallway.

He wasn't proud of taking out his impotent anger on the boy, but his nerves were too raw for control. He wanted to scream out his frustration. He wanted to speed along the street, but he forced himself to creep along, his eyes scanning first to the left and then to the right.

A block and a half from the Barrett house, he heard a dog barking furiously. It was a large dog; he could tell that from the deep, barrel-chested sound. Not normal barking like a dog warning off someone walking past the back fence. This sounded more furious and dangerous.

KATHRYN stared at the old photograph. Gran as a young woman standing tall and proud beside her new house. This house. Only the azalea bushes were tiny, and the car in the driveway, which was gravel instead of macadam, had headlights like bugs' eyes, a square top, and high fenders.

A wave of longing for what had been and would probably never be again swept through her. "Oh, Gran," she whispered, "I wish I could talk to you now. About so many things. My work. Jack Thornton. Heather."

The woman in the photograph didn't answer, of course. Kathryn rubbed her hands over her arms, staring at the material possessions she'd pulled out of the storage closet. Old photo albums. Gran's sterling silver dresser set, carefully wrapped in plastic. Her button box.

Her postcard collection. So many precious things that Kathryn hadn't been able to throw away—because they were the last links to her past. Today she'd felt the need to touch them, look at them once more.

Somewhere outside, the loud barking of a dog drifted toward her. The sound was far away, yet she tipped her head to the side, listening for a moment, feeling a small spurt of uneasiness. The sound faded, and she turned back to the collection of memories.

"I got my values from you, Gran, didn't I?" she murmured. "Work hard. Love your family. Keep your private business private. Stay productive."

Which was why she was sorting through this stuff *now*, she told herself firmly, since she needed a rational explanation for her behavior. She hadn't been able to keep her mind on her job since Detective Thornton had left. And if she couldn't work, then she needed to do something else useful—like figure out what should finally go to consignment shops. Or Goodwill.

"So what about the love part?" she asked, still speaking aloud, as though her grandmother were sitting in the easy chair in the corner. "You were so warm and generous and loving. That's how I know something important is missing from my life. Is that why I've fixated on the first man who knocks on my door?"

Gran didn't answer. If she had, her words would have been drowned out by the sudden sharp noise outside. The dog was barking again. Only now it was louder. Closer. More frantic. It sounded like an animal in trouble. Or an animal about to attack someone.

Jumping up, she ran to the window, craning her neck. Although she saw nothing unusual, the uneasy feeling wouldn't go away.

Stepping over a box of old tablecloths, she hurried to the door, opened it, and pounded down the stairs.

JACK craned his neck, seeing nothing. The noise was coming from off the street. A backyard? Or a wooded area along a stream? An isolated location?

He was out here because he was looking for his daughter, but he'd just encountered another situation. It sounded a lot like the animal had someone cornered, and as a cop—as a good citizen, for that matter—he couldn't simply drive away from obvious trouble.

Pulling to the curb, he cut the engine and started up the blacktop path between two houses. Wind rustled the dry leaves still clinging to the oak trees overhead. Through a screen of tree trunks, he saw a large backyard with a wooden playhouse a handyman father must have lovingly built for his kids. It had wood siding and flower boxes with artificial flowers under the windows. A solid wooden door was closed. The windows had mullions but no glass panes, as far as he could see.

A dog charged around the corner of the house—a Doberman. It was jumping and barking and snapping its teeth, directing its fury toward the little building. When it threw its body against the side, the house rocked.

One of the mullions cracked under the assault. The animal stuck its head inside, and he heard a child's terrified shrieking from within. If the dog got in there, it was obvious he was going to tear the kid to shreds.

If Jack had been able to assess the situation from the street, he would have called for backup. Now he was on his own. And the first thing he had to do was get the dog away from the child cowering in the playhouse.

If he called the dog, would it leave the kid alone? Would it calm down? Or attack him?

He had never been in a situation where it had looked like he might have to shoot a dog. But he drew his Sig before giving a loud shout, "Come on, boy. Come away from there. Good dog. Good dog."

The animal whirled in his direction, teeth snapping in the face of this new enemy. In those first few seconds of confrontation, it was apparent that the animal wasn't going to calm down. A deep growl rose in its throat as it leaped away from its previous target. Focused on

Jack, it picked up speed, its teeth snapping as it headed straight toward the new target.

Jack held his gun in a two-handed grip, pointed at the charging streak of black and brown as he took careful aim.

"Daddy! Watch out, Daddy!"

The child's cry riveted his attention just as the dog leaped.

God! It was Lily in there!

Thrown off his stride, he scrambled to find the dog again, knowing he couldn't risk a wild, random shot in the middle of a residential neighborhood—with his daughter somewhere in front of him.

It was already too late to get the dog before it reached him. He braced for the deep, tearing sensation of canine teeth sinking into his flesh.

But it never happened. Once more that day, the normal course of time seemed to stop. It was like someone had thrown a switch, making everything around him freeze. The leaves on the trees went still in place. The wind stopped blowing. The dog seemed to hang in midair—three yards from him.

Jack Thornton was the only moving, breathing thing in the freeze-frame universe. He had time to bring the gun into firing position, time to pull the trigger before the dog reached him. As he fired, time snapped back into its normal forward course.

The dog yelped once, dropped to the ground. And Jack knew by the way it lay still and the lack of blood on the wood chips that he'd shot it in the heart.

KATHRYN stood transfixed. Moments ago, the angry barking had enveloped her, solidified the breath in her lungs.

Now . . . there was utter silence. Feeling unsteady on her feet, she leaned back against the door frame, staring into the afternoon sunshine, struggling to catch her breath.

She had the strange conviction that disaster had been averted. Yet she had no idea what had happened.

For several minutes, she stood in the doorway, all her senses on alert. But she saw nothing unusual. Heard nothing. With a shake of her head, she stepped back inside, made her way up the steps, clutching the banister. Back into the living room—she blinked, staring at Gran's things still spread over the floor.

Lord, she'd been sorting through this stuff, trying to decide what to keep and what finally to let go of. But she'd forgotten all about what she'd been doing when the dog had claimed her attention.

JACK stepped around the dog, holstering his gun as he rushed toward the playhouse. Pulling open the door, he looked inside and found two little girls. Lily and her friend. They were both white-faced, both sobbing.

He went down on his knees. Reaching inside, he drew them both into his arms, feeling their small trembling bodies press against him as he stroked his hands over their backs.

"It's okay. It's okay," he murmured.

Lily hiccuped, struggled to speak. "Jessica wanted to show me this house on the way home. We . . . we were only going to stay a few minutes. Then . . . then the dog came. He was trying to bite us."

"I know, honey. I know."

She tried to look over his shoulder, but he kept her head down so she couldn't see the dead animal.

Still, her voice quavered as she said, "You shot him with your gun."

"Yes."

He calmed the two girls down, then moved back so he could make eye contact.

"Did the dog bite you?"

"No," both girls answered, although he had to reassure himself by checking their exposed skin. He couldn't find any tooth marks.

"How did you get away from him?" he asked.

"We were playing in the little house when we heard him barking. Then he was running toward us, and we shut the door and pushed that wooden piece down," Lily answered.

"That was exactly right."

"But then he kept jumping at the door and the window, and shaking the whole house. He was going to get in—until you got here," Jessica said. "How did you find us?"

"Well, I was looking for you, and I heard him," he answered, adding a heartfelt but silent "Thank God."

DELIBERATELY, Kathryn focused on the boxes she'd pulled out of the closet, determined to bring order out of chaos. If not her disordered thoughts, then these things.

She'd never use the linen and damask tablecloths, she told herself firmly. Or the box of old fabric. They could go to one of those upscale consignment shops. And the same with the postcards and the little animals that had come packaged in boxes of tea.

She stopped, suddenly picturing herself sitting on the floor, watching a small girl playing with the ceramic lions, monkeys, and giraffes.

Jack's child. She'd just met the man today, under emotionally trying circumstances. But she was back to daydreaming about him—and his daughter.

She dragged in a breath, held it for a moment, and let it out before carefully gathering up the animals and setting them back in the cardboard box. She would save the animals. But was she doing it for the wrong reasons?

JACK glanced at the dog lying on the wood chips, thinking that Animal Services would take hours to arrive.

His alternative was to find a patrol car in the area. Leaving the girls for a moment, he knelt beside the dog, feeling guilty as he stared down at the still form. He'd never shot a dog. And it gave him a queasy feeling now. But there had been no alternative. The animal had been crazed, out of control. After getting the girls into the backseat of the unmarked, he picked up the radio and called for a uniformed officer.

Next he called Emily on his cell phone and told her that he'd found Lily and Jessica. She wanted a full report on what had happened, but he kept it to a minimum, then called the Barrett house.

He got the teenage boy again and said he was on the way back with Jessica, and to tell his mother, if he could get in touch with her.

By the time he had hung up, a patrol car was rolling to a stop in back of the unmarked. Climbing out, he talked to the officer, a guy named Jacobs, telling him what had happened.

Jacobs could have asked him to stay at the scene, since he was the one responsible for the dead dog, but when he explained the situation, and the officer saw the strained faces of the girls in the backseat, he told Jack to take them home.

He drove straight to the Barretts' house. By the time he got there, Mrs. Barrett had just pulled into the driveway. Her face a mixture of fear and relief, she rushed to his car, pulled the back door open, and gathered Jessica to her, hugging her close.

As he climbed out and walked around to the other side of the car, she said, "Mrs. Anderson got me on the phone. She told me about the dog." She raised her face to Jack. "Thank you. Thank you for rescuing the girls. I had a hairdresser appointment, and my neighbor's daughter was supposed to walk them home. But she must have forgotten. I'm so sorry. I should have reminded her in the morning."

Jack gave a tight nod. He wasn't going to say he understood. He only knew Lily wasn't going to the Barnett's again after school.

"Do you know who the animal belonged to?" he

asked. "It was a Doberman. There was a license tag, but no name."

"I'm sorry, I haven't seen a dog like that around here."

"Okay. We'll try to find the owner—and see if the dog's rabies vaccination is current."

Alarm contorted her face. "Did he bite Jessica—or Lily?"

"They said he didn't. And I checked for bite marks. They both seem to be okay, just shaken up. If it will make you feel more secure, you can take Jessica to the emergency room."

Mrs. Barrett nodded. "Do . . . do you want to come in?"

He thought about that for a moment. He had one more thing to say. But he could say it here. He looked from Lily to Jessica and back again. "Don't leave school and walk home on your own." His gaze focused on Lily. "You can always go in the office and call Mrs. A to pick you up. She was worried. So was Jessica's mother."

Lily's face crumpled. "I'm sorry." She gave a gulping sob. "We just thought it would be okay to walk home. And we only stopped for a minute. And . . . and . . . somehow it was more than a minute," she added.

"I know, honey. But I think you see now that it can be dangerous not to be where you're supposed to be."

His daughter was crying in earnest. He returned to her side of the car, opened the door, and hunkered down. She didn't move, and he gathered her close.

"It's okay."

"You're mad at me."

"No. I was worried about you. I'm glad you're safe." He hugged her for long moments, until he felt her calming. Then he looked toward Mrs. Barrett. "I'd like to take Lily home."

"Yes. I understand completely," Mrs. Barrett answered.

He made sure Lily was buckled in, then closed the door and got behind the wheel.

As he started for home, he glanced in the rearview mirror and saw his daughter huddled in a corner of the backseat.

She saw him watching her. "I'm sorry, Daddy. I won't do it again."

"I know."

"I was scared."

"I was, too."

"Is it all right to shoot a dog?"

He dragged in a breath and let it out before answering. "If he looks like he's about to attack someone."

He saw her digesting that. He hadn't liked resorting to his weapon, but he hadn't seen any other alternative—not when the animal was charging him with a murderous look in its eyes.

He took Lily home, where Emily doctored her with chocolate chip cookies. After making sure everything was okay, and filling in the housekeeper on more of the details, he went back to police headquarters. First he called Animal Services and made sure that the dog had been removed. Then he wrote up a report on the incident. Finally, he gathered together the papers he'd started on the DeYoung case and put them in a folder.

He'd kept himself busy. Kept his mind busy. It wasn't until he climbed back into his car that he allowed himself to think about what had happened outside the playhouse.

Not the part about the girls and the dog. He'd been scared, but he'd dealt with that. It was the other part—*The Twilight Zone* part.

He sat for a moment, his hands wrapped around the wheel, his eyes staring toward the redbrick wall of the headquarters building but not really seeing it.

Instead, his vision was turned inward, to the moments when the Doberman had charged him. He'd been ready to fire. Then Lily had called out, and the shock of hearing her voice had totally blown his concentration. He'd thought he was dead meat. Or at least mangled meat.

Before the dog could sink its teeth into his body, something had happened, something so strange that he could hardly believe it—even though he'd experienced it. The world around him had frozen in place. The dog had seemed to stop in midair—hanging there like an inflated toy filled with helium.

He shook his head. That little space of suspended time had given him the chance to get his gun back into firing position.

And it wasn't the only instance when he'd stepped into *The Twilight Zone* today. The first time had been at Kathryn Reynolds's house. Then he'd felt encapsulated in a moment of time with her, felt a connection to her and a jolt of sexual energy.

The sensation had been intense, yet it had made him feel vulnerable—vulnerable to Kathryn Reynolds and vulnerable to his own needs and weaknesses.

He blinked, realizing that he'd been driving without paying attention to where he was going, and he'd missed his turnoff on Falls Road.

He went down to the next development, then circled back to his street.

Ten minutes later he was pulling into his own driveway. As he had at the station house, he sat staring into space.

He'd always had a strong sense of himself. Always believed that he was responsible for his own actions. Twice today, he'd felt as though free choice had been rudely yanked away from him.

He couldn't explain either experience, let alone both of them. Was he going crazy? Becoming delusional? The thought sent a chill skittering up his spine.

It wasn't that! He knew who he was. He knew what he was doing. He was still functioning the way he always had. Yet he couldn't turn off the disturbing thought that some outside force had entered his life.

The very idea was absurd. He tried to shake it from his mind. But it stayed lodged there, like a bullet in soft tissue—festering.

CHAPTER
FIVE

THERE WAS NOTHING like fearing for your child's life to put things into perspective. Lily was shy with him at dinner, but Jack had drawn her out, made sure all over again that she knew how glad he was that she was safe. And after dinner he, Lily, and Craig played the kids' favorite game, Sorry.

Some evenings he knew he neglected his fatherly duties. Tonight he supervised bath time, then read to both kids, holding Lily tight against his side as he sat with her on her bed, still thanking God that everything had turned out all right.

At times over the past three years, he'd felt damn sorry for himself. Now he counted his blessings.

The next morning, he was in a philosophical mood as he drove toward Research Boulevard. So he'd had a couple of really weird experiences. This was another day, and as far as he was concerned, nothing strange was going to happen, if he had anything to say about it.

Nevertheless, when traffic ground to a halt on Gude Drive, his mind went into a little fantasy that his car could fly over the stopped vehicles and land on the other side of the mess.

Of course, he stayed on the road, trapped like everyone else, creeping past a three-car smashup and arriving at work half an hour late.

First he pulled out the number he'd copied from the dog's tag and checked the database at Animal Services.

Some of the terrible weight lifted from his shoulders when he found out that the dog had a history of violence. There were several complaints from neighbors about the owner, Clark Spencer, who had apparently trained the dog to guard and attack. It had bitten two men—both seriously.

Spencer had been warned to keep the animal in his fenced yard. But apparently the dog had gotten away— and gotten into trouble again.

Jack told himself he'd performed a public service by taking a dangerous animal off the streets, yet he couldn't totally let go of his guilt. He was thinking that officers who shot and killed a criminal suspect got counseling from a department shrink. He could probably make an appointment now if he wanted.

Maybe he needed it. But he couldn't quite picture himself talking about his present mental state. What was he going to say—that he'd been experiencing time distortions?

Yeah, right. That would probably be enough to get him pulled off active duty.

With a sigh, he went to his E-mail and started checking the information that had come in overnight on Heather DeYoung. She had four credit cards, all with heavy balances. Her phone was in danger of being disconnected unless she paid the bill. And a collection company was after her to pay up on the large-screen television she'd bought on sale in January. About the only monetary responsibility she took seriously was her rent, probably because she knew that staying on good terms with Kathryn was important.

Make that *Reynolds*, he told himself firmly. *Not Kathryn*.

He leaned back in his desk chair, contemplating his next move. He needed to find out if, by some chance, DeYoung was with her mother. But he didn't want to alarm the woman, since her daughter was an adult who apparently often went off on unexpected trips. And he wasn't bound by law to discuss Kathryn's suspicions with her.

Picking up the phone, he dialed the number that Reynolds had given him.

"Mrs. DeYoung?" he asked.

"Yes," a woman answered. Her voice was thin and weak. She sounded like she was in her eighties. He hated to run a con on an old lady, but in this case he was willing to take any advantage he could.

"This is Jake Thorn at the USA Redemption Center," he said.

"The what? Speak up."

Oh, good, she was hard of hearing. "I'm trying to get in touch with Heather DeYoung," he shouted into the phone, seeing heads turn in his direction in the squad room. Everybody within twenty miles was going to hear his pitch. "She's the grand prize winner in the Win America contest. I'm trying to deliver her prize."

"Why are you calling me? I'm her mother. She doesn't live here. She lives in Maryland."

"I've checked at her residence. Ms. DeYoung isn't at home. We have a forty-eight-hour deadline to deliver her Pontiac Grand Am. After that, we go to the runner-up."

"A car! Oh, my. I'm sure she'd like a new car. She's always complaining about the one she has."

"Well, we'd like her to have the grand prize. So I'm hoping you can help. Her landlady says that she's out of town for a few days, but she doesn't know where she's gone. Could you tell me how to get in touch with her?"

"I . . . I'm sorry. I don't know where she is. Did you check with that fellow she goes around with?"

"Her boyfriend?"

"Yes."

"You don't like him?" Jack asked, catching the woman's tone of voice and figuring he couldn't lose anything by slipping in the personal question now.

"He's beneath her. I think she can do better."

"Well, I'd appreciate your calling me if you hear from your daughter. That's Jake Thorn." He gave her the number of an answering machine that didn't tie into the police switchboard, then urged her to let her daughter know about her good luck, if she phoned. By the time he hung up, he figured he'd done what he could to win the mom's cooperation. She'd put Heather in touch with him—if it was humanly possible. And if she hadn't called back in forty-eight hours, he'd contact her as himself and fill her in on the missing person report.

Next up was the boyfriend, who worked at the Circuit City in Bethesda. Of course, it was possible he wasn't there today. Like he and DeYoung had decided to take off together. But he wasn't counting on it. He'd bet Swinton was in town, and he wanted to interview him before he had time to make up a story.

He took Montrose to Rockville Pike. The traffic was moving well, and he arrived at the shopping center not long after the store opened.

Inside, he found the small electronics section. There were two salesmen in the area. When one of them turned around, he immediately recognized Swinton from Kathryn's description. He confirmed the identity from his white tag with his name in blue letters.

"Gary Swinton?" he asked, walking forward.

"Yes."

"Could I talk to you for a few minutes?"

"What do you want?"

"Montgomery County Police. I want to ask you some questions."

Jack gave him credit for showing very little reaction. "About what?"

"Heather DeYoung."

"What about her?" Swinton looked around and found that the other guy in the department was listening with interest. "Why don't we go outside?" he said. Unlike Reynolds, he didn't ask to see Jack's credentials. Because he'd been expecting this interview?

As they walked through the stockroom and then onto the loading dock, Jack was thinking that for the time being, he might as well play Mr. Nice Guy. Easygoing. Relaxed. Just here to get some facts about a woman who might have skipped town to avoid a bunch of credit card bills.

Swinton reached into his pocket and pulled out a crumpled pack of cigarettes. He didn't ask if Jack minded; he simply lit up.

Jack took a step back. Before the kids had been born, he'd been a smoker himself. But Laura had shown him some articles on the effects of passive smoking, and he'd managed to stop. Usually he didn't crave tobacco. But times like this, when someone was standing a few feet away, puffing like a chimney, it was hard not to bum a smoke. He shoved his hands into his pockets, noticing that Swinton was watching him.

"What about Heather?" he asked again.

"When was the last time you saw her?"

"Last week. Why?"

"Her landlady hasn't seen her in a few days; she's worried."

Swinton shifted his weight from one foot to the other. "That bitch! Did she sic you on me?"

"She said you were DeYoung's boyfriend. What have you got against her?"

"She's self-righteous. Thinks she's better than everybody else."

"She seemed to have a pretty high opinion of Ms. DeYoung."

"Yeah, well, she talks to her against me."

"About what?"

"About stuff that's none of her business."

Jack waited to hear something specific. When nothing was forthcoming, he figured he could come back to the subject later. "So you saw Ms. DeYoung last week. What day?"

Swinton took a drag on his cigarette and expelled the smoke, looking thoughtful. "I was out at her place last Wednesday. We had dinner. Watched some TV. And"—he made a waggling gesture with his hand—"we went to bed."

"You didn't spend the night?"

"No."

Jack filed that away. Sex implied a certain intimacy. Spending the night implied another level to the relationship—unless it was a one-night stand. Or unless one of the participants had young children at home—and wanted to make sure he was there in the morning.

Well, that was certainly an inappropriate thought! He knew damn well it had nothing to do with Swinton and everything to do with his personal interest in Kathryn Reynolds.

"How long have you been going together?"

"A couple of years."

"Do you know where she might have gone? Or why?"

There was a momentary flickering in Swinton's eyes. "No."

Either he was lying, or he was thinking about something incriminating.

"You parted on good terms?"

"Yeah. Why are you asking prying questions?"

"Because she's missing. And I'm trying to establish when she was last seen, and what her state of mind was. Did she seem worried about anything?"

"Her credit card balances were creeping up. She wasn't happy about that."

"Would that make her skip town?"

"I don't know."

"So you don't know where she is?"

"No. I already told you that. Sometimes she goes away on trips."

"By herself?"

"If she feels like it."

"Where does she go?"

"Atlantic City. New York."

"Do you know of anyone who would have reason to harm her?"

Again there was the slight flash in Swinton's eyes. "No," he said, making his voice firm. Then he took another drag on the cigarette.

Well, there was something going on with Swinton, but he wasn't going to find out what it was while they were standing here, and he didn't think that hauling him down to headquarters would be productive at this point.

"Thanks for your time," he said.

"No problem."

Jack walked down a flight of stairs on the loading dock, then around the building to the unmarked.

He would come back to Swinton again. But right now, he was going to attack the case from a different angle. It was time to contact the detectives working on the other three missing person cases and see if he could find anything that would connect them.

KATHRYN reached for the magic wand on her desk and turned it first one way and then the other, watching the stars and moons rise and fall in the blue liquid.

The random patterns usually helped set her mind free, so that she might get a sudden insight into her work that had eluded her as she focused intently on the computer screen.

Today her thoughts jumped back to Jack Thornton— the way they did every time she let down her guard.

She'd never been obsessed with a man. She'd always been slow to get into a relationship—for all the good that had done her with Sam Hastings, her last serious boyfriend. They'd gotten close, and after eight months, she'd thought they were heading toward something permanent. Then he'd been offered a promotion and a big raise if he'd transfer to the Chicago branch of his company immediately. And he hadn't hesitated a heartbeat.

Kathryn had convinced herself that she was in love with him. She'd thought that the job offer might be the event that would tip the balance in the relationship. She'd thought he might ask her to marry him and move with him to Chicago. She'd been nervous about leaving everything familiar and going halfway across the country. But at the same time, she'd been excited.

It had turned out she didn't have to worry about moving. Sam had promised to keep in close touch. After a few weeks, she knew that either he'd found someone else in the Windy City, or he hadn't really been as interested in marriage as she'd thought he was. Or he'd been a damn coward. He'd wanted to break off with her, but he'd been too chicken to say the words. Moving away had given him an easy option.

She'd been sad and hurt. The unceremonious ending of the relationship had been a blow to her self-esteem. But she'd come out of it stronger, she told herself. More self-reliant. More cautious about men. More realistic. She'd let Heather talk her into going to a bar a time or two. She'd dated some of the guys she'd met. But she hadn't connected with anyone who rang her chimes.

Until Jack Thornton. She'd gone to bed fixated on the man. And from the moment she'd opened her eyes, thoughts of him had begun worming themselves into her mind. And not just her mind. She'd awakened aroused, wanting him. And disgusted with herself for the reaction.

She looked at the wand she was having so much fun manipulating, and gave a short bark of a laugh. It was a hard plastic rod about twelve inches long, and it felt good in her hand. A penis substitute?

Was that why she'd been playing with the thing so consistently since he'd been here?

There was no one else around to see her blush, but that didn't stop her cheeks from growing warm. With a shake of her head, she put the thing down. But when she picked up her Koosh Ball, her former favorite toy, and started bouncing it in her hand, the tactile experience was much less satisfying.

Before she could cancel the idea, she moved the ball to one end of the wand and added a similar sized rounded glass paperweight next to it.

Giggling, she stared at her handiwork. A penis and testicles! It had been a long time since she'd indulged in anything so silly. She felt like a little kid drawing dirty pictures on the sidewalk with chalk.

With kids, it was just a naughty impulse. On an adult level, she was able to think in more concrete terms. Like, the wand would make a pretty good dildo. With stimulating ridges spiraling up the side. Of course, it wasn't all that big in diameter. Probably Jack's penis was a lot thicker. At least she hoped it was a lot thicker. Because that would feel so good when it was inside her.

She sucked in a sharp breath, then pressed her palms over her face. Good God, what was wrong with her?

The direction of her thoughts was so out of character that she was almost unable to believe she was behaving this way.

Since when was sex the only thing she could think about? Since she'd met Jack Thornton.

She sat very still, lowering her hands to grip the arms of her chair, because the notion had leaped into her mind that reaching up and cupping her breasts would feel very good right now. Not just cupping them, playing with her nipples that had suddenly gotten hard. Her eyes drifted closed as she imagined Jack Thornton's hands on her. They were large hands, strong hands. But she decided they might be gentle when he caressed a woman. She let herself slip farther into the fantasy, one hand lifting to brush back and forth across a taut nipple.

A small moan escaped her lips.

With a grimace she snapped her eyes open, then pushed her chair away from the desk and stood up, knowing that it would be a very good idea to stop thinking about Detective Thornton touching her, making love to her.

Trying to be as objective as possible, she examined that thought, too. It wasn't just sex she wanted. Not just temporary gratification—although sexual arousal had certainly been heating up her body since yesterday. She was also picturing herself waking up next to the man every morning. Sitting across the breakfast table. Stepping into the role of mother to his daughter.

The fantasy had crept up on her when she'd looked at the ceramic animals. Now she was adding to it, and she knew the daydream was totally unrealistic. Not least because she was sure that she and Jack Thornton had rubbed each other the wrong way during their one meeting. He'd acted like she was a suspect, and that had made her feel defensive. Or was she reading more into the interview than she should?

She gave a mental shrug. What she needed was something else to occupy her mind, now that she'd sorted through the storage closet. Like maybe going down to Heather's apartment and searching for clues.

As soon as she thought about Heather, she felt guilty. She'd met Detective Thornton because she was worried about her friend. She was still worried. And she wasn't going to let her fantasies wipe out her sense of responsibility.

Grabbing the key, she unlocked the door to the inside stairway, then walked rapidly down to Heather's apartment. Once inside, she stood in the dim light, seeing the place the way Jack had seen it. It was pretty messy, and she knew that had prejudiced him against Heather.

She brought herself up short. She hadn't come here to reflect on how Heather's lifestyle struck Jack Thornton. She'd come here to try and find something that would help the police.

Systematically, she began moving her hands through

drawers, feeling clothing that had been thrown inside without being folded. Jack had found the porn magazines and the book in one of Heather's underwear drawers. Kathryn found something else stuffed in between a couple of tee shirts. Something that felt weird.

Gingerly she drew out a plastic bag containing a rectangle of what looked like off-white construction paper. As she turned it in the light, she saw that one side was covered with a series of small yellow squares, each with a picture of a cartoon character in the middle. Each colored picture was about a quarter of an inch in diameter. There were thirty of them on the sheet. And places where she could see that several more had been torn off.

She'd never seen anything like it before, and she didn't know what it was. But she was pretty sure it was something that Heather didn't want anyone to find.

She sniffed at the stuff. It didn't have any odor. She used her fingernail to scratch at a picture, and some of the paper fibers came off. She thought about lifting her finger toward her mouth, then checked herself.

No. Better not taste it. She slipped it back into the plastic bag.

So was this something that she should report to Jack Thornton? Something that had to do with Heather's disappearance?

Or was she looking for an excuse to hear the detective's voice?

She didn't know the answer to that. But she did think she had an obligation to tell him what she'd found.

Back in her apartment, she shoved the plastic bag into her middle desk drawer, retrieved the business card from yesterday, and dialed his number.

"This is Jack Thornton," his deep voice began, and she felt her heart leap inside her chest.

"I'm out of the office right now, but if you'll leave a message, I'll get right back to you. If you need immediate assistance, you can press one to have this call transferred."

She hung up, reluctant to leave a message and wondering if his absence was a sign that she wasn't supposed to tell him about this stuff—whatever it was.

A sign?

It wasn't like her to look for signs and portents. But then, a lot of things she'd done recently weren't like her. Particularly spending a lot of time thinking about a man she barely knew and one she hadn't exactly met under friendly circumstances. And then looking for excuses to talk to him.

CHAPTER
SIX

THE DANGER GREW, like a large black hole opening wider and wider in the fabric of his universe. He could feel it with a sickening pull that brought primal fear bubbling within him. He had never endured this kind of assault. Never feared for his very existence. And he had miscalculated—expended too much of his energy on manipulating the physical world. Stopping time.

The second instance had been justified. He had done it to save Jack Thornton from the dog's fangs. He needed Thornton. It was too late to find another man.

But the first manifestation—when the man and woman had stood in the doorway facing each other— that had been a mere trick. A way of making a point. And now he regretted the effort it had taken.

He was weakened. He needed to regenerate. But he felt wings of fear beating ... beating ...

He must act—soon. And the woman was the key. She had always been the key.

WITH a sense of momentous purpose, Simon stepped into the ceremonial chamber.

The time was close, so close, and he was ready. He stood for a moment, enjoying the feeling of power surging within his body. Through the silk of his black pants, he slid his hand along the hard shaft of his penis, allowing the arousal to build as he gazed admiringly at the details of the chamber he had created. Simply coming here made him pulse with power, but there was more than mere pleasure involved. Much more.

When he'd bought the house, the chamber had been an ordinary basement recreation room. Now it was completely transformed. From floor to ceiling, along the walls and over the small windows, hung yards of gathered fabric. It was black, as was the slate tile on the floor. The room was designed to insulate him from the world. Yet he could still cast his own destructive power outward. And he would soon, very soon. After the sun had set.

Deliberately he let his hand drop to his side, exercising the discipline that was such an important part of his demeanor. Without discipline he had nothing. Sexual satisfaction was a poor goal in itself. It must be nurtured, rationed, used to achieve his ultimate objective.

He stood for a moment, moving his shoulders and arms, loosening the muscles; enjoying the feeling of strength that had already begun to build inside him.

The universe was like a vast ocean. An ocean with great invisible tides. Most people were simply swept along helter-skelter by forces they could never hope to control. Forces they didn't even comprehend.

But some were brave and clever enough to master the cold, black currents that rose from the depths of the universal ocean. He was such a man. A man who could make others bend to the strength of his will.

He walked to the long wooden table, checking the leather ankle and wrist straps attached to the sides.

Beside the long table was a smaller surface, bare except for a folded rectangle of purest white silk. With reverence he slipped his hand inside and gently removed a small dagger. It was very old and very rare, the handle beautifully worked with old Celtic signs. He had found it at an antique shop in Dublin, and from his research, he had known at once what it was—a ceremonial dagger from the time of the Golden Dawn.

It was expensive. But he had gladly paid the price the dealer was asking.

As he turned the weapon in his hand, he admired the balance, the workmanship, the long, tapered line of the blade. It was narrow and delicate, like a woman's finger turned to silver. He pressed his thumb against the point until it pierced the flesh, welcoming the sharp pain as a red drop welled up.

Raising his finger to his mouth, he sucked the sweet, thick blood. His own essence. A small sacrifice.

A prelude.

KATHRYN stretched her arms above her head, then reached to massage the tension in the back of her neck. It was almost midnight, and she'd been at the computer most of today and yesterday, feeling like she was getting very little done. But as she brought up the text and graphics on the monitor, she conceded that the Sunrise Realty brochure had worked out better than she'd expected. She wasn't claiming that the design was her best work. But it was the best she was going to do in any kind of reasonable time frame. She'd already put in about five extra hours that she wasn't going to charge to Sunrise.

Now she was exhausted. It wasn't simply a physical weariness. It was emotional as well.

Three days had passed since she'd reported Heather as a missing person—and her friend hadn't shown up, hadn't called.

With a sigh, she pushed back her chair and stood. But once she was on her feet, it was all she could do to drag herself down the hall to the bathroom, use the toilet, wash her hands and face, and brush her teeth.

She left her jeans in a heap on the braided rug, then tottered across the floor and fell into bed.

Sleep seemed to tug at her with an unnatural eagerness. It claimed her moments after her head hit the pillow.

Her slumber was instantly deep. And only minutes passed before a dream sank its needle-sharp claws into her.

She cried out in her sleep. One moment she was warm and safe in her bed. In the next, she was somewhere else entirely.

Nowhere familiar. Not at all.

Her eyes blinked open. She was in some strange land of swirling, gray mist that obscured her vision and made her feel like she was breathing in water when she tried to drag air into her lungs.

It was cold in this place, cold as a cavern deep inside an iceberg. Perhaps that image came to her because she felt immense weight pressing against her, weight that made it impossible for her to stand erect.

Terror gripped her by the throat, muffling the scream that rose within her soul.

There was no color here. No sound. No solid ground below her feet or sky above her head. And she knew with a terrible jolt of insight that if she stayed here, she would lose her sense of self.

Lord, she had to get away. Had to escape.

Desperately, she forced herself to stumble forward with no idea where she was going. It was hard to walk, let alone run. Her bare feet sank into a thick, spongy surface that shifted dangerously each time she took a step. But fear kept her moving—not simply fear of the environment. Somewhere off to the side, she sensed a presence beside her, keeping pace with her, a presence so terrifying that it robbed her of what breath she had left.

The thing had no body. No form. It was just a huge, indefinite bulk that might swallow her whole if she allowed it to catch her.

She gasped, choked, turned her head away like a
child afraid of monsters in the dark, trying to pretend
that the thing in the mist was simply a construct of her
imagination. But she knew she could never have conjured up the monster or this place on her own.

Her eyes stung as though someone had thrown acid
in her face. Squeezing her lids tightly shut, she staggered blindly forward, each labored breath more choking than the one before. Her lungs burned like fire. Her
heart drummed in her chest. And the pulse pounding in
her head was like the roar of giant waves crashing on
a rocky shore.

Confused, disoriented, she knew only one thing for
sure. This land was not meant for human beings. It
would kill her—soon. She understood that much as she
doggedly put one foot in front of the other, sinking farther into the stuff below her feet with every step she
took.

Then her toe hit something hard, something that felt
alien in this place of bog and mist.

She yelped in pain and surprise—and also relief—as
she staggered forward onto a blessedly flat surface that
held her weight.

After the place of cold, swirling nothingness, the feel
of solid ground and the warmth around her were gifts
almost beyond bearing.

Her eyes snapped open. Reaching out a shaky hand,
she found and gripped a low, solid wall as she dragged
in a breath of clear, pure air. Sunlight streamed around
her with the clarity of a bright summer day.

A deep sigh of relief flowed from her throat. Bending
her head, she slid her fingers over the wall, caressing
smooth marble, seeing the slight variation in the polished stone and the joints where the large blocks butted
against each other.

The stone was warm from the sun. Smiling, she
raised her gaze, and saw the pink blossoms of an oleander bush several yards away. The lower half of the
bush was partially hidden by the backrest of a wide,

circular bench, at the top of a structure that looked rather like a small stadium. No, not a stadium—a lounge; she suddenly remembered the name.

As she looked around at the silent scene, she thought vaguely that there should be two young women seated on the bench. One dark-haired and the other with red hair much like her own. But they were absent.

Beyond the bench and the bush, she saw the sparkling blue of the sea and the lighter blue of the sky.

This place was not in Rockville, Maryland. Not in the United States, she was pretty sure. And yet it was so achingly familiar that she wanted to weep with gladness.

"Under the roof of blue Ionian weather," she murmured. As she mouthed the words, she suddenly realized where she had gazed on this scene before.

The painting.

It was as if she had stepped into the picture that she and Detective Thornton had looked at together.

The sun was hot, and she ran her hand along her arm. It was bare, and she looked down to see she was wearing a sheer, sleeveless gown that cupped her breasts and draped gracefully around her legs.

Part of her knew that she was dreaming. Yet no dream had ever seemed this real, this vivid.

Because her fair skin had always burned easily, she stepped into a shaded marble walkway leading to a part of the lounge that was hidden from the viewer of the painting. Moving forward, she peeked around the corner and saw another long marble walkway. Every few feet, slender columns were topped with vertical wooden pieces covered with gracefully trailing vines.

A flash of movement caught her eye. Far down the outdoor corridor she saw a man striding toward her. He was dressed like a Roman general, in a short, belted tunic and leather sandals. His hair was dark; his bare legs, muscular. His face was in shadow, but she didn't need to see his features to know it was Jack Thornton.

She hadn't seen him since he'd come to her house to

ask about Heather. Yet he'd invaded her thoughts so often that it felt like almost no time had passed since she'd been with him.

"Kathryn!" he shouted, breaking into a run, then stopping abruptly in front of her, his breath coming hard and fast.

From running? Or from the same reaction she was feeling?

She sighed his name, and it was the most natural thing in the world for her to open her arms to him. He reached for her at the same time, gathered her in; and she felt as if she'd finally come home to her long-lost lover, after wandering for centuries in the wilderness.

She was swamped by a raft of sensations. The feel of his hard muscles. The subtle scent of his body. And then his mouth came down on hers, the contact with his lips exquisite and erotic. Waves of heat seemed to come off of him, heat that made her own temperature rise in response.

In that moment, she knew that she was his, now and until the moon and stars dropped from the skies and the seas boiled away.

He was good at kissing. She found that out at once. He nibbled at her mouth, gauging her response before increasing the pressure, taking her lower lip between his teeth, then easing up so that she made a small sound of protest, begging for more.

He drew back, his eyes meeting hers, silently asking how much she wanted.

"All of you," she breathed, knowing it was the truth.

He held her gaze for a long, charged moment, then dipped his head again, his arms tightening around her as he took the level from erotic to mind-blowing in the space of heartbeats. He tangled his fingers in her hair, angling her mouth, making demands that she was happy to grant, swirling his tongue over the sensitive inner tissue of her lips, then probing more deeply, claiming possession as though she were an ancient princess captured by his Roman legions—and his for the taking.

He was the conqueror. But he was no enemy.

They were two halves of one whole, each incomplete without the other. Anchoring her hands over his shoulders, she pressed her body against his to keep from swaying on her feet. She felt as if she had been caught unawares in a strong wind whipping off the ocean, so that staying upright depended on clinging to him. He seemed to have the same problem, because he braced his legs, leaning back against the marble wall. The effect equalized their heights as he slid his hands down her body and brought her aching center against the hard shaft of his erection.

The contact felt exquisite, right.

She had always been a sedate lover—afraid to reveal too much of herself. Now she slid her hips against him, reveling in the wonderful sensations the friction generated. But it wasn't enough. She needed more, needed to feel his hands on her.

His thoughts seemed to follow hers, because he moved her upper body back a few inches, then gently cupped his big hand around one breast the way she'd imagined as she sat at her desk, wanting him.

The scene in her office seemed like a dream now, and this was her new reality.

"Oh!" Through the sheer fabric of her gown, the warmth and pressure of his hand felt wonderful. And when he found the tight bud of her nipple and began to play with it, she felt an arrow of pleasure shoot downward through her body, piercing her center.

He slipped the narrow shoulders of her gown onto her upper arms, lowering the bodice. Pushing the fabric out of the way, he pressed his face against her breasts, turning his head first one way and then the other before finding one distended nipple with his tongue and then his mouth.

She cried out, cupping her hands around his head, holding him to her, swaying slightly on her feet, pressing her sex against his erection.

Nothing in her life had ever felt so good, yet she

needed more. She needed him inside her, needed that
with a desperation that took her breath away. And she
could tell from his harsh breathing that his passion
matched hers.

A wayward thought skittered through her mind. What
was he wearing under that Roman soldier's tunic? Was
it like a Scottish kilt? If she pulled the fabric out of the
way, would she find him bare, find his hot, distended
penis?

She was naked under her own gown. All she had to
do was pull it up and out of the way. Then he could lift
her, fit her body to his.

SIMON stepped into the ceremonial chamber. His eyes
skimmed over the woman, still dressed in her demure
white gown, lying on the long wooden table. Earlier, he
had brought her here from the cell next door. She was
fixed to the table by leather straps that pulled her hands
above her head and secured her feet.

She was also drugged—sleeping. In this important
ceremony, her terror would only be an interference. It
might break his concentration, and concentration was
essential for success tonight.

The room had the feel of a sheltered, secret cave.
Around the perimeter, set on pedestals, were seven can-
delabras. Each had seven arms holding seven slender,
scented tapers. Walking to the closest one, he murmured
an incantation as he touched a glowing light to each of
the seven tapers before proceeding to the next pedestal.

When all the candles were lit, he crossed to the serving table and discarded his only garment, his black silk
pants, hanging them neatly on a bar at the end of the
table.

Then, picking up a crystal pitcher, he raised it high
and poured the water into a silver bowl, listening intently to the gurgle of the liquid, like a mountain brook
flowing over smooth, moonlit stones.

Cleaning his body was a simple ritual, but nonetheless important for his success. Everything must be done in order; everything must be done correctly.

First he wet his hands and wrists. Next he poured the water up his arms, across the network of scars on his smooth white chest, and onto the taut column of his neck. Then he splashed water downward, feeling his excitement grow as the cool water dripped onto his penis.

He was aroused, primed for action, excitement pulsing through his veins.

When he had dried himself with a towel, he picked up the white stick of chalk and stooped. With swift, sure strokes, he drew the magic circle on the slate floor, enclosing himself, keeping him safe from harm.

His eyes smoky now, he stood for several heartbeats, filling his lungs with deep drafts of the thick perfume from the candles while he stroked his penis, building his power, enjoying the mixture of arousal and anticipation.

The room blurred, and his head jerked up sharply. For just a moment, he felt the touch of another presence.

Impossible. Not within the protective circle. Yet his eyes searched the shadows beyond the glow of the candles. For one terrifying moment, he sensed an entity crouching in the corner, a mass of darkness darker than the floor and curtains.

It was the demon. Waiting for him to make some mistake.

But there would be no mistake tonight. He was in control—of himself, of the ceremony. And the demon couldn't really be here. Not yet. Could he?

Carefully he checked the circle. It was intact. Then, ruthlessly, he shut out everything besides the steps he must take to establish his domination over the demon.

First he crossed to the serving table, unfolded the silk cloth, and pulled out the silver knife. Then he walked to the long table. Delicately he inserted the tip of the knife into the white fabric of the dress, cutting a line down the middle of the bodice. With the flat side of the blade, he moved the fabric apart, exposing the woman's creamy breasts.

Nice breasts, he thought, enjoying the view, pretending for a moment that it was Kathryn Reynolds stretched out on the table.

It would have been nice to have her here. But he didn't need it to be her. Any man or woman would do. His victims were not for his physical enjoyment. They were only an instrument to complete the ceremony.

Taking a step back, he began to chant the words he had memorized. The words that would bind the demon to his will at the climax of the ceremony.

His voice was loud and precise. He spoke the first part of the ceremony in Greek, in accordance with ancient ritual, then switched to English.

I have captured your name.
Ayindral.
I will capture your essence.
I will capture your power.
Ayindral.
I call you to my will.
Ayindral.
Ayindral.
I command you to obey.

One hand stroked his throbbing erection as it stood out like a staff from his body; the other hand raised the silver knife.

Once more he stepped to the table. One hand still pleasured himself, the other raised the knife for the killing stroke—aiming for the heart of his sacrificial victim.

But as he brought the knife down, an unexpected image flashed into his head. An image that was none of his doing.

It was a man and a woman standing at the edge of a small marble amphitheater. From their dress and the setting, it looked like a scene that could only have taken place hundreds of years ago.

Yet there was an immediacy to the tableau that riveted him. He focused on the woman's red hair.

Patience. Patience all grown up and with her lover.

He couldn't see her features clearly. The man's head was in the way. But he saw the passionate kiss. Saw hands stroking. Heard moans of pleasure as they aroused each other to a fever pitch.

He strove to dislodge the vagrant scene from his mind. It had nothing to do with him. No place in this room. No place in the ceremony.

Yet the vison compelled him, broke his concentration. And he knew the demon had thrust it into his mind. The words of the chant faltered, even as he realized that it was too late to fight off his own orgasm. He tried desperately to pull himself back from the brink, but the inevitable happened.

Sexual climax overtook him, made his body jerk with the familiar ecstasy of release, yet he knew at the moment when his hot seed spurted onto the table and onto the white dress that he had failed.

The knife had missed its mark, missed the woman's heart. But she was wounded. And his only alternative was to finish her off.

A howl of rage rose in his throat, reverberating off the curtained walls of the ceremonial chamber.

He had been so sure of victory. But in that terrible moment, he knew to the depths of his soul that the demon had outsmarted him.

CHAPTER

SEVEN

JACK FELT KATHRYN sliding her hand up his inner thigh. One minute he was waiting with quivering anticipation for her fingers to clasp his aching cock. In the next, he was clamping his hand on top of hers, stopping her upward progress. "Don't."

Her eyes blinked open. The pupils were dark and dilated, the effect sexy and arousing.

But he could see confusion warring with sensuality—mirroring the emotions that clashed within himself.

He shook his head, striving to clear the sexual fog from his brain. "Something. Something's happening," he managed, speaking between panting breaths.

His gaze focused on her breasts. They were beautiful, the coral-colored nipples tight, the skin flushed. It took all his self-control to gently pull the bodice of her dress back into place.

She didn't move as he took a step to the side, pressing his shoulders against the smooth marble behind him, staring at her across three feet of charged space.

"Jack?" she whispered again. "What was that? What just happened?"

"I don't know! Didn't you feel something? A vibration? A change in the air?" When he said it aloud, it sounded insubstantial.

He saw her swallow. "Yes."

With part of his mind, he ached to close the space between himself and the beautiful woman staring at him with large, worried eyes, pull her back into his arms, and finish what they'd started. But he thought that if he did what he wanted, he would be falling into a trap.

Set by whom? Kathryn? Or some outside force that had been poking its busy fingers into his life for the past few days?

Frustration made him run a shaky hand through his hair.

Her face seemed to echo his own uncertainty.

"This is a dream," she said in a halting voice looking from him to their surroundings and back again. "We can do anything we want. Things we both want. Can't we?"

He blinked, reached down to press his palm against the marble, warmed by the sun but cooling now. It felt so real, so solid. More detailed and real than any dream he could remember in his life.

Then he looked down at the costume he was wearing. It was like something out of a Roman epic. Kathryn, too, was dressed like she'd recently come from central casting.

"Why are we dressed like this? Why are we in this place?" he pressed.

Slowly she shook her head. Her voice grew stronger as she asked, "Do you know where we are?"

"No."

"Come here." She beckoned, and he followed. He would have followed her anywhere.

She led him around the corner, into a small marble amphitheater. It looked vaguely familiar, but he couldn't figure out the context. Behind the last rounded wall he saw a bush with feathery leaves and pink flowers. Beyond that was a jewel-blue sea sparkling in the sunshine.

"California?" he asked uncertainly, trying to put the scene into some familiar context.

She laughed. "I don't think so. Remember the Alma-Tadema painting you admired at my house?"

He did remember, and suddenly realization dawned. "We're in the painting!"

"Yes."

"Both of us," he said.

"So whose dream is this?"

"Mine," she said. "I'm thinking and feeling this."

"So am I. And I'm thinking this is edging into *The Twilight Zone*. Do you remember going to bed—falling asleep?"

"Yes."

He watched her carefully, feeling his chest tighten. This was a dream, yet they shared the reality. And he realized that there was one big advantage in this fantasy world. He could ask questions that wouldn't pass his lips in Montgomery County, Maryland. "Are you a witch?" he blurted. "Did you draw me here with some kind of magic spell?"

She gave a small laugh. "I told you, I'm a graphic artist and a publicist."

"You could still be a witch."

"What, exactly, do you mean by that? Do you think I use that little magic wand to work spells?"

"Do you?" he pressed.

"Of course not."

"Do you have special powers? Can you do things that other people can't? Manipulate the physical world?"

She tipped her head to one side, looking like she was giving his question careful consideration. "I don't think so. I never have. At least as far as I know."

"Should I believe you?" He was desperate to get at the truth.

She had taken her lower lip between her teeth, then eased up the pressure. "Why shouldn't you?"

"Because"—he gestured toward his tunic—"despite this outlandish getup, I'm a red-blooded American cop. Early twenty-first century. And I don't have any other way to explain what's happening to me."

"To us!"

He tried to read her tense features. Her eyes told him she was telling the truth. If he could believe his own observations. Maybe he couldn't. Maybe he was too off-balance.

He dragged in a breath, let it out slowly. "I'm sorry. I'm a little tense here."

"Make that two of us."

The broken sound of her voice and the pain in her eyes tore at him. His own anxiety was making him push her—press her for answers she didn't have.

He reached for her then, folding her into his arms, wanting to hold on to her even as he restrained the impulse to take up where they'd left off.

She moved her head against his shoulder. "Okay—if you want honesty, when I saw you here, all I could think of was making love with you. The way I've been thinking about it since I first laid eyes on you. Then you stopped us, and my mind kicked back into gear. Now I'm scared."

"Me, too," he heard himself admitting. So much for his solid macho image.

"What's happening to us? And what do we do about it?"

"I don't know," he answered. Then an idea struck him. He set her a little away from himself, then took the top of his left hand between the thumb and finger of the right hand. When he squeezed, it hurt.

"What are you doing?"

"Seeing if I can feel pain."

"Didn't you feel pleasure? When we were kissing and touching?"

"Yeah."

"Then why not pain?"

He shrugged, already thinking about another experiment. Jack Thornton, boy scientist! "If one of us gets hurt here, will the injury exist in the real world?"

She gave a little shudder. "What a thought."

He surveyed the scene, looking around for something to use. When he peered over the wall, he saw several sharp stones lying on the dark soil. There was about a yard of ground between the wall and the edge of the cliff. He vaulted over, staying away from the edge.

Kathryn was leaning over the wall, her eyes large with alarm. "Be careful."

"I am." Stooping, he picked up one of the stones and pressed it against the outside of his arm three inches below the elbow.

"Don't!"

Ignoring her, he made a small scratch. "Let's see if I have it when I wake up."

"How could you?"

"Why not? Everything else here is—different from a normal dream." He squeezed the rock in his hand, feeling the solid mass and the sharp edges. He tossed it into the air, watched it plummet downward, then disappear into the water far below. Straining his ears, he thought he heard the small splash.

As he turned back to the marble lounge, he found Kathryn's eyes fixed on him. He looked from her to the top of the wall. The ground was lower on this side, and he decided he couldn't make it over gracefully. So he walked around the end and stepped back into the marble structure.

Kathryn swept her skirt under her and arranged herself gracefully on the curved bench, looking at him with a challenge in her eyes. "Now what?" she asked.

He sat down on the hard surface and leaned back, careful to keep several feet of space between them. He'd been out of his mind with lust for her a few minutes ago. Now he thought he had some objectivity back.

"Now we exchange some information," he said, hoping his voice conveyed that they were back to business.

"Like what?"

"Like you tell me something I don't know about you. And I tell you something about me. And tomorrow, we see if we were both really here."

She lifted her head and looked at him. "So—are you divorced?"

His chest tightened. "My wife was killed in an automobile accident."

Her face registered surprise and compassion. "I'm so sorry."

"I'm coping. It's been almost three years."

"You said you have a daughter."

"Lily. And a son, Craig. Lily is seven and Craig is nine."

"Yesterday you only mentioned your daughter. That must be tough, taking care of two children."

"I have a housekeeper. She's a godsend."

She studied his face. "You look . . . upset. Did something bad happen?"

"Lily went missing yesterday afternoon."

"Oh! Is she all right?"

"It was only for an hour. I found her."

"I'm glad."

He nodded, remembering his panic, suddenly wondering what it would have been like if Kathryn had been by his side, sharing the worry. He could have leaned on her strength, because if there was anything he sensed about her, it was strength.

He caught himself up short. He'd just met this woman. He didn't know if she was involved in the disappearance of her tenant. He certainly couldn't trust her. Not on any level.

Especially since the two of them were sitting here in this fantasy setting, having a conversation that would go over just fine during social hour in a mental institution.

Hi. I'm Jack. I think I'm a Roman general. And you? Are you a vestal virgin? Or something else?

"You've got a strange expression on your face," she commented.

"I'll bet. I was thinking that this dialogue would be perfect for *One Flew over the Cuckoo's Nest*."

She laughed, and he liked the sound.

They shared a grin, probably the first relaxed moments of their short relationship. He wanted to slide toward her, reach for her hand. Trust her. Although he stayed where he was, he asked the question that had been hovering in his mind since their first meeting.

"When I came to your house, and you opened the door, I felt like time stopped. Like we were caught together in some kind of time bubble. Did you experience that?"

"Yes," she whispered. "That's part of what scares me."

"Yeah." Her shaky voice and her admission made it possible for him to add, "It happened again later that day. When I was looking for Lily. I found her and a friend hiding inside a little playhouse. A mad dog was trying to get at them."

"The dog!"

He felt a shiver travel up his spine. "What do you know about it?"

She shook her head. "Yesterday, I kept hearing a dog barking. I felt like something bad had happened. But I couldn't see anything. And then suddenly it stopped."

"You heard it? It was miles from your house."

She could only stare at him, shrug. "Maybe it was some other dog."

"Sure."

"Jack—don't make it sound like I did something wrong. I don't even know what happened. Please tell me."

He sighed, watched her closely. "The dog turned on me, and I thought it was going to snap me in half."

Her exclamation sounded genuine. Like she truly was finding out about this for the first time. Still, he kept his gaze fixed on her as he added, "Then that time thing happened again. The extra seconds let me get my gun into position and fire."

She opened her mouth, and to his surprise, the first thing she said was "You must have hated shooting a dog."

His chest went tight. "Yeah."

"I guess you had to do it. Thank God you're all right. And Lily."

He nodded, caught up in remembered emotions. He jerked himself back with another question. "With you—was the time-stopping experience only once, when I came to the door?"

"Yes."

"So for you it was just when we met. And for me it happened again—when I was in danger."

She had clasped her hands together in her lap, and he saw that her fingers were locked so tightly that they looked bloodless. "What does that mean?"

He shrugged. "My best guess, the first time—somebody wanted to make sure we noticed each other. Then they wanted to make sure I didn't buy the farm."

"Somebody? Who would have the power to do that?"

"Someone with psychic powers."

She gave a nervous laugh. "I thought cops were too down-to-earth to worry about stuff like that. Just the facts, ma'am."

He shrugged. "I used to be like that—until I found out that one of my best friends is a—" He stopped abruptly.

"A what?"

"It's better if I don't go around discussing his situation. He's got enough problems without my blabbing his secret. The important point is that he's made me look at the world a little differently."

"Okay," she agreed—too quickly—and he knew she wanted to ask about Ross. But she didn't, which immediately boosted her in his estimation. He relaxed his guard a little, thinking that there wasn't anything wrong with some personal questions. Once the idea had taken hold, he heard himself asking, "So if this is a dream—is that what you wore to bed?"

"No. A tee shirt. Don't tell me you went to bed dressed like Mark Antony."

"Hardly."

"Then what?"

Trapped by his own line of questioning, he answered, "Briefs."

He had made a mistake, getting personal. His body was starting to respond, and he knew the conversation could get out of hand very quickly. Yet he was unable to resist another intimate querry. "Are you in a relationship?"

"No."

While he was still wallowing in a wave of relief, she said, "I was managing my life just fine—until you knocked on my door. I haven't gotten in any trouble with the law. I support myself. I keep in shape. I'm a volunteer art teacher at the local elementary school."

There was no reason he needed to know any of that. But he was glad to hear those facts and he wanted more.

Inwardly, he cursed himself. He should be sticking to business. Deliberately making his voice hard, he asked, "Did you have something to do with Heather's disappearance?"

Her reaction was swift and angry. "How dare you! I reported her missing."

"That's the way it works sometimes. The person responsible calls the police—to deflect suspicion."

"Thanks for the heads up," she answered, her voice thick with sarcasm.

Before she could marshal more defenses, he shot her another question. "Why were you so on edge when I found that porn material in her dresser? Are the two of you into something together?"

"Of course not!" Anger flashed in her voice—and in her eyes.

"So you're not into whips and chains when you make love," he pressed.

"I'm not like my father, if that's what you're getting

at. I think you have a pretty good idea of what I like when I'm with a man."

His throat constricted, but he stood his ground. Still watching her closely, he switched subjects quickly. "I talked to Swinton yesterday. He told me you talked to Heather about him—about stuff that was none of your business."

"Like her abortion?"

"He wasn't specific."

He had more questions he wanted to ask her, but she cut him off with a brusque "I've had enough of your interrogation."

As she spoke, she got up and walked away, out of the lounge and into the corridor of columns.

"Wait," he called out, then started after her. But when she was about thirty feet away, she vanished into thin air. And he was left standing in an empty fantasy landscape.

CHAPTER
EIGHT

THE SCENE WAVERED. He wasn't sure why he tried to hang on to it, his hands clawing at empty air. But the effort was wasted.

Less than a minute after Kathryn disappeared, Jack was back in his bed, the sheets twisted around his sweat-drenched flesh. His body felt strangely heavy. His mind felt like it might fly right out of his skull.

He glanced at the glowing numbers on the clock radio. It was four in the morning. He knew he wasn't going back to sleep anytime soon.

Heaving himself out of bed, he stood for a moment in the briefs he'd told Kathryn he was wearing, the night air cooling his damp skin. Once he'd slept in the buff, but now that the kids might come bursting into his room at all hours of the night, he'd opted to cover up just a bit.

He reached for his robe, then stopped, remembering something he'd deliberately done in the dream. In the bathroom, he turned on the light and held up his left arm. Below his elbow was a small red line. He knew for damn sure it hadn't been there when he'd gone to bed. It was the mark he'd scratched with the rock—unless he'd somehow scraped himself on the sheets.

He stared at the injured skin, feeling a prickle at the back of his neck.

A dream. But not a dream!

After pulling on his robe, he padded down the hall toward his home office. Before he got there, he stopped outside Craig's room, pushed open the door, and stepped into his son's world.

Stooping, he picked up a tee shirt and a pair of jeans from the carpet and carried them to the hamper in the corner, under a poster of Cal Ripken. There were other posters on the wall. All sports figures. His favorite players from baseball, hockey, football. He was really into sports. Which was great. Better than pot or sex.

Lord, it made his chest tighten to think of those things in the same breath with his son. Yet he knew damn well how young a kid could be and still get into serious trouble.

He crossed to the bed, looking down at the sweet, innocent face, wanting to reach out and make physical contact with his son. Not with a dream, with something real and important.

But he kept his hand at his side, afraid to wake the boy. Long seconds passed before he turned toward the door again.

The warm, fatherly glow was punctured on the way back across the room when he stepped squarely on a Lego piece and had to bite back a curse. Craig might be growing up, but he still played with some of the toys he'd enjoyed as a little boy.

Hobbling into the hall, Jack leaned against the wall and lifted his foot, inspecting the damage. They were overdue for a chat about room cleaning. He'd let that slide, but he had to focus on discipline—as well as the fun stuff.

Until a few days ago, Craig and Lily had been the center of his emotional life. Suddenly, Kathryn Reynolds was taking up a lot of his attention.

He didn't want to think about her now. Not while he was focused on his son—on his children. But he found it impossible to get the redheaded siren out of his mind. And as he stood in the hall, leaning against the wall, he felt his breathing accelerate once more.

Although he barely knew Kathryn Reynolds, there was no way to kid himself about wanting her. He burned to possess her body. And he would have made love with her a little while ago, if something hadn't stopped him. He didn't even know what that was.

A vibration in the air? A sense of some evil presence? He shook his head. He only knew that he'd stopped on the brink of making a bad mistake.

His hands squeezed into fists. He was treating this like it had been real, when it had only been a dream.

A dream. No, much more than a dream, he admitted. An experience with the sharpness and vivid flavor of the most intense reality.

Deliberately he backed away from the sunlit landscape where he'd almost ravished Kathryn and reached back into his own past—trying to recapture the feel of his late teens and his early twenties. Actually, there had been some pretty memorable sexual escapades. Before Laura, he hadn't been into commitment, just getting what he could. But the drive to score had changed with Laura. He'd still wanted to make love. But he'd kept that desire in check, because he sensed that she could mean so much more to him than all the other women who'd passed through his life.

He'd been horny. But he'd been in control.

Now he felt like he was in a speeding truck, heading toward an inevitable crash. Somehow he had stopped. In the dream. In real life, would he have the same control?

He cursed softly under his breath. He should have fucked her a little while ago. In Never-Never Land where there were no real consequences. Instead, he'd pulled away and made it harder—yeah, harder—to maintain his self-control.

Jack Thornton, you're a jerk, he told himself as he strode down the hall to his office, where he firmly closed the door and booted up his computer.

Grim-faced, he accessed AltaVista, then asked the search engine to find web sites that included Lawrence Alma-Tadema.

Some had only essays about the artist. But others belonged to art dealers who offered prints and posters of the artist's work.

Jack paged through them, then came to the scene that was now burned into his memory. The painting was called *Under the Roof of Blue Ionian Weather*. With a strange sense of uneasiness, he studied the details: the marble structure, the bush behind the low wall, the sea, the sky. It was exactly what he remembered from the dream—except that the people were missing. He and Kathryn had been the only two figures in the scene. They hadn't been dressed exactly like the models in the picture. The people had been wearing a bit more. Draped, flowing dresses for the women. And a cloak covering the man's tunic.

But when he paged through other works by the artist, he found women in various stages of undress and Roman soldiers wearing outfits similar to what he'd been wearing in the dream.

He brought back *Under the Roof of Blue Ionian Weather* and stared at the scene. It was the place, all right. And he knew more about it than what was in the picture. He'd climbed over that low wall, used a stone to scratch his skin, then tossed the stone into the sea and heard it splash far below.

Weird.

So how had he and Kathryn gotten there? Had some outside force directed his dream? The same outside force that had stopped time twice?

He tapped his knuckles against his lips. The speculation was absurd, yet he'd learned not to dismiss facts simply because they were inconvenient. Two very strange things had already happened to him. Then the dream tonight.

He glanced at the clock again. It was four-thirty. An obscene hour for a social call. Or even a business call.

Yet he was pretty sure that Kathryn would be as wide awake as he was now. Edgy. Sexually aroused, the way he was, even though he was still trying to ignore the persistent sensations.

Should he call her? Part of him said no. But another part screamed yes.

His hand rested on the receiver, and he was thinking he should go ahead and pick it up.

He had valid reasons. Professional reasons. She was involved in a case, and he couldn't let go of the feeling that she was holding back information. But he knew damn well that professional concerns weren't motivating him now. So he pulled his hand back, then got up from the chair and headed for the bathroom and a cold shower.

SIMON'S jaw was clenched as he drove toward Sugarloaf Mountain. When he'd discovered the place, he'd liked the juxtaposition of the name with his private graveyard.

Sugarloaf Mountain. A confection of a private park. And a great place to get rid of the bodies that tended to pile up from his rituals.

The dead woman from tonight's debacle was in the trunk, sealed in plastic, so there was no worry about bodily fluids or trace evidence contaminating the carpeting.

He drove carefully, not taking any chances of some cop finding his latest victim.

Rolling his shoulders, he tried to relax, but it was impossible to let go of the tight feeling of his muscles. He was angry—with himself most of all.

He'd had few setbacks in his life since he'd clawed his way out of his miserable early years.

He had been born in Dundalk, a poor neighborhood at the northeastern edge of Baltimore. He'd lived in a cramped row house with Mom and Dad and eight brothers and sisters. It had been like living in a chicken coop. He hadn't even had his own bed until he'd pulled off his first job and moved out.

While the rest of the family was gathered around the television set, eating their junk food and watching their mindless sitcoms, he'd withdrawn into the books he got from the public library. Mostly he stayed in the reading room. When it was closed, he hung out on the back stoop of his house, unless it was so cold that his hands began to freeze as he turned the pages.

His interests were far-reaching. He read about theater, magic, faraway places, the finer things in life. Books showed him there was another kind of life besides the dysfunctional family into which he'd been born. The dysfunctional family that laughed at his books and teased the shit out of him.

Ignoring them, he sucked up information like an industrial vacuum cleaner. The magic, particularly, drew him. Not parlor tricks. Real magic. Dark rituals that brought power. But he knew there was danger as well as potency in the ceremonies. He understood that the potential for disaster was greater than the potential for gain. He'd seen that cartoon with Mickey Mouse. *The Sorcerer's Apprentice*. Most people watched it and laughed. He knew it was based on an important truth: a little bit of knowledge was a dangerous thing.

So he studied and bided his time. And the older he got, the more he looked for excuses to stay away from home. He worked in the stockroom and did odd jobs for an antique dealer downtown. And he kept track of the owner's money flow. After a major antique show, he was likely to have a lot of cash around.

Even back then, Simon had been patient. During three years as a trusted employee, he had carefully worked out how to acquire that cash—all the time planning his disappearance into another identity.

It was only a first step, of course. But he'd gotten
away with twenty thousand dollars—a small fortune,
back then. Seed money he'd used to pull off other jobs,
steadily improving his living standard and giving himself the leisure he needed for his most important research—into the rituals of the Golden Dawn.

It was a discipline that fascinated him. A discipline
that few had mastered. He'd put in years of hard work
and watched his success grow. But everything he'd
done so far was only a prelude.

So many magicians down through the ages had tried
to enslave a demon and failed. He'd thought he knew
why. He'd done everything right. Using the sexual energy of orgasm and releasing the life force of a living
sacrifice weren't some half-baked ideas he'd come up
with on his own. He'd studied the nineteenth-century
rituals. And the ancient texts before them. He'd known
what he was doing. But he'd thought that following
everything to the letter would neutralize the demon's
defenses.

He'd been overconfident, and he'd been wrong.

At the turnoff for the park, he switched off his headlights, then stopped to open the chain. After fastening
it again, he drove toward the East View parking lot.

When he reached the far end of the lot, he cut the
engine and sat in the darkness, fighting a tinge of uneasiness.

His eyes probed the shadows under the trees, and he
wondered what he was looking for. Nothing! He was
just overwrought from the fiasco of the ceremony.

After releasing the trunk latch, he climbed out of the
car. It was no problem to heave the body over his shoulder and pick up the shovel he'd brought along.

The ground here was broken by rock outcroppings.
But there were open places where the soil was easy to
turn. He found one and set down his burden.

A few minutes after he started to dig, he felt the hairs
on the back of his neck stir, and he looked up sharply,

his eyes and ears probing the darkness once more.

He saw nothing. Heard nothing. Yet his heart was pounding in his chest.

To his right, the moonlight shimmered on—

On nothing but a place where the tree branches were thick, he decided as he took a step closer.

Still, he couldn't completely let go of his fear.

Could the demon be here?

Impossible, he told himself. The demon couldn't live in the world of men. Not yet. Not until the two of them had established the link of master and slave. And it couldn't come to him of its own will. It had to wait until *he* was focused on *it*.

It couldn't be the demon, he told himself firmly. Yet it was long moments before he felt comfortable enough to return to his business.

Quickly he began to dig. It didn't have to be a deep grave. Just a few feet deeper than the body. If somebody found it a couple of years from now, what would it matter? Simon Gwynn would have a new name and all the power and wealth he needed to maintain his safety.

The shovel bit into the dirt, which he lifted and set in a pile. The motion was automatic, a nice workout. His anger still simmered below the surface, but he had it under control. Anger never did any good. It was a waste of energy.

He had better things to do with his mind while he dug the grave. As he shoveled up dirt, he brought back the image of the couple who had broken his concentration and spoiled the ceremony.

They were dressed for a play or a movie. Like a costume drama set in ancient Greece or Rome. He wasn't exactly sure, because the history of costume wasn't his major field. But he would do some research and figure out the era.

So had he really been viewing an ancient scene? One that the demon had dragged from the past?

Or what?

Something more recent? A man and a woman in costume.

Patience Hamilton and her lover?

Jesus, did the demon know about her?

Or was this something else entirely?

KATHRYN lay in the darkness, her body rigid, her mind churning, her hand clutching Jack's card. She wanted to call him, needed to hear his voice—needed that connection she'd felt to him. But she wasn't going to be the one to pick up the phone.

He should do it. Damn him! Because if she made the call, she was going to look like she was pursuing him. She'd spoken to him candidly in the dream. Too candidly. Now she refused to give him more reason to think she was chasing after him.

Maybe he hadn't phoned because it was only her dream. The abashed, embarrassed part of her wanted that to be true. The needy part wanted him to tell her that they'd connected emotionally in the dream—that what happened between them was all right. So she lay in bed, wide awake, all her senses on alert, which was probably why she heard a noise outside that might not have reached her ears under ordinary circumstances. A quick rattling, as if someone had stumbled over the trowel that she'd left near the back door.

A *zing* went through her nerve endings. Without turning on the light, she slipped out of bed and padded to the window, lifted a slat in the blinds, and peered out into the darkness. Below her she could see a cat streaking across the lawn.

A cat! That was all.

She went back to bed and pulled the covers up to her chin, but she was much too tense to sleep.

Finally, when she heard the newspaper hit the front porch, she pulled on sweatpants under her tee shirt and padded down the inside stairway.

Opening the front door, she took a step outside. Before she cleared the doorway, her ankle hit something taut and invisible.

A scream tore from her throat as she pitched forward, putting out her hands to break her fall as the porch floor came up to meet her.

For long moments she simply lay there on the cold boards, too stunned to move. Then she pushed herself up to a sitting position. First she inspected her hands where she'd hit the painted wood surface. They were scraped, but the damage wasn't serious.

Carefully, she flexed her arms and legs. Then with narrowed eyes, she turned to the door frame. At first she could see nothing. Then she spotted a piece of plastic fishing line stretched across the opening, about eight inches from the sill. On one side it was secured to the door hinge. On the other side, it was wound around a nail head that protruded slightly from the door frame. Not a nail that anybody had hammered into place recently, she knew. The darn thing had been sticking out for months, but she'd never gotten around to fixing it. Too bad!

Who would have done this? Someone who wanted to hurt her? Or someone who had a beef with Heather? That would mean it was someone who didn't know her tenant was missing, since the front door led to both apartments.

And what was the motive?

She had no answer. Back inside, she debated what to do. She'd been ignoring little things. Like the spray paint and the tire tracks over the flower bed. Maybe that had been a mistake. It certainly would be a mistake now, because she wanted this incident on record with the police.

So she dialed 911. When the operator came on, she explained what had happened and that she was in the upstairs apartment.

"We'll have a patrol car out there as soon as possible, ma'am," the woman told her.

How soon was that, Kathryn wondered as she quickly

washed, changed her tee shirt, and pulled on clean sweatpants.

She was pacing back and forth, stopping periodically to lift one of the slats in the blinds, when she saw a cruiser roll to a stop in front of the house.

Hurrying downstairs, she made sure that the officer, whose name was Lorton, didn't trip over the fishing line. After examining it and taking photographs, he unhooked it and put it in a plastic bag. Then he dusted for fingerprints—and found none.

Straightening, he asked, "Has there been any other trouble here?"

"Some vandalism. I didn't think it was all that serious, but this is another matter. I could have broken my neck."

"Yes," he agreed, which didn't make her feel any better.

"Anything else unusual going on?" he asked.

She sighed. "My downstairs tenant has been missing for almost a week."

"You filed a report?"

"Yes. And a Detective Thornton has been out here to talk to me," she said, keeping her hands at her sides so she wouldn't twist them into a knot.

The officer wrote it down.

"Anything else?" he asked, giving her an opportunity to tell him about the strange stuff that had happened between her and Jack. She kept that to herself.

Lorton departed, leaving her with the same unfinished business that had kept her up since she'd awakened from the dream. She wanted to talk to Jack. Now more than ever. She wanted him to tell her what to do.

Finally, swallowing her pride, she picked up the phone and called him. But after all that, once again he wasn't even in the office.

Damn him!

CHAPTER
NINE

JACK HAD BEEN planning to go to Kathryn's in the morning. But as he was shaving, he changed his mind. Maybe he was too chicken to confront her. He preferred to think he should get another perspective. So he decided to exercise another option.

After breakfast with the kids and Emily, he went upstairs to his office and called Ross Marshall.

"Would it be inconvenient if I came over this morning?" he asked.

"You've got some business to discuss?"

"Yeah. I've got to stop by the office and take care of a few things. Then I'll drive over."

He put down the phone, his gaze fixed on the bookshelves in back of the desk. He was still sitting there, staring into space, when he heard a light tap at the door.

"Yes?"

Lily pushed the door open and peeked in. "I came to kiss you good-bye."

He opened his arms, and she scurried into them, holding tight to him. Turning his face, he kissed her cheek. "I love you, honey."

"I love you, too, Daddy." She pressed closer to him. "What?"

In a barely audible voice, she asked, "Are you mad at me, Daddy?"

"No, sweetheart."

"You seem mad."

"Do I? I think I'm just preoccupied."

"What does that mean?"

"I'm thinking hard about a case."

"Oh."

"Thanks for saying something."

"You don't mind?"

He gave her another hug. "Of course not. The only way you can know what somebody is feeling is for them to tell you."

She thought about that and nodded.

"You don't want to be late for school. I'll see you after work."

"I love you, Daddy," she said again, then turned quickly and headed for the stairs, leaving him feeling overwhelmed.

You bring a baby home from the hospital, he thought, *and you don't have a clue about what you're getting into*. Babies turned into children with distinct personalities and a whole bunch of needs. Here he was lusting after Kathryn Reynolds, and he had no idea how she was going to interact with his children.

He snorted. Kathryn again. Invading his thoughts in every conceivable context. So was he thinking about fucking her? Or bringing her home to meet the family? It was a little premature for the latter, he decided as he headed to the office.

He'd been collecting information on the other three missing persons, and he needed to look at the new material coming in. After sorting through the various bits of information, he picked up the bag with DeYoung's tee shirt. He hadn't logged it in as evidence. Not when he knew he was collecting it to give his werewolf detective friend a whiff of her scent.

The thought brought a grim smile to his face. Ross Marshall had an uncanny sense of smell. And he was better than a tracking dog, because he had a wolf's senses combined with a man's brain. A very potent combination.

Ross lived in the western part of Howard County in a still rural area. He'd bought a large piece of property several years ago, with a stream and woods where he could wander as a wolf at night.

The house was at the top of a hill, up a rough road paved with loose gravel and across a wooden bridge that looked like it wouldn't hold the weight of his car. But he'd been over it often enough, and he knew that Ross and Megan regularly crossed it in their SUVs.

He cleared the woods and stopped for a moment, studying the sign that said DITHREABA. It meant refuge in the old Celtic language, the language of Ross Marshall's ancestors.

Taking his foot off the brake, Jack drove up the hill, impressed as always with the setting and with the house that Ross had remodeled by himself. It was a modern structure of wood and stone, with massive windows that faced the meadow on one side and the woods on the other three. Ross had designed the house to bring the outside in—so that he had the best of both worlds, a comfortable interior environment with natural vistas that fed his soul.

After cutting the engine, Jack walked toward the front door. Movement behind the large living room window caught his attention, and he stopped in his tracks.

Through the glass he could see Ross and Megan Marshall. Apparently, they weren't expecting him so soon, and it was very clear that Ross's acute senses were not turned toward the outside of the house.

He and Megan were standing in the middle of the rug, holding each other close, swaying slightly—their mouths fused.

It was a very private moment. Jack knew he shouldn't intrude. But in his hypersensitive state, he couldn't turn away. The waves of sexual energy coming off the couple behind the window caught and held him—and set his own nerve endings quivering.

He'd suspected that there was a high degree of sensuality in the bond between a werewolf and his mate. It appeared to be true. In a moment he expected to see steam coming off the man and woman in the living room.

Ross slid his hands down Megan's back, cupped her bottom, and rocked her body against his.

Jack's breath caught. He was struggling to take a step back when a noise intruded on the scene. It took him seconds to realize it was a baby crying. By that time, Megan was already out of the room and rushing down the hall.

Released from his new role as a voyeur, Jack walked rapidly back to the unmarked, where he dragged in several deep breaths and wiped his damp palms down the sides of his trousers. After taking half a minute to collect himself, he opened the car door and slammed it loudly.

Ross was standing with his back to the window. He didn't turn as Jack came up the sidewalk. And he waited several seconds before opening the door.

His face was slightly flushed.

"I appreciate your seeing me," Jack said.

"You're always welcome here," Ross answered.

They stood awkwardly facing each other until Megan came down the hall, holding the baby.

Jack and Megan had become good friends during the time before her marriage, when she'd been estranged from Ross and wondering if she dared contemplate a future with such a man.

In the end, there had been no way she could turn away from him. Their marriage was strong, he knew. Not just physically, but emotionally as well.

This morning, she seemed to have regained her equanimity more quickly than her husband—but she'd been forced to focus on her son.

When she smiled at Jack, he smiled back.

Joshua had stopped crying, and from the way Megan was cradling him against her chest, Jack could see that the baby was nursing.

Husband and wife exchanged a long, lingering look. Then Megan's gaze came back to Jack again. "Good to see you."

"Yes. How are you doing?" he asked, still feeling like an intruder.

"Well, the son and heir is teething—which is making our life a little difficult," she answered.

"Hang on, and he'll be in a new phase before you know it."

"I hope so." As she spoke, she settled herself in the rocking chair. Ross crossed to the mother and child, standing behind the chair, reaching down to cup his son's head and stroke the fine black hair.

Megan tipped her face up, and they exchanged a look of unconscious sensuality—reminding Jack of years ago when his own children had been babies. Nursing could be a turn-on, Laura had told him. And there had been times when he'd sat beside her on the bed, his hand lightly stroking her shoulder as he waited for her to finish feeding Craig or Lily so they could get back to some rudely interrupted quality adult time.

The eye contact broke, and Ross raised his head. Aware that he had been staring, Jack looked down, watching Megan's knees as she began to rock gently.

"Get Jack a mug of tea," she said to her husband.

"Uh-huh. Tea."

Jack followed him into the well-equipped kitchen, another dividend of Ross's remodeling skills. He'd supported himself while he was in college with two very different jobs. He already had a reputation as a private investigator—using his wolf senses to solve robberies and nail adulterous spouses. At the same time, he was working as a carpenter's apprentice. Both careers built from those fledgling beginnings. Ross continued solving crimes, earning substantial fees. And he used some of the money to start buying and rehabing fixer-upper houses.

His comfortable home in the woods was the culmination of his real estate ventures. Jack knew Ross had expected to live here by himself in this refuge from the world. Then he'd met Megan, and his life had changed.

Ross swept his hand toward the shelf of tea boxes. "What's your pleasure?"

Jack focused on a box. "Ginger-flavored green tea."

"I didn't know you were into green tea."

"A sudden impulse," Jack answered, wondering at his choice, then remembering he'd seen a similar box on Kathryn's counter.

He must have made a face, because Ross paused in the act of extracting a tea bag. "Changed your mind?"

"No."

Ross studied him, then turned to the sink. Apparently he'd added one of those instant hot water faucets, because instead of reaching for the kettle, he simply put the tea bags into two mugs and filled them with steaming water. All the modern conveniences for the descendant of ancient werewolves.

While the tea steeped, Ross asked, "So what kind of case did you come to discuss?"

"Missing person. A woman. I brought along one of her tee shirts. I was hoping you could figure out what's happened to her."

"I can give it a try. But I need more to go on. Like, if she left in a car, there won't be any trail to follow."

"I know. And it won't do any good to check her boyfriend's car. I'm sure she's been in it for legitimate purposes." Jack sighed and looked back toward the great room where Megan still rocked and nursed the baby. "Can we go outside?"

"Sure."

They each picked up a mug and walked to the front door.

"Back soon," Ross told his wife.

About six months ago, Ross had built a fieldstone

patio at the side of the house. Jack suspected that Megan might sit there when her husband was in wolf form, roaming the nearby woods, since she couldn't join him physically.

But he didn't mention his speculation as they settled themselves in Adirondack chairs, facing the forest. Ross sucked in a breath of the early spring air, his expression appreciative, and Jack wondered what scents the werewolf caught that were undetectable to a normal man.

"So what are the details of the case that you don't want Megan to hear?" he asked.

Jack set his mug on the table between the chairs and knit his fingers together. The details of the case weren't exactly the problem. It was his personal involvement, but he knew he was going to ease into that part.

"A young woman disappeared late last week. Her landlady made the report. The missing woman, Heather DeYoung, works as a substitute teacher for the Montgomery County school system. She's got a lot of debts. The landlady doesn't like the boyfriend, and I share the opinion."

As they both took sips of tea, he quickly filled in other facts—leaving out the personal stuff like the time distortions and the dream. But as he felt Ross's keen eyes on him, he knew that his friend was reading between the lines.

"So what do you think?" Jack asked when he'd finished.

"I think you're attracted to the landlady. But you're worried she's mixed up in the case somehow."

Jack let out a breath. "Something like that, yeah. You always were perceptive."

They sat in silence for several moments.

Jack scuffed his shoe against a flagstone, staring intently at the polished brown leather, steeling himself to take the next step. "I need to talk about an aspect of this I haven't touched on yet. Probably anybody else would think I'm crazy. I figure with your particular background, you're going to be open-minded."

"Just spit it out. You'll feel better."

"Easy for you to say!"

"Well, I was the loner who kept his background secret for years. Until I found out I could trust Megan—and you."

Jack deliberately unclenched his jaw and began to speak, describing in stark terms his meeting with Kathryn, the incident with the dog, the dream, leaving out some of the embarrassing details.

"So are you going to send for the guys with the butterfly nets to take me away?" he asked when he'd finished.

Ross's hesitation had his heart pounding.

"I never met a man who had his feet planted more firmly on the ground than you," he finally said.

Jack exhaled the breath he'd been holding. "So—you've got all those books on paranormal stuff. Myths. Vampires. Werewolves. Did you ever run across anything like this?"

"There's always Einstein's theory of relativity."

Jack laughed. "Maybe I should study physics."

"Time distortion isn't so strange. When people are under stress, their sense of time can speed up—or stretch out. Megan told me it happened to her when she took care of me after I got shot. She was sitting on the bed, and I was delirious. I started to change into a wolf. Thank God, I didn't get very far. But she told me later she felt like she was living in slow motion."

Jack hung on his friend's words. "So it was associated with something paranormal. I mean, with your shape-shifting."

"Yeah." It was Ross's turn to laugh. "Let's hope the FBI isn't recording this conversation. They'd haul us both in."

"You and Megan have straightened out your problems."

"That's relative. We've still got some stuff to face. Like, how many of our children the wolf gene is going to kill."

Jack winced. "Yeah. Sorry."

"Megan's doing more genetic studies down at the lab. After hours, when her staff's gone home."

Again they were silent.

Finally, Ross asked, "Did you talk to Kathryn about the dream?"

"Not yet. I was going to rush over there this morning. I came here instead."

"Talk to her."

"I was hoping you could offer some insights. You're the one with the special talents. Do you think Kathryn is a witch—that she's doing this?"

"What's her motivation?"

"Hell, I don't know. Maybe she likes to play with men. Drive them crazy with lust—then suck the life out of them."

Ross laughed, but his hands were rigid on the mug of tea. "Crazy with lust. That's a good description of the werewolf when he meets his mate."

"Are you trying to make me feel better?"

"I'm trying to tell you I understand. At least the sexual part. The rest of it—I don't know. I've never read about anything like what you're describing. And I've read a lot—trying to relate my problems to the literature of the occult and to the literature of human experience."

"Yeah."

"One comment I can make. You're uncomfortable, and you're trying to pin it on her."

Jack nodded, acknowledging it was true.

"I don't think I've been much help."

"Actually you have." Jack heaved himself out of the chair. "I'll leave the tee shirt with you. Her address is in the bag. And the boyfriend's address, if you have time to do some snooping around for me."

"Do you want to borrow some books? General stuff on the occult and witchcraft might give you some ideas."

"Yeah. Thanks."

They went back in and found that Megan had returned the baby to his bed and was warming some homemade cranberry-nut muffins in the oven. Ross and Jack both polished off two while they inspected the bookcase.

He left with an armload of volumes including *Visions of the Occult*, *The Golden Dawn*, *The Black Arts*, *Creatures of the Night*, *The Ways of the Sacred*, and several volumes from the *Time-Life* series, Mysteries of the Unknown.

Time-Life! Maybe he should call the Psychic Hotline, too.

After locking the books in the trunk of the car, he started down the long driveway, then paused at the bottom, checked his messages—and found that Kathryn had called him twice.

Well, he'd been deliberately ignoring her—although there was no way to stop thinking about her. Now he knew that putting off a confrontation any longer only spoke of his own cowardice. And nobody had ever accused him of that. So he checked in with headquarters, then drove back to Davenport Street in Rockville.

AFTER the exercise in the woods, Simon slept for a few hours and woke refreshed.

He'd made a mistake. He'd been too confident. Now he must go back to his textbooks and study the rituals—as soon as he conditioned his body.

He spent an hour in his home gym, splitting his time between the StairMaster and the weight machines. After that, he showered and carefully combed his hair, checking with two mirrors to make sure his bald spot didn't show.

Next came a simple but nourishing breakfast. Blueberry yogurt with a quarter-cup of granola. Half a grapefruit. And a cup of orange spice tea sweetened with a teaspoon of honey—no more.

After rinsing the dishes and stacking them in the dishwasher, he repaired to the library, feeling a serenity descend over him as he pulled out one of the old volumes.

The Golden Dawn, as revealed by Israel Regardie. Complete with a comprehensive index. He didn't need a road map. He'd read and reread the volume so many times that he knew it by heart.

Going back to the basic rituals always soothed him. Just for the pleasure of it, he went through the Banishing ritual of the Pentagram, focusing on eliminating any negative energy that still clung to him.

He was calling up the positive aspects of the Astral Light when a shudder went through his body as the woman's image came to him again. The woman in the ancient setting.

He hadn't seen her face, but it wasn't Patience, he realized, as he focused again on the wild red hair. Of course. That hair was the giveaway. It was Kathryn Reynolds—the one he'd wanted in the first place. He didn't know much about her except that she owned the house where DeYoung had rented an apartment, lived alone, and didn't have a lot of friends.

He'd made it a rule to vary his victims. An older woman. A child. A teenage boy. A younger woman— but a completely different type from his last female victim.

He'd told himself he couldn't have another redhead. Not yet. But now . . .

Now she was involved. She was dangerous. The demon had dragged her into it. He'd turn that back on the creature—and use her in the next ceremony.

He felt excitement coursing through his veins as he began making plans. He'd drive out to Davenport Street this morning. Maybe he'd even be able to scoop Ms. Reynolds up and ask her what the hell was going on. Of course, maybe she didn't understand that the demon had its hooks into her and the man. But that didn't matter. Simon was sure she could give him some information before he sacrificed her.

He stared across the room at the floor-to-ceiling bookcases, but his vision was focused inward. When he'd been in her neighborhood before, he'd been posing as a workman. He'd driven his white van and been dressed in blue coveralls. It would be dangerous to go back in the same persona. He was as careful with locations as with his victims. He never repeated a disguise in the same place. And this was a rule he had no need to break.

The white van was still in the five-car garage. It sat beside the Saab, the Dodge SUV, the Mustang, and the old navy-colored Crown Victoria with the dent in the front bumper and the scratch on the driver's door. Yes, that was the one he'd drive, dressed in a gray wig and a blue striped suit. If anybody asked, he'd be an old guy looking for his nephew's house. But he didn't quite have the address right. Yeah, that would do. Trying to suppress a feeling that bordered on glee, he hurried toward the dressing room where he kept his costume wardrobe and his makeup table.

CHAPTER
TEN

AYINDRAL BLINKED AWAKE. *He had averted the ultimate disaster, but after the ordeal of the ceremony, he had been too weak to do more than drift. Now he knew he must reach out again. Slowly, tentatively, he cast his consciousness into the world of mankind, and a jot of fear dug its talons into the soft, vulnerable part of him, the hidden core that held his essence. He was spent from the terrible effort he had exerted to break the magician's spell. It was vital that he renew his life force now in the way of his kind. Yet his enemy was on the move again. The human—who called himself Simon Gwynn—was even now making plans.*

He was strong. And he was determined. And he was preparing for renewed conflict.

A tremor seized Ayindral, sending currents through the thickened cloud that made up his being. He felt that cloud dissipating, drifting apart into the ether. He wouldn't let that happen. And he would never allow Gwynn to enslave him. If he knew there was no way to avoid defeat, he would gather all his remaining power and send his life force out in a great destructive wave, wiping away a large chunk of Gwynn's universe.

But that would be his last resort. The thought of his own death was fearful; he had always been. He had expected that he always would be. He would try to prevent the end of his existence.

He must resist Gwynn. But for now, he must gather his strength. For this space of time, Jack Thornton and Kathryn Reynolds must cope with the magician on their own.

GRIPPING the handles of the wheelbarrow, Kathryn trundled a forty-pound bag of topsoil out of the old garage at the end of the driveway. The structure had probably been built for a Model T. It wouldn't hold a modern car, so she'd turned it into a storage shed.

She let down the legs of the wheelbarrow with a thump. So far this morning, that bastard Jack Thornton hadn't called her back. Her cell phone was in her back pocket, just in case he deigned to communicate with her.

She'd been pacing back and forth across the living room, her nerves screaming, when she'd finally decided she had to get out of the house. So she'd called the school and asked if any classes might be interested in some art instruction. The secretary had been sorry. She'd love for Kathryn to come over—but not this week or the next, since the kids were prepping for standardized tests.

So she drove to Frank's Garden Center and bought a couple of flats of pansies, one of the few annuals that could withstand the chill of a Maryland spring. By June, the summer heat would fry them. But right now, they were lovely.

She'd picked light blue and yellow, a combination she loved. Still silently cursing Jack Thornton, she set the flats on the edge of the patio while she brought fresh dirt to fill the pots.

She'd learned the rhythms of planting from her

grandmother. In the fall, you emptied clay pots so they wouldn't crack from the soil inside freezing and thawing. In the spring, you filled them with fresh dirt and started planting.

She dug the sharp point of her shovel into the plastic bag of dirt, then spaded the dark soil into the pot. A tingly feeling at the back of her neck made her look up quickly. Across the street she could see Marge Blanco raking leaves that had collected on her lawn during the winter.

Marge waved to her, and she waved back. Then the view was cut off by a navy boat of a car driving slowly down the block. The driver was an old geezer with silver hair and a lined face. He had a slip of paper in his hand, and he was peering at house numbers, then back at the paper.

He slowed to a crawl, staring at her, then rolled down his window. She was sure he was getting ready to speak to her, and she took a step toward him. Then he turned his head in the other direction, and speeded up.

What was that all about? Had Marge spooked him?

With a shrug, she went back to her work. Picking up one of the pansy flats, she began considering where she'd place each plant in the pot. The deliberations were interrupted by the sound of a car door closing. The old guy again?

She looked up and saw Jack standing on the sidewalk, watching her with unnerving intensity. Her hands turned numb. Unable to hold on to the flat of flowers, she felt it tumble to the ground at her feet.

He came toward her, walking slowly.

She'd spent the morning cursing him for leaving her twisting in the wind. Now she was helpless to do anything but speed across the lawn toward him, reach for him the way she had the night before.

Her need for him was beyond her understanding, beyond anything she had experienced in the past. Yet it existed on some deep, instinctive level.

He reached for her at the same time, and she sighed as he folded her into his arms.

"Jack." She had time to gasp his name before his lips came down on hers. Time to clasp his shoulders as his mouth ravaged hers. He tasted of need and passion and some dark seductive ambrosia, sweeter than any wine. The kiss was as potent as it had been in the dream—primal and intense—as if the two of them were caught in an earthquake, clinging to each other lest they lose their footing and tumble to the center of the earth.

When he silently demanded that she open her lips, she did his bidding—then made a low sound of pleasure when his tongue took possession of her mouth, like the Roman warrior from the dream, seizing the spoils of victory.

There was no safety with this man. No way to go slowly. Without conscious thought, she was carried into some dark, erotic realm where nothing but passion existed. In the space of heartbeats, she was lost to everything but Jack Thornton.

He angled his head, his mouth hungry and demanding, demanding more than she had ever given to any man.

Unsteady on her feet, she clung to his shoulders, pressed her body into the heat of his, borrowing his strength to stay erect.

The world contracted around her, walling them off in some private place of their own.

She sensed his toughness and his vulnerability. Tasted his masculine essence. Felt his hard muscles beneath her hands. She forgot they were standing on her lawn, forgot everything but the man who held her in his embrace.

But it filtered into her consciousness that somebody was speaking. Not Jack. Somebody with a high, annoyed voice. An old man, she realized dimly.

"Hey, lady, you too busy to help me out?"

Her head jerked up as she struggled to focus her eyes, then saw the dark blue car that had come down the street before. The old geezer at the wheel was scowling at them, and she felt her face heat.

Jack stiffened, looking as disoriented as she felt. He sucked in a draft of air and waited several seconds before turning. But he didn't break the contact with her. Instead, he slung an arm around her shoulder as he faced the street.

She saw his eyes narrow as he asked, "Can I help you?"

"I hope so. You know this address?" The old guy slammed the gear lever into Park, then slid across the seat, waving a small square of paper at them.

Jack strode forward and took the paper from the man's gloved hand. *Gloves,* she thought, with one corner of her mind. It was too warm for gloves—unless maybe you were an old guy with thin blood.

Embarrassed at getting caught in public in the grip of a passionate embrace, she hung back, watching Jack shake his head.

"You're a cop, right?" the old man was saying. "A big shot detective."

"I'm a detective, yes. How do you know?"

"Your government license plate is a clue. Plus, you look like a dick. So you should know this area."

Kathryn folded her arms across her chest, listening and watching the exchange, sure that the old guy was enjoying himself. He'd liked interrupting their kiss. He liked being rude to a cop—without doing anything illegal.

"That address isn't in this neighborhood."

"Some help you are!" The old guy gave him a caustic look. "What's your name?"

"Detective Jack Thornton."

The man gave him a satisfied smile, then slid back behind the wheel, slammed the gear lever into Drive, and eased away from the curb. In seconds he had disappeared.

Kathryn stared after him, wondering what kind of guy took such pleasure in deliberately interrupting a very personal encounter. At least he hadn't asked Jack if he was on duty—which she suspected he was.

She glanced across the street, relieved that her neighbor was no longer outside. If she and Jack were lucky, maybe Marge had departed the scene before they'd started kissing.

She turned her face toward him. "Maybe we should go inside."

He slipped his hands into his pockets, regarding her with narrowed eyes. "If we go inside, we're going to end up in bed," he said, his voice flat and hard, as though he wasn't very happy about that prospect.

She shouldn't be happy about it either. She didn't know him well enough to make love. That hadn't stopped her in the dream. It was Jack who had stopped then. Jack who had stopped now, and that knowledge was embarrassing. The moment she'd seen him, she'd been out of control. So had he. But he'd pulled himself back.

"I'm sorry," she murmured.

"About what?"

"Getting you in trouble. Do you think that guy is going to call the police department and report you?"

Jack shrugged, but she could see from his face that he wasn't happy about the prospect.

Figuring she had nothing left to lose, she said, "About the other part—ending up in your arms. I'm not sorry about that. I liked it. Are you going to pretend you didn't?"

Instead of answering the question, he said, in a voice that was less harsh, "We need to talk." He walked around the house toward the gazebo, and she followed.

Stepping inside, he leaned his shoulder against one of the posts that held up the roof, looking at her, his hands in the pockets of his dark pants once more.

She leaned against a post opposite him, returning his gaze, thinking again how good he looked to her—whatever he was wearing. He'd been devastating dressed as a Roman general. He was still devastating in his detective's clothing. Above and beyond the sexual compulsion, he had a basic appeal that drew her to him.

Realizing she was too shaky to stand, she sat on one of the benches, drawing her legs up under her, suddenly aware that was how she had sat on the marble seat in the dream. From the expression on his face, she suspected that his thoughts were paralleling hers.

She could dance around the subject. Instead, she said, "You're thinking about the painting."

"Yeah."

"So we both agree that we were there?"

"Tell me something you didn't know before then. I mean something I told you when theoretically we were both sleeping in our own beds."

She looked down at her hands. "You have two children—Craig and Lily. Craig is nine and Lily is seven." Trying for a light note, she added, "And you look very sexy dressed like a Roman general."

"Thanks," he said, his tone sardonic.

Instead of spouting more information, she asked one of the questions that had been deviling her since the night before. "Do you have that scratch you put on your arm?"

"Yeah. I'd show you, but taking off my jacket and rolling up my shirtsleeve out here is only going to raise more eyebrows."

"I'll take your word for it."

Neither one of them spoke for several seconds.

"What are you thinking now?" she asked.

"I'm trained in investigative techniques. I'm trying to apply my police detective skills. Unfortunately, this is like a case where you find a dead body. But nobody saw anything. There's no physical evidence. There's nobody with an obvious motive. So I'm still trying to figure out—why us?"

She shrugged. "I don't know." Deliberately looking him in the eye, she said, "Contrary to what you may think, a wild, irresponsible sexual escapade with a guy I barely know isn't my normal behavior."

She was pleased to see him struggling to bite back a grin. "An interesting way to put it," he said, keeping his voice neutral. Then, "Not my style, either."

She kept her eyes on his. "After I woke up from the dream, I waited for you to call me. Why didn't you phone me last night? Or this morning?"

"I wanted to get some distance."

"I don't think either one of us is going to have much success with that."

"Oh, yeah? What do you know that I don't?" he asked, the challenge obvious in his voice.

"The same thing you know! Stop looking for hidden meanings in everything I say. Are you still accusing me of being a witch?"

"If you're not a witch, then we're back to the other theory—that it's some outside influence."

"You prefer witchcraft?"

"Christ, what a choice!"

In the dream she'd told him she was scared. Pride kept her from saying it again, but she wrapped her arms around her shoulders, rocking slightly as she fought to hold herself together. There was nothing she could say about their shared experiences that would make either one of them feel better. But she did have something to offer him. "Well, I do have some information to give you."

She watched him stiffen. "Like what?"

She dragged in a breath. "Like somebody tried to hurt me this morning."

She had the satisfaction of seeing his face whiten. Maybe— No, she wouldn't let herself hope for any genuine concern on his part. He wanted to take her to bed. But the impulse wasn't his choice. This morning he was just a cop doing his job.

"What happened?" he asked.

She kept her voice steady. "When I came out to get the paper, I tripped over a piece of plastic fishing line strung across the door frame."

"Were you hurt?"

"I scraped my hands—that's all."

"Let's see." He reached for her hands, turned them over, cradling them in his large palms as he looked at the scrape marks. Gently, he ran his thumb over the one where her hand had hit with less force. It was just a light touch. Still, she felt it all the way to her toes.

For long moments, neither one of them moved, until he must have realized that he was holding on to her. He was simply examining the scrapes. But after the wild, erotic kisses they'd exchanged, just his touch had the power to make heat pool in her center.

Perhaps his reaction was as strong, because she heard his breath quicken.

He cleared his throat, turned her hands loose. "Where's the fishing line?"

She snapped herself out of her trance. "An Officer Lorton took it away. It was across the bottom of the front door frame."

"You made a report?"

She raised her chin. "I wanted it on the record."

He strode around the house, bent down to look at the scene of the crime.

"The line was strung between the hinge and that nail," she said, pointing.

"Do you have any idea who did it?"

"Not at all. After the dream—I thought I heard someone outside. Then I saw a cat, and I figured that was what I'd heard. I guess I was wrong."

"Fingerprints?"

"Lorton didn't find any."

"Who wants to hurt you?"

"I don't know! It could be someone who wants to hurt Heather. The front door leads to her apartment, too."

Mentioning Heather made her remember what she'd originally intended to tell him, before events had gotten away from her. "There's something else. Yesterday, I went back to Heather's apartment and did some more looking around. I found something. . . ."

"What?" he demanded.

"I'm not sure. I'm thinking the best thing is to show it to you."

"Is this a ploy to get me inside?"

"You certainly are a trusting bastard."

He heaved a sigh. "Sorry. As I said last night, I'm on edge. Let's go in."

TWO streets away, Simon sat in his car, grinning like Ronald McDonald—only he had a gray wig instead of a bright red one.

With a sharp laugh, he bounced his palms against the steering wheel, pleased with the way things had worked out this morning.

"Hey, lady, you too busy to help me out?" he said, repeating his opening line with an exaggeration of his old man voice.

He'd been going to scoop up Reynolds—until he'd seen that nosy neighbor watching him.

So he'd sped up and turned the corner, thinking he'd try again in a few minutes. Then he'd come down the street the second time and hit the jackpot.

Confrontation wasn't his style. He had always been cautious—stealthy. But when he'd seen the guy get out of his car, he'd known that the last time he'd seen the man, he'd been dressed like a Roman general.

Jesus! He could hardly believe it. The guy who had been with Reynolds in that vision. The vision that had broken his concentration.

Goose bumps had risen on his arms, and he'd known he had to get the hell out of there.

Then reason prevailed. He was in disguise. They had no way of knowing who he was, either dressed like this or dressed like Simon Gwynn, for that matter, and if he played his cards right, he'd come out on top of the situation.

So he'd eased the car forward. The government plate had instantly registered. The guy could have been a county building inspector, of course. Or from the tax department. But Simon had studied cops—and this guy looked like one.

Two seconds of conversation had confirmed that hypothesis. And the stupid bastard had given up his name—just like that. Of course, he probably didn't have a choice. He was a public servant; he couldn't hide his identity.

He was still grinning over the turn of events when the full implications of this couple struck him, and his features turned sharp. They had been in the vision. They had destroyed his concentration.

Which must mean the demon was the one who had brought them together—forged the bond of sexual energy that had destroyed his ceremony.

Once the idea took hold, it began to resonate. Of course the demon was using them! What else could explain last night?

A low sound rose in his throat. They both had to be eliminated—and quickly.

But his original plan to simply kidnap Reynolds was too dangerous. Now that he knew someone would be looking for her—her lover boy police detective. And the cop would be a dangerous opponent.

What he had to do was get rid of Jack Thornton. Which meant making some other quick arrangements.

He started the car again, in a hurry now. As he drove, his mind was busy, already making plans for the ceremony he would perform.

JACK let Kathryn walk past him, then followed her up the stairs to her apartment. Again, he stood aside as she opened the door. He felt the stiffness of his body. The determination that he wasn't going to reach for her again.

Inside, he folded his arms in what he knew must look like an uptight gesture as he stood in the middle of the living room, waiting to find out if she really had something to show him or if she was making an excuse to get him in here.

She opened a desk drawer, took out a letter-size envelope, and held it out to him. He saw she had clamped her bottom lip between her teeth—the way she'd done in the dream, he suddenly remembered. He didn't want to think about the dream. Or anything strange. He wanted to focus on a real case he might have a chance of solving.

He dragged his gaze away from her and lifted the flap on the envelope, pulling out a piece of paper impregnated with colored dots, each one stamped with a picture of a cartoon character in the middle.

"Jesus!"

His exclamation had her gaze drilling into his.

"What?"

"Were you using this stuff with her?"

She looked confused. "What stuff? What is it?"

"You're saying you don't know?"

Her face turned stormy. "Jesus! is right. Every time you have a chance to think the worst of me, you do it. Whatever that paper is, I don't have a clue about it."

"Acid," he said, hearing the anger in his own voice.

"Acid?"

Either she was naive as hell or she was a wonderful actress. "LSD," he clarified. "Did you and she trip together? And now you're feeling guilty about it?"

"Of course not! I didn't even know what it was." Her posture changed as she took in the implications. "You're saying Heather took LSD? People still use that stuff?"

"It's certainly not as big as it was in the sixties. But people fool around with it. Didn't they teach you about it in health class? Didn't people in college do it?"

She sighed. "I guess I was in the wrong crowd in college. And as for health class . . ." She shrugged. "Maybe I was absent when they covered it."

"The cat ate my homework," he muttered.

"What?"

"Forget it."

He saw that Kathryn had picked up the magic wand and was flipping it back and forth in her hand. His gaze was drawn to the damn thing. For several moments, he watched the blue liquid and the suspended sparkly stuff swirl back and forth.

The wand was just a toy. A novelty. It couldn't really have any magic powers, could it?

He strove to wipe that dumb notion from his mind as he slipped the envelope into an evidence bag. Too bad that his prints and Kathryn's were on the paper. He hoped they hadn't obscured some that might be more pertinent. Like maybe those of the boyfriend, Gary Swinton. Was that what the guy had been hiding? That he and Heather had been doing illegal drugs together? Or was there something more?

"Okay, if you aren't worried about my connecting you with Heather's drug use—what are you worried about?"

He saw her face pale. "What, exactly, do you mean?"

"Since the first time I came here, you've acted like you had something to hide. What is it?"

He watched her face harden, watched her struggle to relax. Long moments passed when he thought she wasn't going to answer the question.

Finally she gave a small shrug. "Family tradition, I guess. My mom had some bad experiences with the police."

"Like what?"

"I told you she found that porn stuff that belonged to my dad. After that, they had some pretty violent fights. Mom called the police a time or two before she threw Dad out. Let's just say the cops weren't very helpful," she said, speaking quickly, as though she were trying to get it over with. "Mom was left with a basic . . . dislike for the boys in blue, which she passed on to me. Which made it hard for me to make a report on Heather in the first place. But I did it. And I've continued to cooperate with you." By the time she was finished, she was standing with her hands on her hips and her jaw thrust forward.

She'd made him understand her basic attitude better. "I'm sorry about your mother," he said.

"It was a long time ago."

"But it still influences your thinking."

"Yes."

More gently than he'd spoken before, he said, "Thanks for the information. On Heather."

She nodded.

He half-turned toward the door.

"You're leaving?"

"Yeah."

"Jack—" She took a step toward him, reached out a hand. All it took was that simple gesture for a jolt of sexual need to zing through him.

He stiffened, anticipating her touch, fighting the unwanted reaction. "What?" he asked, his voice and his posture rigid again.

She dropped her hand. "We have to talk about us."

"There is no us!" he said as firmly as he could, willing it to be true. He had children who needed him. He had cases he was working on. He had no time for some kind of crazy sexual compulsion. Before she could engage him in a conversation, he pulled the door open and escaped.

Somewhere in his mind, he knew he was deep in denial. But he couldn't cope with her, couldn't cope with his need. Couldn't cope with what he saw as failure. He was a disciplined man. Yet discipline broke down every time he was with this woman. Rather than take what he wanted—what she was silently offering—he fled.

It wasn't until he was in the car that he remembered somebody had tried to injure her this morning. And, as a cop, he had a responsibility to do something about it.

CHAPTER ELEVEN

AS SOON AS he got back to work, Jack checked with Lorton and found out the officer could add nothing to what Kathryn had already told him. Next he looked at reports from the neighborhood, trying to determine whether the fishing line stretched across Kathryn's doorway was an isolated incident.

He found that over the past few days, there had been several break-ins within a five-block radius. Nothing too big. Someone had jimmied a sliding glass door, gone in, and boosted a television set and stereo equipment. A lawn mower had disappeared from a nearby garage. The older daughter in a Moslem family had been harassed. Kids had stolen several cars. But none of the crimes seemed to have any connection to a fishing line stretched across a door frame.

He had to go on the assumption that someone had specifically wanted to hurt Kathryn—or DeYoung.

He wanted to see Gary Swinton's expression when he asked him about the line. And he was about to leave for Circuit City when Captain Granger asked for an update on the missing person cases.

Not now, he thought with exasperation. What he said was, "I'd be happy to update you."

Glad that he could give a coherent account of the investigations, he spent an hour going over what he knew about each of the three cases that Granger had asked him to try and tie together—feeling uncomfortable at the way the captain was looking at him. He kept waiting for Granger to reveal what was on his mind, but his boss remained silent. So Jack plowed ahead with the facts he'd uncovered when he hadn't been tied in knots by Kathryn Reynolds.

There was still no word on the missing child, Kip Bradley, or his father, Henry Bradley. But Jack had discovered some deep-seated hostility between Bradley and his ex-wife. She said he had taken off for Montana, where he had relatives who were willing to hide him. Jack had contacted the relatives, who claimed not to have seen him. He'd also contacted the Montana State Police, who had gone out to the ranch and failed to find Bradley.

The young mental patient, Stewart Talber, was another matter. Now in his early twenties, Talber had been in and out of mental hospitals and various outpatient programs since he'd been diagnosed as paranoid schizophrenic at the age of fifteen. Most recently, he'd been living in his mother's house out in the county. The mother had died two months ago, and his relatives were worried about him. But when they'd come out to the house with two county mental health workers, Talber had disappeared. Jack had talked to some of his relatives and determined that Talber had a history of disappearing—so there was no proof that anything sinister had happened to him. Jack had intended to check out homeless shelters in D.C. and Baltimore, but he hadn't gotten to it yet.

The case of the young woman, Brenda Quinlin, did bear some similarities to Heather DeYoung. She was single and lived alone. She'd failed to come in to work after a week's vacation. But there still wasn't enough information to link the two cases—except that the two victims were young women who had disappeared when they weren't necessarily expected home. Which could imply that they might have been stalked.

"So that's all you've got?" Granger asked when he finished. "Nothing that would show a connection?"

"I've just started."

"You usually work faster than this."

Jack shrugged. Granger was right, but he couldn't dredge up any excuse that he liked the sound of. "I was just going to interview DeYoung's boyfriend again."

"Okay. Go on."

Jack grabbed some peanut butter crackers from the machine, then drove to Circuit City.

Walking into the small appliance department, he looked around for Swinton. He wasn't there, and Jack's next stop was the manager's office.

"Where can I find Gary Swinton?" he asked.

The secretary stopped chewing her gum and rolled her eyes. "Gary? He was here this morning. Then he said he was sick, and left. He's been out a lot lately. Mr. Victor is probably going to fire him. Only I don't think he really cares. He's been acting like he's got more important things to do."

"Uh-huh. How long ago did he leave?"

"A couple of hours."

"Thanks," he answered. His next stop would be the D.C. apartment where Swinton lived.

He checked the address that Kathryn had given him—it was in the Adams Morgan area, which spread out from the intersection of Eighteenth Street and Columbia Road.

Once it had been a white-bread, upscale D.C. neighborhood. Now it was one of those melting pots where African Americans, Hispanics, Asians, and whites lived together in tolerable proximity. A colorful mix of ethnic restaurants and shops, secondhand stores, older apartment buildings, and row houses lined the main arteries.

Swinton's address turned out to be a small redbrick

apartment house off Columbia Road. Jack found a place to park down the block, then walked up the cracked sidewalk to the building. It wasn't exactly a slum. But some of the hall tiles needed replacing, and the wall could use a new coat of paint.

Swinton lived in 3B. Since there was no elevator, Jack walked up two flights. When he got no answer, he walked down to the basement, where the super lived.

Inside the man's apartment, he could hear a television blaring. His first knock yielded no results. He attacked the door with a noisy fusillade—finally attracting the attention of a wizened old man who opened the door a crack, blocking access with a safety chain.

"You seen Gary Swinton recently?" he asked.

"Who wants to know?" the old man asked.

"The police," Jack answered, showing his badge and ID through the crack in the door.

The super peered at the credentials through thick glasses. "You're from Montgomery County. You don't got no jurisdiction here."

"Actually I do. I'm pursuing a lead in a missing person case. Can I have your name, sir?"

The old guy blinked. "I'm Barry Wagner. Who's missing?"

"Heather DeYoung," Jack answered, showing a copy of the photograph Kathryn had given him. "Have you seen her around here?"

"I seen her here with him."

"Recently?"

Wagner thought about it. "A couple weeks ago, maybe. I don't keep track of stuff like that."

"Swinton left work early, saying he was sick. But he doesn't answer his door. I'd like to get in there."

The super thought that over, then decided to cooperate.

As they walked slowly upstairs, Jack asked, "How big is the apartment?"

"Living room, bedroom, kitchen, bathroom. You want me to come in with you?"

"No. Just open the door. I'll lock up when I'm finished."

The door yielded easily to Wagner's key. "Swinton?" Jack called out as he entered. "Gary?"

There was no answer. As he stepped into the living room, he saw immediately that there was one trait the occupant and DeYoung had in common. They were both slobs. But Swinton outdid her by a factor of ten. The cheap, faux wood coffee table and end tables were littered with discarded fast-food containers.

The kitchen was similar. Food splatters had dried on the counters. The sink was loaded with dirty dishes.

He made a quick stop at the bathroom, wrinkling his nose. Apparently Swinton couldn't aim straight when he peed.

He had trouble picturing a nice young woman in this environment. Someone who lived downstairs from Kathryn. Without warning, his thoughts switched from DeYoung to her landlady. He'd banished Kathryn from his consciousness for the past few hours. Now awareness of her came rolling back like water pouring from an earthquake-damaged dam.

His whole body went rigid, and he squeezed his eyes closed, struggling to wipe her image from his mind. It did no good. He saw her as she had looked in the dream—when they'd been making love. Her red hair a cloud of flames around her head. Her green eyes heavy-lidded. Her lips swollen from his kisses.

He remembered pulling down her bodice and exposing her gorgeous breasts. Creamy breasts with coral tips. He was instantly hard. Instantly angry with himself for allowing the reaction to sneak up on him.

Like a drowning man snatching at a lifeline, he focused on the anger, inch by inch dragging himself under control.

"Fuck!" The expletive tore from his lips. In the next moment he was laughing. Fuck. Yeah, that was what he wanted to do. With Kathryn Reynolds.

He pictured himself leaving Swinton's squalid apart-

ment, driving to her house. Pounding on the door. She
would see him and come into his arms. Ten seconds
after that, they would be tangled together on her Oriental rug.

With a low sound of denial, he cut off the fantasy,
thinking that he'd gone through so many emotional
changes in the past few minutes that his head was spinning—and his cock was twanging like the neck of a
banjo.

For several moments, he stood in the hallway, assur-
ing himself that he was in control of his mind and body.
He knew he was just telling himself what he wanted to
hear. Never in his life had he been more out of control—more surprised by what he found himself thinking
and doing.

When he felt as if he could attend to his job, he
stepped into the bedroom, wondering if he was going
to find a dead man.

The room was empty. He found a rumpled bed, open
dresser drawers. A mixture of more or less clean and
dirty clothing littered the floor. It looked like the place
had been searched. Or like Swinton had cleared out in
a hurry. Jack cursed. If Granger hadn't held him up,
would he have gotten here in time to catch Swinton?
Or somebody else still here?

On the other side of the bed, Jack stopped short. He'd
almost stepped into a vinyl suitcase that lay open on
the floor. He could see knit shirts, jeans, underwear
thrown inside. More evidence that Swinton had been
packing. It looked like he'd abandoned the effort. Or
somebody had interrupted him. Stooping down, he saw
dark spatters on some of the fabric. Blood?

What the hell had happened here? Reaching for his
cell phone, he began to dial the D.C. police.

AFTER the morning's exertions, Simon had changed
into his black silk pants and a comfortable black shirt.
Stroking his fingers over the smooth fabric, he walked

with his characteristic measured steps to the butler's pantry, where he contemplated the rows of wine bottles, each one stored at the proper angle to keep the cork moist.

In cultivating his comfortable lifestyle, he'd introduced himself to the finer things in life. One of those was wine. Over the past few years he'd attended wine tastings so that he had the proper appreciation for the output of the world's wineries. On the whole, he preferred European vintages. But there were some decent products from South Africa—and even some from the Napa Valley.

He'd already considered several bottles and settled on the Georges Duboeuf. Beaujolais-Villages Nouveau.

He'd allowed the wine to breathe for half an hour. Now, from one of the cherrywood upper cabinets, he brought out a long-stemmed red wineglass. After pouring some of the wine into the glass, he held it up to admire the ruby color. Next he swirled the red liquid gently in the glass, then inhaled the bouquet. Finally he took a small, appreciative sip.

There was nothing like a good glass of new Beaujolais, he thought as he took the glass with him into the library and settled into his favorite chair.

Things were shaping up very nicely. Tomorrow he'd call the police department and report Thornton's indiscretion with Reynolds. That should do wonders for the cop's reputation.

Then there were the plans for the upcoming ceremony. It was something he hadn't tried before, but he had worked out the basics. Now he had to settle on some of the protocols he was going to use. This ritual must be perfect. Did he need a protective circle, for example? On the face of it, he thought not. But omitting it might be a mistake—if the demon was hovering nearby, ready to interfere.

For just a moment, a shiver slithered over his skin. He sat up straighter, firmed his jaw. He was in the fight of his life. But there were ways to defeat the demon.

And in the end, Ayindral would be the slave of a great magician named Simon Gwynn.

He had no doubt of that. And no doubt about using his skills to kill the cop—Jack Thornton—now that he had the essential ingredient for such an important ceremony.

Tomorrow evening, he would send his psychic power outward in a dark, destructive wave that would catch Jack Thornton by surprise, sweeping him along and drowning him in its awesome force.

The time frame was short, since he must work quickly to remove the cop before he could go after Reynolds—and use her to enslave Ayindral.

Usually he would have taken at least a week to purify himself. There were many roads to purification. Fasting or restricting food. Abstaining from sexual gratification. Even the old Native American technique of a sweat bath. Some modern magicians might even have denied themselves the wine. But wine was a common ingredient in many rituals. Rituals of the church. And rituals of black magic as well.

More important, he had found that one glass helped relax him.

Taking a sip, he began reading through the section on astral projection in the *Rituals of the Golden Dawn*.

KATHRYN spent the afternoon working on a brochure for a group medical practice in Bethesda, a team of women doctors and other professionals who provided a variety of services to female patients. There were several gynecologists and internists in the group, along with an acupuncturist, a doctor of homeopathic medicine, a chiropractor, a plastic surgeon, and a specialist in laser skin treatments.

They'd gotten a glowing report on her from another client and had asked her to design a brochure that gave a comprehensive overview of their practice, along with selected details of each specialty. She'd been enthusiastic about the commission, so she'd done some preliminary layouts before finishing up the assignment for Sunrise Realty.

The previous work gave her something to start with, thank God. Because most of what she'd done today was sit at the computer and move sentences and phrases around on the screen while she went over every word—every touch—she and Jack Thornton had exchanged.

When she caught herself thinking about driving past his house to see where he lived, she felt the air solidify in her lungs.

What was wrong with her? Was she planning to stalk the man if he wouldn't agree to make love with her? The idea that she would do something so . . . outrageous repelled her. And frightened her.

Pushing her chair away from the computer, she stood up, clenching and unclenching her hands. Finally, she found her walking shoes, put them on, and pounded down the steps. An hourlong walk around the neighborhood would help settle her down.

It was getting dark when she arrived back home. Although she wasn't very hungry, she did fix a little dinner, some cottage cheese plopped onto salad greens and topped with a little bottled blue cheese dressing.

After that she took a shower. Then there was no excuse to stay up. Rummaging in her dresser drawer, she found one of her favorite tee shirts and pulled it on. It was light green, with a mountain meadow of bright wildflowers spread across the front.

Climbing into bed, she looked at the collection of literature on her nightstand. She was in the middle of a romance novel that she'd been enjoying. But she hadn't picked it up in days. Instead, she reached for a gardening book with plenty of pictures.

Ten minutes later, when she felt her attention wandering, she turned off the light and eased down under the covers. For a time she enjoyed some blessed oblivion. Then, like the night before, a dream seized her by the throat. She tried to scream. But no sound made it past her lips. Once again, she was in a strange, gray, formless place where no human being could live.

It was as bad as the first time. Instantly she was cold as death. And engulfed by swirling gray mist that clouded her vision and turned to water in her lungs when she tried to take a breath.

There was no color in the gray mist. No sound. No solid ground beneath her feet. She'd escaped from this place once. Or maybe she'd been allowed to escape. Now she stumbled forward again, her feet sinking into the spongy goop.

Was Jack here, too? Was he waiting for her again?

When she tried to call his name, only a wheezing sound came out.

Jack. Jack. Please help me, her mind screamed.

He didn't answer. Yet words seemed to form in her head.

He isn't here. He isn't here. He isn't here. The statement echoed and reverberated directly in her brain. *You must bring him something. Bring him something. Bring him something.*

No one had spoken aloud. Yet she knew the commands came from the huge, indefinite bulk she'd sensed before. Not a person. Not an animal. Some otherworldly being she didn't understand.

But one thing she knew: It could grab her anytime it wanted. Shake the life out of her body. Still, determination kept her stumbling forward, trying to escape.

Ahead of her, through the gray fog, she saw a tall clear column filled with swirling blue liquid with shiny stars and moons shooting upward, then falling back through the hollow tube.

It was the magic wand, she realized with a spurt of astonishment. Only a hundred times bigger, the action inside more violent. And it was standing there like a guidepost—glowing in the fog.

She staggered toward it, stretching out her hands. For less than a second she thought she felt the smooth plastic surface. Then it was gone. And all at once, she was free. One moment she was in the gray, terrifying place. In the next, she was standing in a dark woods.

She stood with her heart pounding, dragging in gulps of pure, clean air. Her shoulder brushed a tree trunk, and she reached out to press her palm against the rough bark, anchoring herself to something solid.

Last time, when she'd escaped from the place of terror, she'd stumbled into an Alma-Tadema painting. This time was different. She was in a nighttime woods—dark and shadowy but visible in the silver radiance of the moonlight filtering down through the branches above her.

A light wind riffled the foliage overhead, and when she dragged in a breath, she caught forest scents. Heard an owl hooting far away. Closer by, she caught the scurrying of tiny feet in the underbrush.

Now what? Was Jack here? Was he looking for her?

Her heart leaped at the prospect of seeing him again. Then she dismissed the sense of anticipation with a wry laugh. She'd bet he wasn't looking for her. If he was here, he'd probably be running in the opposite direction.

Trying to put him out of her mind, she cast her gaze down to see what she was wearing. She was dressed in the light green flowered tee shirt she'd worn to bed. Now the shirt topped brown stretch pants and the walking shoes she'd worn this afternoon.

It was chilly, and she wrapped her arms around her shoulders, rubbing the goose bumps that had risen on her skin.

This was just a dream, she reminded herself. Yet she knew it was like the last time—more than a dream.

Firming her lips, she began to move through the woods. Dry leaves scrunched under her feet as she made her way forward. In some places she had to detour around large outcroppings of rock. In other spots, brambles tore at her pants.

After tromping through the underbrush for several minutes, she came to a wide trail where the ground was covered with wood chips. It led upward for several yards, then changed to a short flight of stone steps.

She stared at the pathway, thinking how different this scene was from the last dream. It was less static. More like a real place—like the real world. But where? Beyond the steps was a rustic sign, *summit 1,282 feet.*

Well, she was on some mountain, obviously. She could take the path upward. Instead, she kept moving through the trees, avoiding the worst patches of underbrush and the huge rocks. Ahead of her she saw a flicker of movement and went very still. Someone else was here—coming through the trees.

Jack?

Her pulse started to pound. She'd met him in the picture dream. She longed to meet him again—in another dream—where all the controls of the real world were removed. This time . . . This time they would make love.

His name hovered on her lips. But something stopped her from calling out to him. Moving from tree to tree, she made her way closer. When she finally saw her dream companion clearly, she struggled to hold back a gasp. He was a ghostly form, almost transparent, so that when she stared straight at him, she saw right through his body.

His head whirled around, and he looked toward the tree trunk that partially hid her.

She froze in place, wishing she could turn invisible. Or was that almost true? When he looked at her, was she like him—ghostly and transparent?

For long moments, he seemed to be staring directly at her hiding place, and she was afraid to move, afraid to breathe.

Finally, he gave a little shrug and turned back to what he was doing—digging a hole in the ground, working fast, the dirt flying. Then he picked up a plastic-wrapped bundle from the ground, a bundle that looked about five and a half feet long and perhaps a couple of feet wide.

She made a low sound of distress as she saw the shape. It looked like a body! Or some misshapen rug.

As she watched, he dumped the bundle unceremoniously into the hole he'd dug, then began to shovel the earth back in place. He was working fast, breathing hard.

He finished by smoothing out the dirt, then gathering up armloads of dry leaves and scattering them over the fresh-turned ground. For a moment he stood looking at his handiwork. Then he turned and started rapidly down the hill, paralleling the path.

She stayed in back of him, running to keep up. But he had a head start, and he was fast. Beyond the trees, she saw an open area that resolved itself into a blacktop parking lot. By the time she arrived, he was already pulling away—in a car that appeared to her as indistinct and ghostly as the man who was driving it.

She had never paid much attention to the make and model of cars. Now she was too far away to see any of the ghostly insignia. There was no light over the license plate, so she couldn't see that either. Three red taillights mocked her as the car braked, after pulling out of its parking space, and sped away.

She stifled a sob, frustrated that she had no way of knowing who he was. She tried to tell herself that it didn't matter. That he was just some construct of her imagination. That he hadn't really been there at all. But she couldn't fool herself.

She didn't know why he was transparent as mist. But she knew this dream had something important in common with the last one. It wasn't random. She had been brought here for a purpose.

Squeezing her eyes shut, she tried to figure out what she should do. Then she remembered the voice she'd heard at the start of the dream. *You must bring him something. Bring him something. Bring him something.*

Bring him something!

In the darkness, she stumbled down the hill to the parking lot. At this hour of the night, it was empty. But at the far end, she could see another sign.

Quickly, she strode across the blacktop and walked

around to the far side, so that she could see the legend. She had only moments to read the words. Then, the scene around her began to fade.

With an almost physical desperation she tried to hold on to the dream. But it slipped through her fingers. And she was alone in the dark. In her own bed.

CHAPTER
TWELVE

EAST VIEW PARKING lot.

Kathryn's eyes blinked open as she pressed her head against the pillows, bearing down to assure herself that she was back at home and not in the woods.

"Jack," she murmured aloud. She hadn't met him in the dream. Had he been there? In some other part of the woods? Had he missed the main event? Or, this time, had it been only *her* dream?

Pushing herself up in bed, she bent her knees and then circled them with her arms, holding tight.

Lord, now what? What, exactly, had she seen?

She still wasn't sure. But she knew she had to discuss it with Jack. She'd been given a clue. A piece of evidence.

Her sense of purpose deflated somewhat when she swung her head to the right and looked at the clock. The green numbers on the display said three fifty-six.

He wouldn't want her to call him now. Probably he'd be annoyed. And what could she tell him? That she'd seen a transparent man bury a transparent body, and she didn't even know where.

But could she figure it out? What did she know about the place? As she often did when she was thinking about a project, she walked to the window, pulled up some slats in the blind, and stared out. At first she saw nothing of the actual view. Then something outside caught her attention. There was a car parked across from her house.

It wasn't a car she recognized from the neighborhood. Standing in the darkened room, she stared at it, wondering if someone could be inside.

What a notion! Who would be sitting in a car at night on the street?

She tried to dismiss the idea. But it stayed wedged in her mind. With jerky steps she crossed the room and switched on the nightstand lamp. Seconds later, she heard an engine start. By the time she returned to the window, the vehicle was gliding away into the night.

She watched until the taillights disappeared into the distance. It was so much like the dream that goose bumps bloomed on her skin. Yet it wasn't the same car. The shape had been different. At least she thought so. The one outside had been smaller—sportier.

More important, it hadn't been a ghost image. It had been real and solid. And it was impossible for her to dismiss the idea that someone had been out there watching her. Or watching for Heather to come home.

She hated to grasp at that explanation. But it was the one she preferred, under the circumstances.

With a sigh, she turned away from the window and hurried down the hall to the living room. More than ever, she needed to talk to Jack. But she wasn't going to use the car as an excuse. She was going to come to him with something.

During the time it took for the computer to boot up, she paced back and forth across the floor, stopping to pull aside the curtains to look out. The car had not returned, but that didn't give her the expected sense of relief.

After establishing a link to the Internet, she went directly to one of her favorite search engines, then hesitated as she considered what to ask for.

The woods hadn't been a specific place she recognized. But they'd had the look of the local area. Either Maryland or perhaps nearby Virginia or Pennsylvania. Somewhere rural with mountains and rocky soil. The path and the parking lot made her think she'd been in a state park. Or maybe a national park?

Making a decision, she typed in "Maryland" and "parks." A long list of references appeared on the screen. But as she scrolled down through the entries and tried some of the web sites, nothing seemed right.

Over the next half-hour, she looked through more information on parks, seeing nothing that struck a chord with her.

Leaning back in her chair, she contemplated the nighttime scene. She'd seen two signs. One had been near a path and referred to a mountain summit over a thousand feet high. The number had been in her mind when she'd awakened. Now she knew she should have written it down.

Well, what about the other sign? It had said *East View parking lot.*

Trying another combination of key words, she typed in "Maryland," "mountain," "East View." Again, she spent a frustrating half-hour and found nothing.

Damn!

She looked at her watch. It was now seven in the morning. Early. But she couldn't make herself wait any longer.

She'd wanted to come to Jack with something concrete. But she wasn't going to get it. So she might as well call, she decided, as she went into the kitchen to find his card, then reached for the phone and dialed.

"Hello."

The person who answered was a woman, and Kathryn felt her throat constrict—until she remembered that he had a live-in housekeeper.

"Hello?" the woman asked again.

She cleared her throat. "This . . . this is Kathryn Reynolds. Detective Thornton came to my house to ask me some questions about a missing person case."

At that moment a thought leaped into her mind—a thought she hadn't considered before. She'd seen a man burying a body. Oh, Lord, could it have been Heather? She tried to reject that idea. But now it had lodged in her brain.

"Just one moment. I'll see if he's available."

"Thank you."

She waited with her pulse pounding in her ears, wondering if calling him at home had been a good idea.

Then she heard his voice, and she sighed out his name. "Jack."

"What is it? What's wrong?" he asked, sounding like he might care about what happened to her.

"Something's happened. There . . . there was a car outside my house last night," she heard herself blurt, when that wasn't what she'd called about at all. "I turned on the light, and he went away," she added quickly. "But . . . but there's something else. Another dream."

"Oh?"

"I . . . I don't want to talk about it over the phone. Can you come over?"

"Yes. Give me a few minutes to make sure the kids are all set."

She let out the breath she'd been holding. She'd thought he might protest. But he was coming over.

"I'll be there as soon as I can."

"Thank you." As she hung up, she swept her hand through her hair. She'd been up half the night. She probably looked like hell.

The good news was that she didn't have to sit around stewing, waiting for him. She had time to change her clothes, brush her teeth, and wash her face. She was just putting on a little bit of lip gloss when she heard the doorbell and rushed to answer it.

She almost threw the door open, but she had enough

sense to check the peephole and see that it was him.

When she opened the door, he was standing with his arms stiffly at his sides. The look on his face made her throat thicken. The last time they'd been together, he'd pulled her into his arms. This time she could see he was determined not to lose control of the situation.

"Come in." She stepped aside, and he followed.

"Do you want some coffee?"

"Do you have some made?"

"No, but I could use a cup."

There was an unacknowledged intimacy to the encounter. He'd come over to talk about the case. But there was no way to deny the undercurrent of sexuality vibrating in the air. Or to dispel the feeling of familiarity that came from his standing in her living room.

She hurried into the kitchen and filled the automatic coffeepot with water.

"I've got several kinds of coffee," she said over her shoulder. "Kenya. Kona. Jamaica Blue Mountain."

He laughed. "Are you trying to put Starbucks out of business?"

"No. I figure coffee is safer than a lot of other vices."

"Me, too," he answered, and they were both silent as they noted they had something in common besides wanting to jump each other's bones.

She made herself busy, then turned to get the sugar and found him leaning comfortably against the counter, watching her.

Their gazes locked, and she knew how easy it would be to end up in each other's arms again. But she was pretty sure he wasn't going to start anything. And if he could manage it, so could she.

"You're lucky you have someone to take care of your kids," she said.

"Mm hmm."

"Do they take their lunch to school?"

"The school sends out a menu for the week. It depends on what they're having. They love pizza. Macaroni and cheese is another matter."

"Oh," she said, wondering if the conversation could get any more inane.

Finally, the coffee was ready. She took hers with milk and sugar. He took just milk.

When they'd carried their mugs to the table and sat down, he leaned back in his chair and stretched his legs, crossing them at the ankles.

He looked relaxed, but in the time they'd spent together, she'd learned to read him—perhaps because she was so focused on him—and she could see the tension simmering below his calm surface. She wanted to reach out and cover his hand with hers. Just to make contact with him, she told herself, knowing it was only part of the truth. Since the moment she'd met this man, she'd wanted . . . everything he could give her. But she wasn't going to beg. Instead, she kept her hands to herself by clamping them around her mug.

"Someone was watching your house?" he asked.

She gave a small nod. "At least I think so. I can't be sure. All I know is that he was out there. He left when I turned on a light."

"He? You saw him?"

"No. I was just making an assumption."

"I'll arrange to have a patrol car drive by periodically."

"Thanks." She cleared her throat. "You think it has something to do with Heather? . . . Or that fishing line across the door frame?"

"I don't know. But I'll find out."

She clung to the reassurance in his voice.

"Thanks," she repeated. Then added, "I wouldn't have seen him—except that I woke up after another dream."

"Was I there?"

She laughed. "I wish you had been."

The comment generated another moment of silence during which they sipped their coffee.

"Tell me what happened," he said.

"It started like the last one. I was in that gray place where you can't breathe."

"What gray place?"

"It doesn't start that way for you?"

"No."

"Oh, goody. It's just me. I come awake in . . ." She stopped, swallowed. "An awful place. It's like a land of fog." She shuddered as she remembered it. "Not a land where people can live. I can't catch my breath. I feel like I'm drowning, but I'm not underwater." She gave an involuntary gasp. When he reached across the table and laid his hand over hers, she turned her palm up and knit her fingers with his. They sat that way, his hand anchoring her to him.

"It's cold," she whispered. "And creepy. And . . . and there's . . . something watching me." She heard her voice rise at the end.

"Something?"

"A . . . a . . ." She clamped his hand more tightly, unable to speak above a whisper. "I don't know what. But it spoke to me this time."

His eyes widened. "What did it say?"

She gulped, suddenly fighting back tears. "That I should bring you something."

His eyes never left her. "It . . . this thing referred to me? By name?"

She thought back, trying to reconstruct what had happened. Unable to meet his gaze, she whispered, "I was scared. Terrified. I was . . . I called out to you. He . . . it . . . told me you weren't there. But I should bring you something."

Despite her best efforts, the tears leaked out now. She clutched his hand, clutched at her emotions, struggling to rein them in as she heard him swear under his breath.

"I . . . I'm sorry . . . ," she managed.

He let go of her hand, came around the table, and pulled her out of the chair. Cradling her in his arms, he crossed the room and settled on the sofa, holding her and rocking her while she tried to get control of herself.

His hand smoothed her hair as he murmured soft, indistinct words, and she imagined that he might comfort his daughter this way.

She let herself melt against him, letting his strong arms and the masculine scent of his body envelop her. The feeling of safety and closeness helped. By slow degrees she got control of herself. Pushing away from him, she stood, swaying slightly on rubbery legs. When he reached to steady her, she moved to the desk and pulled a tissue from the box.

Feeling more in control, she came back to the living room area. But she didn't trust herself to sit by him again—not without reaching for him. So she settled in one of the easy chairs.

"I didn't even get to the good part," she said.

"Which is?"

"In this dream, I saw a man bury a body. At least, that's what I think I saw. And I think that's what I'm supposed to bring you. Information."

"Okay."

"Only I don't know where I saw this scene. It's in the woods. Somewhere in Maryland—or maybe a nearby state. But I can't figure out where."

"Okay," he said again. "Let's start from the beginning. You were in a place where you couldn't see, and you couldn't breathe. And something spoke to you?"

"Yes." She remembered another detail and added, "Then . . . then I saw the magic wand." His narrow-eyed look had her hurrying on. "It was like the wand on my desk." She stood and crossed the room again, picking up the object in question from beside the computer.

When she held it out, he took it, turned it upside down, and watched the shapes and the blue liquid swirl. "It's just a toy. Isn't it?"

"I always thought so. But it was in the dream. Much bigger. A guidepost—showing me the way out of that terrible place."

"And then?"

"Then I was in the woods. At a mountain. I saw a

trail and stone steps and a sign that said *Summit*. There was a number, over a thousand feet." She watched him write that down.

"It was a park. I'm sure of that. Only I did a web search of parks. And I can't find anything about it," she said in frustration.

"Tell me what else you know."

She gulped. "The man. He . . . he wasn't solid. He was like a ghost. It's hard to describe. I saw him in the woods. Saw what he was doing. But I could see through him. He had something wrapped up—something that looked like a body. He dug a hole, put it in. Covered it over, spread leaves around over the fresh soil. Oak leaves."

He kept writing. "Have you seen him before?"

"I . . . I'm not sure. Maybe there was something familiar about him."

He hesitated for a moment, then asked, "Could it have been Gary Swinton?"

She considered the question. "I don't know. But I don't think so."

"What happened after he buried the body?"

"He started down the hill. To a parking lot. His was the only car; I guess because it was at night. I don't know what kind of car. Something with an odd-looking shape."

"A car you've seen before?" he asked, apparently still trying to tie the incident to present reality. "The car that was outside your house?"

"I don't know!" Helplessly, she shook her head. "In the dream, the car was like a ghost, too. Hard to see. The license plate wasn't lighted. I ran after him. But he got away." She stopped, took a breath, then let it out. "What do you think it means that he was like a ghost?"

He shrugged. "I don't know. Maybe that what you were seeing wasn't real?"

"It was real!"

"Okay." He thought for a moment. "Then maybe it happened at a different time. You were seeing something that had already happened. Or was going to happen."

She considered that. "I didn't think of that! Where did you get that idea?"

He shrugged. "I don't know. I'm just trying to come up with an explanation. What happened next?"

"I walked across the parking lot, and I saw a sign. It said *East View parking lot*."

She watched his eyes brighten.

"Yeah?"

"Do you know where it was?"

"Maybe. Can I use your computer?"

"Of course. Do you want me to get on-line?"

"Yes."

After she'd brought back the connection to the web, he typed in the URL of a search engine. Not the one she'd used, she noted. He didn't start with the information she'd given him. Instead, he typed in the name of a place: Sugarloaf Mountain. There were hundreds of references—some to places in Maryland, others, farther north.

But he zeroed in on a site that included Sugarloaf Mountain, Frederick County, Maryland. The text said the summit was 1282 feet high. When she saw the number, she was pretty sure it was right.

"Why couldn't I find it?" she asked, her fists clenched.

"It's privately owned," Jack said, pointing to the screen. "That's why it wasn't under 'parks.'"

"But how did you know?"

"I've taken my kids there. It's not a bad hike to the summit. Have you been there before?"

"No. Never."

"But you went there in your dream. Apparently you didn't make the place up. How far were you from the path leading up from the parking lot, do you think?"

She cast her mind back. "I wasn't keeping track. It could have been fifty feet. A hundred. But I know it was to the left as you face the parking lot. Through the woods."

She watched him write that down. "So you think what happened to me was 'real.' I mean—that I saw something important?"

"I'm going on that assumption."

She felt goose bumps pepper her arms, and rubbed them vigorously with her palms. "And some strange being who lives in a place of gray mist wanted me to see it—and to tell you about it?"

His face was hard now. "That's one explanation. There are others I can think of."

"Like what?"

"I'd rather not start spouting theories."

He'd spouted theories earlier. Now he was uptight again. She sighed. "Okay, then. Why me? Why us? And what is that thing I sense in the mist?"

"Damned if I know!"

"Are you giving up the theory that I'm a witch?"

"I'll hold that in reserve."

"Is that supposed to be a joke?"

He ran a hand through his dark hair. "I wish I knew. Have you ever had a . . . uh . . . mystical experience before?"

"Never!"

He studied her as if he were trying to decide whether she was telling the truth.

Breaking into his thoughts, she asked, "So now what? Do we go out there, and I try to find the place?"

"No."

"But . . ."

"Think about it! How would I write it up? You reported Heather DeYoung missing. Now you're saying you know where she's buried."

"Heather!" she gasped. She'd been half-thinking that the body was Heather, but she hadn't allowed the speculation to get very far. "You think it's her?"

"Unless this is totally unconnected. Don't you think

it's more reasonable to assume that it's all tied up to-gether?"

"Yes," she managed.

"I have a P.I. friend who has fantastic . . . tracking abilities."

"The man you mentioned before?"

"Yes. I already brought him that sample of Heather's clothing. He can probably locate the grave. I'll go out there with him. If he finds something, I can use him as my source—and keep you out of it. As long as I can testify to a judge that I've used him before, that the information gleaned from him has proven truthful and productive in the past, and that he's credible, I'm in good shape." He explained, then continued as though he were giving a lecture to a new recruit in the detective squad. "I've also got to make a case that revealing his identity would endanger his life or his effectiveness or his credibility.

"Then I've got to come up with corroborating evidence to support the information. It doesn't have to be that much, just enough to show the judge that I've done some background. If Ross says he traced the killer to a wooded area at Sugarloaf Mountain, I can check the vicinity for footprints, fresh-turned earth."

"You think it's worth investigating," she said carefully. "But you'd go to all that trouble to keep me out of it?"

"Yeah."

"Why?

"A lot of reasons. The best one is that I think paranormal evidence is going to get the case laughed out of court. And I want to get a conviction on this case."

He got up, and she knew that she didn't want him to leave. But there was no use trying to give him her reasons. If she told him she thought they'd connected on a more meaningful level this morning, he probably wouldn't want to hear it. But there was another issue, too. A nagging fear that tugged at her.

She found herself trying to prolong the conversation. "You're going out there today?"

"Late this afternoon."

"Why not earlier?"

"My P.I. friend works best at night."

She might have asked him to explain that. Instead she said, "Sugarloaf Mountain must be a big place. You don't need my help?"

"You gave me some good landmarks. It's above the East View parking area. Not far to the left of the trail."

"Yes. But . . ."

"If I need more from you, I'll get back to you."

"Promise you'll call me and tell me what you find."

"I will."

He took two long steps toward the door, then turned. "One more thing. I'm going up there with Ross Marshall. Let me give you his number, just in case."

She felt another flicker of unease that she couldn't explain. "Jack, be careful!"

His face contorted. "I was going to say the same thing to you. I don't like hearing that you saw a car sitting outside last night. Or that somebody tripped you up yesterday morning. Is there somewhere you can go for a few days?"

She felt her chest tighten. "You think I need to?"

"I don't know. It would make me feel better."

She wanted to ask if that meant he cared about her beyond the fact that she was a witness in a case he wanted to solve. But she didn't press her luck. Instead, she said, "I'll keep the doors locked. I won't go out after dark. And you said you'd have patrol cars watching out for me."

"Yeah. You have an alarm system, right?"

"Yes. My grandmother had it. I don't use it much. I'm on the second floor."

He sighed. "Then it's probably not state of the art. Is it connected to a service that will call the police if somebody breaks in?"

"No. It just rings an alarm here."

"Well, turn it on when you're inside. And when you go out."

"All right."

She wanted to go to him, cling to him. She was afraid—not for herself, but for him, although she couldn't explain why. So she stayed where she was, feeling helpless and worried.

After he left, she turned the bolt on the door, then hurried to the window to watch him get into his car, still struggling with fears she couldn't name.

CHAPTER
THIRTEEN

A YEAR AGO, Jack would have turned himself in to the department shrink if he'd contemplated digging up a grave in the woods based on the kind of evidence Kathryn had given him. She'd seen a ghostly figure in a dream. On the face of it, he should dismiss her story out of hand. Yet he'd traveled far enough into the unknown that he took her report at face value. He'd even come up with a reason why the figure had looked like a ghost.

He snorted.

Then there was the nice authentic touch that she hadn't been able to dredge up the location, although she'd obviously wanted to tell him where she'd been.

Sugarloaf Mountain wasn't a sure thing. But if he had to bet on it, he'd bet he was going to find something when he went out there.

In the parking lot at police headquarters, he called Ross from his cell phone.

"I've got a new development in the missing person case," he began. "And I could use your help."

"With?"

"My contact gave me the approximate location of a grave. It's up at Sugarloaf Mountain."

"A nice ride in the country. You want me to do some . . . uh . . . sniffing around up there?"

"Right. I was thinking, we could get there around four. That way, we could do some looking around before dark. Then you could do your thing," Jack said, aware that they weren't on a secure line.

"Yeah. You know the Park and Ride on this side of Frederick?"

"Yeah."

"I'll meet you there."

After hanging up, Jack told Emily he'd be out on an investigation that evening. Granger had started the ball rolling with a request to tie the Heather DeYoung case into several previous missing person cases.

Now, as Jack collected more information on all of them, in the back of his mind he was thinking that if there was one grave up at Sugarloaf Mountain, there might be more. And he wanted to be prepared to do identifications.

Why Sugarloaf, he wondered as he looked up the phone number of the office there, then called to say he would arrive around four in the afternoon on police business and wanted access after hours.

They wanted a fax with the information, so he typed that up and sent it.

His mind was only partly on the work. He kept thinking about the details of the interview with Kathryn.

He hadn't realized her dream experience had been different from his. He'd simply appeared in the Alma-Tadema picture—although he hadn't recognized it at the time. She'd been drawn to a strange, airless world, where an indistinct but massive creature was watching her. He grimaced. A supernatural being?

What did it want with her—and him?

Something.

As he thought on that for a moment, a ready explanation leaped into his mind. He and Kathryn had met because he was assigned to the missing person case. What if the damn thing *wanted* the two of them to solve that case?

But why?

Maybe it was a ghost. One of the victims. And it was in purgatory until the murder was solved. Was that misty, airless world she'd described purgatory?

He pursed his lips, marveling that he was thinking along those lines. If a ghost broke the case, he'd better have a lot more evidence to back it up.

Inevitably, his mind went back to Kathryn. Her magic wand had been the guidepost to her exit. An interesting touch.

The image of something familiar. Something from her world—in that hostile place she'd described.

But why the wand?

He'd spent several hours each evening with the books he'd borrowed from Ross. And he'd learned some pretty amazing stuff—which he hadn't been prepared to share with her, because he could hardly believe he was considering such oddball scenarios.

Of course, some of it was pure twaddle. Like the myth of Atlantis, which he'd read about in several books. But he'd definitely been interested in an essay on hypnosis as a possible explanation of what had happened to himself and Kathryn. Suppose some agency was beaming suggestions to both their subconscious minds? That might account for their apparently sharing a dream, although it didn't explain how it had been done when they'd started out in completely different locations.

He could even fit Kathryn's latest dream into that script. Forget the ghost. Suppose someone had knowledge of the disappearances—now probably murders. And that individual wanted to feed information to the police without getting caught.

Clairvoyance was another mechanism he found himself considering. He'd read an account of the famous mystic Emanuel Swedenborg interrupting a dinner party in the summer of 1759 to go outside. When he came back, he was pale and shaken—insisting that a fire had already burned several houses near his own and that his residence was in danger. The dinner guests were startled by the report, since Swedenborg lived in a city three hundred miles away, an enormous distance in those times. The next evening, a messenger confirmed the mystic's account of the fire.

Something similar could have happened to Kathryn in this latest dream, although she claimed she'd never had any mystical experiences before.

Of course, if he was honest, he couldn't rule out drugs, although he couldn't figure out how someone had slipped the same hallucinogen to both Kathryn and himself. But LSD had turned up as part of the case. Kathryn said she'd found it in a drawer of Heather's bureau. Was she telling the truth?

He grimaced. He was still considering her as a suspect. Probably because he wanted to distance himself from the growing relationship developing between them.

Relationship? No way! This had started off as pure, unadulterated lust. Yet a relationship was what it had felt like this morning at her apartment.

He pulled his thoughts away from Kathryn and back to the investigation of the four missing person cases.

By three, it was time to leave for his meeting with Ross. Just as he was packing up, Granger sought him out again.

"You making any more progress on those cases?" he asked.

"Uh . . ."

"Jack, what's going on with you?" the captain asked.

He shrugged. "I've been a little distracted lately. Lily went missing. I found her, but it was kind of traumatic."

The captain pinned him with a look. "I got a complaint about you this afternoon. From a guy named William Strong. He says you were engaged in public lewdness yesterday morning."

Jack swore. "Oh, yeah? I'd hardly call it that! A kiss isn't lewdness."

"You were with Kathryn Reynolds. Were you on your own time?"

"No."

"I'm going to have to write this up."

Jack felt his chest tighten painfully, until several thoughts occurred to him. He struggled to drag in a breath before he said, "You say a man named William Strong reported me and Reynolds? He claimed he was looking for an address in the neighborhood. So he didn't live there. I gave him my name. How did he know Reynolds's name?"

Granger shrugged.

"Do me a favor. See if his name and address check out before you write it up."

"You think he's not legit?"

"Yeah, that's what I think," Jack said. He didn't have any solid facts—just a hunch and the hope he was right. "Maybe something else is going on," he added. "Reynolds has been having some problems with vandalism. And someone was watching her house last night."

"Did she report it?"

"Yes."

"I'll check that out."

"Fine."

Since he'd joined the Violent Crimes unit, Jack had gotten along with Granger. Now he wasn't so sure. And the captain's next words made him blink.

"I let you drop the Westborn investigation to focus on the missing person cases. Was that because you wanted to spend more time with Reynolds?"

Jack studied his superior. "Wait a minute. *You* asked *me* to try and come up with connections on the missing persons. And if you remember, I didn't even know Reynolds then. You sent me to her house."

Granger ignored the last part, meeting his gaze head-on. "No. It was your idea."

Jack stood there, wondering if he was going crazy—or was it Granger? The captain had told him to drop Westborn, but this was the second instance where he seemed to have forgotten about it.

Jesus, he wished he had some proof of how he'd gotten the assignment. He swallowed. "Can we talk about this later? I have a meeting set up with an important contact."

"Okay," the captain agreed, looking just as reluctant as Jack to continue the conversation. Maybe until he got a line on William Strong.

"I think I'm going to have a breakthrough in the missing person case," he said, hoping to hell it was true.

"I'll be waiting for your report."

Jack nodded, gathering up some papers and shoving them into his briefcase.

He left the building, his pulse pounding.

What was going on?

The old man who styled himself William Strong had called in a complaint. He'd like to check him out. But he didn't have time to do it now.

And Granger was acting like he had early Alzheimer's. Great!

He could come to no conclusions about that, and he tried to bring his thoughts back to the upcoming task as he approached the Park and Ride. Ross was waiting for him, his hips propped comfortably against his Jeep Grand Cherokee.

He waved to Jack, then grabbed his knapsack and loped forward with the easy stride of a predator. A wolf. He looked relaxed and ready for an adventure. Probably he and Megan had gotten the baby to sleep so they could have some quality time together.

The speculation made Jack flash back to his own situation. Why was he resisting the pull of Kathryn Reynolds? They were both consenting adults. Making love with her wasn't going to hurt anybody else.

He recognized the rationalization for what it was as

soon as it surfaced. He wasn't free. He had his family to consider.

"I appreciate your meeting me on short notice," he said as Ross slipped into the passenger seat of the unmarked.

"Well, it's a chance to get out in the woods—for a good cause."

"Yeah."

Ross gave him a long look.

"You appear . . . disturbed," he said.

"As in crazy?"

Ross laughed. "As in worried. Want to talk about it?"

Jack sighed, wondering where to start. "Granger got a report that Kathryn and I were engaged in public lewdness."

"Chasing each other naked around the Rockshire parking lot?"

Jack laughed. "No. Kissing outside her house. Unfortunately, I was on duty at the time."

Ross whistled through his teeth. "Not good."

"The really interesting part is that the guy who reported us claimed to be looking for an address in the neighborhood. He asked my name. But not Kathryn's. Then he included her name in his complaint."

"You're right. Interesting."

"I asked Granger not to write it up until he checked the man's name and address. I'm thinking he'll find they won't exist."

"Which should let you off the hook."

"Yeah. But that's not my only problem." Quickly he filled in Ross on Granger's memory loss.

"Nothing like that's happened before?" Ross asked.

"No."

"So—what do you think?"

"I wish to hell I knew." Jack sighed. "As long as I'm spilling my guts, maybe I can ease into the rest of it."

Ross remained silent. Jack shifted in his seat and said, "I keep running into more paranormal stuff. That's why we're taking this ride in the country. This time Kathryn had her own dream. I mean, I wasn't there. It wasn't a fantasy setting. She was up at Sugarloaf, a location she'd never been to before, but she described it pretty well to me. She saw a guy burying a body a little way up the hill from the East View parking lot. And I'm betting that you'll be able to find the spot."

"I'll do my best."

"There's a strange element," Jack added.

Ross shook his head. "You mean stranger than what you've already told me?"

Jack laughed. "Unfortunately, yes. The guy she saw looked like a ghost."

"So maybe it's a hundred-year-old body."

"That occurred to me when she first started describing what she'd seen. But after the guy finished burying the evidence, he drove away in a late-model car."

"Did she recognize him?"

"Not so she could pick him out of a lineup. But she said there was something familiar about him."

"Mm hmm." Ross took in more details. "Have you been reading the books I lent you?" he finally asked.

"Avidly—when I can snatch the time. I never knew there was so much weird stuff floating around."

"You've led a sheltered life."

Jack laughed again. "There are few people who could say that to a detective who works in Violent Crimes."

"Yeah. It probably takes a werewolf. Or a vampire."

Jack's head snapped toward his friend for a moment, then he brought his gaze back to the road. "You believe in vampires?"

"Why not? The ancient myths must come from somewhere."

Jack felt a wave of cold sweep over his skin. Vampires. And what else?

"I get the feeling you've had a bunch of frightening thoughts over the past few days."

"Unfortunately, yes."

"Like what?"

"Nothing that makes perfect sense. But maybe you

can comment." Jack began summarizing his reading. "So, what do you think?" he asked, trying to breathe around the tightness in his chest.

"None of it seems quite right."

"That's what I was thinking."

Ross was studying him again. "You're in a unique position, you know. For centuries, humankind tried to figure out the secrets of the universe. We had all sorts of mechanisms for explaining the unexplainable—for warding off the devils and the darkness. Modern man, pardon the non-PC designation, feels more secure because he's got science to explain his world. Now you're thrust back into the dark pit of the unknown."

"Gee, thanks for pointing that out. What should I do, have an exorcism ceremony?"

"I wouldn't recommend it. Unless you believe in devils."

"I don't!" Jack insisted, wondering if he meant he didn't want to believe in them. He cut his friend another look. "When you talk about being thrust into the dark pit of the unknown, I take it you're speaking from experience."

"Yeah."

"What did you do?"

"I found Megan. And she helped me make peace with the furies nipping at my heels."

"Don't suggest that I put my trust in Kathryn. She's part of the problem."

"So was Megan, if you remember. But I figured out I needed her." Ross made a low sound. "Okay, that's not quite accurate. She forced me to admit that I could trust her."

Jack nodded, wishing he were free to take his friend's advice. Clearing his throat, he asked, "So, uh, what do you think about beings we can't see, beings we can't imagine? Beings who live in a place that isn't our world. Another dimension. Or another universe. Another—" He stopped, unable to finish the thought.

"Why do you bring up another universe?"

"The dreams start differently for Kathryn than they do for me. She describes a gray place where she can hardly see, hardly feel the ground under her feet, hardly breathe. She knows she'll die if she stays there. And to put the icing on the cake, there's something there—watching her." He shuddered.

"Something?"

"She calls it a presence. Too bad neither one of us has the terminology to describe it."

"So, are you thinking the two of you are being stalked by a creature from another dimension? Actually, it's as workable a theory as anything else. Maybe angels are creatures from another dimension. Maybe devils. Things men admire or fear. Things they can't express any other way."

"So why would a being from this other place be screwing with people from this world?"

Ross shrugged. "Hell if I know. If that's what it is, then I guess you have to figure it out."

Jack grimaced. "Yeah. The easy part. I guess we have to leave that for later. Let's start with dead bodies in the woods."

CHAPTER

FOURTEEN

THEY CHECKED IN at the park gate and got a combination that would unlock the chain across the road after hours. Then Jack drove to the East View parking area, where there were still a few cars.

After climbing out and stretching, he looked toward the hill above the parking lot. It was broader than he'd pictured. "More ground to cover than I remembered."

"Let's walk around up there a little," Ross suggested. "I don't think someone would bury a body within fifty yards of the parking area. So we can start above that level."

"Yeah. Kathryn entered the scene near the path," he said. "She wasn't sure how far she walked. But she knew it was to the left."

They started walking back and forth, their eyes on the ground. After half an hour, Jack began to think that he'd been overoptimistic about discovering anything. But he kept going, because he'd brought Ross all the way out here—and he wasn't going to give up until his friend called it quits.

Another fifteen minutes passed, and the sun began to

set. Jack's hopes were almost extinguished. Talk about looking for a needle in a haystack.

When he opened his mouth to speak, he saw that Ross had stopped and was sniffing the air. Then he moved toward a patch of ground that didn't look much different from the rest of the area. "Here," he said.

"A body?"

"Something dead. Underground. I can tell you better after it gets dark."

"You're going to change?"

"Yeah. But I prefer to do it in private." He hesitated a beat. "You're not going to freak out on me, are you?"

"I think I can keep it together," Jack answered, with more bravado than he was feeling.

"We won't be able to talk, of course."

Jack nodded. Of course the wolf couldn't talk.

He thrust his hands into his pockets, feeling a chill travel over his skin as he watched his friend disappear into the woods. He'd established a bond of trust with Ross, a bond that went deeper than he'd realized.

He wasn't sure how long he waited. He only knew that the light was almost gone when a gray wolf stepped carefully from behind a tree.

He was a magnificent animal. Large and proud and beautifully marked. Still, Jack felt the hairs on the back of his neck tingle as keen yellow eyes regarded him. It was one thing to know that Ross Marshall was a were-wolf. It was quite another to stand face to face in the woods with an animal that could tear him to shreds.

"So, let's go hunting," he said.

It was eerie to see the wolf nod, then move forward to sniff the ground where Ross had said a grave was located.

Jack switched on the large flashlight he'd brought, watching the animal paw up some of the leaves.

Picking up a stick in his mouth, he turned his head and jabbed it at the dirt.

Jack came forward to anchor the marker more firmly

in the soil—which was loose and easy to probe, as though it had been turned recently.

When he finished, he looked toward the wolf again. The animal had lifted his head and was sniffing the air once more, before moving to another location not far from the grave. Again he pawed up leaves, then turned his head toward Jack, who moved forward to meet him.

"Another grave?" he asked.

The wolf nodded, as Jack found a second stick and probed the dirt. Again, it was not packed down.

The wolf was already moving in a rough circle around the general area. Once more, he stopped and pawed.

"More?"

The animal confirmed the question with a nod. By the time he was finished, he had indicated five separate locations, and Jack had marked them all with sticks.

The wolf stopped, making eye contact once more.

"You think that's all?" Jack asked.

The animal nodded, then trotted away in the direction from which he'd come. Minutes later, Ross Marshall emerged from the woods, tucking his shirt into his jeans. "I make five graves," he said.

"That's more than I expected. The captain sent me off to investigate three previous missing person cases. Plus the recent one."

"Somebody's been busy."

"And he likes this burial ground. Which is one of the few patterns I've picked up. Before this, there was almost nothing to connect the cases. A woman who looked nothing like DeYoung. A boy. And a young man. I can't even be sure these are all his victims."

"But you can be sure Heather DeYoung is here."

Jack's head snapped around. "You're sure?"

"You gave me that tee shirt. Her scent is here."

"Okay. Good. Well, not good. I'm sorry she's dead. But at least I've got something to run with."

He gave Ross a direct look. "Thanks for helping me."

"You looked a little spooked, at first. But it worked out."

Jack laughed. "Well, think how you'd feel if I opened a door to another universe and a fallen angel came riding through on a fire-breathing dragon."

"When you put it that way, I can see your point. But you've got to admit that one little wolf doesn't equal a fallen angel and a fire-breathing dragon."

"Some people would think so."

They started back to the parking lot. "So, now I need to notify the Frederick County cops that I think I've got a graveyard from a serial killer in Montgomery County. Although, as I said, we can't be sure who else is buried here. And we can't be sure if the perp lives near his victims or is traveling down to our area from up here." He thought for a moment. "On top of that, I've got to think of a good reason why I came up here. The best solution would be if we could have found something of DeYoung's up there in the woods."

Ross gave him a penetrating look. "You're thinking of planting evidence?"

Jack sighed. "Yeah, listen to me! But that would give me something concrete to start with—rather than a psychic dream from Kathryn Reynolds. And we know the damn bodies are here."

"Do it any way you want. Remember, before that killer scooped up Megan, I refused to tell you *how* I got my information. You were willing to work with me. Some detectives weren't quite so happy about it."

Jack nodded, remembering his conversation with one of Ross's former police contacts. The man had been sure he was guilty of murder, but he hadn't been able to prove it.

Thinking about that made him feel edgy. He'd given Kathryn a rationale for using Ross as a source of information on this. But he knew he needed more than his friend's testimony.

His mood hadn't improved forty-five minutes later as

he turned in at the Park and Ride and thanked Ross again.

Ross had stopped asking questions, electing to remain silent during most of the ride. Now he said, "Are you okay?"

Jack cut the engine and sat with his hands wrapped around the steering wheel, feeling that he needed to anchor himself down—although he wasn't quite sure what that meant. "Not exactly," he said slowly.

"You want me to ride back home with you?"

"You think I need baby-sitting?" Jack asked, more sharply than he'd intended.

"I wouldn't put it that way," Ross answered easily.

Jack made an effort to relax. "Sorry, I'm sort of pre-occupied. I'm not very good company right now. I'll call you tomorrow and let you know what happened."

"Yeah, I understand." Ross studied him for a moment, as if debating whether to let him drive himself home. "Just be sure to call."

"Of course."

Jack watched Ross climb out of the unmarked and return to his SUV, feeling relieved to be alone. The relief lasted only a few minutes. Once he was back on the road, the tension gripped him again. He couldn't stop thinking about ancient myths and creatures of the night, and what you did to escape when you thought some supernatural force had you in its talons.

SIMON stood in the hallway, breathing deeply. He felt the blood pumping in his veins, felt his excitement building. Excitement he would turn into destructive energy. But along with the power, he felt raw nerves poking through his skin like a mass of small spikes.

He hated to admit the last part. There was no reason to worry, he told himself. He had prepared carefully. He knew he was in control of the ceremony. Still, he felt those sharp little wounds in his skin. Self-inflicted wounds, he told himself.

Mentally, he went over the preparations he'd made. The protective circle was in place—except for the break in the line where he would enter it.

And his victim was ready, too. Laid out on the table. Lightly sedated. But the guy wasn't going to stay that way. For this ceremony, Simon wanted him awake. Wanted him to know what was happening to him, and what *would* happen. This time, the victim's pain and fear were an important part of the process.

A tall candelabra stood on a table beside the door. It was an antique that he'd bought at an auction of furnishings from a Catholic church. The irony had always warmed him when he thought about how the priests would react if they knew what he was doing with their precious artifact.

Sitting beside the candelabra was a box of old-fashioned matches. Simon struck one, then touched it to the wick of a taper, watching the small flame flicker to life. Swiftly he lit the rest of the candles, then drew in a deep breath and let it out before opening the door and stepping into the ceremonial chamber.

It was a sacred place. Sacred to him. Not a church, but a space he had created where his purposes could be achieved.

The candles flickered, and he felt a cold wind moving his hair and the fabric of his pants.

A curse sprang to his lips.

Ayindral was here. Watching. Somehow, he was here, in this world.

Well, there was nothing the bastard could do, he assured himself as he stepped into the room and set down the candelabra. With a hand that shook slightly, he picked up the strips of tanned animal skin that would complete the circle. Stepping inside the protective line, he knelt and swiftly completed the defensive perimeter. Then he stood, and walked to the man strapped down on the table.

*   *   *

JACK kept his gaze focused on the road as he headed back toward Montgomery County. He tried to give all his attention to simply driving himself back home, but the need to escape clawed inside his chest like a wild animal desperate for freedom. Escape from what? He didn't even know.

He told himself to calm down. And as they had so many times during the past few days, he found his thoughts turning to Kathryn. He knew he'd made a decision. He was going to stop by her house and get a piece of Heather's jewelry. It was a good solution to the problem—a piece of evidence that he could say he'd found at a burial ground—but it also made him feel slightly queasy. He'd always been a straight-arrow cop. Now he was getting ready to turn himself into Mark Furman.

He thought about calling Emily and telling her he was going to be later than he'd expected. But how late? He didn't want to think about how long he might stay at Kathryn's and what he might do there.

He grimaced. No matter where his thoughts strayed, they kept coming back to her. To making love with her.

KATHRYN stood in her kitchen, her heart thumping in her chest. Hardly knowing what she was doing, she grabbed a mug from the shelf, filled it with water, and dropped in a bag of green tea. With shaking hands, she set the mug in the microwave. The turntable began to move, and a spark arced off the rim of the cup.

"Oh, shit!" she exclaimed, pushing the Off button. She'd grabbed a mug with a gold rim, and the metallic paint had set off a reaction inside the microwave.

The machine stopped, and with shaking hands, she opened the door and pulled out the mug, cradling it in her palms as she looked down, unseeing, at the cold water and wet tea bag.

She felt a terrible tightness in her chest, and an almost palpable vibration in the air around her.

"Jack?" she whispered. "Jack?"

He didn't answer, of course. He wasn't here. Yet she felt connected to him—as though an invisible wire were tugging at her, pulling her closer.

This was like the dreams. Only she was awake, the way she had been when she'd heard the dog barking. Then she hadn't understood what was happening. Now she knew she was waiting for some dire event.

With eyes squeezed tightly shut, she stood very still, barely breathing, trying desperately to make the connection with Jack stronger. So she could warn him? Be with him?

She didn't know her specific goal. She only knew that she had to get closer to him.

All at once, she could see him. He was in his car. Driving down a narrow road, coming to her.

Or was it all her imagination? Was she seeing him in his car because she ached for him to be with her?

She stood in the middle of the kitchen, gripping the mug, telling herself that everything was going to be all right—even when she knew it was a lie.

THE traffic on Route 270 was heavy, and Jack decided to turn off onto a secondary road.

As he negotiated a turn, he heard a man scream.

What? It sounded like the guy was in the car with him. His gaze bounced to the passenger seat. Nobody was there, of course.

But he couldn't stop himself from craning his neck to look in the back of the car.

The scream of pain was followed by a plea. *"Jesus Christ, don't do that!"*

"Ah, you're awake," another man said, his voice crackling with excitement. *"I want you conscious for the ceremony."*

Jack blinked, shifted lanes rapidly as the honk of a car horn brought his attention back to the road. The other driver shook his fist at him as he sped past—then shot into his lane and hit the brakes.

Jack hit his own brakes, narrowly avoiding rear-ending the son of a bitch.

The other car sped away. He thought about pulling out his flasher and giving chase, then forgot about the idea as another high-pitched scream of pain filled the car.

"No! Stop! For God's sake, stop."

This time, he thought he recognized the voice. Jesus! It was Gary Swinton!

"Swinton?" he called out, knowing in some part of his mind that the man wasn't in the car.

All he heard now was the chanting of words— smoothly flowing words in some language he didn't understand. They rolled on, filling his head.

The road in front of him dimmed, and he saw a room—a room draped in black, lit by flickering candles.

The scene was sharp and clear. As sharp as the dream with Kathryn. Sharper than reality. Swinton lay naked, strapped to a wooden table, his body slick with sweat, his face contorted with pain and fear. Another man leaned over him—naked to the waist, wearing black trousers in some thin, slinky material. His back was crisscrossed by scars. One hand gripped the edge of the table where Swinton lay. The other hovered over the naked man, holding a candle in an elaborate candlestick, tipping it to the side so that hot wax dropped on the man's midsection. Overlaying the scene was the sound of a voice, chanting smoothly, relentlessly.

Jack had the sensation of standing in back of the chanting man, staring at his blond hair, carefully combed over a bald spot. Though he strained to change the angle of the picture, he couldn't see the man's face.

He forgot where he was, what he was doing. All his attention was focused on the scene in the dark chamber as the hand slowly brought the candle lower. The strangeness and the horror of the scene riveted him.

"Jack! Jack!" Kathryn's voice pierced the bubble

around him, and the danger to himself came back in a sharp zing of awareness. Abruptly, his attention snapped back to his own reality—to the car he was driving. He felt his right front tire bite into gravel. He was on the shoulder, and he yanked desperately at the wheel.

But it was already too late. The road curved in the wrong direction, and he shot off the highway. He whipped across a patch of weeds, then down a sharp incline.

There was no question of steering. He rode the vehicle down the hill like a runaway locomotive. The car struck an obstruction he couldn't see, then skidded and rolled over, so that his head hit the column at the edge of the windshield.

That was the last thing he remembered.

CHAPTER
FIFTEEN

THE MUG IN Kathryn's hand crashed to the kitchen floor, the shattering of crockery mingling with the scream that tore from her throat.

"Oh, God, Jack! No!"

She saw the wild plunge of the car, saw the vehicle turn over. But she couldn't see inside, didn't know what had happened to Jack.

For long moments she couldn't move. Then, carefully, she stepped around the broken crockery and headed for the phone.

She didn't even know whom she was going to call until she had picked up the phone number Jack had left her. With wooden fingers, she punched in the numbers.

After several rings, a woman answered.

"Hello." In the background, a baby was crying.

"I . . . I'm sorry," she stammered. "I must have the wrong number."

"What number were you calling?"

"Ross . . . Ross Marshall."

"This is his wife, Megan Sheridan. Can I help you?"

Kathryn dragged in a breath, then let it out in a rush. "There's been an accident."

The woman gasped.

"No, no—not Ross," Kathryn managed. "It's Jack. His car went off the road and crashed. He went out with . . . with your husband. Does Mr. Marshall know where he is?"

"You say there's been an accident. But you don't know where?" the woman asked carefully.

Kathryn made an effort not to start shouting. "I'm in my living room. I . . . I saw his car go off the road. I saw it turn over. I don't know how I saw it. But I know it's true. It's what happened."

There was only a moment's hesitation on the other end of the line. "Okay. Ross was stopping on the way home to pick up some groceries. Let me give you his cell phone number."

"Thank you!" Kathryn gripped the pen so hard that she felt the plastic giving as she scribbled down the number. To make sure she'd gotten it right, she repeated it back. When Megan Sheridan had confirmed it, Kathryn hung up and then immediately called the private detective.

She waited with her hand clamped on the phone as it rang once, twice, three times. Finally a man answered.

"Mr. Marshall?"

"Yes."

"This is Kathryn Reynolds."

"What's wrong?" he asked immediately.

Again she had to drag in a breath and let it out before she could speak. "Jack's car has gone off the road. It's turned over. Do you know where he is?"

He didn't question her source of information. Instead, he said, "I think he was going to your house. That would put him on 1-270."

"No. He's on a secondary road."

"Okay, he must have turned off. Which is the best route to your house?"

"West Montgomery Avenue."

She had snatched up her purse when Marshall said, "Don't go there. You'll never get through in the traffic." He paused for a moment. "I'll report the accident, if somebody hasn't done it already. They'll take him to Montgomery County General Hospital. I'll meet you there."

"Yes. Thank you." Kathryn hung up, then stood for a moment, telling herself she had to get a grip. If she crashed her car, she wasn't going to do Jack any good.

As she charged out the door, her mind went back over the conversations. Megan Sheridan had been surprised to hear from her, but she'd been cooperative. Ross Marshall hadn't questioned her story or her need to get to Jack. What had Jack told them about her? Specifically— what had he told Marshall?

She couldn't answer the questions. She could only pray silently as she drove to Montgomery General Hospital.

The emergency room was full of people. Some looking sick. Others were obviously injured. Still others were waiting for word about loved ones. As she stepped through the door, she scanned the crowd and found a tall, dark-haired man standing with his shoulder propped against the wall, watching the entrance.

The moment she walked in, he came toward her. "Kathryn?"

"Yes. How did you know?"

"Your hair. Jack told me you have wild red hair." He held out his hand, and she shook it. "Ross Marshall."

"I'm glad to meet Jack's friend. I'm just sorry—" She broke off before she could finish the platitude, and began again. "Is he here? How is he?"

"He's here. I don't know his condition." He reached to clasp her shoulder. "Take it easy. Jack said you're a strong woman."

"He did?"

"Well, that was the implication."

She gave a tight nod. "Have you seen him?"

"He's in the back. They're working on him. I'm going to tell the nurse that you'll be here waiting for information." He stopped, ran a hand through his hair. "I'm going over to his house—to tell Mrs. Anderson. She'll have to tell the kids."

"Craig and Lily." She pressed her fingers against her lips. "Oh!"

He nodded. "They lost their mother in an automobile accident. This is going to be tough on them."

"He's going to be okay!" she said.

"Yeah. Jack's tough."

He cleared his throat. "I gave the receptionist your name and told her that you're Jack's fiancée. That way they'll give you any information available."

She caught her breath, feeling her face go tight.

Again, he clasped her shoulder. "I know the two of you have gotten close."

"Not because Jack is comfortable with that."

"Are you?"

"Well, if you know the circumstances, you know it's hard to be exactly comfortable. But I'm a woman; I think in terms of relationships. Jack's a man; he thinks in terms of avoiding entrapment."

Marshall laughed.

She gave him a considering look. "I get the feeling you've been there yourself."

"Yeah, but I got over my male reluctance. Now I'm happily married." His expression grew serious again. "As I said, I know you're close. No matter how it started."

"What did Jack tell you about us?"

He swallowed. "Let's not get into that now. What's important at the moment is that I think you're entitled to the latest information about his condition."

She sighed, told herself he was right. "Yes. Thank you. But maybe you'd better go get his family. I'll stay here and wait."

"Okay. And I'll tell Mrs. Anderson that you're a good friend."

"She already knows I'm involved in a missing person case. I talked to her this morning," she murmured.

An expression flashed across his face, an expression she read all too well. Gasping, she reached out to grab his sleeve. "What did you find at Sugarloaf Mountain?" she demanded.

He kept his gaze steady on her. "I'm sorry."

"You found Heather up there?"

"I can't tell you with one hundred percent certainty. But I'm pretty sure that's true."

As she swayed on her feet, he caught her and led her to a plastic chair, easing her down. She was aware that people were staring at her, but she didn't care.

"I'm sorry," he said again.

"I was . . . afraid of that," she whispered. "I guess I've already started coming to terms with it."

He nodded. "I'll be back as soon as I can."

She watched him disappear into the parking lot, then turned her attention toward the door where patients were called for treatment.

When she'd first set eyes on Jack, she'd felt like time was standing still. Now, each second seemed to stretch into a century.

She leaned her head against the wall, closed her eyes. Maybe some protective mechanism helped her doze off, because she felt herself jerking awake. Someone was calling her name.

She jumped up, hurried toward the voice, which belonged to a rumpled-looking man in a white coat.

"Ms. Reynolds?"

"Yes. Can you tell me about Jack?"

"I'm Dr. Hammersmith. Detective Thornton has a concussion and a dislocated shoulder."

"A concussion!"

"He's awake. We'd like to keep him for a day or two, to observe the head injury. Under the circumstances, I'd say he escaped with a minimal amount of damage."

She nodded, trying to take that in. "Can I see him?"

"Yes. For a few minutes. We're going to admit him to the neurological floor. That's the second floor."

"But he's out of danger?"

"Things look pretty favorable. But we need to keep him under observation."

"Okay. Thank you," she answered, thinking that the doctor was expecting Jack to recover, but he wasn't willing to say that for sure.

He led her into a busy open area where personnel were rushing off on various emergency errands. They stopped at the entrance to a treatment cubicle, secluded from the main area by curtains. Jack was lying in a hospital bed, low rails raised on either side of the mattress. Her gaze shot to his face. One of his eyes was swollen closed. His complexion was deathly pale, except where it was discolored by bruises turning purple. His arm was in a sling, strapping across his chest.

She must have made a noise when she saw him, because his good eye flickered open and focused on her.

His lips moved, and she thought she heard him whisper her name. Seeing him like this made her insides clench. And, at the same time, it made her realize that her feelings for him ran strong and deep.

"Jack." Swiftly she crossed the room. She wanted to gather him into her arms, but she was afraid to hurt him. So she restrained herself, leaning over him, reaching for his good hand and squeezing it gently.

This time when he whispered her name, she heard him clearly.

She bent to brush her lips against his cheek. "Just rest."

He sighed, closed his eye again.

"Ross went to get Mrs. Anderson."

He made an effort to rouse himself. "Better if the kids don't see me this way."

"I'll tell them you're mending."

The brief exchange seemed to have exhausted him. His good eye closed again, and she felt his fingers loosen.

Once more, she brushed his cheek with her lips, then stepped back. She wanted to stay, but she knew that he needed to rest.

Out in the waiting room, she spotted Ross again. He was standing with an older woman and two children, a boy and a girl. The boy looked achingly like Jack. The girl had more delicate features. Probably her mother's.

The trio must be Craig, Lily, and Mrs. Anderson.

Her heart turned over when she studied the children's pale, pinched faces. They'd lost their mother a few years ago in an automobile accident. Now their father was in the hospital for the same reason, and they had to be scared—no matter how much their housekeeper had contributed to their stable home.

Kathryn wanted to rush to them and offer what comfort she could. But when Ross waved his hand to usher her over, she saw the older woman's expression turn disapproving.

The negative reaction made her throat tighten. But she understood it. Mrs. Anderson had talked to her about a case Jack was working on. Now she was suddenly being billed as a close friend of his. And she'd been allowed to go in and see him—while his family was still in the waiting room.

Instead of hurrying over, she came slowly toward the little group. "Hello, I'm Kathryn Reynolds, Jack's friend. We talked this morning, Mrs. Anderson."

The woman gave a tight nod.

"And this must be Craig and Lily."

"Yes," the boy answered.

She started to offer her hand to the housekeeper, then thought better of it when she saw the woman's unfriendly expression had hardened.

"Is my daddy going to be okay?" a trembly voice asked.

Kathryn lowered her gaze toward Lily. "Yes, I just saw him. He said he's feeling pretty good," she said.

"I want to see him."

"I'm sorry. They don't let children into the emergency room, and I think your daddy's taking a nap now," she said, remembering that Jack hadn't wanted his children to see his battered face.

The little girl's lower lip trembled. She looked so miserable that Kathryn bent down and folded her close, feeling the little girl cling to her. "It's going to be okay. Your daddy told me to tell you not to worry."

"He's not going to die," Craig said emphatically. Then turned it into a question. "Right?"

"That's right," Kathryn answered, praying that it was true.

The housekeeper's hard voice interrupted. "I can take care of Craig and Lily."

Knowing she'd been put in her place, Kathryn stood up again, her eyes going to Ross. "I think I should go home now," she said.

"There's no reason you can't stay," he answered, but he sounded uncertain.

"No. I know when it's time to leave," she said, her voice barely above a whisper because she was afraid she was going to burst into tears if she tried to manage more volume. "You stay here with Mrs. Anderson and the children. They need you. I'll be okay."

Quickly she turned away, blinking to clear her vision. Without waiting for a reply, she started for the door—then saw that a broad-shouldered man had come in and was looking around. Ross spotted him, too, and rapidly crossed the tile floor. The man looked grim, and Ross drew him aside, away from the family that was now seated on a plastic couch.

She couldn't hear what they were saying. But when Ross glanced in her direction, she made her way over to the alcove where the two men were talking.

"This is Captain Granger, Detective Thornton's superior," Ross said. "Kathryn Reynolds."

The captain studied her, his expression not exactly friendly. "Aren't you the woman who filed the missing person report in the DeYoung case?"

"Yes."

"What are you doing here?"

"Detective Thornton and I . . ." She spread her hands, not knowing exactly what to say, particularly since Ross had introduced the man in very formal terms.

"How did you know Jack was here?" he asked.

It was Ross who answered the question. "I have a police scanner in my car. I heard what had happened, and I called Ms. Reynolds because she was waiting for word on what Jack and I had discovered."

Kathryn struggled to keep her expression steady. That wasn't exactly the truth. But she knew why Ross had to give the answer he did.

Granger looked like he was having a bad day. "So my detective runs off the road in a one-car accident—in his company car," he muttered. "Which is always fun to explain to Internal Affairs—and the press."

Kathryn opened her mouth, then thought better of protesting.

Granger was already speaking to Ross again. "How did you two end up at Sugarloaf Mountain?"

"I had some information pertinent to the case."

"Yeah, you come up with some pretty amazing leads," Granger said in a voice that didn't make it sound like a compliment. "So you and Thornton spend the afternoon up at Sugarloaf. Then he comes back and crashes his car. What were you doing up there? Having a party?"

"Of course not," Ross snapped. "You can have his blood alcohol checked. And you can have a drug screen done, too."

"I will. And how, exactly, did this particular expedition come about, if you don't mind my asking?" Granger pressed.

"I found a piece of Ms. DeYoung's jewelry up at the mountain location."

Kathryn blinked.

Granger issued an immediate challenge. "Jack didn't say anything about that."

"I guess he was planning to put it in his report." Ross

slipped his hand into his pocket and pulled out a small plastic bag. In it was a circle pin that Kathryn recognized.

Lord, had he really found it up there? Or what? She could only stare at the piece of jewelry. "That's Heather's," she managed as he handed the bag to the captain.

Granger's head swung toward her. "So you can conveniently corroborate the information."

"Yes. I've seen her wear it. Is that bad?"

Granger scowled. "Convenient, as I said. There's something going on here that I'm not picking up, isn't there? Are the three of you in some kind of conspiracy or something?"

Ross cocked his head to one side. "Like what?" he asked, keeping his voice mild. In the face of Granger's accusations, Kathryn might have shouted the question.

"You tell me," Granger muttered. "What's your story—that you were hiking up at Sugarloaf and found this jewelry? That you knew it was related to a case Jack happened to be working on?"

"That sounds right."

Granger snorted. "Okay. We'll get back to that later."

"The important point is that both Jack and I believe you'll find DeYoung's grave up there. As well as several other graves—all related to the missing person cases Jack has been investigating."

Granger's gaze swung toward Kathryn. "You don't seem surprised."

"I was starting to feel like Heather wasn't coming back," she murmured. "Then, before you got here, Ross told me he was almost sure she was dead."

"Convenient," Granger muttered again.

"Are you accusing her of something?" Ross asked, his voice low and level.

Granger gave him a hard look. "What are you, her lawyer?"

"No. I'm just trying to figure out why you're coming on so strong," he said, sounding deliberately controlled.

"Because Thornton hasn't been himself since he asked to get into the missing persons investigation. And then, this afternoon, I got a complaint about him—and Ms. Reynolds."

Kathryn sucked in a sharp breath.

"And you checked out William Strong?" Ross asked.

Granger stared at him. "Thornton told you about that?"

"Yeah, he did. And he told me he thought the guy was going to turn out to be bogus. Was he?"

A slight flush spread across the captain's cheeks. "As a matter of fact, the name and address don't check out."

"So it looks like somebody who wanted to make trouble for Jack or Kathryn."

"That doesn't excuse the behavior."

"Pretty innocent behavior, the way I heard it."

Again Granger looked at her. "Is that right?"

"Yes," she managed, feeling her cheeks flame. Bending the truth had never been her strong suit, yet in the face of this man's attack, she felt like it was her best choice—if she wanted to help Jack.

"Maybe we should get back to your missing person case." Ross's voice cut through her discomfort. "You need to identify the site, so I'll be glad to go up there with a crime scene team and show them where we marked the graves."

Granger was looking at him thoughtfully. "I'll contact Frederick County and apprise them of the situation. When we get a court order, I'll let you know."

"Fine," Ross answered.

Kathryn stood there, taking it in, thinking that there was a subtext to the conversation that she couldn't quite read.

Ross turned to her. "I appreciate your meeting me over here. But you might as well go on home." He sounded impersonal—like she'd merely come out of duty or something. But the look in his eyes as he met her gaze was intense. And she was pretty sure he was trying to get her out of there without any more questions. "Probably the captain will want to express his sympathy to the family."

Granger scowled at him.

"Okay. Thanks," she said.

"I expect you to make yourself available if we have any more questions," the captain said.

"Of course."

Granger strode off to see Mrs. Anderson and the children. Kathryn couldn't hear what he was saying, but his voice sounded milder.

"Is there anything else I can do for you?" Ross asked.

She thought about that. With his unqualified defense of Jack and his kindness toward her, this man had earned her trust in a very short time—unlike Captain Granger, who had earned her instant dislike. Keeping her voice low, she said, "Jack told you what's been happening to us? That we've . . . shared a dream? That I dreamed about going up to Sugarloaf and seeing the man burying the bodies? Only I guess it wasn't happening at the same time that I was there. It was something that was going to happen. Or had happened."

"Had happened," Ross supplied.

"You don't have any trouble with any of this weird stuff?"

"What did Jack tell you about me?"

"Not much. You're his good friend. You have extraordinary detective skills. And I guess you have some secret that you don't talk about much."

"Yeah." He hesitated for a moment, then lowered his voice so that she had to lean forward to hear him. "The ER waiting room isn't the place to talk about my background. Let's just say that my mind is open to stuff that other people might consider over the top. So when Jack talked about the two of you having the same dream, I didn't dismiss it as paranoid psychotic ravings."

"I'm glad to hear that. Did you have any insights for Jack?"

"Nothing of any immediate help."

She glanced toward the group at the other end of the

room and saw Mrs. Anderson looking at her as she spoke to Granger. She would have liked to know what the woman was saying. It couldn't be anything good.

"I'd better go," she said to Ross.

"I'll meet you here in the morning."

"Yes. Thanks." Turning, she started for the door, keeping her gaze focused straight ahead. She'd been on the verge of tears before the captain had walked in. And she'd kept herself together in the face of his interrogation.

Now she was close to breaking down again. She wanted to talk to Jack. And if not Jack, Ross. He had some things to explain to her. Like how he'd gotten Heather's circle pin. But she couldn't ask him now.

The cold reality of the conversation with Ross and Granger began to sink in as she stepped into the parking lot. Heather was dead. And Jack—

Jack was beyond her reach. By the time she got to her car, tears were streaking down her cheeks. She wiped them away with the back of her hand, then made an effort to get control of herself so she could see to drive.

All the way home, she kept thinking about her relationship with Jack. She'd come rushing down to the hospital like she had a right to be there. But seeing his family had made her realize how badly she was kidding herself. He had a son and a daughter who were his first responsibility. What part could she play in that life? She and Jack had been drawn together by circumstances neither of them understood. From the first moment they'd laid eyes on each other, there had been a wild, out-of-control sexual pull between them.

Jack didn't think that meant anything beyond the physical—because some outside force had pushed them together. She could understand his point of view, although it wasn't true for her. What she felt for Jack went a lot deeper then sexual compulsion, but she couldn't expect—or demand—the same from him.

Telling herself the truth only deepened her misery.

By the time she turned onto her street, she was sobbing. She pulled into the driveway, cut the engine, and hunched over the wheel, struggling to calm herself.

Kathryn! Someone called her name. Not aloud. The voice resounded inside her skull.

Raising her head, she looked around, not knowing what to expect—until a noise behind her had her whirling in her seat and craning her neck so she could see in back of her.

She stared in confusion when she saw that a car had pulled in front of her driveway, blocking her in.

She gasped when she recognized the angular shape. She still didn't know the make and model, but she was almost certain it was the car she had seen up at Sugarloaf Mountain. The car that had been driven by the man who'd buried Heather's body.

CHAPTER
SIXTEEN

IN THE LIGHT from the streetlamp, she saw the car door open. A man climbed out and jogged toward her.

Something was in his hand. As he drew closer, she saw it was a gun pointed toward her.

Her heart blocking her windpipe, she acted instinctively, twisting the key in the ignition.

When the engine roared to life, she threw the car into Drive, spinning the wheel as she came around in a tight circle across the grass. The vehicle clipped an azalea as she crossed the lawn, sank into the grass, then mowed down a flower bed. But she didn't slow down. Crossing the sidewalk, she bumped down the curb onto the street, not bothering to turn on the headlights.

When she risked a quick glance in the rearview mirror, she saw the man was running toward his car. Seconds later, his vehicle lurched after her.

Desperate to escape, she took the corner on two wheels, driving through the night with her headlights off.

Twin beams came toward her out of the darkness.

When the driver spotted her, he honked, but she ignored him.

Her eyes flicked to the rearview mirror, and she saw lights behind her. Was it the guy? Or somebody else? In the darkness, she couldn't tell.

Teeth clenched, she made a quick turn at the next block, then another turn, and another, weaving through the neighborhood like a drunken snake, thankful that she knew the twists and turns so well.

She kept glancing back. The lights had disappeared, and as far as she could tell, there was nobody following. But she didn't allow herself to relax. He could have turned off his headlights, too. And he could be coming up on her fast. A sob welled in her throat. As long as she was in the neighborhood, she wasn't safe.

When she reached Route 28, she was forced to turn on her lights or risk an accident. Hands gripping the wheel, she eased into the stream of traffic, watching the rearview mirror as closely as the road in front of her.

She didn't see the familiar shape of the car. But she still didn't feel safe. She headed for Rockville Pike, driving toward Bethesda. After several miles, she turned in at one of the well-lighted, busy shopping centers that lined the Pike, then used the off-road exit connecting it to the next strip mall.

In the second parking lot, she pulled up to the curb and sat with the engine running in case she had to make a quick getaway.

To stop herself from shaking, she wrapped her hands around the wheel. Reality was finally sinking in. The men who had buried Heather had been parked on the street, waiting for her to come home. And he'd probably been there last night, too, in a different car.

She tried to figure out what to do, but after everything that had happened, her brain felt almost too numb to function. First she'd seen Jack's car crash. Then she'd rushed to the hospital. After a few minutes with him, she'd had to deal with both Mrs. Anderson and Captain

Granger. Then she'd gone home, and the man who had killed Heather had almost gotten her.

The logical thing was to call the police. But she couldn't bring herself to do that, not after her interview with the captain. He hadn't bothered to hide his anger with Jack—and her, too, she was pretty sure.

If she started talking to the cops, there was no way to keep Jack out of it. And when she started trying to explain all the weird stuff that had happened to the two of them, she was going to sound demented. Which wasn't going to do Jack any good—or her, either. So the best thing was not to get started.

Did her reasoning make sense? She couldn't be sure. She only knew she couldn't go to the police. Not now. Not until she could consult Jack. And there was no chance of that until he was better.

Then what?

Ross's face swam before her. Ross would help her, but his phone number was at home, and she couldn't risk going back there.

A sob welled in her throat, and she knew that she was on the edge of hysteria. Pressing back against the headrest, she took several shallow breaths, ordering herself not to come apart.

When she was feeling a little calmer, she exited onto the Pike once more and drove toward D.C.—until she spotted the low profile of a motel on her side of the road.

After pulling under the lobby entrance canopy, she looked in back of her again. The guy wasn't there.

She knew if the killer had followed her, getting a room would be a dangerous idea. But she was almost certain she'd lost him. Since he didn't know where she was, spending the night here would be a lot safer than going back home. In the morning she'd figure out what to do. Right now, all she wanted was to feel safe.

She was deciding which credit card to use, when her mind canceled the decision. You could trace people through their credit card transactions. Which meant that she should pay in cash.

Luckily, she was prepared for that eventuality. Long ago, after Gran's purse had been stolen, she'd tucked emergency money—three fifty-dollar bills—under the floor mat of her car. Before getting out, she found the money, then went inside and rented a room for the night. The place was one of those two-story motels where you registered, then drove to your room. So she didn't have to explain why she was arriving without any luggage.

After locking the door, setting the chain, and tipping a chair back under the doorknob, she looked around the room. It wasn't anything fancy, but it wasn't too bad. At least the blue spread, curtains, and carpeting looked clean.

But the air was cold, and she suddenly felt chilled to the bone. Shivering violently, she crossed to the bathroom, and turned on the shower with a shaky hand.

She stayed under the hot water for a long time, using the soap and shampoo provided by the management. Finally, feeling better, she got out and dried herself, then put her tee shirt back on. After using the hair dryer mounted above the light switch, she washed out her underwear and hung it on a towel rack.

By the time she was finished, she was so worn out that she could barely move. She'd been going to see if she could get Ross's number from information. But now it didn't seem worth the effort. If she'd been thinking clearly, she might have decided she was being compelled to go to bed. But coherent thought had been washed away with the hot water. She could only stagger across the room, turn off the lights, and crawl into bed, pulling the covers up to her chin like an animal seeking refuge in its burrow.

She was asleep almost as soon as her head hit the pillow. And there was almost no opportunity to rest. Almost at once, she was in the strange, airless land where humans had no place.

The fear was still there, nipping at her heels. But this time it was less, because she knew where safety lay. The huge incarnation of the magic wand was shining in the distance. She staggered toward it, gasping as she reached the milestone, then broke free of the thick fog.

As soon as she stepped into untainted air, she knew where she was. Not Sugarloaf Mountain, thank the Lord. Instead, she was back in the Alma-Tadema painting. Well, not exactly. It was the landscape of the painting. Only now the brilliant midday sunlight was gone—replaced by the softer light of early evening.

And she wasn't alone.

A man dressed in faded jeans and a dark tee shirt was standing at the edge of the marble structure, staring out to sea, his hands stuffed into his front pockets. She saw him only from the back, but she knew who it was.

"Jack!"

He turned, and a smile of welcome broke out on his face. A relaxed, open smile that was achingly new to her.

"Kathryn. I was hoping you'd come."

She walked swiftly toward him, stopping a few feet away, thinking that she was going to show him she wasn't controlled by passion—that the two of them could have a conversation without grabbing each other.

Hours ago, when she'd seen him in the hospital, his face had been bruised, one eye swollen closed. His arm in a sling.

That image faded as she stared at him. He looked as he had before he'd left for Sugarloaf. Well, not exactly the same. He looked happier, more relaxed than she'd ever seen him. He wasn't in his persona of Jack Thornton, police detective. He was off duty. At ease.

As she took him in, she saw him doing the same with her. For the first time, her focus shifted away from him. She looked down at her own garb and saw that she was wearing only the tee shirt that she'd put on in the motel. It was a long tee shirt, skimming her hips, but much too revealing to be wearing out here in the open.

His warm look told her that keeping their hands off each other might not be so easy.

"I was going to say 'We have to stop meeting this way,' " she managed.

"You mean just when I've decided it's a good idea?"

"A good idea," she breathed, trying to keep her tone light, but he must have seen something on her face that disturbed him. And she recalled that he was excellent at reading people.

"What's wrong?" he asked. "I mean, beyond the usual problems?"

"What . . . uh . . . do you remember before this?"

She watched his thoughts turn inward, watched his features cloud, knew the moment when comprehension dawned. "Oh, Christ!" he exclaimed. "I went off the road." He gripped her arm. "What happened to me? Am I dead? Is this heaven?"

Her throat clogged. "Heaven? I hope not. If this is heaven, then we're both here. And I didn't think he got me."

His hand tightened on her flesh. "You don't think who got you?"

"I . . . I shouldn't have said that."

"Yeah, but you did. What happened to you?"

"The man I saw in my last dream. He was waiting for me when I got home from the hospital. When I pulled into the driveway, he blocked me in. At least I'm pretty sure it was him."

"Shit!"

"It's okay. I drove around him. I . . . I got away. Then I went to a motel on the Pike."

"You're sure he didn't follow you?" he demanded. "You checked?"

"Yes. I'm fine."

"Thank God for that." His face contorted. "But when you wake up, I don't think I'm in any kind of shape to protect you." His expression clouded. "My car turned over. What happened to me?"

"You have a concussion. And a dislocated shoulder."

"Oh, shit."

"You're going to be okay."

"Yeah, well, I've screwed things up pretty good. I'm not going to be on active duty anytime soon. Damn! I was driving to your house. To get something of De-Young's—to salt up there at the grave site." He stopped, cursed again, his expression contrite. "Sorry, that's a wonderful way to tell you that your friend is dead."

She reached for his hand, knit her fingers with his. "Ross told me. He . . . he already got something of Heather's. A pin. He showed it to Captain Granger."

"Granger! You talked to Granger?"

"He came to the hospital. He was . . . pretty hostile."

"I'll bet." He shook his head. "Something's going on with him. I can't figure it out. He asked me to try and connect the missing person cases. Then somehow he decided it was *my* idea."

She stared at him. That's . . . weird."

"My thoughts exactly."

It was a strange discussion. They were both talking quickly, exchanging information as though it were perfectly normal to be meeting in a dream. But then, for them, it was!

"There *is* some good news," she told him. "You were right about William Strong. He doesn't exist, so . . . uh . . . Granger couldn't write you up."

"That's something, anyway."

They discussed the captain for a few more minutes, coming to no real conclusions. Yet she felt the tightness inside her chest easing. All too often, she had felt she and Jack were antagonists. Now, they were trying to figure things out together.

"How did you hook up with Ross?" he asked.

"I called him and asked him to meet me at the hospital."

"*You* called *him*?"

She gave a small nod. "I . . . I saw the accident. Like a . . . a vision. I saw you go off the road."

His reaction was more matter-of-fact than she might have expected. "Just like I saw the ceremony."

"What ceremony?"

He grimaced. "I saw two men in a room hung with black curtains, and one of them . . ." He stopped. "You don't want to hear about this."

"I think I have to." Her fingers clamped on his. "Jack, we're in this together. We're tied together by this thing. You understand that, don't you."

"Yeah. I understand it." His grip tightened on hers. "I was just trying to skip the gory details. But, okay. One man was wearing black trousers and standing over another man, strapped naked to a table. The one in the trousers was torturing the one who was strapped down."

She felt her throat close, understanding why Jack had wanted to hold the information back. He gathered her to him, cupping the back of her head and pulling her face against his shoulder.

When a shudder went through her, he pulled her closer, then leaned back against the wall and took her with him.

She stayed in his arms for only a few moments. Then, struggling to show him that she wasn't going to go to pieces, she eased away and pressed her shoulders against the opposite wall. "Did you see his face?" she asked.

"Which one?"

"Either."

The man with the black pants had his back to me. All I saw was a network of scars on his skin and a bald spot at the back of his blond hair. The man on the table was Gary Swinton."

"Oh, my God! Swinton? You're sure?"

"I interviewed him a couple of days ago. He was hiding something, but I didn't know what. I went to talk to him again after you gave me that paper with the acid, but he'd left work. When I got to his apartment in D.C., it looked like he'd been packing—then gotten interrupted. There was blood in his suitcase."

"Oh, Lord!"

"What I'm thinking is that he helped Black Trousers capture your friend."

"Black Trousers?"

"That's what I'm calling the guy whose face I couldn't see. My guess now is that Swinton drugged her. Probably he got her used to doing drugs with him, so she wasn't worried about what was happening."

She sucked in a sharp breath.

"Swinton must have worked out some deal with the other guy to be paid for his services. Then it turned sour. Maybe Black Trousers was angry that I was investigating Swinton."

The thought of The Swine handing over Heather for money turned her stomach. "Unfortunately, that sounds like something he might do."

"It looks like he paid for it. I wouldn't want to bet he survived the session in that room."

She nodded tightly. "I should have called the police sooner. I mean, when Heather first disappeared."

"Jesus! Don't blame yourself! You had every reason to think she was just off somewhere having a good time."

She didn't want him to make excuses for her. "Maybe you would have found her."

"Probably not in time. This guy has been hiding his activities for months—maybe years."

Quickly, he stepped forward, reached for her, and she came back into his arms, relief flooding through her as he folded her close.

In some corner of her mind, she warned herself that this wasn't real, that maybe nothing between them was real. But reality had never been more achingly immediate.

His deep sigh matched hers as he pressed her to him. His hand swept down her back, encountered the edge of the tee shirt, and continued downward, stroking her bare bottom.

The passion she'd struggled to contain, flared. Ter-

rible things had happened today. Too much to take in.
She didn't want to think about the real world. She only
wanted to be with this man—to take comfort from him
and give him comfort in return.

"Jack?"

For a long, charged moment their gazes locked, and
she saw the smoldering heat in his dark eyes.

CHAPTER
SEVENTEEN

HE LOWERED HIS head, brought his mouth down to hers, his lips moving urgently, potently in a passionate kiss that swamped her senses.

She had wanted this from the moment she had set eyes on Jack Thornton. Now she wanted so much more. Everything.

But she would take what she could get.

His fingers stroked up and down her arms, then found the sides of her breasts. She couldn't hold back a small sob of gratification and surrender. She heard wind roaring in her ears and understood that it was her blood rushing in her veins.

He raised his head, and her eyes snapped open.

"I think we need to find somewhere more comfortable than a marble bench," he muttered.

"Yes." Kathryn smiled at him. She had never been in this place before the first dream encounter. Hardly ventured beyond the boundaries of the painting. But she was confident as she took him by the hand and led him down the marble colonnade, stopping to grab a sprig of the fragrant vine that trailed from the horizontal beams above them.

She twined the stem around her wrist and Jack's, binding them together.

"Handcuffs?" he asked with a smile in his voice.

"Uh-huh. I'm not going to let you get away this time."

"Not a chance."

For now, she thought. *At least for now.*

Her heart squeezed, and her fingers tightened on his. He returned the pressure, and she wanted to pull him to a stop—make him promise that they could turn dreams into reality. But she kept moving—hurrying lest he come to what he considered his senses.

Halfway along the walk, she turned between the columns, leading him through a field of pale white flowers swaying gently in the shimmering moonlight, then up a small hill toward a round marble pavilion. They were both in a hurry now, taking the flight of three steps at a run and ducking under gauzy hangings into a rich, private enclosure—a bedroom fit for one of the Greek gods. A bedroom dominated by an opulent round bed covered with plum-colored silk.

"Clever of you to bring me here," he murmured.

She nodded wordlessly, unable to explain how she'd known this place would be waiting for them.

He turned her toward him. One of his strong hands tangled gently in her hair, playing with the strands as he angled her head so that he could ravage her mouth.

"God, I love your sweet mouth and your red hair. It's so wild and sexy, and thick," he said, teasing her lips with his as he spoke the words.

"And I love everything about you. Not just your body. All of you. The better I get to know you, the more I understand how extraordinary you are, Jack Thornton. You're a hero to me."

He grimaced. "I'm no hero. I'm full of very human flaws."

"Everyone has human flaws. You have fewer than most people."

When he opened his mouth to protest, she went on quickly, "I don't think we came to this nice bedroom to argue, did we?" She had never thought of herself as a bold lover. Now she slid her hand slowly, seductively down his body, stopping when she found his erection. Cupping her palm over the hard shaft, she rocked her hand against him.

"Ah, Kathryn, are you trying to drive me crazy?" he growled.

"I'm trying to . . . get what I've wanted since I first set eyes on you."

"Oh, yeah."

His eyes locked with hers, and for wild heartbeats she thought she might drown in the scorching intensity of his gaze.

Then he swept her into his arms and took her down to the horizontal surface of the bed, and she sighed out her triumph and her relief. This time . . . this time there would be no turning back.

She felt her body tune itself to the wordless vibrations rumbling deep within him. Vibrations that touched every part of her—physical and spiritual. And she knew he felt her response as he rolled to his side, clasping her against his heat and hardness as he devoured her mouth with kisses.

He tugged at the tee shirt, breaking the kiss only long enough to pull the garment over her head and toss it away, leaving her naked on the bed.

"Lord, you are so beautiful," he said, his voice husky, his hand tracing the curve of her hip, then drifting upward as he reached to circle her hardened nipple with his forefinger.

"Oh!"

He smiled, leaning forward to repeat the caress with his tongue. The sensations were exquisite, and even more exquisite when he sucked the nipple into his mouth.

She clasped his head in her hands, her breath coming broken and fast as he built her pleasure—with his hands, with his mouth.

She had thrilled to his kisses. Now she thrilled to his knowing touch. She had thought that when they made love, it would be sharp and fast—out of control. But the pace slowed to a long, sweet exchange of pleasure.

Together they took off his jeans and shirt, touching and kissing all the while. When she had him naked, she stroked her hands greedily over his body, loving the texture of his skin, the thatch of dark hair spread across his chest, his narrow hips, the jutting shaft of his penis.

He was beautiful and hard. Aroused—for her. And she gloried in his reaction. Whatever happened later, she would have this moment in time to remember.

His hand slid down her body, finding the moist, swollen flesh of her sex, and she arched into his caress, rocking against his fingers, increasing the wonderful sensations.

Her blood had turned molten, but her physical response was only part of what she felt. She was with him—soul and body—as they drove each other higher and then higher, until the urgency was beyond bearing, and she knew that she would die if she didn't feel him inside her.

"Jack, now. Please, now," she begged, reaching to clasp him, guiding him to her.

He entered her, and her breath caught.

For a long moment, he stared down at her, his eyes dark with passion. Then he began to move inside her, and she climaxed almost at once, calling out with the wonder of it.

Waves of pleasure took her, but it wasn't enough. Not nearly enough. Just a taste of paradise. Eagerly, she surged against him, with him, asking for more.

His hand moved between them, stroking and pressing as he kept up the rhythm—taking her up, up beyond the sun.

The second climax tore through her, carrying her

away on a wave of ecstasy so intense that she dug her nails into his shoulders.

Her joy was complete when she heard his shout of release and felt him go rigid above her.

She clung to him, tears gathering at the backs of her eyes. Making love had been wonderful. Beyond anything she had ever experienced. Beyond anything she could have imagined. Now she could only anchor herself to him, vibrating with the aftershocks of pleasure that still quivered through her.

Clasping her to him, he rolled to his side. The physical storm had left her limp. The emotional storm was even more intense. There was so much that she wanted to say; but, for the moment, the words remained locked in her throat.

He held her, stroking his hand over her damp shoulder.

"That was incredible," she said, hearing the thickness in her voice.

She felt him nod, and knew that he still couldn't acknowledge the glory of it. So she simply cuddled against him, floating in the aftermath of exquisite pleasure.

She dozed. A dream within a dream. Peaceful at last after the past few days of tension.

Sometime later, her eyes drifted open.

Jack had drawn away from her and was lying with his hands behind his head, his gaze focused on the gauzy canopy above them.

"Jack?"

He turned his head toward her, and she saw that the barrier he'd let down a little while ago had snapped back into place.

Her disappointment was like a physical blow. But she was determined not to let him know how much he'd hurt her by closing himself off again.

Tangling her fingers in the sheet, she murmured, "Relax. It's only a dream. You don't have to feel guilty about making love with me."

He stared at her, trying to read the expression that she was struggling so hard to keep unreadable. "It's a dream. But it's more. We both know that."

She gave a small nod.

"A reality dream," he muttered. "An altered reality—that we're able to share."

"Okay. Yes."

"But the sixty-four-thousand-dollar question is—How did we get here?"

She didn't want to say what she was thinking, but she had told herself that she was going to be honest with him—whatever the cost. "I guess someone brought us here."

"Right. Like maybe Black Trousers. I mean the guy who was torturing Swinton."

She winced, wishing he hadn't brought that up *now*.

Jack got up, pulling on his jeans as he plowed on. "We have to find out who he is. He was . . . intoning . . . words I couldn't understand. It sounded like he was working a magic ceremony."

"To have some effect on us?"

"On me. To make me crash the damn car. Apparently it worked. I heard him, saw him; and I forgot where I was and what I was doing. Like now. We've both forgotten the real world, haven't we?"

She didn't quite understand the analogy, and quickly dipped her head so he couldn't see the hurt in her eyes.

"What are we supposed to do?" she whispered.

"I don't know! I don't like being manipulated."

She saw the frustration and anger bubbling inside him and said quickly, "We were brought here. But once we got here—we acted of our own free will."

"Did we?"

The two words were the cruelest he'd ever spoken to her. Still unable to speak above a whisper, she managed to say, "I don't know how we got here. But I know how I felt when I saw you. I was so happy to be with you. And I won't let you take away the joy of our making love." She swallowed. "Only the two of us were in bed together. Giving each other pleasure—showing each other how much we cared. At least that's how it was for me. I didn't feel like I was with a man operating under some outside influence. I was with a man who was totally focused on me—on making love."

She couldn't meet his gaze, didn't want to see the expression on his face.

Feeling very vulnerable and very naked, she climbed out of bed, pulling the sheet with her. There were low chests of drawers at one side of the enclosure. In one, she found a pair of silky white slacks and a matching top, which she quickly donned.

When she turned back to Jack, he was gripping one of the marble pillars.

"Did you see my children? Did they come to the hospital?" he asked.

His children. Of course he would want to know about Craig and Lily.

"Mrs. Anderson brought them." She looked down at her hands.

"What? Are they all right? What happened?"

Ashamed that she'd let her own emotions intrude, she said quickly, "They're fine. I was thinking that Mrs. Anderson wasn't too pleased to see me."

He nodded.

She was still looking at him when she caught a subtle vibration in the air. A wrinkle in the texture of the dream.

"You feel that?" he asked, his voice low and urgent.

"Yes," she answered. Then her eyes went wide as a shape loomed beyond the gauzy curtains that formed the walls of the pavilion near her. They parted, and a figure stepped into the room.

It was a man of medium build, medium height. The lower half of his body was clad in the black trousers Jack had described. His chest was bare, the pale skin covered by a network of scars. And his face was a horror mask, distorted by a stocking or something similar pulled over his head.

His right arm was bent across his chest, and she saw he was holding a silver knife. He moved the weapon in front of himself, swinging his gaze from her to Jack and back again.

"Get away from him," Jack shouted at her, but her feet were rooted to the spot.

The man shifted his weight from one foot to the other, then lunged at her, the knife flashing.

Finally released from her trance, she ducked away, grabbing a pillow and throwing it at the attacker's face as Jack charged forward. The man swung to the right, and Jack was too far away to stop the knife from slashing at her, slicing through the fabric of her gauzy shirt, cutting into her skin.

She screamed, screamed again as the weapon flailed toward her a second time.

Before the blade reached her, Jack caught the man by the shoulders and pulled him away from her.

The two of them rolled across the floor. With her foot, Kathryn reached out and stamped down on the arm with the knife, sending the weapon clattering across the marble floor.

Black Trousers cried out in pain. "You bitch."

Jack grabbed his hands, pulled them above his head. "What do you want with us?" he shouted. "Did you bring us here?"

Kathryn didn't expect an answer, but he gave a high-pitched laugh. "Me? Me? Don't you have a clue what's going on?"

"No. Enlighten us."

"Not a chance," he spat out.

And then the dream began to dissolve around her.

"No! Oh, God, no!" she screamed, unable to hear the sound of her own voice.

"No!"

One moment she and Jack were grappling with the invader. In the next, she was gone from the frantic scene—lying in bed, panting, crying out in terror and frustration.

In bed.

Not her own bed.

Where was she? Some new dream? Alone.

New panic seized her by the throat.

God, where was Jack? Was he all right?

She leaped from the bed, then remembered where she was. A motel room, where she'd gone after Black Trousers had tried to grab her.

Black Trousers. Oh, Lord! He was the man with the knife. Somehow he had gotten into the dream with them.

As the reality of his presence flooded through her, she felt pain slice across her midsection. Looking down, she saw a dark stain had soaked into the fabric of her tee shirt. She gasped, then rushed into the bathroom and turned on the light. Blinking in the brightness, she examined the stain.

It was blood. And when she pulled up the shirt, she found what she expected to see—a slash across her midsection.

Jack had scratched himself with a rock. But she'd never seen the injury. Now she had her own proof of what would happen if she was injured in one of what he'd called their reality dreams. She turned on the water, grabbed a washcloth, and washed away the blood. The wound wasn't deep, thank the Lord, since she had no way at the moment of treating it beyond cleaning it with soap and water.

She hurried through the first aid, then stared at her bloody tee shirt. It was the only thing she had to wear, but it looked like she'd been in a street fight.

Her stomach clenched. She couldn't stay here. She had to get to the hospital and make sure Jack was all right.

Quickly she reached for the underwear she'd washed the night before. It was still damp and clammy, and the feel of it made her cringe. With a grimace, she tossed it onto the edge of the tub, then pulled on her jeans and shirt again.

Was she going to keep this room? She didn't know. But she'd paid for it until eleven this morning. So she stuffed the key card in her purse as she headed for the door. Minutes later, she was driving up Rockville Pike toward the hospital.

The lights of an all-night drugstore shone from one of the shopping centers. After a quick debate, she pulled into a parking space and entered the store—speeding down the aisle toward the clothing section, where she snatched a black tee shirt and a package of underpants off the rack. The clerk didn't even glance at her bloody shirt when she paid for her purchase. Back in the car, in the darkness of the parking lot, she scrunched down below the dashboard, dragged on underwear, and changed her shirt.

Minutes later, she was pulling into the hospital parking lot. The doctor had told her where to find Jack. Acting like she had every right to be there, she marched through the emergency room, then took the elevator to the second floor.

CHAPTER

EIGHTEEN

AS THE ELEVATOR started upward, Kathryn was torn between wanting the car to go faster and dreading what she'd find when she arrived on the second floor.

Nobody was at the nurse's station, so she went behind the counter and found Jack's chart—with his room number.

In the movies, they put guards outside of a cop's room when he was in danger. But this wasn't the movies. And nobody besides the two of them knew what had really happened to him.

Her heart was pounding as she stepped inside the private room and crossed rapidly to the bed. When she looked down at him, her chest tightened. She was shocked to see his bruised face and the sling strapping one arm to his chest. He was sleeping, an IV line attached to the other arm. Was he still in the dream? Was he in danger? Should she wake him? Or was that the wrong thing to do? Anxiously, she studied his face. He looked peaceful, but what did that prove?

She'd been cut, and a dart of fear stabbed at her. Pulling back the sheet, she raised his gown, examining his chest and stomach—looking for slash marks.

His good hand caught her wrist, scaring the spit out of her.

Her gasp of alarm was met by his curse. "Jesus! I thought it was him." Then, "What are you doing?" he demanded in a voice that sounded stronger than it had the day before.

Lifting her gaze to his face, she found he was staring at her—a mixture of emotions on his face. Relief. Surprise. Uncertainty.

Her own voice wasn't quite steady as she pulled his gown back into place and said, "I was looking for knife wounds."

"I'm fine." His gaze went to her midsection, and she noted that the swelling had gone down on the eye that had been closed the day before. "But I think *you* got cut. At least, I remember his slashing at you."

"Yes."

His expression turned stormy. "How bad was it?"

"Not bad, just a slash across my stomach. I washed the blood off."

"That bastard!"

A sound at the door made them both look up. It was a nurse, and Kathryn waited to be told she had to leave. But apparently the unit was pretty relaxed. The nurse only said, to Jack, "You're awake. Good. Let me check your pupils and your vital signs."

Kathryn stepped out of the way, waiting tensely while the woman went efficiently through her routine. She relaxed a bit when it looked like everything was okay. Finally, they were alone again, and she said, "Tell me what happened after I left."

"I was trying to get some information out of him. Then—there was a . . ." He trailed off. "I don't know what. Something else was there. Something I couldn't see. But I sensed it, like a huge storm cloud hovering over both of us. Some kind of . . . being." He stopped, swallowed, looked angry. "Black Trousers sensed it, too. I could tell he was scared. He . . . he disappeared and the dream disappeared, too. And I was back here."

She nodded. "The thing you described. It . . . it sounded like what I told you about—in that place where I can't breathe." She went very still, her mind taking another leap. "It's there every time I have one of the dreams. And this time you were aware of it, too. Do . . . do you think it could be what's dragging us in there?"

His face contorted. "We're talking about something you can't see except as a large, dark shape? If it's causing the dreams—and the other stuff we've been experiencing—how the hell do we fight it?"

"I don't know how—but we will."

He studied her closely. "Lord, you look so fierce. If you can fight this thing, so can I."

"You had the stuffing knocked out of you—I'm still on my feet."

"Okay, I'll accept that excuse."

"It's not an excuse!"

"Then let's get some work done. Can you describe the thing any better?" he asked.

She thought about it. "I can't describe it physically. I can't really see it. Like I said, it's got no shape. No features. But I feel like it's watching me. And it's spoken to me. Spoken in my mind."

"What else?"

"It lives in that place where I start the dreams, I think. Or maybe a place that's even less hospitable to humans—but the thing changed the conditions a little so I can be there, at least for a little while."

She saw he was listening intently, also saw that the short discussion was taking a lot out of him. Pressing her hand over his, she said, "We can talk about it later."

"No. This is important. We need to talk about it now. While it's fresh in our minds."

"Jack, I can see you're worn out. If you don't get some sleep, you won't be in shape to discuss anything."

He considered the advice, then gave a tight nod. "Maybe you're right."

"I'll stay here." She looked around, saw the bulky plastic easy chair in the corner. "I'll get some rest, too. And when you wake up, we'll talk again."

She could see he didn't like it, but she also saw that his energy was draining away.

Settling down in the chair, she watched him slip into sleep and knew he must have been making a tremendous effort to stay conscious. Her own energy level was pretty low.

As her eyes started to drift closed, a voice whispered in her head. The voice she had heard before. *Stay awake. You must stay awake.*

She sat up straighter, gripped the arms of the chair. It was the thing she had encountered in the dream—the thing they had just been talking about—speaking to her again. Only this was no dream. It was reality.

"Why?" she said aloud.

If you both sleep at the same time, he will find you.

There was no doubt in her mind about whom the voice was referring to. It was Black Trousers.

Somehow, he had found them together in their last dream. He could do it again.

She shuddered, pressed her spine against the chair back. There was no reason to believe a voice whispering in her head. Yet she believed.

"What does he want?" she asked.

To kill both of you.

"Why? What did we do to him?"

There was no answer. "Why?" she repeated. Then, "Are you trying to help us? Hurt us?"

Again, there was only silence. She could choose to dismiss the warning, but she elected to keep herself awake. So she sat in the chair, watching Jack, telling herself she must keep him safe.

Twice a nurse came in and roused him, checking his pupils and taking his vital signs. Each time, he went right back to sleep, and she was thankful for that. And thankful the nurses didn't ask her to leave.

Sleep tugged at her, and she dug her nails into the

palms of her hands, then stood up and crossed to the small bathroom, where she splashed water on her face.

Around six, she was standing with her hips propped against the window ledge when Jack opened his eyes again.

He looked toward the chair, and the disappointment on his face gave her a small jolt of hope. Then he found her, and his features smoothed out again. So he felt something! But he wasn't going to tell her about it. At least that was how she decided to interpret his behavior.

"Did you sleep?" he asked.

"No."

"Yeah, sleeping in a chair isn't all that great."

"It's not that. It's . . ." She trailed off, then started again. "I might as well tell you straight out. The thing spoke to me again. Here."

His expression sharpened. "Oh, yeah? What did it say?"

"That if we both sleep at the same time, he can find us again."

"Oh, shit! You believe that?"

"Yes."

He swore again. "Crank up my bed, will you?" He looked around. "Better yet, help me get to the bathroom."

She eyed the IV line. "Is it all right for you to get out of bed?"

"It better be." He pushed himself up, swung his legs to the side of the bed, and she hurried to move the stand with the IV line so it wouldn't pull out of his arm. On his feet, he swayed slightly, and she reached to steady him.

He grimaced as he looked at the tubing. "I feel like an old guy in a nursing home."

"No, you feel like a guy who was in a car that rolled over," she corrected him, thinking he was probably uncomfortable with her helping him. Slowly, they crossed to the bathroom, her arm around him. After easing the IV stand inside, she closed the door and waited outside.

The toilet flushed, then she heard water running. When he came out, his face was damp, and she assumed he'd splashed it with water—and probably also taken a drink.

They reversed the trip, and he sat down heavily on the side of the bed. "I could use some civilized clothing," he said, gesturing toward the hospital gown. "It's disconcerting to have a breeze blowing on your butt."

She laughed.

"Maybe I should call Mrs. Anderson. She can bring me some pajamas—and some clothing to wear home." He looked at the clock on the wall. "And I can talk to the kids before they go to school."

He lay back down, and she cranked up the head of the bed so that he was sitting comfortably. Then she moved the phone to the long table that swung across the bed.

After dialing the number, he leaned back and closed his eyes. "Emily," he said when the housekeeper answered.

Kathryn watched him, torn between drifting out of the room and listening to the conversation. When he didn't tell her to give him some privacy, she decided to stay.

"Yes, I'm much better," he said, then was silent, apparently listening to a long monologue.

"Kathryn and I have gotten close," he said, and she knew he must be responding to some complaint about the night before.

Close. That was a bland description of what she felt, but she had no right to argue the point—not when he had other people in his life to consider.

Again there was a lengthy comment that she couldn't hear. Instead of responding, he said, "Why don't you put Craig on?"

In a moment he was speaking to his son, his voice steady and reassuring, and she felt her heart squeeze.

When she volunteered at school, she got to see lots of kids—and lots of parents. So she knew Jack was a good father—as good as any child could hope for.

"Yes, I'm fine. Yes, I miss you, too," he was saying. "I'll be home as soon as I can. Craig, I love you. You don't have to worry about me, I'm fine. Well, my arm's in a sling, and my face is kind of bruised. But I'm going to be as good as new." After a bit more conversation with his son, he said, "Let me talk to Lily now."

He repeated what he'd said to Craig, reassuring his daughter in a warm, deep voice that made Kathryn feel good just listening to it.

Then he asked to speak to Mrs. A. again, and requested the pajamas he rarely wore and some trousers and a button-down shirt that he could wear home.

When he was finished with the phone call, he flopped back, his eyes closed.

"You're a great father," she murmured.

"I try my best. Sometimes I worry it's not good enough."

"Just from meeting them here, I can tell they're good kids."

"That's as much Emily's doing as mine."

"She was upset that I got to see you, and she didn't."

"Yeah."

She waited for him to tell her what the housekeeper had said. Instead, he asked, "How did you manage to see me, by the way?"

"Ross told them I was your fiancée."

"Oh." He looked down at his hands, and she wanted to assure him he could put an announcement in the paper saying it wasn't true.

It was almost a relief when he changed the subject. "You were telling me about the thing watching you. The thing with no body. No shape. What else do you know about it?"

He had come right back to where they'd left off.

"It's intelligent. Not like an animal. Not like a person. Not anything we can understand. It doesn't have senses in the way we think of them. It doesn't want to be here." As she struggled for some other way to describe the creature, another voice chimed in.

"It sounds like something that doesn't belong in this universe." The observation came from Ross, who was standing in the doorway.

"How long have you been eavesdropping?" Jack demanded.

"Long enough to know that you need some distance from the present subject. So why don't you tell me what happened when you went off the road?"

Jack sighed. "Okay, maybe you're right. But I'm counting on your not thinking I've plunged off the deep end."

"We've gone past that, don't you think?"

"Yeah," Jack answered, then told Ross about the ceremony that had captured his attention while he was driving.

When he finished, Ross looked thoughtful. "It seems like you're up against a guy who knows how to use magic to alter reality."

"You think that's possible?"

"You're telling me it is."

Jack sighed. "Yeah. I was working my way toward something like that."

"I don't know much about black magic. But from what you describe, it sounds like he sacrifices a victim as part of his ceremony."

Kathryn sucked in a sharp breath. "You think that's why . . . how he killed Heather."

"I'm afraid so."

"Heather and Swinton. And at least four other victims. There were five graves up at Sugarloaf," Jack muttered, then leaned back and closed his eyes. "Apparently Black Trousers has been practicing his craft for a while."

Kathryn studied his face and posture. He was looking exhausted again. "I think you need to sleep some more."

"I'm fine," he said automatically.

"We'll go get some breakfast," Ross said. "And you get some rest. Then we'll continue the conversation."

Before Jack could object, Ross gestured toward Kathryn. "Let's get some food."

She hesitated. She knew Jack needed to sleep, but all at once the idea of leaving him alone made her chest tighten.

She told herself she was being ridiculous. Nothing was going to happen while she and Ross were downstairs for a little while.

Still, her steps were slow as she exited the room. She wasn't sure she could eat, but she dutifully let Ross lead the way to the cafeteria.

"You don't look so great yourself," he said, as they stepped out of the elevator.

"I didn't get much sleep." She stopped, realizing that Ross didn't know what had happened after she'd gotten home. Quickly she filled him in on the man who had tried to block her car in the driveway. "I'm pretty sure it's the same guy I saw digging Heather's grave. The magician."

He whistled. "He's been busy. You can't go back to your house. At least alone. After breakfast, I can take you back there to get some clothing. Then you can stay in our spare room."

"I can't."

"Why not?"

She swallowed. "God, I keep forgetting that I've lived a thousand lifetimes since I saw you last night. After I checked into that motel, I went to bed—and Jack and I met in a dream again. This time, the magician showed up. He attacked both of us with a knife."

"Jesus!" Ross exclaimed.

"The bad part is that if we get hurt in one of those reality dreams, the injury is real. He gave me a slash across the stomach. It's not bad," she added quickly. "But I was pulled out of the dream before Jack. That's why I rushed here so early—to make sure he was all right."

Ross nodded.

"Then when I sat down in the chair beside Jack's bed,

the . . . the thing we were talking about when you came in spoke to me. It said that if Jack and I slept at the same time, the magician would find us again. So I have to stay near Jack—so we can figure out whose turn it is to sleep." She grimaced. Then asked the next logical question. "What does the otherworldly creature have to do with the magician?"

"I don't know. But we'll find out."

He sounded so sure that Kathryn felt some of the hopeless feeling lift.

"The two of you need to come to our house—so Megan and I can torture you to keep you awake." He laughed. "Actually, if you come home with me, Joshua may not let either one of you sleep."

"Joshua is your little boy?"

"Yes. He's seven months old."

She smiled at him. "You sound like you have such a normal life. I can't get over how you accept all these nutball explanations without acting like I'm crazy. I tell you a creature from another universe talked to me while I was in Jack's hospital room, and you don't even blink."

They had reached the entrance to the cafeteria. Over to one side was a small walled courtyard filled with tables. It was probably more appealing in the noontime sun, so none of the tables was occupied at the moment.

"Let's go outside for a minute," Ross said, holding the door open.

When the door had closed behind them, he turned to face her, his gaze appraising. "Well, the reason I don't have any trouble accepting your wild story is that I've got my own wild story." She saw him shift his weight from one foot to the other, watching her.

"You don't have to tell me anything you don't want to," she said quickly. "It's enough that I know you're on our side."

"What did Jack say about me?"

"That you could find Heather—if anybody could. That you'd be able to find the body I saw him bury. He didn't say it in so many words, but I know he trusts you implicitly." She swallowed. "And I gather from what he said that you have . . . something in your background that you'd rather not talk about."

"Yeah. That's right." He scuffed his foot against the concrete.

"Ross, I don't need to know what it is."

He sucked in a breath and let it out. "Under the circumstances, I think you do. The reason I'm good at sniffing out graves is that I'm a werewolf."

Kathryn stared at him, wondering if she'd heard him correctly. But the tight expression on his face told her that he'd just given up a deeply hidden secret. Still, she heard herself saying, "You're not making that up?"

"Sometimes I wish I were. It can be a difficult burden. So maybe you want to reconsider my invitation to come home with me."

She shook her head, still trying to wrap her mind around his admission. Probably she should be more shocked. But she knew she'd been prepared to hear something extraordinary about Ross—prepared by the aura of the man and by what Jack had hinted at.

But more than that, she'd changed over the past few days. When she'd first met Jack in that painting, she'd literally stepped out of the ordinary world and into a universe where anything was possible. "You've been a good friend to me. I thought from the first that you were someone I could trust," she said.

"So you can deal with a friend who's a werewolf?" he pressed.

She saw the tension in his face and reached to clasp his hand. It was a large hand but, aside from that, totally ordinary. She didn't allow herself to imagine it as anything else—a wolf's paw, for example. "You've shown me what you're like. And I know that Jack trusts you with his life."

"Thank you."

She couldn't hold back a small laugh. "Jack said you'd be good at investigating the grave up at Sugarloaf. I guess I understand why. You've ... uh ... probably got a sense of smell that's way beyond anything ..." She had started to say a sense of smell that was way beyond human capacities, but realized at the last moment how that would sound.

He breathed out a small sigh. "Yeah."

"Thank you for telling me. I'm sure you don't broadcast the information."

"No. But I wanted you to understand why I'm open to strange scenarios. Jack came to me, worried about what was happening. I listened and told him that anything is possible." He reached for the door. "Come on, you need to eat something."

Allowing him to change the subject, she followed him back into the cafeteria. When she would have settled for picking up a cup of coffee in the cafeteria line, he ordered her bacon, eggs, and toast, then made sure she ate some of the breakfast.

"Heather's circle pin. How did you get it?" she asked after she'd chewed a bite of toast.

"Before I picked up Mrs. Anderson and the children I stopped at your house and found the key under a rock near the door." He lowered his voice. "I know Jack was planning something similar—to keep you out of his report. So I went ahead and did it for him." He gave her a direct look. "He's a good cop. He's never done anything like that before."

She nodded, then tried to eat a little more of her eggs. But the longer they sat there, the more anxious she got. She'd thought it was all right to leave Jack; now she was regretting that decision.

"I have to go back upstairs," she finally said.

"Okay. I'll meet you in Jack's room."

They both left the cafeteria. Ross stepped into the men's room, and she hurried to the elevator, then waited impatiently for it to reach the first floor. Back on the neurological floor, she practically ran down the hall. Ahead of her, a man in a white coat was checking the numbers on the doors. He looked like he was one of the hospital staffers, a doctor or an orderly. Or a male nurse.

She couldn't see his face, but from a distance, he looked vaguely familiar. He was brown haired, about medium height and medium weight. Had she seen him when she was in the emergency room last night?

The man stopped in front of Jack's room. Stiffly, he reached for the door handle and walked inside.

She felt her breath catch. Then she was running toward the room.

CHAPTER
NINETEEN

JACK WAS DOZING when he heard someone running down the hall, then come bursting into his hospital room.

He saw two things simultaneously. Kathryn pelting into the room, her breath coming in jagged gasps, a look of terror on her face—and a brown-haired man in a white coat and black slacks standing calmly beside his bed.

He took it all in with one swift glance. With one hand, the man was reaching for the IV line attached to Jack's arm. In the other he held a hypodermic.

The man's serene expression changed in response to Kathryn's noisy entry.

"No," she screamed.

Instinctively, Jack lurched up in the bed, lunging at the intruder, knocking the hypodermic into the air—and sending a jolt of pain through his recently dislocated shoulder.

The hypodermic flew up in an arc, drops of liquid flying into the air.

Striking that one blow used up all his reserve of

strength. He put up his arm as the man came toward him. But it was like trying to stop a tidal wave with a paper boat. The man flung him back onto the bed, and he gasped as the violent landing jolted his shoulder again.

He saw Kathryn dart to the bedside, pick up a water pitcher, and fling it at the intruder, scoring a direct hit on his forehead.

The man howled in pain, cursing as he lunged around the bed and shot toward her.

Without many options, Jack pressed the call button, hoping that for once, the nurse would arrive and take the guy's attention away from Kathryn.

He watched her jump backward with the agility of a gymnast. She pulled on the wheeled table that extended over the bed, putting it between them, then savagely pushing it forward.

It struck the intruder in the midsection, and he howled again, then pushed the table out of the way before turning and leaping for the door.

Before he could make a clean escape, he crashed into a nurse coming into the room.

Flinging her out of the way, he dodged past as she fell to the floor, screaming.

Kathryn was trying to get out the door and follow the guy, but the nurse grabbed her and hung on.

"Let me go! He tried to kill Jack. We have to get him," she gasped. But it was already too late.

She freed herself and made it into the hallway, but came back moments later with her shoulders sagging. She was followed by Ross.

"What happened?" the P.I. demanded.

"Someone was here," she gasped out. "He tried to kill Jack."

"Which way did he go?"

"I don't know."

"Probably the stairs."

The nurse had recovered her composure and was leaning over Jack. Grabbing his wrist, she started to take his pulse. He couldn't hold back a sharp laugh. When in doubt, fall back on basic medical procedures.

Kathryn came up behind the nurse. "Is he all right?" she demanded, her voice urgent.

"As far as I can tell. I'll call Dr. Samenow."

"We need to test that hypodermic and find out what's in it," Jack said.

"Yes." Kathryn moved to the far side of the bed and started to stoop down.

Fear leaped through him. "Don't," he shouted.

When her head swung toward him, he said in a calmer voice, "We don't know what's in that thing. I don't want you anywhere near it."

He looked at the nurse. "Get some gloves to pick it up, and bring a box to put it into. Something where the needle can't stick through."

"A container for biohazards?"

"Yes. I don't want anyone getting a dose of poison on my account."

Wide-eyed, the nurse scurried off.

Kathryn leaned toward him as he held out his good arm toward her. Well, "good" was a relative term. It wasn't the arm in a sling. But it was still tangled up with the IV line. He wanted to pull the damn thing out, but he didn't want to cause any more damage. So he left it in place as he folded her into his embrace.

He was overwhelmed by her courage. Overwhelmed that she'd put her own life on the line for him.

But he would have done the same for her. And that knowledge, too, was overwhelming.

He couldn't tell her what he was feeling. He could only hold her tightly. For long moments, neither of them moved—or spoke.

Finally, he said, "It looks like you saved my life."

She kept her face buried against his neck. "Lord, what if I hadn't come back in time?"

He swallowed with some difficulty. "You did."

She turned her face so she could press her lips to his

unshaven cheek, and he turned his head so that his lips met hers.

The kiss wasn't passionate. It was more an acknowledgment of words he couldn't speak.

A throat-clearing noise from the doorway made Kathryn look up. Emily Anderson was staring at them as though they'd just been photographed nude in bed together. Neither one of them was nude, and he was the only one in bed—although he wouldn't want to get up in front of her, with his butt hanging out of his hospital gown.

Kathryn stepped away from him, turning to confront Emily.

The housekeeper gave them a long look before making a *tsk*ing noise. "I . . . I'm sorry if I interrupted something," she said, sounding like she was actually glad that she'd arrived in the nick of time to prevent Kathryn from climbing into bed with him. "You asked me to bring you some clothing." She held up a small bag.

"Someone . . . someone just tried to kill Jack," Kathryn said. "I . . . I'm grateful that he's all right."

Jack saw Emily's expression change as she tried to work her way through the statement. "Oh, my," she said, dropping the bag onto the tile floor.

Jack gave her a direct look. "Kathryn risked her life to save mine."

"Oh!" His housekeeper's gaze swiveled from him to Kathryn and back again.

Jack sighed. "Emily, you're an important part of my family. I'm sorry that I haven't had a chance to talk to you about Kathryn, but a lot has been happening quickly. I was investigating a missing person case. It's turned into a serial murder case. One of the victims is Kathryn's tenant. That's how we met." He paused, considering what to say next. "We've been working together, and we've . . . realized that we care about each other."

As he watched his housekeeper absorb that information, he continued, "It looks like the murderer tracked me down here. And she chased him off a few minutes ago."

He saw Kathryn staring at him, probably wondering what he meant by "caring about each other." He wasn't sure he knew the definition himself, but he did know that denial was becoming more and more difficult.

At that moment, the nurse walked back into the room, carrying a plastic box. A doctor was right behind her, presumably Dr. Samenow. Behind him was Ross. It was suddenly very crowded in the small room.

His hand covered by a surgical glove, the doctor bent down and carefully picked up the hypodermic. Just as he'd set it in the plastic box, a uniformed police officer walked into the room. It was Carl Boswell, and Jack gave silent thanks that he'd worked with the guy before and they'd gotten along well.

"I'm responding to a call about a murder attempt on the patient in room 321," he said. His eyes widened when he saw Jack. "You're the intended victim?"

"Yeah. It's a long story. I was working on a kidnapping case that's turned into a serial murder." He repeated what he'd told Emily. "At least, it will be when somebody digs up the graveyard at Sugarloaf Mountain. I was on my way back from there when the murderer tried a little vehicular homicide."

"He caused your accident?" Boswell asked, obviously struggling to assimilate new information.

"Yeah. I'll get back to that in a minute. Right now, the important point is that the murderer tracked me down here and decided to make a second attempt to get me off his back. At least I have to assume it was him."

He was aware that everybody in the room was staring at him.

Kathryn and Ross were both waiting quietly for his story. He wasn't going to talk about magic ceremonies. But he wasn't going to let the connection go, either. Putting the experience in terms anybody could understand, he said, "Last night, he ran me off the road near

Damascus." As he uttered the statement, he silently told himself that in a way it was true.

He also noted that Ross was struggling to hold back a grin at the way he'd put it. Lord, was he doing it again—twisting facts to suit his purposes? But he couldn't think of any other way to connect the two incidents.

At the same time, he was thanking God that there hadn't been any other cars in sight when the accident had happened. So there was nobody to dispute his version of events.

"His car hit yours?" Boswell asked.

"No, he edged me over to the side. I was trying to stay on the pavement, but I lost control of the vehicle when the road took a sharp turn."

Boswell wrote that down, along with a few more imaginary details. When he'd finished, Jack went on to what had happened after he'd opened his eyes and found the guy standing over him, ready to inject something into the IV line. He raised his head toward the doctor, who still held the hypodermic ensconced in its plastic box. "You can turn that over to Officer Boswell. The sooner he gets that stuff to the police lab, the sooner we'll know what it is."

Samenow looked reluctant, but he handed over the evidence.

"Did you tell the officer who arrived on the scene of the first attempt?" Boswell asked.

"I wasn't thinking too straight right after the accident. I had a concussion, and the details eluded me. Dr. Samenow can confirm my medical condition last night. After I was admitted, some of it came back to me."

"What kind of car was he driving?"

"A 1985 Ford Crown Victoria," Jack answered, naming the car driven by the guy who had called himself William Strong.

Kathryn gasped. "You . . . you think it's the same person as the old man who drove by my house?"

"Yeah, I do," he answered, the conclusion taking on

more weight as he continued to speak. "I think he alters his appearance, which is one reason we haven't caught him yet."

He saw her vision had turned inward. "You have something to add?"

She swallowed. "I'm pretty sure I saw him in my neighborhood before Heather disappeared. He . . . he was dressed like a workman. He had a white van, but there was no name on the side. I think he must have a closet full of disguises."

Jack gave her his full attention. "What else have you been processing while I was lying here in bed?"

"Nothing," she said in a thin voice, and he was sure she wasn't telling the truth. Well, there was plenty of stuff *he* didn't want to talk about in front of the people crowded into his hospital room. She probably felt the same way.

"We both saw him a few minutes ago, although he was doubtless in some sort of disguise, probably a wig and a mustache."

Kathryn nodded tightly.

Jack turned back to the doctor. "I'd like to get out of here."

"If you're well enough to leave," Kathryn jumped into the discussion.

"I'd better be. Because it's obvious I'm not safe when someone can walk in wearing a white coat and try to inject something into my IV line." He gave her a direct look. "And you aren't safe, either."

He saw her complexion go a shade paler, felt his own blood run cold as several terrifying thoughts struck him. This guy not only knew a lot about both of them—but he also had means beyond normal human capacity. He'd slashed Kathryn in a dream, and she had the mark to prove it. And there was no doubt he'd caused the accident on the road—even if he hadn't physically been there.

Jack swung toward Ross, ready to beg an urgent favor. But he stopped short as he looked around the crowded room.

"I need to speak to Ross alone. It's important. But first I hope we can get this thing out of my arm," he said, gesturing toward the IV line.

Kathryn turned and walked out the door. He knew she was hurt, knew she was wondering why he didn't trust her. But he couldn't talk about his motives now.

The rest of the crowd followed Kathryn out, except Ross and Dr. Samenow, who walked to the side of the bed and detached the IV drip before removing the needle from his arm.

"How long do I have to wear this sling?" Jack asked.

"Three weeks."

"Shit! That's just what I need."

"You can remove the sling to take a shower, if you hold your arm in that position," Samenow offered.

"Yeah, thanks. That's something. But it's not going to help my accuracy with a gun," he said, thinking that if he was going to be facing Black Trousers with his right arm tied to his chest, he'd better get some practice on his left-handed shooting skills.

"I want to check your eyes and your reflexes," the doctor said, "before I sign you out."

Jack sighed. He'd conveniently forgotten why they'd kept him in the hospital overnight. Not because of his arm—but because he'd suffered a concussion.

Samenow glanced at Ross, then went through an examination routine.

"I can clear you to leave," he said.

"Good."

"And I'll write you a prescription for pain medication." He scribbled on a prescription form and left the slip of paper on the bedside table.

After the doctor had departed, Ross closed the door. "What do you need?" he asked.

"Kathryn and I have to disappear until this guy is caught. I've already asked a lot of you, but could you go with Emily and get my kids out of school? Then . . ."

"Then they can stay at my place," he said quickly. "After I pick them up, we'll stop by your house and get some clothing. And I'll make damn sure nobody is following us."

Jack let out the breath he'd been holding. There was nobody he trusted more than Ross Marshall to keep his children safe, but he understood that having houseguests wasn't easy for a man who prowled the woods at night as a wolf. "Are you sure that won't be cramping your style?" he asked.

"No," his friend answered, his tone unequivocal.

"There's the supernatural angle," Jack said, wanting to make sure he touched all the bases. "That's how he got to me on the road. That's how he got into our dream."

"I'm better equipped to handle the supernatural element than most."

"Yeah. Right. I can't thank you enough for this. I owe you one."

"It will be a long time before we even that score," Ross answered. "Do you need some cash?"

Jack thought about that. "I can raid an ATM on the way out of town."

"Do you know where you're going?"

"I'd rather not decide yet. And I think it's better if you don't know. The fewer links my kids have to that guy, the better."

"Right."

"I'll think of some way to thank you," Jack said again. Then, "Could you ask Kathryn to come in here?"

"Will do."

Kathryn walked slowly into the room, her head lowered. "I was starting to think you might trust me. I guess I was wrong," she said.

"I trust you."

"But you wanted me out of the room when you talked to Ross."

"I needed everybody out. I didn't want to waste time making selections."

"Okay."

"I asked him if he'd take Emily to pick up the kids at school. I want as few people as possible to know where they are. Not even the cops."

Her expression turned contrite as she took several steps toward him, then stopped. "Oh, Jack. I'm sorry. I thought . . ."

He cut her off ruthlessly, because he'd dealt with as many emotions as he could handle this morning. "You and I have to get out of here, too."

"Where are we going?"

"Let's hold off talking about it."

She nodded tightly.

"So, could you help me get dressed?"

"Yes."

He kept his directions brisk. "Take the sling off, so I can get my shirt on."

"Is it all right to take it off?"

"Not for long. The doc said I could take a shower, if I kept the arm across my chest. But I'll wait on that. I want to get us out of here." He stopped, and gave her a direct look. "You asked if I trusted you. It goes both ways. We need each other to get Black Trousers off our backs. And his friend," Jack added, his eyes seeking hers.

He could see from her pinched features that she knew what he meant. The being she'd tried to describe.

"YES," Kathryn murmured, tacitly agreeing. They needed each other at the moment. But he wasn't making any plans for the future. Well, they were together now. With a killer and an otherworldly being after them. She was scared, yet at the same time, she felt as if she'd been handed a chance to be with Jack—in the real world.

She struggled to keep her expression neutral as she carefully worked his sleeve up his arm. She could see that moving his shoulder hurt, but he was struggling not to show the pain. At the nurse's station, they reclaimed his property, then got his Sig from a safe downstairs. He stuffed the shoulder holster into the bag that his housekeeper had brought, then tucked the gun into his belt—on the right side—and pulled his shirt over it.

"Can you shoot left-handed?" she asked.

"I need some practice. Can you shoot at all?"

She laughed. "Grandma believed in self-protection, so she dragged me to a target range every few months."

"Good for her!"

When they reached the car, he said, "I'd like to get out of town right away, but I need to stop by police headquarters. I want to check out a laptop computer, so I can get into the databases I use."

She unlocked the door, then waited while he cursed as he buckled the seat belt.

"Make sure nobody's following us," he said as they pulled out of the hospital parking lot.

She looked in the rearview mirror, then looked again as she pulled out into traffic. As far as she could see, no car was sticking behind them.

"Nobody I can see, unless he's using a magic spell to track us," she murmured.

"Let's hope to hell not."

SIMON was still seething with anger. Things weren't working out the way he'd been sure they would. The cop hadn't died when he'd driven off the road.

But he was right there in the hospital—hurt and helpless. With his closet full of disguises and fake ID's, it had seemed like an easy matter to finish Thornton off. And he'd been so close to breaking the demon's unholy alliance. Then the woman had come charging into the room, stopping him from injecting the insulin into the IV line. It wasn't a poison; it had legitimate medical purposes, which was the beauty of it. The authorities could think that someone had made a mistake. Except that Miss Bitch, Kathryn Reynolds, had come in and fucked up his plan. He'd sprinted for the stairs and gotten out of the building. Then some dark-haired dude had come charging after him, but he'd escaped and driven home, wanting to speed but staying under the limit.

Jesus! That had been close. He'd thought he'd had the perfect solution. Now . . .

Well, he wasn't exactly back to square one. He was aware of Kathryn and the cop even now. The demon had established a connection among the three of them—a connection that went more than one way. Simon had used it to find them in that sexual fantasy of a dream last night. They'd had sex. And they'd dropped their guard. He smiled as he remembered the expression on their faces when he'd joined them in their wet dream. And he would do it again, the next time they both slept. Meanwhile, they were in his mind, like a background buzz. They were both awake, so he couldn't go to them now. But he was working on it.

He thought about Sugarloaf Mountain, and anger flared again. He'd had a bad feeling about the place since he'd buried Heather DeYoung's body. He wouldn't go back—ever again. But there was still the matter of Gary Swinton. Well, there were plenty of other places besides Sugarloaf. He'd used some before. He'd get rid of Swinton's body somewhere else tonight. Most of his body.

KATHRYN turned right, toward police headquarters.

Ten minutes later, Jack directed her to a parking space in the detectives' lot, saying, "It would be better if I had the unmarked."

"Do you want me to wait for you?"

His answer was sharp and instantaneous. "Not out here! Come up to the waiting area. I'll be as quick as I can."

She could see his energy was seeping away, see that he was in pain. He left her on a bench in a wide hallway and was back in twenty minutes, carrying a black case that she presumed held the computer. He still looked like he should be in bed—which was where she was going to put him as soon as they got where they were going.

Before they could make their escape, the door he'd come through opened again, and Captain Granger stepped into the hallway.

"Where are you going with that computer?" he asked.

Jack turned to face him. "I need it for research."

"But you're on medical leave."

"That doesn't mean I'm going to stop looking for the serial killer."

"I've assigned Dave Culligan to the case."

Jack leaned back against the wall and took several quick breaths. She wanted to turn and scream at Captain Granger to leave him alone. But she managed to keep silent.

"Good," Jack said. "But I want to do some research on my own. I've been in direct contact with the perp. Culligan hasn't. You should be getting a report from Carl Boswell. The guy who told you his name was William Strong came into my hospital room this morning and tried to eliminate me. There are several witnesses. The lab will give you a report on the stuff he tried to inject into my IV line. And, FYI, he was the cause of last night's accident."

"Did you put that into the accident report?"

"Like I told Boswell, I was concussed last night. My brain's functioning better now. The perp has found me twice. Once on the road and once in the hospital. Apparently he's been stalking Kathryn, too. So we're going to disappear for a while. Maybe when you dig up those bodies, you'll get some clues to his identity. If I hear you've arrested him, I'll get back into contact with you."

"How will you hear?"

"On the evening news. In the newspaper."

"I can't just have one of my detectives disappear."

She saw Jack's mouth tighten. "If I don't—if we don't—he'll get us. Because it looks like he's made this personal. You want to be responsible for our deaths?"

CHAPTER
TWENTY

KATHRYN WATCHED CAPTAIN Granger shift from one foot to the other as he pondered how to respond. "I can put a twenty-four-hour guard on you," he finally said.

"In this case, that's not going to work," Jack answered.

"Why not?"

Jack looked like he wished he'd kept his mouth shut. He shrugged. "Okay, if you want to know, it's because this guy is psychic," he said, punching out the answer. "And he's using his powers to fight us."

The captain goggled at him. "You got hit on the head last night. Did the doctor discharge you, or did you leave against medical advice?"

Kathryn's gaze swung between the two men.

"My brain is working fine. I'm not delusional," Jack growled. "The guy used his psychic powers to find me on the road last night. He didn't follow me. He just came out of nowhere."

"More like you didn't know he was on your tail," Granger countered.

Jack didn't bother to argue. Instead, in a quiet voice, he said, "When you catch up with him, you'll find that he's using the victims he murders as a part of magic ceremonies."

"Jesus!"

Jack sighed. "I guess I can't blame you for thinking I've gone off the deep end."

Kathryn had held her tongue because this was between Jack and his boss. Now she couldn't stop herself from jumping into the conversation. "If he's gone off the deep end, so have I. Because we've both experienced the same weird phenomena since this guy came after us."

Granger pivoted toward her, looking her up and down. "Oh, yeah? Such as what?"

"Such as sharing the same dreams," Jack answered. "And when we wake up, we've exchanged verifiable information. Stuff we couldn't have known before we discussed it in the dream."

Granger looked like he'd swallowed a bottle of vinegar. "You expect me to believe that?"

"No," Jack answered. "Because I think he's messing with your mind, too."

Granger's face darkened. "You'd better explain that."

"Okay. You remember that *I* wanted to compare the various missing person cases and see if I could find any link between them. The way I remember it, *you* asked *me* to drop the Westborn suicide investigation and look into the missing person cases."

"You're still on that kick?"

"Yes. I was busy with my own stuff. I didn't even know we had that many missing person cases until you brought them to my attention. Until you pulled the files and gave them to me. What would be my motive for launching an investigation? You know I'm not a glory hound. I'm just a working stiff detective who already had enough on his plate."

Kathryn took in shallow breaths as she watched the captain consider that. Instead of responding directly to

Jack, he said, "You signed out the computer?"

"Yeah."

"Then take it. And get out of here before I change my mind about your sanity."

Jack followed his advice. Pushing away from the wall, he picked up the black case and headed for the exit.

Neither Kathryn nor Jack spoke until they were back in the car.

"What if he comes out here and asks what the guy's motive was for getting into his mind?" she asked as she started the engine.

"I guess he hasn't gotten that far yet. Good thing, because then we'd have to tell him it wasn't the killer—it was the being from the other universe who did that!"

It struck them both funny, and they started chuckling. She sat with her hands gripping the wheel, laughing hysterically.

Jack stopped first.

"I suppose you're going to tell me it only hurts when you laugh," she said.

That set them off again. Jack leaned his head back. "Actually, it does hurt," he finally said between puffs of breath.

She immediately turned serious again. "You need something for the pain."

"I need to keep my head clear."

"Do you have a prescription?"

"Yeah."

"Let's fill it, then go pick up some of my clothes, if you're planning for the two of us to get out of Dodge."

"That's what I'm planning. But I wasn't including a stop at your house."

She swung her head toward him. "We have to stop there."

"Why? You can pick up what you need at a cheap department store."

She didn't want to answer the question out loud. Just hearing the words in her own head made her chest constrict. But she felt like she had no choice. "I need my magic wand," she said in a low voice, watching his eyes narrow.

"You're kidding, right?"

"Unfortunately, no."

"You need it for—what? Casting spells?"

"Are we back to thinking I'm a witch?" she asked, hearing her voice go high and thin.

"You said it—not me."

She dragged in a breath. "I said it because I knew it would be a serious mistake to leave it behind. I don't know why I need the damn thing. I just do. I'm sorry, but I have the terrible feeling that if I leave it at home, we're both going to be sorry."

She watched him consider that. Lifting one hand off the wheel, she pressed it over his. "This is like your discussion with Granger," she said. "We're talking about something that can only be taken on faith."

He sighed. "Okay. You can get the damn thing. I just hope Black Trousers isn't waiting at your house—the way he was last night."

"You want to skip it?"

"No!" He sounded angry. Probably he was in pain. As she drove away, he closed his eyes.

She was torn. She hadn't been home since her frantic drive across the grass. But she knew with gut-tightening certainty that the wand was important.

So she drove home, casting frequent glances at Jack, seeing the tension in his jaw. The jaw relaxed, and he looked like he could be sleeping, but his eyes blinked open when the car slowed. Sitting up, he looked around.

"Drive around the block," he said, "I want to check out the neighborhood."

"Okay." She followed directions, her eyes scanning the streets, the houses, the cars, looking for one of the vehicles she remembered. The strangely angular car, the old Ford, or the white van. None of them was on the street. Everything looked peaceful and normal. But she had learned that looks could be deceiving.

The last time she'd been in the driveway, she'd almost been killed—or kidnapped. The thought of being trapped made her throat close. After a quick glance at Jack, she pulled to a stop at the curb and cut the engine.

He opened his door and stepped out, swayed slightly, and reached to steady himself against the car.

She was almost to the door when something lying on the porch caught her eye. At first, all she saw was a ring. The ostentatious gold ring with the round diamond that Gary Swinton always wore on his right hand. She'd asked him about it once, and he'd told her with considerable pride that he'd won it in a poker game.

She'd never seen it off his hand. Now it was wrapped around something pale and white that lay slightly curled on the porch like a bleached slug. She stared at it, trying to comprehend what she was seeing. At first her brain refused to take it in. When she finally did, she let out a high, bloodcurdling scream and backed away, bumping into the wall of the house and lurching to a stop.

Jack was instantly at her side, his gun in his left hand as he turned in a circle, checking the area for invaders.

When he saw nothing, he came back to her. "What is it? What's wrong?"

She pointed to the porch floor.

"Jesus!" Stooping, he examined the object—which she had recognized as a human finger—circled by the gaudy ring.

She tried to speak, heard her voice crack, and tried again. "That's Swinton's ring. I . . . I guess . . . that he must be . . ." She couldn't say it.

"You're sure it's his?" Jack asked, his eyes fixed on the grisly object.

She pressed back against the wall. "Yes. He was really proud of it. He always wore it."

"Okay. This should help Granger focus his mind on the case."

Jack ushered her inside, away from the porch. When she started up the stairs, he called out, "Wait! I want to check the apartment first."

"Okay." She eyed the gun in one hand and the other arm strapped to his chest. "I guess I'd better unlock the door for you."

"Details!"

They made their way up the stairs, where she opened the door, then stood back with her heart pounding while he entered the apartment and checked out the interior. The door had been locked—but that didn't prove Black Trousers wasn't inside.

Her breath was fast and shallow as she waited for him to deliver his verdict.

"All clear," he said when he returned.

She felt like a great weight had been lifted off her shoulders as he tucked his gun back into his waistband. "You've got ten minutes to grab what you need. Then we're out of here."

While she hurried into the bedroom, he pulled out his cell phone and began punching in numbers. She could hear him saying that he and Kathryn Reynolds had found a human finger wearing a ring belonging to Gary Swinton outside her house, then asking for a crime scene team.

The unnerving conversation continued in the background while she threw shirts, pants, and underwear into a small bag, then grabbed the magic wand off her desk. She was going to shove it right in with the other things, but the feel of the hard rod in her hand stopped her. It was only a plastic toy, but it felt almost alive in her grasp.

Jack had finished his phone call, and was watching her. "You sure you don't work spells with that thing?"

She flushed. "Not so far."

"But you're planning to."

"I don't know *what* I'm planning," she insisted, her voice coming out more strident than she'd intended. "I just know that this thing is important. Remember, I told you I saw it as a guidepost when I was in that . . . that place . . . where we think the creature lives."

"Speaking of which—I notice he hasn't put in an appearance lately."

"Actually, in the hospital, he told me I shouldn't sleep at the same time you do."

"Why not?"

"He said if we do, the magician will find us."

Jack grimaced. "You're sure it was him? And not the magician trying to trick us?"

She slumped against the wall. "No! I'm not sure of anything. We could assume it was my imagination," she offered, even though she was pretty sure that wasn't the case.

"I guess I'm beyond that point," he replied, his voice gritty. "It was one of them. I'd just like to know which one."

She studied him, hardly able to believe the conversation.

"You mean you've gone from a true doubter to a true believer?"

"Christ, if I could walk away from this mess, I would. But it feels like I don't have any choice. Neither of us does!"

She swallowed. "I guess not."

"So tell me—where's the fantasy creature now?"

"I don't know. Sometimes he goes away."

"You keep track?"

"I've started thinking about it. I guess he was the one who . . ." She stopped, sucked in air. "Who stopped time so you could escape from that dog."

He gave a tight nod.

"But he wasn't here when the old man came by my house and lit into us," she said without making any reference to what had actually happened on that occasion.

"I guess not."

She felt a strange tingling on her skin, like small electric prickles. At the same time a thought popped into her head. "You said Ross lent you a bunch of books. Maybe . . . maybe we should ask him for some more. Maybe we'll find something . . . that will explain this."

She could see he was considering the suggestion. "Yeah. We need to understand what's going on. And like Ross said, we don't seem to be getting very far by ourselves." His brow wrinkled. "When we went up to Sugarloaf, I asked him to meet me at the Park and Ride on this side of Frederick. . . ."

A sound outside made them both start. Jack drew his gun and moved to the window, staying next to the wall as he looked out.

When she saw him put the weapon away, she let out the breath she'd been holding.

"It's the cops. Unless the perp has a patrol car," he added. Then, "No, I recognize the officer. It's Dick Hamilton."

Several long moments passed before the officer came up the stairs. After he and Jack greeted each other, he said, "I saw the finger. Nice calling card."

"For a serial killer. You know that the guy is after me and Ms. Reynolds?" Jack asked.

Hamilton nodded. "Yeah, it's gotten around the department pretty fast."

"Okay. That's why we don't want to stick around. Can I leave this crime scene to you? It's just the porch. He hasn't been in here. The door was locked, and there were no signs that anything had been disturbed. Captain Granger said Dave Culligan has been assigned to the case—since I'm officially out on sick leave. So you'll want to inform him."

"You've got it. I'll secure the scene."

"Thanks."

Hamilton started for the door.

"We'll be right with you," Jack said. When the officer had left, he used her phone to call Ross. The P.I. had already arrived home with Mrs. Anderson and the kids, which was obviously a relief to Jack. They arranged to meet at the Park and Ride in about an hour.

Kathryn locked the front door behind them, thinking

that Black Trousers could probably get inside if he wanted to.

Hurrying across the porch, she studiously directed her gaze away from the . . . ring.

After sliding behind the wheel, she waited while Jack spent several more minutes talking to the officer. By the time he climbed back into the passenger seat, she saw that his skin was flushed.

"You need to rest," she murmured.

She expected him to offer a macho protest, but he only gave a tight nod.

"Are we going to pick up clothing at your house?"

"No, we're getting out of town. Where's the closest ATM?"

"The shopping center a couple of blocks away."

When she pulled up near the machine, he got some money, then started to protest when she did the same.

"Consider this enforced vacation a Dutch treat," she told him. "I'm from the generation where the women pay their own way."

"The Montgomery County P.D. should be treating us," he growled.

"Maybe we can collect later. Right now, where to?"

"A cheap department store—Target, maybe."

"Can you tell me where we're heading after we meet Ross?"

"I've been thinking about that. Somewhere near Harper's Ferry or maybe Shepherdstown. Somewhere rural—but where we can get back to the city pretty easily."

"Do you care which?"

"Take your pick. Just check the rearview mirror—to make sure we've made a clean getaway."

In a few minutes she looked over, and was glad to see that he was dozing. She wanted to get him into a bed, where he could get some real sleep. But she settled for his nodding off in the car while she drove. It looked like they'd made a clean getaway, yet she kept having the feeling they were being followed. Every few minutes, she glanced in the rearview mirror, watching for a car she recognized or a car that stuck with them. When she saw nothing, she ordered herself to relax. By the time she pulled into a shopping plaza about twenty minutes later, she had damped down her fears, but they were glimmering below the surface—small internal prickles like the little electric shocks she'd felt on her skin earlier.

SIMON was calmer now, in complete control. Anger had no real purpose in his life. It only got in the way of effective action.

He had made a mistake going to the hospital. He'd pictured the detective alone and helpless. Too bad that hadn't been the case.

But no harm done. He had learned an important lesson. Overconfidence was dangerous. He must stay calm and steady. Then he would get what he wanted.

He sat in his favorite chair, sipping a glass of Jekel Vineyards chardonnay. Usually one long-stemmed crystal wineglass was his limit. This afternoon he'd allowed himself two, in celebration. He would defeat the demon soon. He knew it. The creature was weakening, expending too much energy fighting him. Soon it would exhaust its resources, and he would bend it to his will.

Meanwhile, he had to deal with Kathryn and Thornton. He closed his eyes, projecting his mind outward, searching for them. It was getting easier now, easier with every passing hour.

They were in a car. In a parking lot. At least that's what he thought he saw. He couldn't be absolutely sure. Not until they dreamed together. Then he would come for them again.

KATHRYN was aware of the moment when Jack's eyes snapped open, and he looked around. "Where are we?"

"The Target in Sykesville."

"As good as any place." He reached for the door handle.

"You just got out of the hospital. Tell me what sizes to buy, and I'll pick up some basic clothing for you."

She saw him hesitate, torn between machismo and fatigue. Fatigue won.

"Okay. Get stuff that's easy to get in and out of. Sweatpants would be good." As he spoke, he dug his wallet out of his pocket.

She wanted to refuse the money, but she'd told him they were going Dutch. So she went inside with a list of items and headed for the men's department. If the circumstances had been different, she would have enjoyed the shopping expedition. It was a pleasure to pick out shirts that she knew would look good on him. She couldn't stop herself from savoring the intimacy of buying items like underwear, shaving cream, and disposable razors. Picturing him in tight, white briefs gave her a sexual jolt. Immediately she told herself to cool it. They weren't going on their honeymoon; they were hiding out from a serial killer. And, as she'd pointed out to him, he was just out of the hospital. He needed rest, not sex.

Before leaving, she made a quick pass through the grocery department, where she stocked up on canned soup, cheese, salsa, corn chips, nuts, pretzels, peanut butter, and jelly. Bread. Mayonnaise, tuna fish. And a selection of drinks—from instant coffee and tea bags to sodas. For fun, she threw in some candy bars and cookies.

In less than half an hour, she was back at the car—stopping short as she saw Jack slumped in the front seat. He looked so vulnerable that she felt her heart squeeze.

She tried to tell herself they had escaped from Black Trousers. But had they? He'd reached out and found them in a dream. What would stop him from finding them again?

Jack sat up with a start when she slipped back into the driver's seat, then blinked. "Finished already?"

"And ready to meet Ross."

"You know the Park and Ride?"

"Yes."

The assurance was all he needed to let himself doze off again. He didn't wake until they pulled into the parking area.

Ross was waiting for them. A large cardboard box sat on the hood of his SUV. He hoisted it up and brought it to the car, where he stowed it in the trunk alongside their clothing.

"The kids are okay?" Jack asked.

"Yes." But he didn't look entirely sure.

"What's wrong?" Jack asked anxiously.

"Nothing. Lily wants to play down by the creek. I told her she has to stay inside."

"Yeah, she's been a handful lately."

"We'll try some tempting indoor activities."

"Tell her I said for her to mind you."

"Will do."

Jack looked torn.

"We could stop and see them before we leave," Kathryn offered.

"No. That's too dangerous," Jack answered immediately. "I don't want them anywhere near us until the bastard is in custody."

She gave a tight nod, knowing how hard this was for him.

Minutes later, they were on the road again.

While he slept beside her, she headed toward Harper's Ferry, then on the spur of the moment veered off to Charles Town, West Virginia.

"Where do you want to stay?" she asked Jack when she saw his eyes had blinked open again.

"A motel on a secondary road. Nothing fancy. The best would be a place with individual cabins—where half the units are empty."

She laughed. "I'll try."

She came close to his requirement about twenty miles outside of town, in a rural, wooded area. A faded sign advertised cabins, and she pulled up a short, rutted driveway to a rustic office.

"I'm kind of conspicuous with this arm in a sling."

"Then I'll register."

"As whom?"

She'd been going to use her real name. Now she stopped and reconsidered.

"As Mr. and Mrs. James Taylor?"

He laughed. "That will do."

Leaving him in the car, she stepped into the office. A heavy woman wearing black stretch pants and a pink sweater with multiple pulls in the weave said they could rent a very nice cabin with a kitchen unit. The price was so low that Kathryn expected to see cockroaches scurrying across the floor. But the one-room cabin was clean and neat, with a charming old quilt covering the double bed, and a small kitchen area where she stowed the groceries.

The place had a warm, country appeal, and she liked the way she and Jack fit into the picture. She looked up to see him setting his bag down near a battered old dresser, and was struck with a mixture of emotions.

She'd dared to daydream about going off with him to a cabin in the woods—just the two of them. In her imagination, she'd made it a sexy little adventure. She'd gotten her wish—with a twist. They were here to fight for their lives. Against Black Trousers. And . . . something else, a being from another world who was somehow tangled up with the magician.

Jack looked up and found her watching him. "Your turn to sleep."

"I . . ."

"Don't argue. I've been sleeping off and on half the day. I'll get you up in a few hours. While you're sleeping, I'll do a little light reading. And eat some of this nice nourishing food you've thoughtfully provided."

"You like my taste in junk food?"

"It's perfect."

He crossed to the kitchen, opened the freezer compartment at the top of the refrigerator, dropped ice cubes into a glass, then added Dr. Pepper. After carrying the drink and a bag of onion and sour cream chips to a table in the corner, he settled into the Morris-style easy chair and started sorting through the box of books Ross had brought.

Kathryn wanted to cross the room, lean over the chair, and wrap her arms around him. Instead, she closed the curtains across the windows, used the bathroom, then pulled off her jeans and crawled into the double bed, wearing just her tee shirt and panties.

She knew Jack was watching her, and she liked that, liked the fact that her legs were long and sleek below the tee shirt.

The lamp behind his chair cast a warm pool of light. She watched him pretend he hadn't been very aware of her, watched him settle back and open the bag of chips. Then reach for a book.

He looked up, saw her regarding him, and smiled. "Sleep."

"I like watching you."

"An old broken-down cop?"

"Stop fishing for compliments. You're not old. And you're not broken-down."

He gestured toward the white sling. "I wouldn't be much good in hand-to-hand combat."

"If you came over here, I'd show you how wrong you are."

"Oh, yeah?"

"Yeah."

A grin flickered on his lips, and she thought for a moment that he might actually come to her. Instead, he said, "Grab some sleep while you have the chance."

She wanted to ask what could happen later. But she tucked that thought away and snuggled down under the sheet and quilt.

When she closed her eyes again, exhaustion took over. She'd been operating on nerves for hours, and letting go was suddenly a luxury.

Quickly she left the world behind and slipped into oblivion.

JACK watched her, wanting to join her in the bed and strip the tee shirt off her. Sure! One-handed would be a little awkward. Resolutely he turned back to the pile of books. There were so many volumes. What should he read?

As he shuffled through them, one felt hot when his fingers touched the cover.

He blinked, pulled his hand away, then gingerly touched the cracked and faded blue leather again. It felt like a stove burner. Only it looked perfectly normal.

The title was *Portal to Another Universe*. By Jonathan Zacarias, written in 1787. With clumsy fingers, he flipped through the pages. They fell open in his lap to page 28, and he stared down at the old print, his pulse starting to pound.

FOR a short time, rejuvenating slumber cradled Kathryn.

Then she awoke. Well, not awoke, literally. She was *there* again—in that place of dim light and unbreathable air. The place of fear. The place where a huge, dark presence hovered over her like low, storm clouds bringing the fury of a tempest.

"No," she gasped, struggling to pull herself back to the world. But the land and the being held her captive as surely as if she'd stepped into a steel trap.

Relief flooded through her when she saw the magic wand. Eagerly, she staggered toward the beacon shining in the gloom. But this time when she reached it, there was no sense of relief.

She was on a grassy hill. Under a blue sky. But still her lungs burned.

Then suddenly ropes captured her hands, pulled her

backward, bound her to the plastic post that till now had been a symbol of safety.

She saw that faggots of wood were piled around her. And as she watched in terror, flames sprang up, leaping at her, reaching for her flesh.

A tongue of fire licked at her, and she screamed at the burning pain.

"No! Please stop! Why are you doing this to me?"

You ran away.

"No."

Go back where you came from.

"No. We can't. He'll find us."

You think he won't find you here? He wants to enslave me! You must stop him.

The fire receded, and images came to her then—hazy, ghostly. Like at Sugarloaf Mountain. Only now she was seeing the chamber Jack had described. A ceremonial chamber, hung with black. But it wasn't Swinton tied down on the table in the specteral scene. She gasped when she saw it was Heather—unconscious. Wearing a white dress slit down the middle to bare her breasts.

Black Trousers stood over her, chanting, a knife in one hand, his other hand . . .

She gagged. His other hand was on his erect penis, stroking in time to the words he was chanting.

In a corner of the room, the dark presence hovered. And then interspersed with the scene was another—herself and Jack that first time, he in Roman military garb. She in a sheer white gown.

They were kissing, touching, totally absorbed in each other. And all at once she knew that the scene had flashed into Black Trousers's mind, making the downward stroke of his knife falter.

He climaxed then, his seed spewing onto the table— even as he cried out in rage. And she understood the ceremony had failed.

Then the flames leaped around her once more. And she screamed in pain and terror, screamed again, then struggled against the force clamping her in place.

CHAPTER
TWENTY-ONE

"KATHRYN! KATHRYN!"

"No! Don't! Please don't! Oh, God, please stop," she gasped, trying to wrench away from the force that held her.

"Kathryn, it's just a dream. You're all right. You're with me. With Jack."

Finally, the words penetrated the horror and the terror. Her lids blinked open, and she found herself staring up into his worried eyes. It was his hand on her shoulder, holding her down.

As soon as he saw that she recognized him, he eased up the pressure. She blinked, her eyes filling with tears, and she clutched at his shoulders. When he grimaced, she realized she must be hurting him, and relaxed her grasp. "I'm sorry," she whispered. "I didn't mean to hurt you."

"I'm okay. What happened? One minute you looked like you were sleeping peacefully. Then you were flailing around, moaning. It was another one of the dreams, wasn't it? Another one by yourself," he said between gritted teeth.

She nodded, her mind spinning back to the dream. There were so many things she needed to say.

"A magic ceremony," she gasped out. "I saw a magic ceremony. Like you did when you were driving. Only it wasn't Swinton strapped down to the table. It was Heather. It was like up at Sugarloaf. I could see them. But they were ghostly." A sob escaped her lips as she recalled that picture.

Jack reached for her, folded her close. "I'm so sorry."

She nodded against his shoulder, wanting to wipe the terrifying image from her mind, yet knowing that it was important. All of the dream was important.

"You don't have to tell me any more."

"Yes I do. I have to tell you the rest. It's the key to what's been happening, I think. It wasn't just the ceremony. And I saw us, too."

"Us? In his clutches? He's going to get us?"

"Oh, Lord, I hope not. No. That's not what I mean. I saw us . . . from that first dream in the painting. Remember, you stopped kissing me because you thought something was happening?"

"Yes."

"Well, I think I know what it was. I . . . I . . . think the magician saw us while we were there. And seeing us messed up the ceremony for him." She knew she was babbling, knew she must barely be making sense, but she couldn't stop. "But that wasn't all of the dream. He was punishing me. That's how I know. . . ."

Jack interrupted her, his voice urgent. "Who was punishing you? Black Trousers? Or was it the demon?"

Her eyes widened. "What demon? What are you talking about?"

"The creature. That's what it is. Well, not one of Satan's minions, if that's what you mean by a demon. It's what you've been telling me—a being from another universe."

She gasped. "How . . . how do you know? I thought I was alone in the dream. Except for that thing."

He turned and gestured toward a book that lay

splayed open on the floor. "While you were dreaming, I was reading about it in *A Portal to Another Universe*, by Jonathan Zacarias. One of the books from Ross. I was shuffling through them, trying to decide what to read, and that one felt like a hot brick."

She sucked in a sharp breath before telling him the rest of it. "Hot. Right. I was hot, too. In the dream. I was tied up at a stake—burning. And the stake was the magic wand."

"Jesus! That bastard!"

Fearfully, she held up her hand, inspecting the flesh. It was whole, unburned. "At least it didn't carry over into the real world this time. I guess he just wanted to give me a warning."

"A warning about what?" Jack asked, his voice grim.

"He . . ." She stopped, readjusted her thinking. "The demon thing was angry. He told me to go back home. He wants us to save him from Black Trousers."

She waited for Jack to make some objection.

Instead, he looked toward the book he'd dropped on the floor.

"Yeah. I was reading about it."

"You were?"

"It's hard to make sense of the text. The writing is pretty convoluted. But it was talking about a magician trying to enslave a demon with a magic ceremony."

She took a gulping breath as the pieces of the puzzle fell into place in her mind. "I think it's what I told you. I saw him *doing* the ceremony. Black Trousers. He had Heather strapped down on a table. He was going to kill her, and at the same time he was . . ." She stopped, gulped again. "He was masturbating."

"Jesus!" Jack said again, making no attempt to hide his revulsion.

"But we stopped him. He saw us, and he lost his train of thought. So maybe that's what's going on. The demon brought us into it. And now he wants us to go back and stop Black Trousers again."

"Okay, after reading the book, I can buy that. But

why us?" He gestured in frustration with his good hand. "Why is he giving us all this information *now*? And why the hell doesn't he just give us the guy's name, so I can arrest him?"

She shared his frustration. "Maybe he's finally telling us stuff he didn't want to reveal because he's gotten desperate. And . . . maybe there's a magic spell that keeps him from telling us Black Trousers's name."

"That's just great." Jack muttered. "The problem is, we're screwed either way. If we don't stop Black Trousers, the demon keeps torturing you."

"Not just me. Us," she corrected.

"Yeah, well, right now it looks like you're taking the brunt of it. But that's nothing compared to what happens if Black Trousers does get it right. If he succeeds with his damn ceremony, we don't want to be anywhere around."

Kathryn took in the ominous tone of his voice. "What happens?"

He gestured in anger toward the book. "Jonathan Zacarias wrote *Portal to Another Universe* as a warning. His friend succeeded in the ceremony, but the demon wasn't willing to let himself be enslaved. You've heard of the Nemes explosion when they thought a big chunk of southern France was incinerated by a meteor. Well, that was the demon avoiding capture. And there's no reason to assume this one won't take the same route. Which means the explosion is going to be like a nuclear weapon landing on Rockville."

Kathryn gasped. "That's what you read in the book?"

"As near as I can figure it out—yes."

"You've got to call Granger."

"And tell him what—that a demon is going to blow up Rockville? He'll put us in the loony bin for sure, and then we *won't* be able to do a damn thing."

She looked around the warm, cozy room, feeling trapped. "What are we going to do?"

He ran his good hand through his hair. "I wish to hell I knew."

The anger in his voice made her raise her head. "Jack, I'm so sorry."

"For what?"

"I got us into this."

He smoothed her damp hair back from her face. "How do you figure that?"

"I reported Heather missing. Then you came to my house. That's how all this started."

His jaw muscles tightened. "You had to make the report. It was the right thing to do."

She breathed out a small sigh. "But look at the consequences."

"You mean, I got to meet you?" he said, his voice low and husky.

She felt her heart stop, then start up again in double time. Somehow, she managed to say, "You made it pretty clear you wished you hadn't."

"That was when I was freaked out by the . . . bond forming between us. It was too fast. I couldn't deal with it."

"The bond, yes," she said softly. "Are you saying you can deal with it now?"

"Not completely. I don't like knowing that outside forces are operating on me—on us. But there are compensations. I've found out what kind of woman you are."

"What kind?"

He grinned. "Are you fishing for compliments?"

"Maybe I need some."

"You're the bravest woman I've ever met."

"How?"

"What you go through every time you step into one of those dreams would have driven a lot of people crazy. And then there was the way you threw yourself at Black Trousers in my hospital room."

"I had to!"

"Why?"

"You were in danger. And, Jack, I care very much what happens to you."

"Kathryn." His hand stroked gently down her cheek. She turned her head so that her lips brushed his fingers. He went very still. Watching him intently, she opened her mouth, using her teeth, then her tongue, to play with his flesh.

Desire flared between them—desire and something so much more profound that her breath caught. "Jack, please. I don't want to think about magicians and demons and terrible explosions right now," she whispered.

"Neither do I."

"Oh, Jack." She clasped her arms around him and found his lips with hers.

When the kiss broke, he said her name, his voice thick with emotion. Yet in the next moment, she heard him make a rough noise.

"Oh, Lord, Jack, is your arm hurting?" she asked, abashed that she'd been thinking about making love when he had just gotten out of the hospital that morning.

"It's not that. I was sitting across the room, watching you sleep, thinking about how much I wanted to make love with you. But I can't help comparing myself to how I was in the dream—when I didn't have my damn arm strapped to my chest. I'm afraid I'm not going to be much good to you, sweetheart."

She gave him a slow smile. "If that's your only problem, then lie back and relax, and we'll see if we can work something out."

His gaze locked with hers, he did as she asked, easing to his back, giving her control of the situation. Feeling powerful and alive, she bent over him—kissing his mouth, his cheek, his hair, gentle kisses that were as full of warmth as they were filled with desire.

She ached to tell him she'd fallen in love with him. But she kept the words locked inside her, trying instead to show him how she felt.

Carefully she reached down to unbutton his shirt, spreading the fabric apart so she could slide her hand over his chest, under the sling, playing with the thick hair covering his warm skin, and finding his nipples with her fingers.

Each time she touched those dark nubs, he sucked in a quick breath, and she grew more confident in her power to please him.

When she moved away from him, he made a sharp sound of protest, but she only smiled at him as she pulled her shirt over her head and tossed it onto the floor. Nerves stopped her for a few seconds. Ignoring them, she reached around to do the same with her bra.

His heated gaze made her nipples harden as if he'd touched them.

"Sweetheart, you are so sexy. So beautiful."

She felt beautiful. She felt like a sex goddess. Holding his gaze, she reared up on her knees and skimmed her panties down her legs.

Naked, she bent over him, sweeping her breasts back and forth across the part of his chest that she could reach and the fingers trapped in his sling.

"Kathryn, dear Lord," he gasped out, then gasped again as her hand slid down his body to find the rigid shaft of flesh behind the fly of his jeans.

He arched into her touch, and she heard his breath catch as she rocked her hand against his erection.

She had never held a man more firmly in her power, and she took complete advantage of him, slowly lowering his zipper.

She gave him a lazy, provocative smile as she reached inside his pants, her touch going from light to firm and back again, her whole being caught up in the excitement of giving him pleasure. She had never been so bold with a man, never felt her own excitement grow as she teased and aroused and pushed him toward the edge.

"Kathryn, please," he moaned.

Quickly she skimmed his jeans and his briefs down his body, and he helped her kick them away. He was still wearing his shirt, but she wasn't going to take the time to get rid of it.

She had much better things to do, she decided, as she lowered her head to his erection, caressing him with her face, then using her lips and tongue and finally taking him fully into her mouth.

He made low, incoherent sounds as he used his good hand to play with the silky flesh of her bottom, then reached between her legs to find her most sensitive flesh, stroking and caressing and turning her molten while she indulged her appetite for him.

"Kathryn, stop. I want to be inside you when I come," he grated.

"God, yes."

Raising her head, she looked into his smoldering eyes, her gaze locked with his as she straddled him, using her hands for balance as she lowered her body onto his.

He cried out—half curse, half thanks—as she brought him inside of her.

Going very still, she stayed where she was, her eyes drifting closed, as she focused on the wonderful feeling of his penis filling her so completely.

"Look at me," he demanded, his voice husky.

She opened her lids to see that his eyes had darkened with passion. He gave her a slow smile as he took a visual tour of her body, starting with her face and slowly moving downward.

She might have felt vulnerable and exposed. But his words were too warm for that. "Lord, what a beautiful view," he whispered.

"Of you, too. You are so beautifully made. So masculine."

Slowly she began to move, building her own pleasure and his. With his good hand, he reached up to caress first one breast and then the other, his touch inciting her to quicken the pace.

His eyes held hers as she climbed the high peaks, knowing he was taking the journey with her.

She felt his body go rigid below her, heard his shout of pleasure. Then she was driving for her own climax,

her movements frantic now until release seized her. Her
whole body seemed to vibrate in a series of strong con-
tractions that shook her to her very core, then left her
limp and panting.

She would have collapsed on top of him, but she
remembered his injured shoulder and shifted to his left
side, sliding down onto the bed beside him.

His arm came up to clasp her close. Her eyes drifted
closed, and she dozed, warm and relaxed in the aftermath of passion.

SIMON sat in his easy chair, reading more on astral
projection. But his mind was only half on the book. He
was open, alert, waiting for the opportunity he knew
would come. This morning he'd felt the need for action.
Now he knew he only had to wait for the next time the
redheaded bitch and the cop dreamed together.

The minutes ticked by as he crouched like a spider
in the center of its web, waiting for a hapless insect to
come along.

Finally, it happened. The delicate strands of the web
sent out a vibration. His body jerked, and he knew the
time had come. They were both sleeping. Their guard
was down.

His face contorted. They'd been having sex again. He
could feel that, too, feel the satiety and the lazy relax-
ation of their minds and bodies. And feel their vulnerability.

They had fled Montgomery County. He had felt them
moving farther from him—in distance. But they could
never get far enough away.

They were his.

He closed his eyes, watching them. They were in a
rustic-looking room. Snuggled together in a pine bed
covered with a much-washed quilt.

They thought they were safe. Let them dream on—
for a few more minutes—until he got there. This time
he sensed that they were sleeping in the dream world,

too. He could sneak up on them, plunge his knife into the woman, and be gone before the cop could do anything about it. And then the triangle would be broken— and he would be free to go after the demon.

Quickly he left the library and hurried down to the ceremonial chamber, ready to say the spell that would bring him into their dream.

JACK stirred. He had been lying snug and warm, his arms around Kathryn. Both arms, which meant this must be a dream, because in some corner of his mind he remembered that he'd been in an automobile accident, and his right arm was in a sling.

But when he reached for her, she wasn't there.

He heard her scream—a bloodcurdling sound that he felt from the roots of his hair to his toes.

He was out of bed in an instant. Not the bed in the cabin. The bed in the Greek pavilion where they'd first made love.

He dashed outside, looking wildly around—seeing a wall of flame shoot up to his right. And through the flames, he could see Kathryn, tied to a stake, the fire licking at her white skin, searing her flesh even as he watched.

"No," he cried out, running at full speed toward her, determined to snatch her from the inferno. Before he reached her, the dream dissolved around him, and he shouted out again in renewed panic.

Then his eyes blinked open, and he found himself in the bed again. Kathryn was lying beside him, tears leaking from her eyes.

"Oh, God, sweetheart, sweetheart," he crooned, holding her against himself as best he could, cursing the damn injury that kept him from pulling her fully into his arms.

He felt her trying to rein in her tears and finally bring herself under control.

"It's okay," she finally murmured.

"What do you mean, okay? How the hell is that okay? You were in the middle of a fire—tied to a stake."

She gulped in air. "It saved us. Black Trousers was coming, like he did the last time we dreamed together, and the thing woke us up in time."

Jack stared down at her. "You saw him?"

"I felt him. At the end, I felt him. He had to wake one of us. He seems to pick on me."

Jack let loose with a string of curses. "And he's getting more violent. What the hell does he want from us?"

"You know what he wants! We have to find Black Trousers. Because either he's going to get us—or the demon is going to push us beyond what we can take."

"Yeah. Great." Jack heaved himself up and reached for the jeans that had ended up draped over the foot of the bed.

Kathryn pulled on the tee shirt and panties she'd been wearing. She was covered up before he'd finished struggling into his jeans.

"Find Black Trousers. Sure," he spat out as he paced back and forth across the cabin. "He's been killing people for months, maybe years, and nobody's found him. He's a clever bastard. He makes sure his victims don't fit any particular pattern. He uses a bunch of disguises. He has different cars and vans. Which probably means he has plenty of money." He stopped, and dragged his good hand through his hair. "And I can't protect you from him. I can't protect my family. I had to leave them with Ross Marshall."

She crossed to him, took him in her arms.

"Do you know how it makes me feel that I can't protect you?" he asked.

"Yes."

"How do you know?"

"You said you'd discovered what kind of woman I am. I always knew what kind of man you are. Steady. Responsible. Strong. And beating himself up for not cracking this case. Jack, you're the one who figured out he's a serial murderer."

"With your help."

"Okay, then. We make a good team. So let's get to work."

Easing away from him, she walked to the kitchen, where she began opening bags of snack foods. Willing her hands to steadiness, she poured pretzels, cookies, corn chips, and salsa into bowls she found in the cabinets.

By the time she'd carried it all to the table, she was feeling more grounded. "Something to drink?"

"Dr. Pepper. It's perfect for this place."

She poured the drinks while he brought his laptop computer to the table.

"Come sit over here, so you can look at the screen with me."

"What are we going to do?"

"See if two brilliant minds can come up with his picture."

"But he's always been disguised."

"Let's see if we can work around that."

She pulled over a chair, drawing close to Jack. He turned and kissed her ear, and she snuggled closer. "I like working with you, Detective," she said.

"But I'd better keep my mind on business." He brought up a program that let victims of crimes build a picture of the perpetrator. Pulling the computer close to his body, he typed with his left hand and used the fingers protruding from his sling to press the shift and control keys.

"Want me to type?" she asked.

"I can do it."

"Okay. Then I'll be right back."

Probably, he thought, she was going to the bathroom. Instead, she opened her overnight bag and got out the magic wand. Jack watched her carry it back to her chair, then turn it slowly in her hand as they began to work.

"You think that will help?"

"It can't hurt."

He turned back to the computer, starting with a general face shape.

"Long but not too narrow," she said, pointing with the wand to one that looked right.

They progressed from that to hair—dark and long.

She and Jack both had excellent visual memories—she because of her art background, he because he'd trained himself to observe people. And they had no trouble building a picture of the man who'd come to the hospital room.

As his face emerged, Kathryn felt goose bumps raise themselves on her arms. They were finally getting somewhere! Doing something constructive.

Unless he'd worn contacts, he had gray eyes. Narrow lips. An average sort of nose. Slightly hollow cheeks. A face that looked smooth—except for a big mustache.

"Take the mustache off," she murmured. "It doesn't look right."

Jack followed directions.

"That's him," she whispered.

Jack didn't seem so certain.

"What?" she asked.

"The hair is wrong," he mused. "It was long and dark in the hospital. But remember, I saw him doing that ceremony in the privacy of his own torture chamber. He's got short blond hair." With a few keystrokes, he changed the hair. "Yeah. That's better."

Jack copied the face into another file, then added other details—coming up with the old man who had stopped to ask directions, then reported them to the police department.

Again, Kathryn felt spooked. "He changes his looks, but when you've got the eyes and mouth, you can see it's the same guy."

Jack nodded and saved the files. "You want to go on and do the workman you saw around your neighborhood? The man in coveralls?"

"I don't think we have to bother. He looked like a cross between the young image and the older one."

"Okay. Then bring me the phone," he instructed.

Kathryn watched him unhook the instrument, then plug the computer into the connection.

"A modem?"

"Yes." He wrote Granger a memo, explaining that these were two composite pictures of the guy who had tried to murder him—one as he usually looked and one in his old man persona.

Almost as soon as he'd sent them, he was surprised to receive a reply, thanking him for the pictures and adding, "The lab identified the drug from the hospital as insulin. In sufficient quantity, it would be lethal. We're not sure how much he was intending to inject into your IV line because some of it spilled on the floor."

After returning the captain's thanks, Jack rocked back in his chair. "Sounds like he's joined the team."

Kathryn seesawed the wand in her hand. "Want to tell him about the demon?"

Jack laughed. "Sure! Just when he's acting like we're not insane. Let's see if we can feed him some more information." He switched to a web site with various makes and models of automobiles.

"We already know he's got an '88 Crown Victoria."

"How did you know that?"

"I'm a cop. I know cars. So let's figure out the one you saw at Sugarloaf and across your driveway. What was the shape?"

"Angular. With a strange kind of projection at the rear window. Something unusual."

"Speaking of the rear—how many taillights? Three—or just two?"

She answered quickly. "Three."

"Then it's a newer model—after the upper taillight law came into effect."

He brought up another web page with premium models, and they began paging through the pictures.

*   *   *

SIMON clenched and unclenched his fists. He had missed his chance to kill the woman while she was in the dream. The demon had woken her up. With fire.

He'd felt the heat. Heard her gasps of pain. That was something, anyway. The demon didn't mind hurting her. The damn thing was getting desperate. Driving Reynolds and Thornton to the limit. Maybe the creature would make a mistake and kill them.

Simon chuckled. That would be a nice irony. The demon was flailing around in its death gasp—and it didn't care whom it hurt. Even the man and woman it had chosen to save its miserable hide.

He felt a tug on his consciousness, and the focus of his thoughts quickly changed.

For a moment, a picture of his own face floated in his mind. Not a photograph. A drawing—that looked like it could have come from a computer.

Reynolds and Thornton had worked up his image. And not just one drawing—two. Himself as he looked now. And himself as the old man.

As he stared at the two images in his mind's eye— so real, so accurate—he felt his heart blocking his windpipe.

He'd been careful with his disguises. But he'd made a mistake at the hospital. He'd figured nobody was going to identify him. So he'd only relied on the mustache and the wig.

Christ! They'd nailed him.

The walls of the library seemed to close in around him, and he took several breaths, then crossed to the window and flung it open.

He stood staring out at the woods in back of his house. He'd thought he had time to plan his attack.

And now he was going to have to move fast. Very fast. Not just with magic ceremonies. With modern technology.

CHAPTER
TWENTY-TWO

HE SAT FOR a long time, sending his thoughts toward the man and woman in the small, rustic bedroom.

A cabin in the woods. About an hour away, he guessed.

He smiled, thinking that the connection was growing stronger—thanks to the demon. The creature had thought it was so clever, sending their image to screw up his concentration the night he'd used Heather DeYoung in the ceremony.

But it worked both ways. He could watch them easily now. They had finished with the composite drawing. And they were looking at pictures of cars.

He cursed again. They had looked at the Ford the old man had driven. They had the make and model.

He gritted his teeth, ordering himself to think this through. He was so close to success. One more ceremony, that was all he needed. The demon was weak. It couldn't hold out against another direct attack.

He looked around the library. He loved this room. Loved the house he had decorated to his own specifications.

Was it time to leave? Yes, he'd better go to one of his other residences. For now. When he had all the power a man might need, he would come back and reclaim his rightful place.

But first he had some things to do.

JACK brought up some pictures of Acuras.

"Any of those look familiar?"

She peered at the shapes. "I don't think so."

They went on to Mercedes-Benzes.

She leaned forward, peering at the screen. "Not that."

When he brought up Saabs from the early '90s, she gasped. "Yes!"

"It's got the strange projection over the back window, all right. And there's nothing else quite like it. I should have thought of it myself."

He was typing in another web address. It turned out to be the Department of Motor Vehicles. After giving his police authorization, he waited for a menu to appear.

First he went into the database of vehicle registrations. In the state of Maryland, there were only eight men who owned all of the cars in question—an early '90s Saab, an '88 Ford Crown Victoria, and a van.

Jack marked their names, then went to the register of licensed drivers.

Kathryn watched, her heart pounding, as he brought up the driver's license of the first guy, James Butterworth.

They stared at the picture. Butterworth was a sixty-year-old black man. Definitely the wrong guy.

They went on to Timothy Folger. He was white. But he had close-cropped red hair and had gotten his license only two years earlier—as soon as he was of legal age.

"Simon Gwynn." Jack read the next name on the list, then brought up the picture on his driver's license.

Kathryn gasped as she stared at the color picture. "That's him. Without the wig and the mustache or the old-man makeup."

Jack let out the breath he must have been holding. "One and the same."

They looked at each other, and she felt the sense of triumph bubbling between them. He jumped up, picked up his cell phone from the table, and pressed the activation button.

"You're calling Granger?"

"Yes." He punched in the number, then waited, tapping his foot. When the captain came on the line, he said, "I've identified the bastard through his car registration and driver's license." He walked back to the computer screen. "His name is Simon Gwynn. He lives at 2935 Tilbury Way. A pretty swanky address."

In response to something Granger said, he answered, "Then bring him in for questioning. Kathryn and I will come down there and identify him as the guy who tried to inject the insulin into my IV line."

He hung up, turned to her. "Granger is sending Culligan and two uniformed officers to bring him in."

"So we're going back to Rockville?"

"Let's wait until we hear from the captain." He looked at the phone in his hand. "I want to stay out here where Black—uh—Gwynn won't be looking for us, and I want to see how the kids are doing at Ross's."

He punched in another number, and the phone was answered almost immediately.

"So how is everything going?" Jack asked.

She saw him grin, then listen some more. "We may be able to pick them up tomorrow. But don't say anything yet. I'd like to talk to Craig and Lily, if they're not too busy."

She smiled as he spoke to each of his children in turn. It was obvious that the kids still needed reassuring. And Jack told them that he'd be seeing them soon.

When he had completed the call, he looked better than she'd ever seen him. More at ease. "When Granger picks up Gwynn, he'll call us." He looked at his cell phone. "There's no reason why we can't go out for something to eat."

"Okay," she agreed, when what she really wanted to do was stay here, holed up with him. "Do you want to shower first?" she asked.

"Yeah. But you're going to have to help me in and out of my shirt—and sling."

"I don't mind."

In fact, she enjoyed the intimacy of being close to him, helping him with simple, everyday tasks.

Then she took her own quick shower. They stopped at the office, where the manager recommended an old inn up the road, where they could go dressed in the casual clothes they'd brought.

The restaurant was charming, with log walls that contrasted nicely with crisp white linen. The waitress found them a table in the corner by a fireplace.

The crisis was over, and she wanted to talk about what might happen between them now. But they were both worn out, and she didn't want to put any pressure on him. So they were mostly silent, except when she asked about his shoulder. Or when they discussed what food to order.

They had finished an excellent bruschetta appetizer when his cell phone rang.

With a look of anticipation, he answered. She watched his expression quickly change—heard his low curse.

"Shit!"

Every muscle in her body tensed. From what she could hear of the conversation, she gathered that Gwynn hadn't been home when the cops had arrived.

Jack hung up and took a swallow of the red wine they'd splurged on.

"I guess the celebration was a little premature," he said.

"What happened?"

"Gwynn skipped out on us."

"Because we chased him out of the hospital?"

"Maybe. All the cars we identified were in the garage. Granger went back to his DMV record. It turns out that he also owns a Dodge SUV and a Mustang. He's in the SUV."

"Strange he didn't take it to Sugarloaf," she mused.

"I guess he wanted to travel in style when he was going up there to bury bodies."

"Have they dug up the graves?"

"The Frederick County cops have excavated two of the sites that Ross and I marked. There are three more."

Their meal came, and Kathryn was sorry she'd asked about the burial ground. The chicken cacciatore that had sounded so wonderful tasted like paste.

Silently they picked at their food. Then Jack pushed back his chair. "I can't eat any more. But you go ahead."

"That's okay. I can't either."

Outside, they paused in the garden, and she looked around. The feeling of being watched was strong, and she drew closer to Jack.

"What?"

"I just feel . . . spooked."

They drove slowly around the parking lot. There was no Dodge SUV. And no person who looked remotely like the old man or the real Simon Gwynn—which proved nothing, of course.

Still, it was hard to wipe away the dread hanging over her.

"You think he's looking for us?"

"That would be a logical assumption."

"Do you feel like we're being watched?" she whispered.

"Yeah. But not necessarily by Gwynn."

She felt the hairs on her arms prickle. "The demon?"

"I was hoping that if the police picked up Gwynn, he'd leave us alone. Now I have to assume he's still around."

"We haven't seen him recently."

Jack shrugged. "You mean since he set you on fire in that last dream?"

She made a low sound. "Right, since then. I've felt

like he wasn't in this world. Maybe he can't stay here for long periods of time."

"Maybe."

They rode silently back to the cabin, where she watched Jack set his gun and his phone on the table, then settle down in front of the computer. "You sleep for a couple of hours," he said. "I'm going to see what else I can find out about Simon Gwynn."

He was right; they had to take turns sleeping. So she crawled under the covers, conscious of the scent of lovemaking. She glanced over at him. For almost an hour he'd been happy and relaxed. Now his face was as grim as she'd ever seen it. It hurt to look at him, so she rolled onto her side and pulled the covers up to her chin.

This time, there was no interference with her sleep. As she drifted off, her last thought was that she was being given a precious gift.

It was dark, with the only light coming from the cracked bathroom door when Jack gently shook her shoulder. She sat up and rubbed her eyes.

"I hate to wake you."

"It's okay." She turned her face, kissed his cheek.

His hand came up to stroke through her hair. "I was going to let you sleep all night. Then I figured I'd better get some rest."

"Yes. You need to sleep, too." She wanted to lie beside him. Just hold him while he slept. But she knew that was too dangerous.

So she climbed out of bed and forced the conversation back to business. "What else did you find out about Gwynn?"

He eased under the covers. "As far as I can figure out, the name is an alias he adopted six years ago."

"Oh."

"I have no idea what his real name is. Probably he's used other names, too."

She nodded, still standing beside the bed, looking down at the man she loved.

His next words were hardly romantic. "The gun and the phone are on the table."

"Yes. Thanks."

He lay back and closed his eyes. She carried the weapon into the bathroom while she used the facilities. By the time she came back to the bedroom, it looked like Jack was already asleep.

After switching on the lamp, she picked up the book that he'd been reading earlier, *The Portal to Another Universe*.

It was hard going—full of convoluted sentences. The best she could do was thumb through it, picking up various bits of information.

"The magic circle was a bastion, its protection paramount, a girdle of tutelage against the cosmic forces which waited in the ether to overwhelm him and tear him asunder. There were yet forces which might leap the moat and challenge him."

She shook her head as she tried to work her way through that. Was it English? Sort of. But she could translate it into clearer terms: The magician protects himself within a magic circle, yet the circle doesn't offer absolute protection.

She set the book on the table, got up, and walked restlessly around the room. But she was drawn back to the volume. Opening it to another section, she read:

"The magician must make his bargain with the forces of the universe in a bubble of utter and serene calm. He must subjugate all external abstractedness to his will. Distraction from his purpose is the fatal flaw in the attainment of his goal through magic agency, and may lead to the disharmony of all he strives to achieve."

Okay—so that seemed to be saying that the magician had to concentrate fully to make his ceremony work.

She wanted to get up and pace again. Instead, she stayed with the book. Despite the convoluted language, she was gaining some understanding by reading it.

A passage caught her eye, and she felt her breath go shallow. "The sacrificial victims are of two discrete

modes. One is passive—rendered unconscious by the
magician. That is the way of safety. But the victim's
consciousness is the bolder stroke, for the terror of the
one to be sacrificed is a powerful enhancement to the
working of the spell."

She shuddered. That was pretty clear. You could have
your sacrifice unconscious—or awake. Awake was better, because then you could use her fear as part of the
ceremony. The downside was that you'd have trouble
controlling her.

She felt nausea rise in her throat, trying to picture
what kind of person would want to follow this advice.
She huddled in the chair, fighting the feeling that someone was watching her. Her and Jack.

Around the edges of the curtains, gray dawn was filtering into the room. But there were still dark shadows
gathered in the corners. She kept turning her head
quickly, her gaze probing those corners and the line
where the ceiling met the wall. The notion came into
her head that the demon was here—that it had been
reading over her shoulder. Or, even more spooky, that
it had been picking the passages it wanted her to know
about.

She struggled to release the claws of fear jabbing at
her. All along Jack had felt some outside force was
using him—them. And he'd been right. The thing had
burned her. Terrified her. But it had also saved Jack
from the dog. And she had to thank it for that. If the
truth be told, she had to thank it for bringing them together.

She looked over at the man sleeping on the bed, one
arm strapped to his chest. So many of her relationships
with men had turned out to be disappointments. This
one might turn out the same, yet what she'd found during the short time with Jack was precious to her.

"So, why did you pick us?" she asked, her breath
stilling as she waited for an answer. "Why did you
throw us together?"

If the thing was here, it didn't choose to answer the question.

Dawn had broken outside the window, and she lowered her voice, thinking that it would be a shame not to give Jack a few more hours of sleep—if he could get them.

"Why couldn't you just tell us Gwynn's name?" she asked.

A jumble of images flooded her mind then. She saw Gywnn, standing inside a circle, a circle she knew gave him some kind of protection—from humankind and from the demon's kind as well.

So what could you do to the circle to make it less effective?

She was pondering that when the cell phone on the table suddenly rang, making her jump.

Jack instantly sat up, and she brought him the instrument.

Pressing the Transmit button, he said, "Hello."

She saw his face drain of color. "You lying bastard!" he shouted, but he kept the phone pressed to his ear.

CHAPTER
TWENTY-THREE

JACK'S VISION BLURRED as he listened to the gloating voice on the other end of the line.

"I have your daughter."

"I don't believe you, you scum," he answered, because he didn't want it to be true.

"Well, I'd let you talk to her, but she's sleeping at the moment."

He couldn't hold back a strangled protest.

"Call your friend, Ross Marshall. I'll be back in touch with you in fifteen minutes. And don't call the cops. The second you call in your cop buddies, she's dead."

The phone clicked off, and he was left with the feeling that he would never draw another full breath.

Kathryn came into focus.

"Please—tell me what's happened," she breathed.

"The bastard says he has Lily."

"Oh, God," she gasped, and moved to his side, wrapping her arm around his shoulder even as he began punching numbers again. He felt the tension in her arm. When he finished, he pressed his hand over hers.

Ross came on the line almost immediately.

"Is Lily there?" Jack asked in a voice that was barely under control.

He heard his friend make a sharp, anguished sound. "Jack, she's not in her bed."

"You're supposed to be watching her!"

"Jesus, you don't have to remind me of that."

Jack struggled to get control of his anger as he listened to Ross's explanation.

"Yesterday, she wanted to go down and play at the creek, and I told her she had to stay up here. She was . . . upset about that. We've gone down there before, but I told her it wasn't a good idea this time, and that she needed to stay in the house unless Megan or I went out with her. I thought she was okay with that."

He dragged in a breath. "Then, a few minutes ago, Craig came into our room to say that she was missing. We've torn the house apart. I was just going down to the creek to check."

Jack closed his eyes, imagining it. Lily had promised she wouldn't get into trouble again. But now she was under a lot of stress. She'd lost her mother three years ago, and she was worried about her father. It seemed the combination was too much for her.

"Maybe she's down at the creek," Ross was saying.

"Yeah. Let's hope so. Unfortunately, I got a call from the killer. He says he's got her."

"Jesus." Ross stayed on the line, and Jack could hear his friend breathing hard as he sprinted outside. There was the sound of an engine turning over, then tires squealing on gravel. He waited centuries for the car to skid to a halt again, then pictured the bridge across the creek and the shallow water running over rocks underneath.

When he heard Ross curse, he felt his heart stop. "What! What is it?"

"I smell him. He was here, all right."

"Oh, Christ."

"Jack, I'm so sorry."

"I know. It's not your fault." He forced himself to

say the words that must be said. "You told her to stay in the house, and she went out. She's . . . she's in a phase . . . where she makes her own decisions."

"I should have kept better watch on her."

"I should have told you that she hasn't exactly been a model of obedience lately, but I thought we'd worked it out. A few days ago, she and a friend were going to the other girl's house after school. They took a detour—and got into some trouble." While he spoke, he heard noises on the line and knew that Ross was already back in his SUV.

"Jack, I don't think she's been gone long. I'll go out on the road. See if I can spot him. Do you know what he's driving?"

"A Dodge SUV. He's going to call me back"—he looked at his watch—"in three minutes. I'll let you know what he says."

"Okay."

Kathryn had been standing stone still. Now she turned and wrapped him in her arms.

"Oh, Jack. I'm so sorry."

He let himself lean into her, laying his head against her shoulder, trying to hang on to the tattered shreds of his emotions.

When the phone rang, he almost jumped out of his skin, then glanced at his watch. Not three minutes.

He eased away from Kathryn, needing the space. Should he answer? What if it was Granger? If it was, he couldn't answer the call.

He debated in an agony of indecision, then pressed the button. "Hello."

"I see you talked to your friend."

"What are you doing, monitoring my calls?" he asked, already knowing the answer to the question. The curse of the cell phone, he thought. But he hadn't figured the guy could get to him that way.

"You can probably get to work out how I'm doing it. If you have the time. But I think you're going to be too busy."

"I want my daughter back."

"She would make a good sacrifice. Youth and innocence count for a lot."

"No!"

"The thought of my killing your little girl distresses
you?"

"You bastard!"

"Keep a civil tongue in your head when you talk to
me."

Jack swallowed, struggled to stay calm and clear-
headed—and to remember everything he knew about
hostage negotiation. Not enough. "Okay," he answered.

"I'll use your beautiful little daughter if I have to.
But she's not the one I want. You can get her back."

"How?"

"By trading her for Kathryn Reynolds."

A curse sprang to his lips. "No."

"It's your decision. You know, like that movie *Sophie's Choice*. Um—didn't Sophie end up killing herself?" Gwynn continued in a silky voice. "I'll give you
a few more minutes to think about it. Meanwhile, if you
call the cops, I'll kill her. And if you call Ross Marshall
back, I'll kill her for that."

The phone went dead, and Jack was left listening to
empty air, feeling like a wrecking ball had hit him in
the chest. He struggled to catch his breath, struggled not
to scream out his anger and his anguish.

"What does he want?" Kathryn asked, her arm moving toward him, then falling back, as though she weren't
sure what to do—how to help him.

There was nobody who could help him now. He
didn't want to tell her, but he understood that keeping
silent was not an option. Slowly, he raised his eyes to
hers. "He said he was willing to trade Lily for you."

He saw the blood drain from her face, felt his own
spirit shrivel. He had to drag in a breath before he could
manage to say, "God, I can't lose her. And I can't lose
you."

"Oh, Jack." She moved swiftly then, reached for him,

clung with a terrible strength. "It's all right. I can do it."

He felt too numb to answer. Lord, had he heard her right? Without a moment's thought, she was volunteering to trade herself for Lily. A sound of anguish welled from deep inside him as he used his good arm to pull her closer. He wanted to tell her not to do it. But he couldn't say that. "Kathryn," he managed. "Why?"

She drew back so she could meet his eyes. "Jack, I met her at the hospital. She's such a good kid. She doesn't deserve to be dragged into this."

"She went out of the house when Ross told her to stay inside!"

"I know, but she's just a little girl."

"Oh, God, Kathryn, what am I going to do?"

"Let me get her back for you."

"She could already be dead," he said in a choked voice. "That would be just his style."

"Don't think that way!"

He could only stand there, despairing.

"Jack, she can't fight him off. But I can."

He found himself arguing with her when he still felt so numb that he knew his brain hadn't caught up with his mouth. "How? Nobody's fought him off. Heather is dead. Swinton is dead. And a bunch of others. We don't even know how many."

She stroked her hands gently over his back. "Jack, I won't lie to you. I'm scared. But *there is no alternative*. Is there?"

He fought the sick feeling threatening to surge up his throat. Defeated, he whispered, "No."

"I know more than Heather. More than Swinton. We've been into this thing for days. And I . . . I was reading that book Ross gave us. It's got a lot of information."

He pulled away from her. "Information! Christ, if this were about information, we'd have him in custody," he shouted. Then, more quietly he said, "I can't ask you to do it."

"I know you can't. But I will."

"God, no. I can't lose her—and I can't lose you," he said again, because it was the only thing he *could* say.

"Which is why you can't be the one to make the decision. Jack, I love you," she whispered. "I wasn't going to say that. But I want to say it now. Maybe it sounds crazy, but I saw your family, and I loved them, too."

Before he could answer, the phone rang again, and he felt dizzy. "Hello," he said.

"What's your answer?" Gwynn said.

"Kathryn is willing to come to you."

"Excellent."

"How do I know you'll keep your end of the bargain?"

"You don't. You'll have to take my word for it."

He bit back another oath.

"We'll have an exchange. When I have Reynolds, I'll tell you where to find your beautiful little daughter. But don't make any calls."

"All right."

"Bring Reynolds to the old Caldwell farm. It's on Route 97. After Logan Road. When you're coming from the Frederick area, start looking for a mailbox with the number 9507. It's about a quarter-mile farther on. Then an eighth of a mile up a gravel lane to the farmhouse. The front door is unlocked. Put Reynolds in the living room and leave. I want her tied up, by the way. You'll find rope there. Leave as soon as you drop her off—and start driving toward Damascus. After I have Reynolds, I'll tell you where Lily is. And remember, no phone calls—or I kill the kid. You have all that?"

"Yes."

"Repeat it back to me," Gwynn ordered.

In a low, gritty voice Jack repeated the instructions, watching Kathryn. She looked so beautiful. So calm. Yet he saw the tightness around her eyes.

"Leave Charles Town right away."

"You know we're in Charles Town?"

Gwynn laughed. "I know everything. That's why I always get what I want."

The phone went dead, and Jack was left feeling as though he'd stepped into a frozen arctic wasteland, the cold wind burning his skin to the bone.

He saw Kathryn watching him.

"We have to go," she said.

He closed his eyes, clenched his fists, fighting not to scream. He felt her cross to him, felt her brush her lips against his. He pulled her close, crushing her mouth to his, devouring her, drinking in the taste of her.

She was the one who pulled away first. Crossing to the luggage, she opened her bag and took out the magic wand.

"If you take that with you, he'll find it."

"I'm giving it to you."

"Why?"

"I don't know. I think you'll need it." She held the wand toward him.

He took the other end, and for a moment they stood there, each holding one end of the hard plastic. It should feel cool, but somehow heat seemed to pulse in the depths of the blue liquid.

He felt like he was in one of their dreams as he shoved his gun into his waistband, then left the cabin and walked toward the car.

Dark clouds had gathered in the sky, the gloom hanging over him like a shroud.

When Kathryn started to climb into the driver's seat, as she'd been doing since he'd left the hospital, he stopped her. "No. I'd better drive."

"Why?"

"Because I have to drive away from the damn farmhouse. I'd better start doing it now. Thank God you've got an automatic."

He was grateful that he had something to focus on. After dropping the wand on the seat beside his hip, he leaned forward, shifting into reverse with his left hand, then let go and turned the wheel, thinking he'd better be careful and not crash the car.

Then he pulled around and down the narrow lane that led to the highway.

Kathryn was sitting beside him, her hands folded in her lap.

"I love you," he said. "I never thought I'd say that to any woman again."

She turned toward him, her eyes shimmering with tears. "Thank you for telling me that. I know it makes this harder for you."

His voice was steel as he said, "I'll get you out of this. I promise."

"I know."

"Did you see *The Last of the Mohicans*?"

"Yes."

"Do you remember what he said to her when he had to let the Indians take her captive? He said, 'Stay alive. Stay alive, and I will find you.' "

"Yes."

"Do it!"

"I will."

"I'll beat the crap out of you if you don't," he said, knowing he was speaking nonsense.

She laughed, moved closer, and laid her head on his shoulder.

"There's stuff I want to tell you. Stuff I'm thinking about how I'm going to get you back. But I can't tell you any of it. If I do, he might get it out of you."

"I understand." Closing her eyes, she murmured, "Let's talk about something else. Tell me what I have to look forward to."

He swallowed hard. "Will you marry me?"

"Oh, yes."

"You're not afraid to be a stepmother?"

"I'll have Mrs. Anderson to help me—if she lets me in the house."

"Oh, she will!"

She nodded against his shoulder. Then whispered,

"Well, since I've got you in the position where you can't say no to me, tell me we can have a baby together. You have two wonderful kids. I want one of your children."

"Wonderful! A couple years ago it was Craig who was acting out. Now it's Lily. I want to strangle her," he grated, his hand clamping on the wheel as he struggled to keep his anger from breaking through.

"Just hug her when you get her back. Hug her for me."

He nodded, because he knew if he tried to speak, he would start to sob.

He wanted to scream. He wanted to drive the car into a tree so he wouldn't have to drive to that farmhouse. Then the choice would be taken away from him. Instead, he kept the vehicle pointed toward the cliff at the end of the world, while they kept talking about the future—each clinging to what hope the other could give.

All too soon, he was turning onto the rutted drive. He kept hoping against hope that the farmhouse wouldn't be there. But it was where Gwynn had said it would be.

SIMON watched them from the dark shadows of the woods, his excitement growing to almost overwhelming proportions. They were here! He hadn't been absolutely sure they would show up. But they were here, and he had won. In a little while, he would go get the woman, and then he would complete the ceremony.

He'd thought about whether he was going to give back the little girl. He'd decided to do it for now. She'd keep Thornton busy.

Later, when he had the demon in his power, he would finish off Thornton—and his family.

But not yet.

He watched them get out of the car, watched their jerky movements. They were scared. Good.

He stayed where he was, watching from a distance.

He wasn't going to take a chance on Thornton pulling something tricky. He'd acted like a man who knew he was defeated, but his cop instincts could still kick in.

So Simon would wait until Thornton left, then wait twenty more minutes before going down to the house to get the woman.

Still, it was hard to stay where he was. Hard to contain his excitement.

STIFFLY, Jack got out of the car, the magic wand stuffed into one side of his waistband and the gun into the other. His footsteps rang hollowly as he climbed the sagging wooden steps, vividly aware of Kathryn right behind him.

The door opened, and he stepped into a bare room, then cursed.

"What?"

"I should have brought a blanket for you to sit on."

"I'm sure I won't be here long."

She looked at the rope lying on the floor. "He wants you to tie me up."

"Yes."

Her face blank, she sat down, took the cord, and used it to tie her ankles. He was hardly able to watch her, hardly able to believe she was preparing herself for her own kidnapping. Then they both worked at tying her hands, since the sling would have made the maneuver impossible for him to do it alone.

When he was finished, he could barely breathe as he stared at the bonds. He reached toward her, but she shook her head.

"You have to go," she whispered. "You have to go to Lily."

"Oh, God, Kathryn. I *will* get you back."

"I know."

He prayed he wasn't lying. Quickly he kissed her and walked out of the room, because if he didn't do it quickly, he would never do it.

The tears in his eyes made it almost impossible to see as he staggered outside. It had started to rain, the cold drops pelting him as he walked woodenly to the car and lurched it down the road. It took several moments before he realized he'd forgotten to turn on the windshield wipers.

He switched them on, and the windshield cleared, but his vision was still blurred by tears as he drove toward Damascus—his heart pounding as he waited for the phone to ring.

CHAPTER
TWENTY-FOUR

HE SCREAMED CURSES he would never have used in front of Kathryn, pounded his good hand against the steering wheel. Cursed the bastard who had put him into the fires of hell.

He didn't know what made him pull the magic wand from the waistband of his jeans.

As soon as his hand closed around it, it felt burning hot. He held it up, looking at the swirl of blue and the flecks of shiny stars and moons. The damn thing looked as cool as it ever had. But it felt like a white-hot poker.

He shoved it into the sling so it rested along his arm, grasping the hard plastic with his right hand.

Then he started driving through the rain again, the burning wand giving him a strange kind of comfort.

He came to a crossroad, sped past, then gasped as the rod turned from furnace to ice in his hand.

"Jesus!"

When he screeched to a stop on the wet pavement, it warmed again. When he made a U-turn, the temperature increased. It grew even hotter when he turned right on the crossroad.

His heart leaped into his throat. Daring to give himself a sliver of hope, he kept driving through the pounding rain, braking again when the rod turned freezer cold.

It was telling him which way to go. He knew that in his gut. Like the child's game. "You're getting warmer." Only this was no game.

"You're showing me where to find Lily?"

There was no answer—just the burning plastic against his hand.

He hadn't thought beyond Gwynn's phone call. Now he knew there was something else he could do. Turning in at a gas station, he leaped out and fumbled the correct change into a pay phone, rain pelting his back as he called Ross.

"Where the hell have you been?" his friend demanded.

"Gwynn told me he'd kill Lily if I called anybody. I figured he's got a line on the cell phone. I hope to God he's not using magic to monitor every pay phone in the area. I'm at a gas station on Woodfield Road." Quickly he told his friend what had happened. "The magic wand is leading me to Lily. Meet me out here. When I know she's safe, I'll go back for Kathryn. He won't be expecting me back so soon. He thinks I'm going to be driving miles out of my way. But I'm close to her. Very close."

"I'm on my way. I called Granger. Where's Kathryn?"

Jack gave the address. "For God's sake, tell him to be careful."

"He understands."

Jack splashed back to the car, then sped down the road again, his tires throwing up curtains of water as he let the hot and cold temperature of the wand guide him. To his daughter—he hoped.

While he drove, he muttered out loud. Talking to the demon, he supposed. "You bastard, what do you want from me?"

If you let him get me, you and your family are all

dead. The words were very faint, only an echo in his mind. Maybe he'd made them up, but he didn't think so.

"Why did you let him get her? You could have stopped him," he shouted.

No. Too weak. You must do it.

Jack cursed, then braked as the rod clamped in his fingers turned to ice.

KATHRYN sat with her head pressed against the wall, the hard surface anchoring her to sanity. Her bound hands were crossed in her lap; her heart was pounding.

She'd gone from calm acceptance to pulsing fear and back again. She'd helped Jack tie her up. She'd volunteered for this. Now she was covered with ice-cold perspiration and wondering about her own sanity.

Except that she saw no alternative. She couldn't let Gwynn use Lily in his ceremony.

But, oh God, now what?

She had to think. But her brain felt like a big bowl of rice pudding. Closing her eyes, she listened to the sound of rain drumming on the roof as she ordered herself to take shallow, even breaths.

Stay alive, Jack had said, *stay alive*.

If her hands and feet hadn't been tied, she might have jumped up and run like hell.

But that wasn't an option. She had volunteered to come here, and she couldn't leave.

So how was she going to keep this bastard from killing her? By being docile? By fighting him? By talking back? Stroking his ego? She didn't know what approach was best.

Above the roaring in her ears, she thought she heard footsteps splashing through the rain outside, and her eyes snapped open.

She was looking into the gray eyes of Simon Gwynn, and down the barrel of a gun.

Except for the wig and mustache, he was the man

she had seen at the hospital. Instead of a white coat, he was wearing a black silk shirt and black trousers.

She wanted to tell him that black was the wrong color for blonds, but she decided to keep that observation to herself.

Somehow she held her gaze level, somehow she kept from clenching her bound hands as every rational thought fled from her brain.

He studied her for painful heartbeats, the silence making her skin crawl. "So good of you to sacrifice yourself for the child," he finally said. "But then I thought you would. Gary told me so much about you— how nicey nice you were, how you were always so concerned for Heather DeYoung. You know, the irony is that it was you I wanted all along. But I had to be careful. I couldn't take another redhead so soon, so I decided Heather would do. And Swinton made it easy for me. All I had to do was offer him a lot of money, and he drugged her and brought her right to me. And he kept you distracted by those nasty pranks of his, like the trick with the fishing line." He laughed. "Of course, he did it because he hated your guts. He told me all that when he was trying to get me to let him go—instead of using him in that nasty little ceremony where I drove Detective Thornton off the road.

And now you're here because you think your detective is going to come back and rescue you? Well, you'll be long gone from this place before he gets back."

She couldn't stop her throat from closing, and she knew he sensed her fear.

He stared at her, and she tried to read the expression in his cold gray eyes. Should she keep him talking? Flatter him? Beg? She canceled that. One thing she knew—begging wouldn't work.

"Jack thinks I'm on his side. I could . . . you know . . . change sides . . ." she heard herself saying. "I want a strong man. You're stronger than Jack."

He laughed. "That's right. But I don't believe you. You're like Patience."

"Who?"

"The girl who tricked me so long ago. You look a lot like her with that pretty red mane."

She struggled to hold back a moan as he hunkered over her and wound his fingers in her hair, holding it up and letting it fall back into place, before he slapped a piece of duct tape over her mouth. Next he pulled a hood over her head, and she was thrown into terrifying darkness.

JACK went back to the crossroad and howled in agony when the damn thing stayed icy. Then he figured out he'd turned the wrong way.

Five minutes later, he was driving up another rutted lane—his tires sinking into puddles as he skidded to a halt. Throwing his door open, he dashed through the cold rain and charged into another abandoned farmhouse.

His wet shoes almost sent him sprawling on the wooden floor as he sped through the house. He found Lily in one of the bedrooms, curled on her side, sleeping. She whimpered when he picked her up and gathered her close with his good arm, crying out his relief as he rocked the precious bundle against him.

He had her. Thank the Lord, he had her. He slid down to the floor, cradling her in his lap as he took a colossal risk and called Ross, praying that the magician was too busy now to be monitoring phone calls.

Jack gave Ross his location and asked him to come get Lily. Hanging up, he leaned against the wall, holding his daughter in his lap, trying not to weep. He was stroking her silky hair, listening to the sound of her breathing, when Ross charged through the door.

Lily stirred against him, and Jack tensed. But she didn't wake. He was torn. He wanted to talk to her, assure himself that she was all right. And he knew she would want him there when she woke. But he couldn't have everything.

"Take her to the hospital. Make sure she's all right. And call Emily, get her to meet you there," Jack said, stroking his lips against Lily's soft cheek, then lifting his head, his gaze burning into Ross's. "I'm going back for Gwynn."

His friend gave him a critical look. "You're in no shape to go after him on your own."

"Granger's on the way. You take Lily."

"Okay."

Ross picked up the child, cradling her in his arms. Jack stood with his shoulders pressed to the wall, trying to catch his breath, taking one last look at his sleeping daughter before trotting back to the car.

For a time, the magic wand shoved into the wet fabric of his sling had been just a hard rod of plastic. Now it burned his flesh again.

He started the car, heading back toward Logan Road.

When the phone rang, he pulled onto the shoulder and answered as quickly as he could.

"Hello."

"Your daughter is at 9037 Carter Drive."

Pretending he didn't already have Lily, he shouted, "You're not lying to me?"

"Go pick her up."

I already did, you bastard. And now I'm coming to get you, if Granger isn't already turning in to the drive.

Jack drove as fast as he could through the pounding rain—one hand on the wheel and the other wrapped around the magic wand. It was hot again, and this time it was directing him toward Kathryn.

Only he didn't need magic. He knew where he was going to find Gwynn.

Just a few more miles, he kept chanting in his mind. Gwynn wasn't expecting him to have picked up Lily and come back so soon.

The phone rang again, and he cursed as he pulled to the shoulder so he could answer.

It was Granger. "Jack, I'm sorry. The house your friend sent us to is empty."

"Empty!"

"He's cleared out."

"God, no!" he shouted into the phone. He had been so sure that, with his head start, he could get back to Kathryn before Gwynn took her out of there. He'd been counting on that advantage. He'd been wrong.

Granger was speaking, and he realized that he'd missed part of the conversation. Then the phone went dead.

"Fuck!" He stared at the instrument—pressed buttons. Nothing happened, yet the battery showed enough of a charge to receive a message. If he'd been in his unmarked, he would have put in the spare battery, but he was in Kathryn's car. He opened the glove compartment, rummaged through gas station slips and her owner's manual, but found nothing useful.

"Fuck!" he said again, because there was no other way to deal with his frustration.

Then he forgot about the phone as the magic wand flared hot, then went ice cold, then hot again.

"What the hell?"

You must go to her. Hurry.

"Did you turn off my phone?"

Yes.

"Jesus, what are you thinking? You think I don't need Granger's help?"

You must do it by yourself.

"Why?"

No others may see.

He shouted out another oath, then pulled back onto the road and pressed his foot on the accelerator—following the heat of the wand.

HE was strong. Kathryn had found that out when he'd picked her up, slung her over his shoulder, and carried her to a car.

She lay there on the backseat in her damp clothing,

forcing herself not to scream when he tightened the knots on her bonds.

Cold and shivering, she heard him talking to Jack— telling him where to pick up his daughter.

A scream bubbled in her throat.

Jack had to go get Lily now. Then he'd come back to the farmhouse, and it would be too late for her.

Jack. Oh God. Jack, find me. Please, find me.

The phone call was over quickly. He clicked off, drove on. All too soon they were slowing down again. Cutting the engine, he climbed out and opened the back door, and she steeled herself to feel his hands on her again.

If she could have screamed, she would have. But the duct tape kept her terror locked in her throat.

He picked her up, carried her through the cold rain, then under some kind of shelter.

A porch? She heard a key turning in a lock. A door opened, then slammed behind them as he walked across a hard floor that magnified the sound of his footsteps.

Then they were going down a flight of steps.

Her heart pounded. The spit in her mouth had turned to stone.

Another door opened. Seconds later, he laid her on a hard surface. She felt him cutting the cord that bound her legs, and kicked out at him.

"Is that how you plan to help me?" he growled as his fist pounded into her stomach. The pain made her gasp. By the time she could breathe again, he'd secured her legs to rings at the end of the table.

It was all happening too fast, and there was no way to fight the terror.

He fingered the cord on her hands, then pulled them above her head and secured them to a metal ring.

When she was immobile, he pulled the hood off her head, a smile flickering on his lips as his gaze swept over her.

The breath froze in her lungs as she stared up at him. When she'd told Jack she would change places with

Lily, she had never in her imagination thought that she would end up strapped to a table.

She was going to die here. She knew that now. Unless . . .

Please, she silently begged. *Please take the gag off my mouth.*

"You just relax," he said. "I must purify myself for the ceremony. I'm sorry you can't see the chamber in my primary residence. This is just a poor substitute—a room I fixed up in case I needed a cozy place to work away from home." He stopped and laughed, reaching out to stroke his fingers against her hair.

"Such beautiful hair," he murmured. "I love red hair—like Patience. Since we broke up, I've had a thing for redheads. I was going to take you that morning—before I caught you and Thornton on the lawn. But now everything's worked out the way I wanted."

His hand moved down to her cheek, and she struggled not to cringe.

"Heather had a pure white ceremonial gown. I don't want to take a chance changing your clothes. Not when I already have you tied down. But that wet shirt and sweatpants certainly don't look appropriate for an important ceremony."

He turned from her, and when he pivoted back, he had a knife in his hand, the knife she'd seen in the dream.

She gasped behind the gag and tried to twist away, but her bonds kept her in place.

He inserted the knife tip in the damp fabric of her shirt, ripping a line down her side, parting the material and pulling it away. He cut other slashes in the knit, cut the shirt away from her body, then severed her bra straps. In moments, she was naked to the waist.

"Nice," he murmured, looking down at her, tracing the curve of her breasts with his finger.

Unable to stand the look of satisfaction on his face, she squeezed her eyes shut.

When the knife blade touched her thigh, she couldn't

hold back a whimpering sound. But he was only cutting away her sweatpants and panties, leaving her naked on the table.

His hand skimmed the triangle of hair at the base of her legs. "It's a shame we don't have more time," he murmured. "But since time is of the essence and you came to me of your own free will, I'll make it easy on you. We'll do it as soon as possible. You won't have to wait too long for me to plunge my knife into your heart."

As she listened to him, every muscle of her body felt like it was fighting an electric current. Then he was gone, and she flopped back against the table.

Jack had told her to stay alive. It didn't look like she was going to manage that. She felt tears stinging the backs of her eyes, but she was too proud to let them leak out.

CHAPTER
TWENTY-FIVE

JACK PULLED BACK onto the road, relying on the same method he'd used to find Lily. In the back of his mind, he knew it was the demon controlling the magic wand. But he didn't let himself dwell on that. If he let himself think about what he was doing, he would start to scream. He had started out hating and fearing the creature that had interfered in his life. He still felt those emotions. Yet he knew that he and the creature must work together now, if he was going to save Kathryn's life.

Obscene images rose in his mind. Ruthlessly, he shut them out because they could only drive him mad. With a single-minded purpose, he concentrated on the feel of the hard plastic rod where it nestled inside the sling.

He was learning how to use the damn wand. When the plastic was hot, he sped forward, slowing down when he reached a crossroad, feeling for a subtle change that would tell him whether he should go straight or turn.

He wasn't even paying much attention to the route—just driving like an automaton, through the driving rain, following the directions of the wand. The directions of the creature.

Somewhere in the western end of the county, he blinked, came out of his dreamlike state as the wand pulsed in his right hand, stinging his skin, shocking him into full awareness.

He was on a narrow gravel lane, much like the lane he'd traveled less than an hour earlier, only longer and wetter.

Coming around a curve, he caught his breath. The SUV was parked in front of a redbrick rancher. A house about forty or fifty years old, he judged. Nothing remarkable.

He looked down at the wand, wondering if it had led him to the wrong place. This couldn't be Gwynn's house. It wasn't grand enough. Yet the wand had told him he was going to find the guy here.

He started to hit the brake hard, then checked himself, slowing gradually so as not to give himself away with a squeal of tires and a shower of water and gravel.

A new thought struck him, then. Maybe Gwynn wasn't even in the house with Kathryn. Maybe he had planted the car here and gone somewhere else.

He craned his neck, saw that the road ended here. But was there another structure hidden back in the woods?

He didn't have time to make mistakes. He had to act. And the wand was burning so hotly that he could barely stand to keep it inside the sling. But he left it where it was, because the pain helped focus him. Stepping out of the car, he moved quickly toward the house, splashing through a puddle and onto the floor of the porch.

His heart speeded up as he saw a trail of wet footsteps. When he looked through the window, he saw they continued across the floor of the empty living room.

The door was unlocked. Stepping inside, he followed the wet trail across the floor and down a hallway to another door.

* * *

KATHRYN lay on the hard table, her skin covered with goose bumps, her nipples tight from the damp and cold. She was alone, but somewhere nearby she could hear Gwynn moving around. Could hear water splashing. Was there still something she could do? Some way to save herself?

It took every scrap of will she possessed not to weep in terror. Holding on to her self-control, she turned her head, looking around for some source of help.

She was in a room like the one she'd seen in the dream. It must be in the basement, judging from the flight of steps he'd carried her down. Black curtains hid the sharp angles of the walls, and candlesticks stood on tables around the room. But none of the candles were lighted. The illumination was low and came from a small lamp on a table in one corner.

This was where she was going to die, she thought with a kind of strange detachment.

Jack, I love you, she murmured inwardly, trying to send the thoughts out to him. *It could have been so good. No. I mean it was good. It just didn't last long enough. I'm so sorry we couldn't have had more together.*

It seemed like only moments later that Gwynn was back. He was naked to the waist, his only garment a pair of silky black trousers.

The trousers were thin, and she saw that he was aroused.

She swallowed, tried to look somewhere else besides that thick rod at the front of his pants. But she couldn't take her eyes off his erection.

When he lowered his hand to stroke himself, she felt the breath solidified in her lungs. Reaching out, he touched one of her tightened nipples with a fingertip. "You want me?" he asked.

The obscenity of the question clogged her throat. She

longed to cringe away, but there was nowhere to go,
nowhere to hide.

Summoning every scrap of courage that remained,
she raised her eyes to his face, seeing the tension and
the triumph in his expression.

Please, take off the gag, she silently begged. *You
think you know what's going to happen. But let me tell
you the truth. You're not going to like it.*

Her hopes crashed as Gwynn turned away. She heard
him chanting in a language she didn't recognize,
watched as he finished inscribing a white circle on the
black floor.

When he was finished, he walked back to the table,
still chanting.

Her eyes riveted on the silver knife in his hand. He
had used it to cut away her clothing.

Now there was nothing between her flesh and that
knife. Not even a thin scrap of fabric.

But he wouldn't just kill her—would he? He'd make
it part of his ceremony.

She clutched at that as he bent over her.

With his free hand, he ripped the tape off her mouth,
and she bit back a scream of pain.

Dragging in a steadying breath, she let it out in a
rush and began to speak—quickly, urgently, knowing
that keeping Gwynn's attention was her only chance to
do what Jack had asked her to do—to stay alive. "You
can hold your ceremony. You can kill me, but you
won't get what you want. The demon will kill himself—
kill everyone within miles of here—before he lets you
capture him."

She saw at once that she'd scored a point. He'd been
looking like a man in total control of events. Now a
flicker of uncertainty invaded his features.

"What do you think you know about it?" he demanded.

She forced herself to meet his gray eyes. "More than
you want me to know. Have you read a book called
Portal to Another Universe?"

"No."

"Pity," she said, hardly able to believe that she could talk coherently. She was naked, totally vulnerable, totally under this man's control. But she wasn't going to give up. *Stay alive. Stay alive.*

"I've heard of the work. It's been lost for centuries."

"You're wrong. My werewolf friend lent me a copy," she tossed off. "I was reading it last night."

"No. You're lying. What do you mean—your werewolf friend?"

"He's Jack's friend. He found your graveyard at Sugarloaf Mountain. And if you get out of this room alive, he'll find you and tear you to pieces."

JACK stood rigid on the other side of the door, his teeth clamped together to keep himself from screaming.

He'd silently turned the knob and pushed the barrier open a crack—then held back a curse as he took in the scene before his eyes. Neither of the people in the room knew he was there. They were too focused on each other.

Kathryn was naked, secured to a table. Gwynn was dressed in his black trousers, leaning over her.

It was all he could do to stop himself from bursting into the chamber and drilling the fucker. But not when he was holding his gun in his left hand. And not when Gwynn was standing over Kathryn with a knife.

Instead he strained his ears. They were talking, and he felt a surge of pride and gratitude. She was doing what he'd asked her to do. Keeping herself alive. Gwynn hadn't started the main part of the ceremony, but he could kill her if he thought he was cornered.

He saw Gwynn's hand move, and he almost leaped through the door, but he forced himself to hold back.

With a snarl of rage, the magician slapped her across the face.

She cried out, then, incredibly, started talking again.

"It won't do you any good to get angry with me. You

should have read the book before you got into something too big for any man to handle. It tells about a
magician who was trying to do what you're attempting.

"He died. So did a lot of other people. When the
demon knew he would lose the struggle, he blew himself up. The description makes it sound rather like a
thermonuclear explosion."

"No!"

KATHRYN kept her eyes focused on the magician's
twisted face—knowing that some part of him believed
her. "You don't have to take my word for it. Go ahead
with what you're doing, and you'll find out."

"You can't stop me with your lies," he flung at her.

"I'm not lying. You're welcome to try it—if you
think you know more than the last stupid bastard who
made the attempt."

"Shut up. Just shut up," he shouted. Whirling away
from her, he stood stiffly, chanting again, his voice rising, the tone no longer under his control.

The room seemed to shimmer with a blue light—
everywhere except a large area near the top of the far
wall, where it looked like a gray cloud had gathered.

She felt breathless, felt a terrible pressure against her
chest. It was one of the sensations she had experienced
in that place where the creature lived. The demon.

And something else was happening. In the air above
her she saw dancing shapes, floating like motes of dust,
only larger and shiny.

She stared at them, seeing moons and stars—like the
moons and stars from her wand.

Despite everything, an exclamation of wonder welled
in her throat, just as the door burst open, and she saw
Jack step into the room. He had a gun in his hand.

"POLICE, freeze," Jack shouted.

Gwynn whirled toward him—his arms outstretched—

and a tongue of fire that looked like it came from a flamethrower shot from his fingertips, hitting the gun, making it fly out of Jack's hands. The weapon landed on the floor, melted into a twisted shape.

Jack stared at the ruined weapon as he screamed out a curse and staggered back.

The magician whirled away from him, began a louder chant that filled the room, and Jack knew he had launched into the ceremony—hurrying through the preliminaries so he could reach the ending more quickly.

"No! You fool, you'll die with us," Jack shouted.

Gwynn ignored him, his words coming faster and louder as he stepped toward Kathryn, raising the knife above his head.

The air in the room pulsed and thickened, holding Jack in place. Making a tremendous effort, he shook himself free and charged toward Gwynn. Before he reached the magician, he hit the circle on the floor, hit an invisible barrier, and was flung back against the wall—sliding to the cold cement as searing pain reverberated through his shoulder and down his arm.

On the table, Kathryn screamed and struggled, desperate to escape. But she couldn't break free of her bonds.

Jack pushed himself up and somehow staggered to his feet, the clawing pain in his shoulder almost more than he could bear.

The rational part of his mind howled in despair. The magic circle had stopped him, flung him back. But some core of him refused to give up even in the face of what seemed like certain defeat.

Let me in! The words echoed in his head. Low and urgent, the creature's power flared in one last desperate command.

Jack went very still, his eyes fixed on the terrible scene unfolding before him. Gwynn was rapidly building to the climax of his ceremony. And there wasn't a damn thing Jack Thornton could do about it.

He had reached the point of desperation. There was

no way he could save Kathryn, nothing left besides surrender to a force that had terrified him from the first
moment he had considered the idea that he was no
longer in control of his own destiny.

He had battled against that fear. And at the same
time, he had fought for his free will with every fiber of
his soul, of his body, of his intellect. Yet in this terrible
moment of defeat, everything changed. With no other
way to save Kathryn, he didn't hesitate to surrender his
soul.

"Yes," he screamed, throwing aside his carefully
marshaled defenses, inviting the one thing he had fought
with strength born of primal dread.

For one moment of unimaginable fear, he was open
and vulnerable to powers beyond human imagining. In
the next, he felt as though shards of glass had lodged
themselves in the tissues of his brain, filled the inside
of his head, tearing at each cell with steel claws.

The shock of slicing pain was too great for any human to withstand, and he blacked out for several seconds, standing with his shoulders braced against the
wall. Then his eyes blinked open, and he found that
somehow he could endure the knives stabbing into his
mind.

He saw the scene through a grainy, gray haze that
wrapped itself around him. He felt his skin turn icy cold
and, at the same time, hot as the fires of hell. Words
came to his lips. Words in some ancient language he
had never heard and didn't understand. His own magic
chant giving him power that no human being had ever
possessed or would ever possess again.

His voice rose in strength, filling the room. Gwynn
whirled to face him, his features contorted in a mask of
shock and rage, his lips moving in a frantic stream of
words. But Jack could no longer hear the syllables
above the screeching in his ears.

He was almost blind. Almost unable to stand against
the tremendous force pressing down against his shoulders. When he tried to draw in a breath, he felt as

though his lungs were filling with water. And he knew this was what Kathryn had endured every time she entered one of the dreams.

But she had stood it. And so could he. It took a tremendous effort to raise his arm. Still, he managed it—pain tearing through his injured shoulder as he brought the wand into position. Into firing position.

He had no idea what would happen next. In amazement he watched a stream of molten flames flare from the tip of the plastic tube—like the flames that had come from the magician—only hotter, a mixture of blue and gold like the interior of the wand. As though there had never been a barrier, the flames arrowed past the protective circle, striking Gwynn in the chest.

The magician screamed in agony, his face a mask of rage and shock. For heartbeats, he stayed on his feet. Then he swayed sideways and toppled to the floor, his body lying in a crumpled heap.

The darkness in the room swelled and swirled, like a living, writhing presence. Jack gasped for breath, struggling to pull air into his lungs. Then a shock wave threw him to the ground, followed by a thunderclap that sounded as though the very fabric of time and space had been torn open.

The dark, swirling substance in the room rushed toward a jagged, gaping hole that opened in the air, tugging and pulling at him, so that he thought he would be swept along with it into a dark, airless place where no man could live.

He tried to call Kathryn's name. But once more he lost consciousness.

For long moments, there was only blessed nothingness. When he came back to himself, Kathryn was calling his name.

He opened his eyes, turned his head toward her, blinking as he took in the scene.

"Jack, oh God, Jack. Are you all right? Jack, answer me!"

He pushed himself to a sitting position, staring across

at her. She was naked, her cheeks streaked with tears. "Kathryn."

He got to his feet, teetered unsteadily as he crossed the room—crossed the circle that had stopped him moments earlier. First he knelt to check Gwynn, finding no pulse in his neck. Then he staggered to Kathryn.

Leaning over, he delicately touched her hair, pressed his cheek to hers, then turned his head and kissed her on the lips, relief and gratitude surging through him.

"Jack. Thank you for saving me."

"It wasn't just me," he said in a low voice. "The demon led me here. The demon worked that trick with the wand."

"And now he's gone," she said.

"Yes," he answered, realizing as he said the word that it was true. They'd been entwined with the creature for days. Now there was a void where the presence had been.

He let that knowledge sink in as he worked awkwardly to free Kathryn from her bonds, "Did Gwynn . . . hurt you?"

"No," she murmured. "I'm fine—now."

When he'd freed one of her hands, she helped him with the other side.

Once he'd freed her, he kissed her again, then pulled down some of the black drapery and spread it over her naked body, hugging her to him.

Finally, he turned to look around the room. The first thing he saw was the gun. He'd seen it melt. Now it was intact again. And when he picked it up and checked the clip, he found that one round had been fired.

"Jesus!"

Kathryn sat up, clutching the curtain around her. "What?"

"Did you see my gun lying in a melted heap on the floor?"

"Yes."

Quickly he crossed to Gwynn and rolled the magician over. Instead of a burn mark on his front, there was a bullet hole in his chest. A perfect shot to the heart.

"It looks like I shot him," he muttered as he came back to Kathryn. "Is that what you saw?"

"I . . . I saw fire shoot out of the wand."

"Yeah," he answered, picking up the gun and shoving it back into his waistband. He pulled out the wand and looked at it. It was unblemished, the beveled plastic clear and bright, the stars and moons swirling in their blue liquid.

"You said the demon did that?" she asked. "How?"

"I let him into my mind, and he killed Gwynn."

She stared at him. "You let him in? Lord—that must have been . . ." She fumbled for the right word.

"Scary," he supplied. "But it was the only way I could save you—save us."

"Oh, Jack!" She pressed her cheek against his middle, and he stroked his fingers through her hair.

In the distance he heard sirens. He hadn't told Granger where he was going. He hadn't even known. But it sounded like somebody had called the police.

Kathryn pushed herself off the table, swaying on her feet as she pulled the curtain around her like a toga. He steadied her, held her to him.

"We'd better get our stories straight," he said quickly. "I mean—you saw me shoot Gwynn. Because that's the only way anybody's going to believe us."

"Yes." She turned her head. "And how did you find me?"

He ran a hand through his hair, at a complete loss. "Jesus. I don't know."

"You'd looked through records to see what other property Gwynn owns?"

"Yeah. Right. Let's hope he owns this place."

His arm slung around her, they climbed the steps. "We'd better go out," he said. "Before they come in here with guns blazing."

The rain had stopped, and the sun was fighting its way past the clouds as they staggered together onto the porch. Jack slung his good arm around Kathryn as two police cruisers roared into the yard.

Granger jumped out of the unmarked, looking them both over. "I see I missed the excitement," he said.

"Gwynn's down in his ceremonial chamber—dead. I shot him." He pulled out his Sig. "You want this, I assume."

"Yeah."

Granger bagged the gun, and two uniforms entered the house.

"He shot him to save my life," Kathryn said. "He was going to kill me in one of his ceremonies. Like he killed Heather. He cut off my clothing and he was going to stab me in the heart."

Granger nodded, then turned to Jack. "Why didn't you tell me where the hell you were?"

"The phone went dead! I guess you found this place the same way I did—by checking other properties he owned."

"Right," Granger agreed, then looked toward Kathryn. "Do you need medical attention?"

"No." She looked down with distaste at the black curtain. "Do you have anything I can put on?"

"I'd give you my shirt, but getting out of it is a major effort," Jack said.

"I've got some clean gym clothes in the back of my unmarked. If you don't mind a guy's sweats," Granger offered.

"No. That would be fine."

He brought her the clothing, and she disappeared into the bathroom.

While she was gone, the two uniforms emerged, their eyes wide as they reported on the ceremonial chamber and the table where Kathryn had been tied down naked.

Staying on his feet had become too much effort for Jack. He sat down heavily on the damp steps. When Kathryn returned, she sat down beside him, locking her fingers with his good hand.

"He should be back in the hospital," she said, raising her eyes to Granger.

"An ambulance is on the way." The captain scuffed his foot against the gravel of the driveway. "I'm sorry," he said in a low voice. "You were right about this case. I was wrong."

Jack gave a tight nod.

Kathryn raised her chin. "We figured out it was Gwynn who turned in that complaint on us. He was driving past my house, getting ready to kidnap me. But he saw Jack there, and he took an opportunity to try and get Jack off his back."

Granger muttered his agreement with her scenario.

Afraid that Kathryn was going to push the captain harder, Jack tightened his grip on her hand.

She picked up on the signal, looked toward him, then pressed her lips together. And he thought she was going to make a very good cop's wife.

"BEDTIME," Jack said.

"I want to stay up with Kathryn," Lily protested

"I know. But we're practicing listening to what adults tell us."

Lily gave a little nod, her gaze fixed on Kathryn. "But she'll still be here in the morning."

"Yes," Jack said, feeling the thickness in his throat. He'd been torn. He'd never thought that a man with children should move his fiancée into the house. But the thought of her alone in her duplex had made his stomach knot. Intellectually, he knew the danger was over from Swinton, from Gwynn, and from the dreams. Yet he simply couldn't allow her out of his sight. So he'd insisted she move in with the family.

Things were working out pretty well. Emily had volunteered to find a new position. He'd convinced her that the family needed her. And Kathryn had added her voice to the warm assurances, telling the housekeeper how wonderful it was to move into a smoothly running home. But Emily could have some more time to herself now. So the women were working out their relationship. As were the kids and their soon-to-be stepmom.

Craig was a little prickly. Probably because he felt he had to keep the memory of his real mother alive. But Kathryn was dealing with that, too.

"Let's go up, and you can tell me what story you want me to read," Kathryn said to Lily.

"The King's Stilts."

"Okay. And tomorrow after school, we can get some more books out of the library. I'll pick you up, and we'll go right there."

Lily's eyes sparkled. She was sucking up the attention that this new woman in her life seemed to love lavishing on her.

"We can call you when we're ready," Kathryn said to Jack.

"I'll come up with you," he answered, heaving himself off the sofa. He'd reinjured the shoulder in the fight with Gwynn and set back his recovery. But he'd also learned what was important in life.

He wasn't going to miss the moments with his family. So while Kathryn supervised Lily's bath, he stepped into Craig's room and made sure his son's homework was finished, then talked about the Orioles game they were going to attend.

He was coming back down the hall when the conversation in his daughter's room stopped him in his tracks.

"And the same bad man that kidnapped me, kidnapped you," Lily was saying.

"Yes."

"Were you scared?"

"Yes. But I kept thinking your daddy would come rescue me."

"Me, too."

Jack's chest was so tight he could barely breathe. They'd agreed it was better not to tell Lily why Kathryn had ended up in Gwynn's clutches. Maybe when his daughter was older, he'd explain that her stepmom had saved her life. Right now, that was too much of a burden for her slender shoulders to bear.

He stepped through the door, and they both turned to face him. "Sit with us while Kathryn reads," Lily demanded.

"I'd like that," he said, thinking that they'd have to be a little stricter with his daughter. But not now.

A half-hour later, they'd finally turned off the lights, gone into the master bedroom, and closed the door.

It was a masculine room. He'd swept away any feminine overtones a year ago. And he was glad that no traces of his previous relationship lingered here. He'd already told Kathryn she could redecorate any way she wanted.

"Things are going pretty well," he said.

She nodded.

"You're good for Lily."

"I love her. And Craig. And you. And I feel like Emily and I have come to an understanding. She knows she'll always be the kids' grandma, which is wonderful, since neither one of us has any parents left."

He reached for her with his good arm, holding her close as best he could. "I love you so much. When I first saw you, all I could think about was getting you into bed. Now there's so much more I want with you. Lord, I was lucky to find you."

"It's the same for me."

For long moments, they simply clung to each other, caught up in the joy of being alone.

"So—how soon do you think we can manage a wedding?" he asked in a voice that wasn't quite steady.

"Oh, pretty quickly. If we just have Emily and the kids. And Ross and Megan."

"I want you to have a wedding you'll remember. Something fancy."

"Fancy. Right. Just your style." She thought for a moment. "Well, I've heard about a fancy wedding pavilion down at Disney World. Would that do?"

"You're kidding?"

"No. I think it would be fun. And easy. I'm sure they provide all the trimmings—except that I want to splurge on a dress." She warmed to the idea, adding details. "And if Emily will take the kids off for tours of the theme parks after the ceremony, I think we'll all have a wonderful time. We can rent one of those—what are they called?—tree houses. So we end up with a bedroom door that locks."

"Yeah, a door that locks. That better be in the contract."

She snuggled against him, then raised her head and laughed.

"What?"

"Maybe we should film it, so we show it on a Valentine's Day segment of *Oprah*. You know—couples telling how they met."

He chuckled. "Yeah, right. A demon brought us together."

"We never did find out his name." The name was important, they had discovered from reading *Portal to Another Universe*. It was kind of a compulsion, learning all the gory details. The book explained that the magician had to know the demon's name to capture him.

"I just think of him as the SOB," Jack muttered. "He put us through hell."

"Which makes heaven all the sweeter," Kathryn whispered, raising her mouth to his for a long, eager kiss that quickly turned passionate.

Jack looked toward the bed, then back to Kathryn. "I'm sorry you're leaping into the reality of parenthood. But it will be safer if we let the kids settle down for a half-hour first."

"I found that out last night, when Lily stood outside the door, twisting the knob," she answered. "They're curious about us—alone together."

"I know, but things will settle down."

They kicked off their shoes and stretched out on the bed in their clothing—touching and talking and making plans for the future until the heat building between them was too great. Kathryn got up and wove her way on shaky legs to the door, where she checked the lock— then returned to Jack.

As he lay on his back, watching her standing over him, slowly starting to unbutton her blouse, he thought that he was the luckiest man in the world.

Turn the page for a preview of
Rebecca York's new novel,

Witching Moon

Now available from Berkley Sensation

THE LAST GUY who had walked in his shoes was a dead man, Adam Marshall thought as his booted feet sank into the soggy ground of the southern Georgia swamp. But he didn't intend to suffer the same fate. He had advantages that the previous head ranger at Nature's Refuge hadn't possessed.

Still, something was making his skin prickle tonight, Adam silently admitted as he slipped one hand into the pocket of his jeans. Standing very still on the porch of his cabin, he listened to the night sounds around him. The clicking noise of a bullfrog. The buzz of insects. The splash of a predator slipping into the murky waters of the mysterious marshes that the Indians had called Olakompa.

The Indians were long gone, but an aura of otherworldliness remained in this pocket of wetlands, which had managed to withstand the encroachment of civilization. It was a place steeped in superstition, and Adam had heard some pretty wild tales—of people who had been swallowed up by the "trembling earth" and of strange creatures that roamed the backcountry.

In the darkness, he laughed. He'd taken all that with a grain of salt. But maybe he could contribute to the myths while he was here.

This was a very different setting from his previous post in the dry desert country of Big Bend National Park.

He liked the change. Liked the swamp. For now. He never stayed anyplace too long. It didn't matter where he lived, actually. Just so he had the space he needed to roam free.

He looked up and saw the moon filtering through the branches of the willow oaks and cypress trees. It was huge and yellow and full, and he knew there were people who would think that the large orb in the sky had something to do with his unsettled mood. But it wasn't that.

He dragged in a long breath, detecting a scent that was out of place in the sultry air. Nothing he had ever smelled before, he thought, as he walked down the steps, then into the shadows under the oak trees.

Whatever it was had a strange tang, a pull, an edge of danger that he found disturbing. Of course, he was affected by odors as few people were. And by other things most folks took in stride. Coffee, for example, made him sick. And forget liquor.

Later tonight, he'd probably have a cup of herbal tea. By himself, since he was the only staffer who lived in the park—in the cozy cabin thoughtfully provided by Austen Barnette, who owned this three-hundred-acre corner of the swampland, along with a sizable portion of Wayland, Georgia.

Barnette was the big cheese in the area. And he'd gone to the expense and bother of hiring Adam Marshall away from the U.S. Park Service to show he was serious about running Nature's Refuge as a private enterprise. But there was another reason as well. Adam had a reputation for solving problems.

Most recently, at Big Bend, he had shut down a bunch of drug smugglers who had been bringing their cargoes across the drought-shrunken Rio Grande. He had tracked them to their mountain hideout and scared the shit out of them before turning them over to the border patrol.

He had done a good job, because he always demanded the best from himself as far as his work was concerned. It compensated for the other area of his life where he wasn't quite so effective—personal relationships. But he was damn well going to find out who had killed Ken White, the previous head ranger.

He walked to a spot about a hundred yards from his cabin, a place where he often stopped and contemplated the swamp before going out to prowl the park. It was a good distance from the house, where he was sure nobody would find his clothing.

Standing in the shade of a pine, he sniffed the wind again as his hands went to the front of his shirt. He unbuttoned the garment and dropped it on the ground, then pulled off his shoes and pants, stripping to the buff.

The sultry air felt good on his bare skin, and he stood for a moment, digging his toes into the springy layer of decomposing leaves covering the ground, caught by a push-pull within himself. The man warring with the animal clamoring to run free.

The animal won, as it must. Closing his dark eyes, he called on ancient knowledge, ancient ritual, ancient deities as he gathered his inner strength, steeling himself for familiar pain, even as he said the words that he had learned on his sixteenth birthday—the way his brothers had before him. As far as he knew, the only Marshall boys still alive were himself and Ross. But he didn't know for sure because he hadn't seen his brother in years.

It was when he prepared to change that his thoughts sometimes turned to Ross, but he didn't let those thoughts break his concentration.

"Taranis, Epona, Cerridwen," he intoned, then repeated the same phrase and went on to another.

"Ga. Feart. Cleas. Duais. Aithriocht. Go gcumhdai is dtreorai na deithe thu."

On that night so long ago, the ceremonial words had helped him through the agony of transformation, opened his mind, freed him from the bonds of the human shape. Maybe they were nonsense syllables. He didn't know. Ross had studied the ancient Gaelic language and said he understood what they meant. Adam didn't care about the meaning.

All that mattered was that they blocked some of the blinding pain that always came with transformation.

While the human part of his mind screamed in protest, he felt his jaw elongate, his teeth sharpen, his body contort as muscles and limbs transformed themselves into a different shape that was as familiar to him as his human form.

The first few times he'd done it had been a nightmare of torture and terror. But gradually, he'd learned what to expect, learned to rise above the physical sensations of muscles spasming, bones changing shape, the very structure of his cells mutating from one kind of DNA to another. At least that was how he thought about it, because he didn't understand the science involved. In fact, he was sure modern science would have no explanations for his family heritage.

But the change came upon him nevertheless.

Gray hair formed along his flanks, covering his body in a thick, silver-tipped pelt. The color—the very structure—of his eyes changed as he dropped to all fours. He was no longer a man but an animal far more suited to the natural environment around him.

A wolf. Where no wolves had made their home for decades. But now one had command of Nature's Refuge. It was his. And the night was his.

Once the transformation was complete, a raw, primal joy rippled through him, and he pawed the ground, reveling in the feel of the damp soil under his feet. Then, raising his head, he sucked in a draft of air, his lungs expanding as his nose drank in the rich scents that were

suddenly part of the landscape. To his right an alligator
had gone very still. And a bear had stopped and raised
its head, sensing the presence of a rival.

The large black beast stayed where it was for a moment, then ambled off in the other direction, unwilling
to challenge the creature with whom he suddenly shared
the swamp.

Adam's lips shaped themselves into a wolfish grin.
He wanted to throw back his head and howl at the small
victory. But he checked the impulse, because the mind
inside his skull still held his human intelligence. And
the man understood the need for stealth.

Dragging in a breath, he examined the unfamiliar
scent he had picked up. It was nothing that belonged in
this natural world. Men had brought something here that
was out of place.

The smell was acrid, yet at the same time strangely
sweet to his wolf's senses. And it drew him forward.

Still, he moved with caution, setting off in the direction of the odor, feeling the air thicken around him in
a strange, unfamiliar way as he padded forward.

Each breath seemed to change his sense of awareness.
His mind was usually sharp, but the edges of his
thoughts were beginning to blur as though someone had
soaked his brain with a bottle of sweet, sticky syrup.

The air stung his eyes now, and he blinked back
moisture, then blinked again as he caught his first
glimpse of fire.

The flames jolted him out of his lethargy.

Fire! Where no fire should be. Out here in the open—
in the middle of the park. The swamp might be wet, but
that wouldn't stop a blaze from sweeping through the
area, if the flames were hot enough. He'd read as much
as he could about the Olakompa in the past few months,
and he knew that in the winter of nineteen fifty-five,
wildfires had burned eighty percent of the swamp area.

Fires were usually due to lightning igniting the layer
of peat buried under some areas of the swamp.

He'd seen no lightning tonight, but it wasn't difficult

to imagine a conflagration roaring unchecked through the park. Imagine birds taking flight, animals scattering for safety, the water evaporating in the heat.

His mind fuzzy from the smoke, he kept moving forward, toward the center of the danger. But when he took a second look, he saw that the flames were contained. A bonfire. Deep in the wilderness.

Tall, upright shadows moved around the flames, and in his bleary state, he could make no sense of what he was seeing. Then the wavery images resolved themselves into naked human figures—dancing and gyrating in the glow of the fire.

He shook his head, trying to clear away the fog that seemed to swirl up from the sweet, enticing smoke. For a moment he questioned his own sanity.

He'd heard people describe hallucinations that came from drug trips, heard some pretty strange stuff. Had his mind conjured up these images? Against his will, the circle of fire and the gyrating figures drew him, and he padded forward once more, although caution made his steps slow. He had come upon many strange things in his thirty years of living, but never a scene like this.

He blinked, but nothing changed. The naked men and women were still there, chanting words he didn't understand, dancing around the fire, sometimes alone, sometimes touching and swaying erotically together, sometimes falling to the ground in twos and threesomes—grappling in a sexual frenzy.

The thick, drugging smoke held him in its power, compelling his eyes to fix on the images before him, making the wolf hairs along his back bristle.

Getting high was deliberately outside his experience. He had never tried so much as a joint, although he had been at parties where people had been smoking them. But just the passive smoke had made him sick, and he'd always bailed out, which meant that he was ill-equipped to deal with mind-altering substances. Street drugs were poison to the wolf part of him. He was pretty sure that even some legal drugs could bend his mind so far out of shape that he would never be able to cram it back into his skull.

But the poison smoke had a stranglehold on his senses and on his mind. He was powerless to back away, powerless to stop breathing the choking stuff.

He took a step forward and then another, his eyes focused on the figures dancing in the moonlight. The smoke obscured their features. The smoke and the slashes of red, blue, and yellow paint both the men and women had used to decorate their faces and their bodies. He licked his long pink tongue over his lips and teeth, his eyes focused on sweaty bodies and pumping limbs, his own actions no longer under the control of his brain. Recklessly, he dragged in a deep breath of the tainted air. The fumes obscured the raw scent of the dancers' arousal. But he didn't need scent to understand their frenzy.

He watched a naked man reach for a woman's breasts, watched her thrust herself boldly into his hands, watched another woman join them in their sexual play, the three of them dancing and cavorting in unholy delight, the firelight flickering on their sweat-slick bodies.

His gaze cutting through the group of gamboling figures, he kept his heated focus on the threesome. He saw them swaying together, saw them fall to the ground, writhing with an urgency that took his breath away.

His own sexual experience was pretty extensive. But he'd never participated in anything beyond one man/ one woman coupling. And some part of his mind was scandalized by the uninhibited orgy. Yet the urge to join the gang-shag was stronger than the shock. He felt as though his skin were cutting off his breath, restraining him like a straitjacket.

He had to escape the wolf. And in his mind, in a kind of desperate rush, the ancient chant came to him, and he reversed the process that had turned him from man to wolf.

"Taranis, Epona, Cerridwen," he silently chanted, the words slurring in his brain.

"Ga. Feart. Cleas. Duais. Aithriocht. Go gcumhdai is dtreorai na deithe thu."

His consciousness was so full of the sweet, sticky smoke that he could barely focus on the syllables that were so much a part of him that he could utter them in his sleep.

But they did their work, and his muscles spasmed as he changed back to human form, the pain greater than any he remembered since his teens.

He stood in the shadows, his breath coming in jagged gulps, his eyes blinking in the flickering light, his hand clawing at the bark of a tree to keep himself upright when his knees threatened to give way. The sudden urgent sounds from the campfire twenty yards away snapped his mind into some kind of hazy focus.

"There! Over there," a man's voice shouted.

"Someone's watching."

"Get him."

"Kill him!"

"Before he rats us out."

The orgy-goers might have stripped off their clothing in the swamp, but they hadn't abandoned the protections of the modern world.

A shot rang out. A bullet whizzed past Adam's head.

Without conscious thought, he turned and ran for his life, heading for the depths of the swamp where either safety or death awaited him.

Also from
Usa Today Bestselling Author

REBECCA YORK

THE MOON SERIES

KILLING MOON

EDGE OF THE MOON

WITCHING MOON

CRIMSON MOON

SHADOW OF THE MOON

NEW MOON

GHOST MOON

ETERNAL MOON

"Action-packed...
and filled with sexual tension."
—*The Best Reviews*

penguin.com

Penguin Group (USA) Online

What will you be reading tomorrow?

Tom Clancy, Patricia Cornwell, W.E.B. Griffin,
Nora Roberts, William Gibson, Robin Cook,
Brian Jacques, Catherine Coulter, Stephen King,
Dean Koontz, Ken Follett, Clive Cussler,
Eric Jerome Dickey, John Sandford,
Terry McMillan, Sue Monk Kidd, Amy Tan,
John Berendt…

You'll find them all at
penguin.com

*Read excerpts and newsletters,
find tour schedules and reading group guides,
and enter contests.*

Subscribe to Penguin Group (USA) newsletters
and get an exclusive inside look
at exciting new titles and the authors you love
long before everyone else does.

PENGUIN GROUP (USA)
us.penguingroup.com

M224G1107